A MAJOR PUCK UP

BRITTANÉE NICOLE

A MAJOR PUCK UP
the revenge games

BRITTANÉE NICOLE

Copyright

This is a work of fiction. Names, characters, places, and incidents either are the product of the author's imagination or are used fictitiously. Any resemblance to actual persons, living or dead, events, or locales is entirely coincidental.

A Major Puck Up © 2024 by Brittanée Nicole

All rights reserved. No part of this book may be reproduced or used in any manner without written permission to the copyright owner except for the use of quotations in a book review.

First Edition May 2024

Model Cover Design by Ali of Dirty Girl Designs

Illustrated Cover Design by Cindy Ras of cindyras_draws

Formatting by Sara of Sara PA's Services

Editing by Beth at VB Edits

BOSTON BOLTS

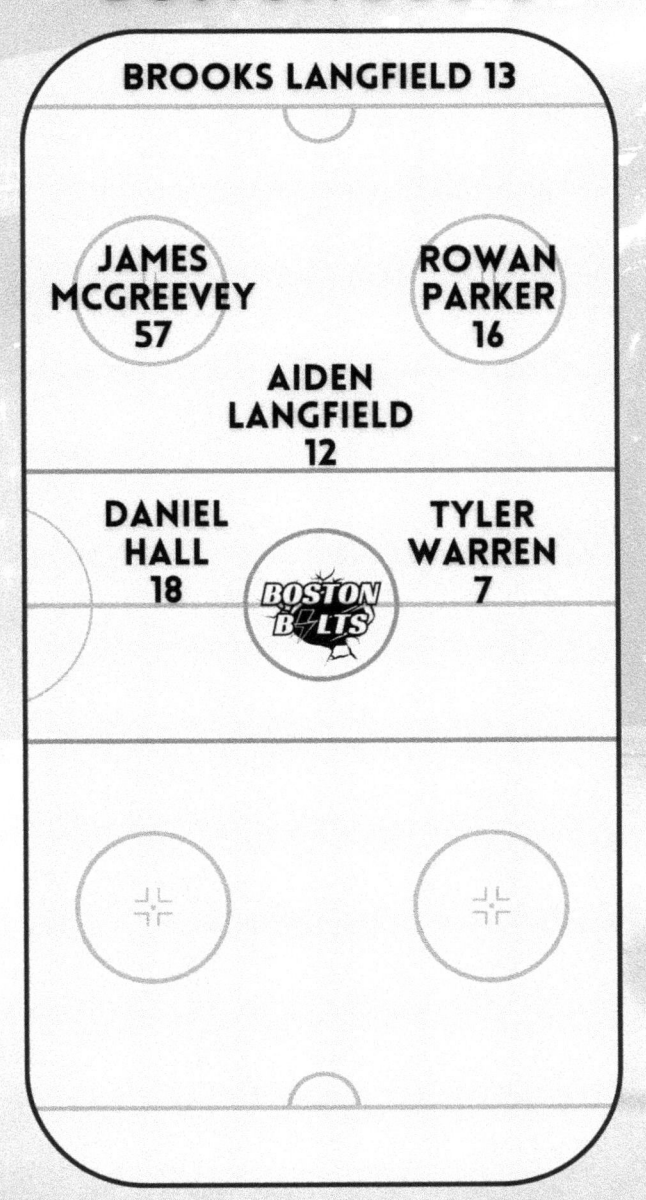

BROOKS LANGFIELD 13

JAMES MCGREEVEY 57

ROWAN PARKER 16

AIDEN LANGFIELD 12

DANIEL HALL 18

TYLER WARREN 7

COACH: GAVIN LANGFIELD 0

PLAYLIST

Please Notice - Christian Leave
The Prophecy - Taylor Swift
In the Kitchen - Reneé Trapp
Infinitely Falling - Fly By Midnight
Slow Dancing in a Burning Room - John Mayer
All the Best - Layup
Witchcraft - Frank Sinatra
Reckless Driving - Lizzy McAlpine, Ben Kessler
get him back! - Olivia Rodrigo
Addicted to You - Sped Up - Picture This
Alchemy - Taylor Swift
would've been you - sombr
What If I Wasn't Done Loving You? - Fly By Midnight
Feels Like - Gracie Abrams
Paris - Taylor Swift
Peaches - Jack Black

DEDICATION

*The best revenge is no revenge.
Move on. Be happy. Find inner peace.
Flourish.
-Anonymous*

FOREWORD

Dear Reader,

With each book I write, the world I build becomes more connected and complex. You will see some character overlap and since I know many of you enjoy the easter eggs I hide and prefer to read in order, here is a suggested reading order as it comes to this world:

Revenge Era: Ford Hall and Lake Paige
Mother Faker: Beckett Langfield and Olivia Maxwell
Pucking Revenge: Brooks Langfield and Sara Case
A Major Puck Up: Gavin Langfield and Millie Hall
A Pucking Disaster: Aiden Langfield (coming 9/21)

All of these books take place in the Boston Billionaire World so you will see or hear about those characters as well.

I hope you enjoy this world as much as I enjoy writing it.

XO,
    Brittanée

CONTENTS

The Hockey Report	xv
1. Gavin	1
2. Gavin	9
3. Gavin	21
4. Millie	29
5. Gavin	51
6. Millie	59
7. Gavin	65
8. Millie	77
9. Gavin	85
10. Gavin	97
11. Gavin	101
12. Millie	105
13. Gavin	115
14. Millie	125
15. Gavin	135
16. Millie	141
17. Gavin	147
18. Gavin	159
19. Millie	169
20. Gavin	179
21. Gavin	183
22. Millie	191
23. Gavin	199
24. Gavin	207
25. Gavin	219
26. Gavin	231
The Hockey Report	239
27. Millie	243
28. Gavin	251
29. Millie	257
30. Gavin	271

31. Gavin	281
32. Millie	287
33. Millie	295
34. Gavin	305
35. Gavin	311
36. Millie	323
The Hockey Report	329
37. Gavin	333
38. Millie	343
39. Gavin	351
40. Millie	357
41. Gavin	365
42. Millie	371
43. Gavin	379
44. Millie	383
45. Gavin	389
46. Millie	399
47. Millie	405
48. Gavin	411
49. Millie	421
50. Gavin	427
The Hockey Report	433
51. Millie	435
52. Millie	441
53. Millie	449
54. Millie	457
55. Gavin	467
56. Gavin	473
57. Millie	483
58. Millie	487
59. Gavin	497
60. Millie	501
Epilogue	509
Acknowledgments	515
Also by Brittanée Nicole	519

THE HOCKEY REPORT

"Good Morning, Boston. I'm Colton, and this is my cohost Eliza. We're here to bring you the Hockey Report."

"And what a good morning it is, Colton. Can you believe the Bolts are only two months away from the playoffs?"

Colton laughs. "And under new management."

"So true. For those of you who have been living under a rock for the last month, a few weeks ago, Bolts fans were stunned when their favorite good-boy goalie knocked out his coach. Brooks Langfield was suspended after the incident, and many of us were concerned that it would be the end of his career."

"It was a real worry for many hockey fans in Boston, Eliza. His own brother, Gavin Langfield, nearly fired him."

"Then, of course, we learned that Coach Lukov had used his position of power inappropriately with one of the younger staff and had failed to disclose to her that he was married," Eliza adds.

"And since Coach Lukov's wife is a shareholder in Langfield Corp, it came as no surprise that Gavin Langfield fired him once those details had been revealed."

"No, that was most certainly not a surprise, Colton. What was a surprise, though, was that Gavin Langfield named himself head coach."

"I've got to admit," Colton says, "I didn't see that coming. With one Langfield brother covering the net and another playing center, I have to wonder if Gavin can really handle keeping both of his younger brothers in line and leading the team."

"And, more importantly," Eliza says, "does he have the experience needed to take them to the playoffs again?"

"All I know is everyone in Boston is wondering if he can do it or if he's just another rich guy playing out his fantasy at the expense of what has been a great team."

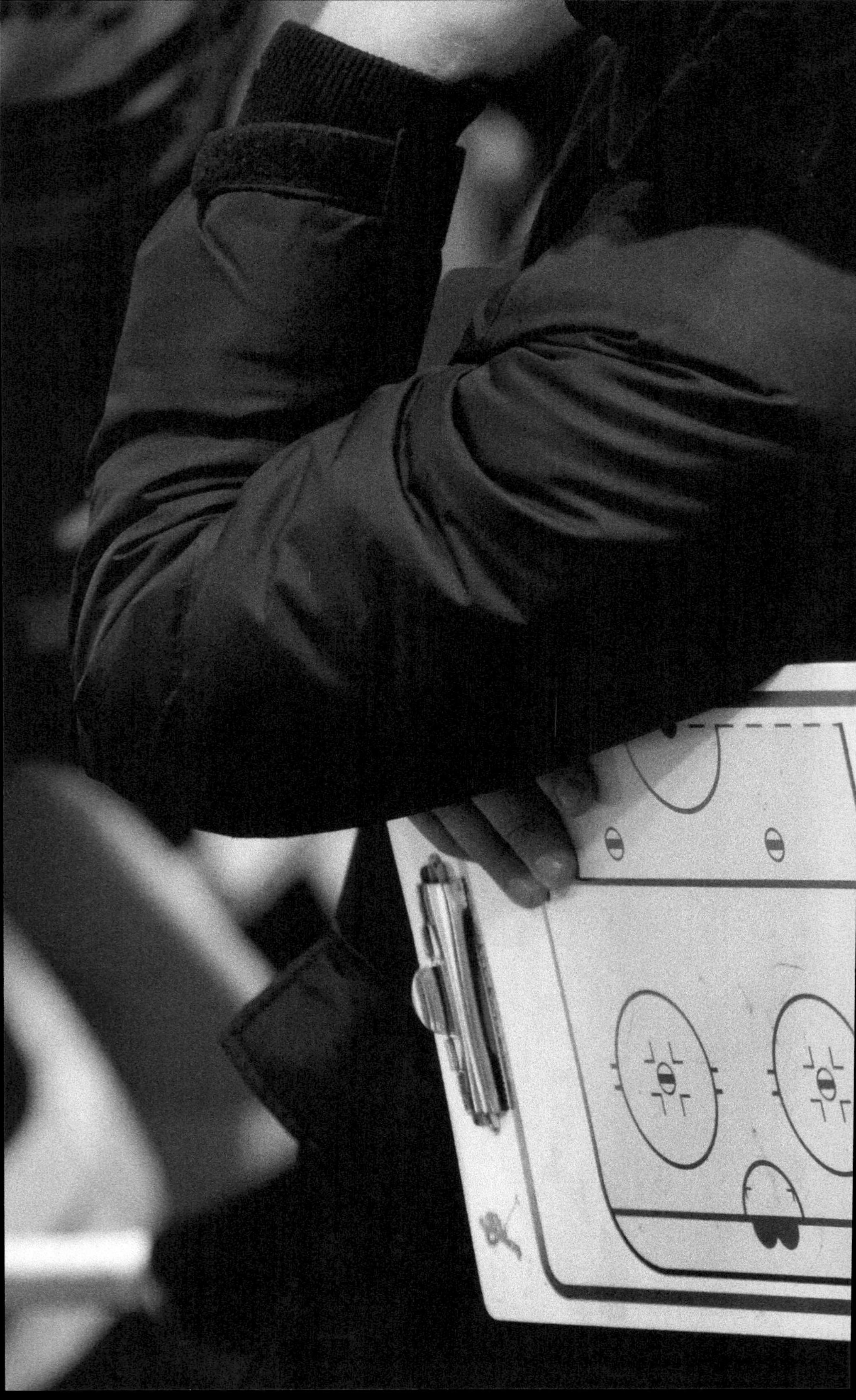

CHAPTER 1
Gavin

Me: I'm at your front door.

Aiden: Mine?

Me: No, Beckett's.

Aiden: What are you guys doing?

Me: Taking Finn to the park.

Brooks: Have fun. Need me to bring anything for dinner tonight?

Aiden: Can I come to the park? Which one? I can be there in ten minutes.

Me: No.

Brooks: LOL

Aiden: Why? You nervous Finn will be more interested in hanging out with me? That he'll leave your grumpy ass sitting on the bench while we play tag?

Brooks: Aiden, remember he's your coach now. That's why he's grumpy.

Me: I'm not grumpy.

Beckett: You really are. It's weird when I'm known as the fun brother.

Aiden: You're not. Don't worry. That would still be me.

Beckett: Duck you.

Me: Still standing at your door. You gonna open it anytime soon?

Beckett: It's open. Livy and the babies are asleep upstairs, so grab Finn and get out.

Me: LOL. See? You're still the grumpy one.

Beckett: No. I'm the tired one. You'll understand when you have kids.

Me: Yeah, that's not going to happen. And no way would I follow in your footsteps and end up with 25 of them.

Beckett: I have five. You going to come inside or what?

Aiden: Beckett, want me to pick up Addie and Winnie? I am the favorite uncle, after all.

Beckett: Sara and Brooks are taking them so I can nap with my wife. Any other questions?

Aiden: Jeez. You are the grumpy one.

I CHUCKLE as I pocket my phone and head inside the brownstone, where my brother lives with his twenty-five kids. I tease him because, for a while, he really did live with a shit ton of kids, but truthfully, I'm jealous of the life he has now. Up until this year, I didn't think I wanted that kind of life. Had zero interest in settling down or having kids. But now?

Well, now the only woman I want that with is gone, and everything in my life is wrong because of it.

I scrub a hand over my face and push her from my mind. There's no going back.

"Uncle Gav!" Finn shouts loud enough to rattle the walls. At the same time, Deogi comes bounding toward me. He's some type of oversized mutt Beckett brought home as a surprise for his kids last year. Liv was less than impressed, but she certainly had a surprise of her own when, that same night, she told him they were having twins.

I give the dog some loving while eyeing my brother.

Beckett throws his head back, defeat and exhaustion evident on his face and in his drooping posture. My brother, who is always well dressed, without a hair out of place or a whisker on his face, is covered in a five o'clock shadow gone wrong. So very fucking wrong.

"Your beard is gray," I say, and that little dig makes me feel a modicum better. God, I am grumpy.

"And your face is ugly. Let's not point out obvious facts."

A low laugh rumbles out of me. Jesus, I need to spend more time with Beckett. He might be the only person I like these days, and that's only because messing with him makes me feel slightly better about myself.

"Sure you don't want to come to the park with us?"

He's crouched down, giving Finn a quiet talking-to. The way they are together, the way my brother is Finn's whole world, creates an ache inside me that I don't understand.

I'm the cool uncle. Finn loves me. I don't need to be a dad to be content with my life.

Right?

Beckett stands, head still dipped, and holds out a fist for Finn to bump. Then he looks up at me. "No. As much as I'd love some time with my favorite guy"—he looks at Finn and gives him half a smile—"I need sleep."

I thumb toward the door. "All right, we'll get out of your hair. Want me to keep the kids tonight? The team is coming over for dinner, but they wouldn't mind."

"Nah, Winnie is sleeping over at Delia's, Finn is going to Shayla's, and Addie is going to Dylan's. We'll just have the twins, and since you don't have boobs, you can't handle them."

Huffing a laugh, I turn to the window and survey the houses that surround Beckett's. Last year, my brother moved into the house down the street with his wife and her best friends. They lived that way for a while, in a house overrun with kids. Now, though, Delia, Shayla, and Dylan, along with their husbands, have houses on the same block, meaning my brother and his family have help close by.

He has me and the boys too. Aiden may be my biggest pain in the ass, and Brooks might still be on my shit list because of what his lies this past year nearly cost the team, but I love them and know they'd do anything for Beckett and his kids.

As would I.

Finn slides his aviators over his eyes and starts for the door.

"Coat," Beckett growls.

Finn turns around, decked out in his newest favorite style choice. For more than a year, all he wore was fatigues and tutus. Interesting combination for sure. But he recently transitioned to a new look that he calls his jean tuxedo. It's literally a jean jacket buttoned all the way up, washed-out denim pants, white sneakers, and his aviators. The boy also likes to wear shiny jewelry.

He's hysterical.

"Bossman," he says, sliding his glasses down on his nose so Beckett gets the full impact of his incredulous expression. "You don't cover the fit." The six-year-old runs his hand up and down his body, as if to put himself on display.

"You do when it's thirty degrees out in Boston," my brother reminds him, pulling a puffy black jacket off a hook at the door.

The way Finn grumbles as he puts it on has me chuckling as I follow him out the door.

We stop at McDonald's, which is not at all part of the diet I normally follow. As the new head coach of the Boston Bolts, a team my family owns and I oversee, I typically enforce the same kind of dietary constraints on myself as I do on my players. But sometimes a guy just needs an Oreo McFlurry and fries.

"What do you think? Should I text her?" I turn to Finn on the park bench, still scrolling through the chain of text messages that stopped months ago when I told my girlfriend that it was over. Not because I don't love her or because I want anyone else, but because I couldn't keep up with the secrets and lies.

Finn twists his lips and studies me, french fry midway to his mouth.

A laugh from my other side gets my attention. The man seated at the end of the bench is wearing an unzipped oversized jacket over his thin frame. White scruff covers his face, and he's got a navy-blue Bolts beanie pulled over his ears.

"You tell your problems to a kindergartener?"

"Hey, I'm in first grade!" Finn defends.

He huffs a laugh but gives Finn a nod of apology.

My nephew peers up at me, his brow scrunched. "He has a point. You've been telling me about Princess Peaches for a long time."

"Just Peaches. Princess Peach is from the Super Mario game," I say, deciding it's probably best to ignore the old man and his judgment.

Finn shrugs, his legs swinging. "That's how I picture her. Does she drive a cool car at least?"

I snort. "Ya know, Finn, I don't know if she drives at all."

That makes my chest ache a bit. That's the kind of thing I probably should know, but I've never seen her drive a car. She lives in Paris, so she walks or takes taxis. If she lived here, maybe I'd know.

I shake my head. She doesn't live here, and that's just one of the millions of issues we had.

"You got any great advice?" I ask the old man.

He cocks his head and studies me, his wrinkles deepening. "About what?"

"You've clearly been listening, and you were quick to judge my choice in a confidant, so you got any suggestions?"

He narrows his eyes and purses his lips. "I'd need you to start from the beginning."

Finn spots a group of kids on the playground and takes off without a word, leaving me with the judgmental stranger. I stare at the man and wonder if it's even worth it. Then I remember the moment I first saw her. And every moment after that.

Every moment is tattooed onto my brain, forcing me to relive it daily. Maybe I just need to say it all out loud. Maybe going backwards will free me...

Or maybe I'm a glutton for punishment and I'm just looking for someone else to talk to about Peaches.

"Well, it all started two years ago..."

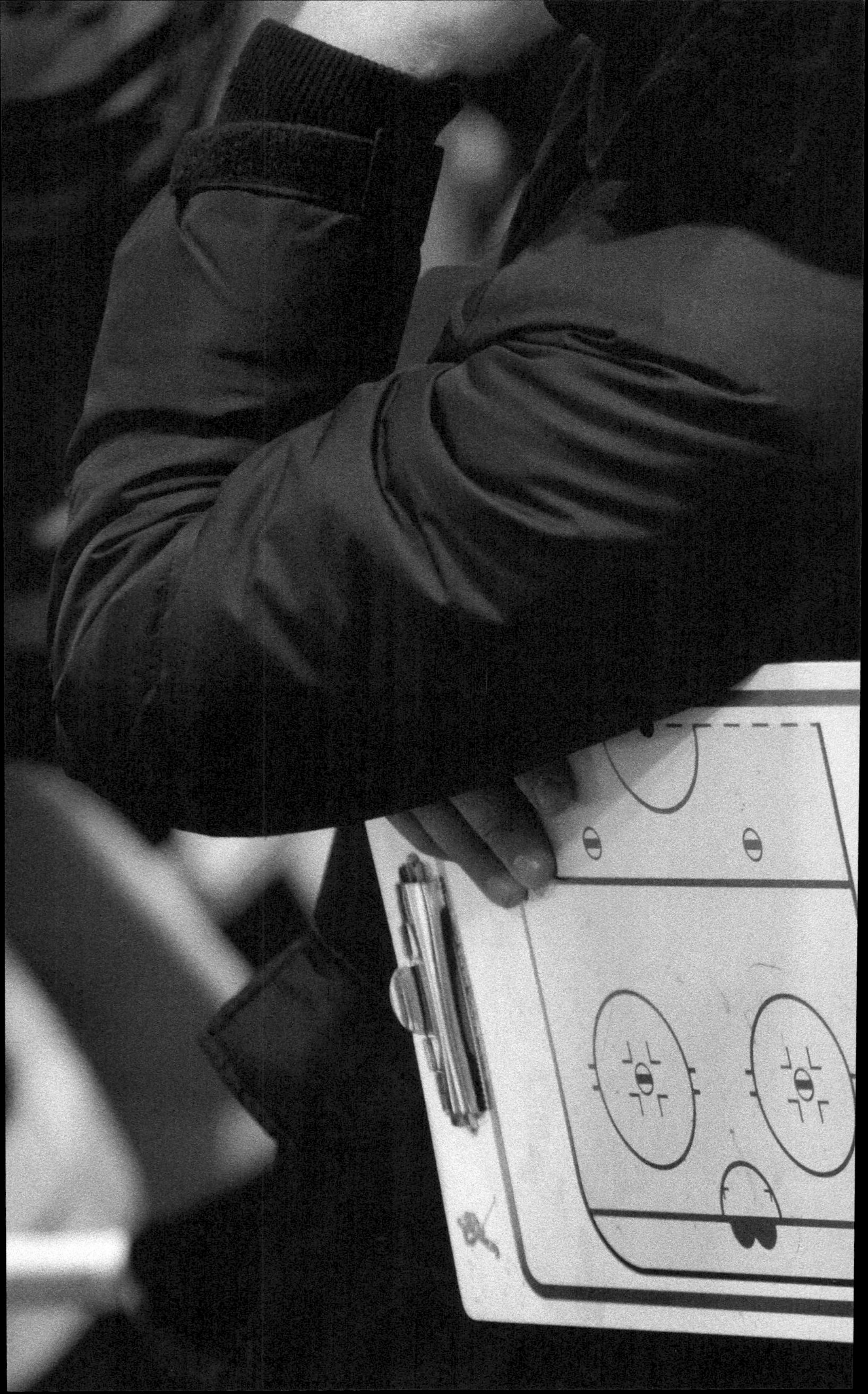

CHAPTER 2
Gavin

MARCH

Me: Are you guys coming?

Brooks: Can't. Seb has me working with Fitz tonight, since I'll miss two practices while we're traveling for the wedding.

Aiden: I met a girl. I think I'm in love. Can I bring her to the wedding?

Beckett: You can't invite people to someone's wedding at the last minute. Especially the wedding of a fucking pop star. They vetted everyone who is coming to the island.

Aiden: No plus-ones?

> Beckett: Aiden, you are not in love. Sorry, Gav. I'm stuck in the office with Liv. We just ordered food.

I chuckle to myself as I pocket my phone. Despite being annoyed that they aren't meeting me at the bar, thinking about Beckett and his insane obsession with Olivia Maxwell always makes me laugh. My poor besotted brother and his unrequited crush.

I look out the window at the rain pouring down in sheets. I should go home and have a quiet night before I have to get on a plane and head to Aruba for Ford's wedding. My best friend is marrying Lake Paige. Yes, that Lake Paige. America's sweetheart, one of the biggest musicians of our time, and his son's ex-girlfriend. It's going to be a huge weekend, and between the events and parties and dealing with my brothers, I doubt I'll be getting much sleep.

I *should* go to bed.

Should turn in early and rest.

But ever since Ford started dating Lake, I've been restless. The way he looks at her, with contentment and a happiness I've never experienced before, has messed with my head.

The one-night stands aren't cutting it either.

Women in general aren't cutting it. I don't know; I need something more than just a warm body. I need a challenge.

As the general manager for the Boston Bolts, I should feel challenged at work, but the opposite is true, really. Work is easy. I go into an office, make deals, talk to my friends about advertising spots, hang out with my brothers. I love it. I couldn't ask for more. But it's not challenging.

I'm not sure a woman or a job has ever challenged me.

"Sir, would you like to go home?" my driver asks.

I cringe. Jacob has been working for me for the last year. He's young, and I hate that he calls me sir.

"Gavin. Please call me Gavin." While I'm almost forty, I'm most definitely not a sir.

Jacob laughs. "Right. Gavin. You going into the bar or...?"

With a sigh, I button my jacket and reach for the door.

"I'll get that." He scrambles for the door handle, but before he can get out, I grasp his shoulder, pulling him against his seat.

"I'm not an old man. I won't melt in the rain or slip and break a hip. Go home. I'll call you when I'm finished or, ya know, walk across the street." My apartment is literally one block over. And maybe a walk in the rain will get me out of the funk I'm in.

This mood, this bitter taste in my mouth, is it jealousy? God, I've never been jealous of a thing in my life. I have more money than I could ever spend, a body cut from stone that I don't particularly need to work hard for—even at my age—and my face, fuck, my face is beautiful.

And I'm the funny one. I make everyone laugh. Everyone loves me.

I'm just not so sure *I* love me.

Ignoring that familiar pang in my chest, I push the door open and rush out into the cold rain, reminding myself that it could be worse. It's March in Boston; I'm lucky it's not snowing. As I enter the warm bar, music from the piano filters into the night air, instantly draining the tension from my body. I recognize the tune immediately, "Witchcraft" by Frank Sinatra, though the voice is female—alluring, raspy, and somehow magical.

Just inside the doorway, I zero in on the piano in the corner. Where Benny usually sits behind the keys is a woman whose dark hair falls like a curtain, obscuring her face. It's a deep auburn color and wavy like it was styled for an old Hollywood film, though it spills over her shoulders. Her dress is low cut, and with the way she's bent over and playing, I get an eyeful of her cleavage.

Utterly mesmerized, I freeze at the door, dripping onto the mat, until the song ends. She stands, and like a magnet, I feel a tug toward her. But before I can approach her, the hostess steps in front of me. "Mr. Langfield, may I take your jacket? I've got a spot available near the fire."

I nod and shrug off my jacket, all the while scanning the bar for the piano player who seems to have disappeared into thin air.

"The piano player—" I say, scratching at my jaw. "She's new?"

The hostess frowns. "No, Benny's playing tonight."

"A woman. There was just a woman playing."

She tilts her head and hums. "Was there? Sorry, it's been so busy I didn't even notice. Maybe he allowed a friend to play. He does that every once in a while."

Behind her, Benny settles on the bench and strings chords together. Damn, where'd that witchy girl go?

The hostess is right. It seems half of Boston is seeking refuge in my favorite bar tonight. Luckily, my family name and reputation mean that wherever I go, no matter how busy the place, I'll have a table. And tonight, it's the best one in the house. A spot at the end of the bar near the fireplace. The perfect spot to settle and warm up. The perfect spot to search for that piano player. She couldn't have gone far.

As soon as I settle at the bar, the bartender sets a whiskey in front of me—Hanson, of course. A couple of my best friends own the company. I take a sip, and then I pull out my phone and tap on my other best friend's contact.

I met Ford Hall a decade ago at a concert at my family's arena. The headliner was one of his artists, though the singer has since fizzled out. Back then, before he signed Lake Paige, the artists Ford worked with at his label weren't the kind who packed stadiums. These days, his label is the hottest in the industry.

When we met, Ford was divorced, and for years, he stuck to one-night stands and casual hookups like I have. He's got three kids who he's totally devoted to.

I just recently convinced Ford to let me offer his younger son, Daniel, a spot on my hockey team. For now, he's our third-string left winger, but I wouldn't be surprised if he's starting by next season. The kid is a beast on skates and one of my proudest drafts.

That's the part I love most about my job. Scouting. Looking for talent.

I'm a bit more hands-on than most owners. I attend practices often so I can keep an eye on the guys as they hone their skills. And there's nothing I love more than the actual game. Watching my team fight it out on the ice. Watching them win.

It's the best feeling in the world.

Ford's other son, though? God, that's going to be awkward. Wonder if he'll actually show up to the wedding. Maybe he'll bring his boyfriend.

I chuckle as I take another sip of my whiskey. The idiot dated Lake first and was stupid enough to cheat on her. So Lake hooked up with his dad to get even. And now she's marrying him. It's nothing short of savage. Ultimate revenge.

> Me: Ready to get hitched?

> Ford: Hell yeah.

> Me: You're so gone for her.

> Ford: Have you seen my future wife? Of course I am.

I laugh, but the humor fades quickly, because there's one thing that's still keeping them from being 100 percent happy.

> Me: Your daughter RSVP yet?

> Ford: No. Daniel is still trying to talk to her. I asked her to meet us for dinner last night, but she didn't show.

I wince. The only thing that made Ford hesitate before he finally took the leap with Lake was his daughter's anger over the situation. Despite how perfect he thinks his daughter is, she's acting like a spoiled brat. If Paul can get over his father marrying his ex, then why can't Millie deal with it? Of course I'd never say that to my best friend. To him, Millie is perfect.

> Me: She'll come around.

> Ford: Maybe. All right, my fiancée is calling out to me from the hot tub. This place is gorgeous. Can't wait til you guys get here. Have a safe flight.

That damn pang I've been forced to ignore more and more hits me again as I place my phone down on the bar, face down. What I would do to find that person I'd want to rush to if she were calling my name.

"Another whiskey?" the bartender asks.

I glance down at my glass, surprised to see that it's empty. Tapping it on the bar, I give him a nod. "Yes, thanks."

I'm engulfed in an intoxicating fruity scent as someone sits beside me, and as I turn my head in her direction, a smile forms on my face unbidden.

The woman, though, keeps her attention on the bartender who has just slid my glass in my direction and looked up at her.

She gives him a soft smile. "Peach margarita, please."

He mimics the expression, though his smile is a little more starry-eyed, like he may be as tongue-tied as I am over the gorgeous creature who's just appeared.

It's not just her long dark hair or the slinky black dress that barely covers her full tits. It's not the cranberry stain on her lips or the alluring light-brown eyes with hints of gold speckled within them or even the damn beauty mark on her cheekbone. No, it's the way her lips quirk, as if she knows she's ensnared us both. The way she shifts on the barstool, moving her gorgeous ass in a way that leaves me instantly hard. This woman knows precisely what she's doing. Seduction in a black dress, curves that are meant to suffocate every working brain cell.

She's young. That's obvious.

I'm just not sure how young. Legal, yes, but otherwise, I'm not sure I want to find out.

I'd rather not know if it'll cause me to actually use my brain tonight. For the first time in at least a month, I'm met with a woman who has piqued my interest. Now let's just see if she can keep it.

"Peach margarita? Bold for such a cold night," I say, sipping my whiskey.

She peeks in my direction. Only one glittering eye is visible. The other remains hidden behind that curtain of dark hair. "I know what I like."

Fuck, why is that hot?

Even when they're my age, most people don't really know what they like. Hell, I'm beginning to wonder if I even know what I like. I drink Hanson whiskey because my friends own it. I run the hockey team because I couldn't play professionally and my father handed the reins over to me. I live in a huge penthouse with an incredible view of the Boston skyline because I was told it was the most expensive unit in the city. If it's the most expensive, then it's the best, right? And as a Langfield, I'm expected to own the best.

"Can you make me one of those too?" I ask the bartender as he pours my seatmate's drink into a margarita glass.

Her lips quirk almost imperceptibly, and damn if the knowledge that I'm making her happy doesn't have me growing harder.

That's new.

Sinatra was onto something. It's gotta be witchcraft.

The bartender slides her drink toward her and then gets to work on mine. While I wait, I keep my eyes trained on her. It might be creepy, and I should probably stop, but if the way those gold flecks in her eyes are dancing are any indication, she's amused rather than bothered by my attention.

I'm used to being the entertainment, the funny brother, so I don't mind in the slightest being hers.

The music starts up again—this time it's John Mayer. The room grows quiet, as often happens when Benny plays. For a Boston crowd, this one is subdued. This is exactly why I frequent this bar. I appreciate Benny's relaxing vibe after a long day. There's no one waiting for me at home, so most nights, if I'm not at a hockey game or watching the local MLB team—my older brother's baby; I oversee the Bolts, and he oversees the Revs—I either drag my brothers out or end up here by myself.

When my new drink is placed in front of me, the woman to my left angles herself toward me and presses her lips together in a hint of a smile as she waits for me to take a sip.

I can't stop the cringe that overtakes me the moment the tangy sweetness hits my tongue. "Oh god. That's awful."

The bartender's eyes go wide and panicked.

Coughing, I hold up my hand. "It has nothing to do with your skills. But fuck, I don't like that."

The woman beside me giggles, then turns back to face the bar—away from me.

I wince. "It's not that it isn't a good drink, it's just—"

"Not for you."

The bartender slides a glass of water in front of me, so I snatch it off the bar top and down it.

"Yes. It's not for me at all. Sorry," I say, nodding at the man behind the bar this time.

He chuckles and shakes his head. "'Nother whiskey?"

I sigh. When was the last time I drank anything other than Hanson whiskey? "You have a menu?"

"You seemed to be enjoying your whiskey," the woman beside me says.

"What's your name?" I ask her, shifting her way.

She assesses me, eyes narrowed and lips pressed together, as if to say *why the hell do you want to know?*

"I'm Gavin," I offer.

She shakes her head and picks up her glass. "Not interested."

I cough out a surprised laugh. "I was just being polite."

"No you weren't." Her cranberry-painted lips tip up into that knowing smirk. "What's with the drink menu? We both know you'll only end up with another drink you dislike. Clearly, you are a man of habit who always drinks whiskey."

Amusement flits through me. "You been spying on me?"

She delicately licks the edge of her glass, her tongue peeking out just enough to swipe at the salt, then hums and takes another sip. I realize then that her eyes aren't truly brown. As the light hits her perfectly, the golden specs seem to blend together, revealing a rich, mesmerizing rose gold. They fix on me as she sets her drink down again. "No. Just know your type."

"Well, you happen to be wrong, witchy woman. I am a man who likes to try new things."

She smiles. "Witchy woman?"

"That was you playing when I came in, right?" I play dumb, as if I didn't know precisely who she was the minute she sat down.

She presses her hands against the edge of the bar and pushes back, as if she's going to leave. "I don't play games, Gavin. Have a good night."

On instinct, I grasp her elbow, holding her in place.

She looks down at my hand, and her brows furrow before she looks back up at me.

Stomach sinking, I let her go, holding my hand up, fingers splayed. "I'm sorry. I just—You were incredible up there."

Her face softens, and she might even be blushing under the praise. Like maybe she isn't used to being complimented for her talent. So far, she's been bold, confident. She's comfortable in the revealing dress, like she knows exactly what she's working with. But when it comes to her ability to sing and entertain a crowd with her piano playing, she's suddenly shy.

And damn if the juxtaposition isn't intriguing.

"Thank you."

"Will you stay?" I ask, because damn, do I want her to. I'm not ready for her to walk away. "Help me find what I like?"

She watches me with a thoughtfulness so profound it's hard to comprehend. Like she sees something in me, understands me in a way I don't even understand myself. She's an old soul. That much is clear. I'm afraid that if she looks too closely, she'll realize I'm shallow and have nothing to offer, that if she sees the real me, she'll pull back and say good night.

So I'm pleasantly surprised when she instead settles back on her stool and motions to the menu that's been placed in front of me. "Well, what are we trying?"

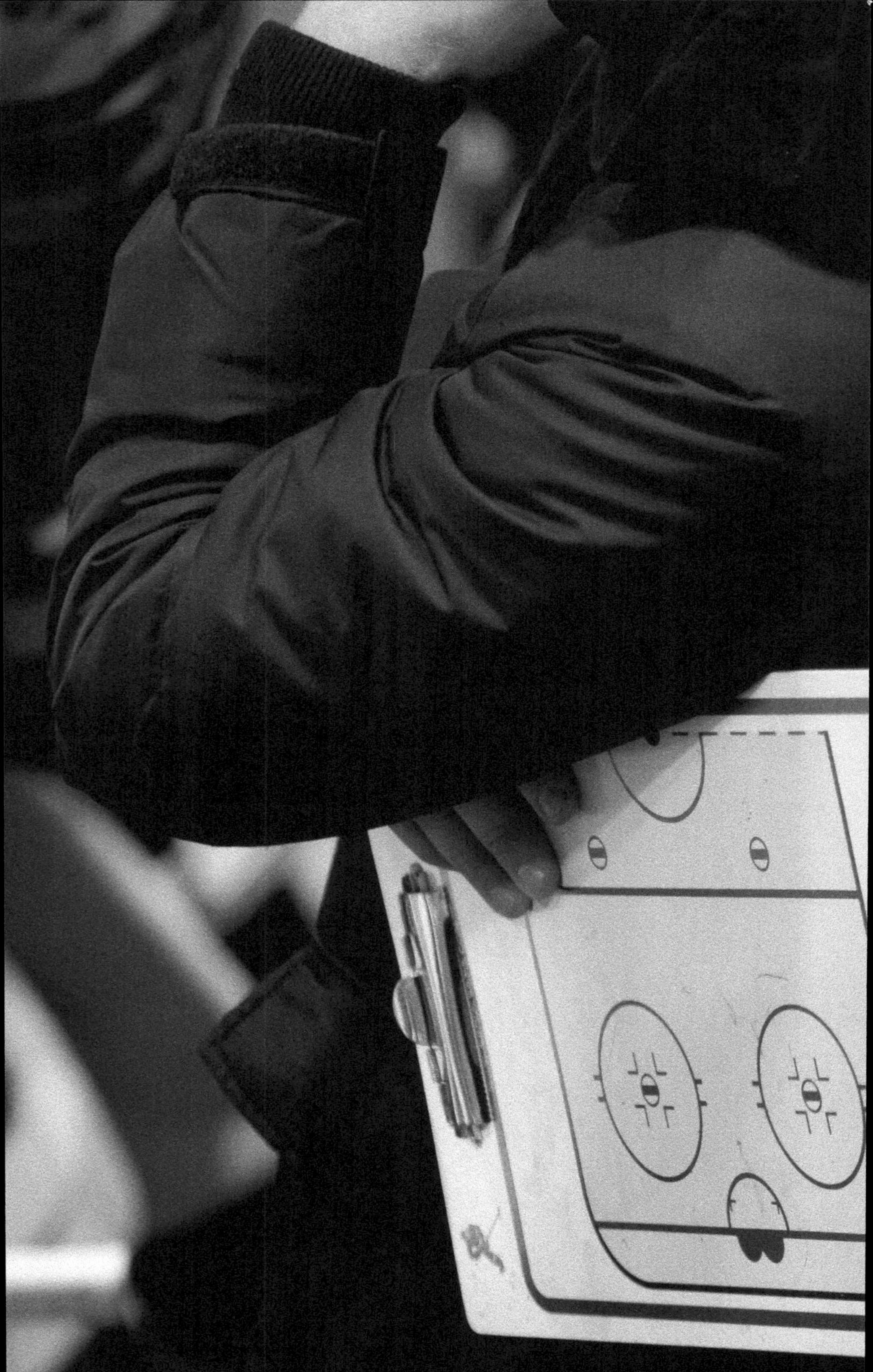

CHAPTER 3
Gavin

"HOW DO YOU FEEL ABOUT TEQUILA?"

"Makes my clothes fall off, but I'm not opposed," I tease.

She grins and taps her lip as if she's trying to decide whether that's a good thing. "Eh, what the hell. Mikey, give us two shots of Jose."

I scoff. "Mikey, top shelf, please."

She giggles. "So bougie. Okay, tell me something else about you."

"How come you keep getting things out of me but you still won't give me your name?"

She shrugs one shoulder and tilts her head to the side in this cute little way, like she knows I'm obsessed and enjoying myself.

"Um," I say, because, of course, I can't deny her. "I have three brothers."

"*Oh*, are they hot?"

"Not as hot as me."

She giggles. "That's what everyone says."

"Is that what you'd say about your siblings?"

She bumps her shoulder against mine. "I see what you're doing. Trying to get me to divulge personal details."

I laugh. "Of course. You've given me nothing so far."

"And yet I have a feeling you'll take everything," she sings softly, a gorgeous smile lighting up her face.

When Mikey places two shots in front of us, I scan the surface of the bar. "No lime?"

"Aw, you need a chaser, do ya?" she teases.

With a sigh, I clink my shot glass against hers and then, without looking away from the vixen by my side, I toss it back.

It burns on the way down, enough to make me wince, but her expression remains neutral, so I school mine too.

"What do you think? Tequila your drink?"

I cough out a laugh. "Fuck no."

"Ready to go back to whiskey and admit that you're just a whiskey guy?"

"Why do you say that like it's a bad thing?" I cock a brow at her. "So what if I am? Does that make me boring?"

She shrugs, the picture of innocence. "You said it, not me. You go to the same bar most nights. Drink the same drinks. I bet the only thing that changes is the woman you sleep with from one night to the next."

Another cough of a laugh escapes me. "Women don't sleep in my bed."

She smiles like she's proud of herself. Like I just proved her point.

I close my eyes in defeat. "That came out wrong."

"But did it? Think about it, Gavin. When was the last time you took a risk? Really did something you weren't supposed to?"

The taunting in her tone doesn't seem intentional. I may be conjuring it myself because I agree with her. When was the last time I took a real risk?

Fuck it. I like this girl, and I want to kiss her. So with a hand on the edge of her barstool, I pull her close.

She inhales sharply as she watches me, and then she licks her bottom lip. Another taunt. Another dare.

I wrap my hand around her neck and press closer.

Her eyes are wide and full of heat. "What are you doing?"

Instead of responding with words, I press my lips to hers in answer.

I'm kissing her. That's what I'm doing. Kissing a woman I really want to kiss. Not because she's gorgeous or because I want to get laid tonight. Those are truths, yes, but I kiss her because I like that she sees through the show I normally put on and calls it like it is. Because she's the first person in months to make me want to take a risk. To make me want to make the effort.

Her soft whimper as I slide my tongue against hers has my heart beating wildly in my chest. In response, I suck on her tongue, which only makes her moan louder.

"Now tell me your name," I murmur against her mouth. I don't give her a chance to respond, though, before kissing her again.

Fuck, I can't stop. Her lips are pillowy soft, and she tastes like a fucking dream. Don't even get me started on her fucking sounds. Her soft, warm skin beneath my fingertips is the most comforting thing I've felt in months. Maybe years. And it's right up there with the way she allows me to hold her close. Every single second with my lips against hers is perfect, and I don't want it to end.

She pulls back and takes a heady breath, her eyes locked on mine. "No."

I'm not even surprised. "Then I suppose I'll just have to call you Peaches."

She quirks a brow. "Why's that?"

"Because of how you taste." I lean in and kiss her again, groaning at the flavor of her on my tongue. Peach and tequila and *her*.

"Thought you hated the drink," she teases.

"And yet it's my favorite thing when it's mixed with you." Unlike the drink, she's made for me.

She eases back and, lashes lowered, gives me just a hint of a coy smile.

"Makes me wonder what you taste like in other places."

That smile turns challenging. "And you think you'll have the opportunity to find out?"

"Oh, I know I will. The question is, will I lay you out on my bed to do it? Or maybe my kitchen counter, or the bathtub? Or maybe, since you seem a bit sinful, you'd prefer out on the terrace?"

The way her eyes flare at my last suggestion tells me precisely where she wants it.

"Oh, you're a greedy little thing."

"I haven't even agreed to another kiss," she whispers, even as the smile on her lips and the desire in her eyes make it obvious she's begging for another one.

I'd like to see her beg. That thought has need ripping through me.

It only compounds with my next thought. Because, fuck, I'd like to get down on my knees and beg for her.

Keeping my focus fixed on her, I slide my card over to the bartender. "I'll cover the bill of every person in the bar right now, plus I'll tack on a 40 percent tip for you and every other employee working tonight if you can clear the place in fifteen minutes."

Peaches' golden eyes glow in excitement. "Whoa, money man. You know that'll probably cost you ten grand, right?"

The bartender, who's tapping away at the touch screen behind the bar like he wants to get my request processed before I change my mind, coughs out a laugh. "More like a hundred."

"Grand?" she cries, her eyes going wide. "Are you insane? Tell him to stop."

I simply lean back and smile. "Totally worth it."

"Why? What in God's name do you think I'll do to you that would warrant dropping over a hundred thousand dollars so you can spend time alone with me?"

I sip my drink as I study her. She's beautiful. Her skin is tinged pink from the alcohol and from her outrage over my extravagant spending.

"It's not about what you'll do to me. It's what I'm going to do to you." I lean in until my lips brush the shell of her ear. "I'm going to lay you out on this bar, and then I'm going to pull off your panties and drink right from the tap."

She scoffs, but it's breathy and sensual. "What?"

"Yes. I've finally decided on what I want, and it's not on this menu. It's you. One kiss told me the only thing that will satisfy me is you. That spot between your legs, if I'm being honest."

"You're insane. That's—" She shakes her head, the move jerky. "That's disgusting."

That only pulls a laugh from me. She doesn't truly believe that.

"Really? You're telling me that the idea of me licking you clean, the idea of me using my tongue to play with your clit and pressing my fingers against your G-spot is *disgusting*?"

The color in her cheeks has darkened, and her chest is heaving now.

I push closer and twine my fingers through her long, wavy hair. Grasping the back of her neck, I tug her so close that when I speak, my lips brush hers. "You telling me that my tongue on your pussy isn't exactly what you've wanted since the moment you sat down next to me? That you didn't come to this bar with that plan in your head?"

Her lips part on an exhale, her warm breath fanning my face.

With a groan, I lick at the seam, all while keeping my eyes open. "You telling me that you haven't been fantasizing about me fucking you since the moment you sat down next to me? That the mere thought of it doesn't have you dripping for me right now?"

"Yes," she whispers.

"Yes, you're telling me the thought hasn't crossed your mind? Or yes, you're admitting that if I slid my hand up your dress and dipped my fingers between your legs right now, I'd feel just how drenched you are for me?"

"That," she stutters. "That one. Yes."

"Mmm." Grasping her thigh, I lean back and holler "you've got five minutes" to the bartender.

And then my lips are on hers. The room around us goes hazy as we exchange kisses for oxygen, our desire for one another overpowering common sense. Common decency. I slide both hands up her legs to her waist and pull her close, positioning her between my thighs. No one but me gets to see the way her nipples pebble beneath this slinky black dress. No one but me gets to see the way she grinds down against the chair, needy and ready.

And as soon as I hear the snick of a lock at the front of the bar and the slam of the door in the back, I pull her up onto the bar and make good on my promise. I push her back, shove her dress up to her hips, and pull down her panties. Then I feast.

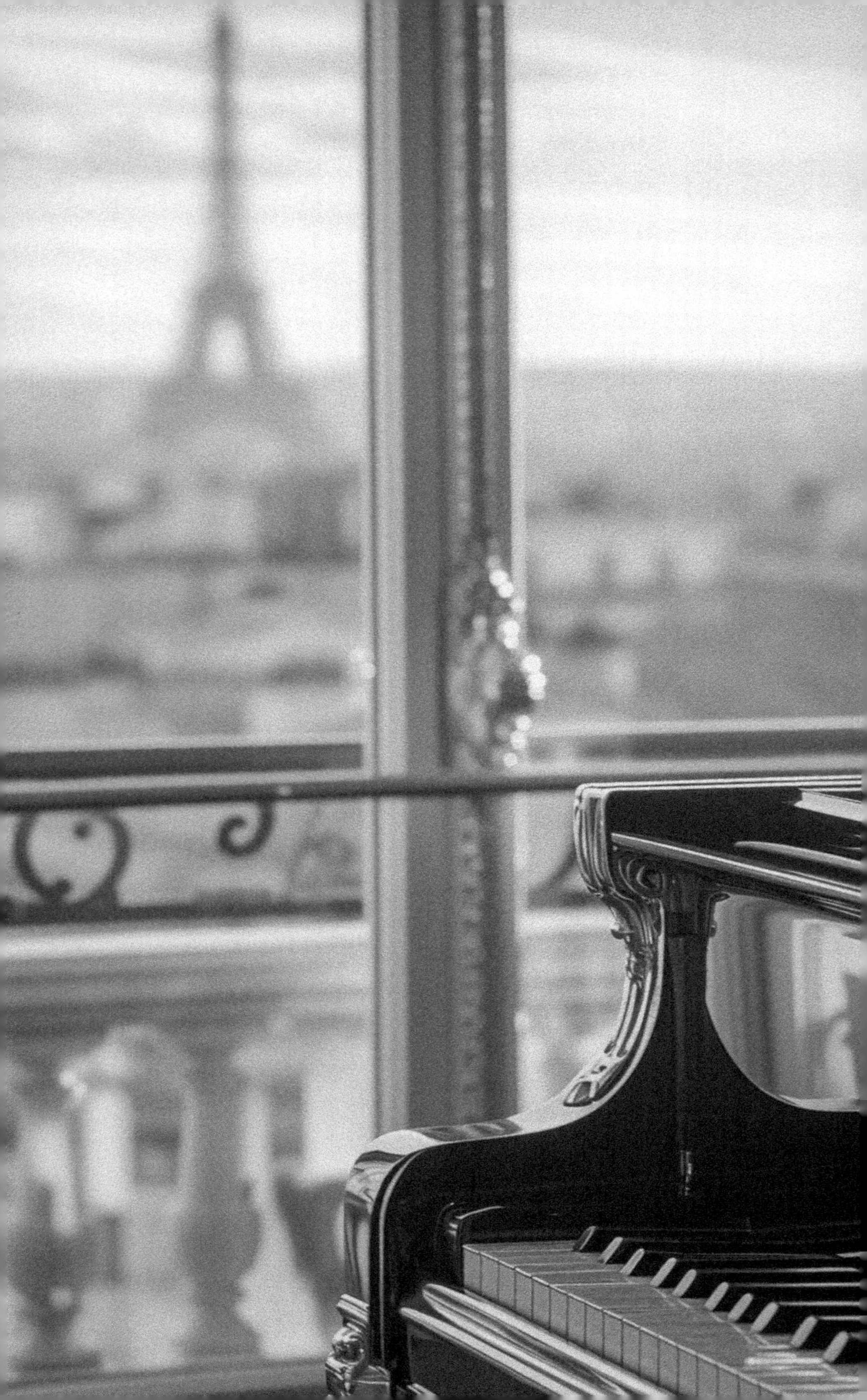

CHAPTER 4
Millie

HOLY SHIT. My dad's best friend is tongue-fucking me on a bar top in the middle of Boston.

Despite Gavin's assumptions, this is not how I expected the night to go. Yes, I came in here to seduce him. Yes, I knew precisely who he was when he walked in. And yes, I had every intention of giving him my virginity in a big fuck-you to my father.

But god, I had no idea it could feel like this.

The bar is completely empty and dark. The only light is coming from behind the bar. The way it shines on us leaves me feeling like I'm on a stage.

Not that I could perform right now if I tried. The man has me strung up. His tongue moves over my clit, achingly slow, like he's savoring every moment with me, and god, is it unbelievably hot.

Another thing I didn't plan on.

I figured that I'd have to kind of grin and bear it when I seduced him. Not because he isn't good-looking. The man is gorgeous. And I chose him because he had a nice smile. That was the thing I noticed each time I saw him in photos with my father.

According to my dad, he's the funny one. The fun one. The playboy of the group. Figured he was an ideal choice because, let's be honest, it'd be nice if my first time didn't suck. I've heard stories from friends who said most boys couldn't even find their clit, let alone their G-spot.

But holy hell, Gavin sure knows his way around the female anatomy, and he's hitting me right where it counts.

"Holy shit, that is..." I lose my words as he adds a finger and curls it upward. How in God's name is he doing that? I feel...I can't form a coherent thought. I blink a few times, hoping to ground myself. I'm supposed to be seducing him, not the other way around. "Gavin, please," I beg, clamping my thighs down on his hand.

With a low chuckle, he nudges my thighs apart with his shoulders and holds them wide open. His dark eyes are molten as he watches me from between my legs. The sight is absolutely sinful. He's still seated on his barstool, still in his crisp white button-down. Though he's rolled his sleeves, and holy forearm porn, is that hot.

He splays one large hand across my bare leg, squeezing and kneading my flesh. "Need something, Peaches?"

Damn, I love that nickname. And I love that he has no idea who I am. I wasn't sure I could pull it off at first, despite going with contacts instead of the big black-framed glasses I normally wear and styling my hair in loose waves instead of the bouncy, adorable natural curls.

Yes, on a regular day, I look like a sixteen-year-old Shirley Temple. I'm constantly carded, and for a long time, I was teased by the girls who pretended to be my friends because they were obsessed with my hockey star brother. Or my music executive father. Take your pick. Even now, people use me based on what they want. And honestly, for most of my life, I've let them, if only because it meant I'd be included.

Once my other brother started dating Lake, the hangers-on really came out of the woodwork. Suddenly, all of my supposed friends wanted to know if I could get them tickets to concerts. The students in my music program begged me to give her their demos or ask her to come to events on campus so she could listen to them.

Never mind how Lake's appearance in my life only cast a bigger shadow over me and the music I was writing. Not that I ever told my family or Lake about my music.

Then, when Lake dumped my brother and started dating my dad, the comments and the way people treated me got vicious.

Right now, though, the last thing I should be focusing on is the way I lost my so-called friends left and right. Suddenly, everyone had a comment about my life. About my father. About me.

Tonight I've pushed aside that mousy girl who's always hidden behind the scenes, watching life pass her by. I straightened my hair, then curled it into long waves. I traded my glasses for contacts, covered my freckles with foundation, and stained my lips a deep cranberry. The makeup and the dress both help me look my age, if not older, rather than like a starry-eyed teenager. But it's the attitude that I think makes the most difference. I've finally stopped giving a damn. Or at least I'm giving the impression that I have.

I figured Gavin wouldn't recognize me. He and my father are good friends, but their friendship has always revolved around meeting for drinks, and since my brother is a hockey superstar, it's safe to say he comes up in conversation far more than me. He doesn't come to family parties, nor was he around when I was growing up.

Right now, though, every ounce of his attention belongs to me, and damn if it isn't going to my head.

To have a man as powerful, good-looking, entertaining, and charismatic—a man who, by all accounts, is the center of attention everywhere he goes—pay to have the bar cleared so he can have me to himself? That is going to my head.

The way he's making me feel, though, can't be normal. It's like I'm about to come out of my skin, like I'm slightly ticklish but also euphoric. Is that—oh god—is that what an orgasm is? Am I—

"I think—" I pant, gasping for air. "I think I'm coming."

Gavin doesn't stop. He doesn't slow. Eyes hooded, he watches me come apart beneath his fingertips. He wrings pleasure from me, and just as I'm balancing on the precipice, he leans down and sucks on my clit.

I thrash against the bar, hands splayed against the slick surface, unable to control myself. Head whipping from side to side and my body taking over, I kick him back, sending him hurtling toward the floor.

"Shit!" Gavin coughs out a laugh. "That's a first."

I scramble upright and find him sitting on the floor, his head hanging and his elbows on his knees.

Mortified, I grasp at the fabric of my skirt and tug to cover myself. "I'm *so* sorry."

Shit. Shit. Shit.

He's probably seconds away from hauling himself up and walking out.

My first male-induced orgasm—maybe my first *ever* orgasm—and I kicked him in the freaking stomach. What the hell is wrong with me?

"Are you okay?" I jump off the bar and land with a thud beside him.

Gavin makes a wheezing sound in response. My heart drops, and I cover my mouth, mortified. But when he tips his head back, his brown eyes dance with humor and his lips are pulled into a full smile.

"Holy fuck." He lets out a deep, loud laugh that instantly forces my heart back to its rightful place in my chest. "That was insane."

Arms crossed, I huff out a laugh and bump his leg with the toe of my shoe. "Ass. I thought you were hurt!"

"I could have been with the way you maimed me, but I'll take your reaction as a sign that the orgasm I gave you was explosive."

"Shut up," I argue, though I'm laughing now too.

I cover my face. My skin is on fire, which means my freckles are getting darker. Too dark for my makeup to cover. I should go. This was enough revenge for tonight.

Disappointment clangs in my chest at the prospect. Now that I've spent time with Gavin, I wish it could be more than what we just did. He was fun. And more than that, I was fun. The person I conjured tonight is a person I like, and I don't want to say goodbye to her. I don't want to revert back to the woman I haven't particularly liked much lately.

When he pushes to his feet and our eyes meet again, I find myself wanting to lean in closer to him. To sink into him and be kissed by him again. It's unexpected. *He* is unexpected.

It's suddenly clear that I didn't think my plan through as thoroughly as I should have. Because every expectation I had has been obliterated by his smile.

He's kind. And I'm an asshole for thinking I could go through with this to spite my father.

This isn't me. Using this man. Or maybe it is. I'm awful.

Gavin's smile falters as he steps closer to me. "What's wrong?"

"I'm embarrassed."

He cups my cheek, and when he caresses me softly with his thumb, I melt beneath his touch.

"Please don't be. I'll remember that moment for the rest of my life. The way you owned that orgasm. The way you exploded for me. Fuck, I love how responsive you are. How you know what you want. How you enjoy life. I see it in everything you've done tonight." His dark irises are deep pools of sincerity as he dips a little closer so I'm forced to look at him. "Honestly, I've been in a bit of a funk for the last few months, and if you hadn't called me on it, I'd still be. But god, you knocked me on my ass tonight."

I giggle, my eyes falling shut. "I mean, I did."

He laughs, and when I open my eyes, he's pressing his lips to mine again. It's gentle and explorative. Like he's testing the waters. I taste myself on him, which is new, but I don't exactly hate it. When I moan in response to the tingles coursing through me, he nips at my lips.

"Can I take you back to my place?"

My breath catches, and I take a step back. I'm not surprised by his request, but I'm not sure it's a good idea. I want to spend more time with him. I want to sleep with him. And my reasons have nothing to do with my father. I understand Gavin. I relate to him. What he said before, about being in a rut, that's been me. Tonight, for the first time in months, I've felt anything other than anger and hurt.

But it can't go past tonight, and I'm not sure if I'll be able to walk away once we sleep together.

"I'm not sure."

The genuine smile that splits Gavin's face almost takes my breath away. "What if we just go for a walk?"

I eye the stained-glass windows near the entrance. Each is a different color—red, green, blue, and purple—and impossible to truly see through, but I can hear the rain coming down heavily outside. "A walk in the rain?"

Gavin's face falls. "That was dumb. Sorry."

"No." I swallow, searching for an explanation that would make any sense at all. "It's—I'm just—"

"You don't have to explain yourself." He's giving me a smile again, but his shoulders are slumped and his eyes are sad. "I just liked hanging out with you."

I bite my bottom lip.

He leans close and kisses me once more, his warm palm still pressed to my cheek. "It's okay, Peaches. I had a great time with you tonight. Thank you." He clears his throat. "I'll call my driver, then I can take you home."

He pulls away, and already, I'm second-guessing myself. As he takes out his phone and murmurs what I assume are instructions to his driver, all I can think is that I'm not ready for this night to end.

My phone buzzes, and I regret looking at the message as soon as I pull it out.

> Mom: Your father posted a photo of Lake with a view of the beach behind her on Instagram. Gag me. I can't believe he's really doing this.

In rapid succession, they continue.

> Mom: What time will you be home?

> Mom: I bought a bottle of wine and rented the new J. Lo movie. Or we could look up ways to covertly ruin a wedding. He'd never suspect it was you. LOL.

I roll my eyes, even as my heart sinks. I don't understand why my mother is taking my father's engagement so hard. They haven't been together in over a decade, and mom has been in plenty of relationships over the years. Though she always has loved drama, and she's exceptionally good at putting my siblings and me in the middle of her fights with Dad.

Tonight, my family drama is the last thing I want to think about. Which is ironic, considering that I came in here seeking revenge for exactly that.

My father and my brothers have moved on with their lives, while I'm stuck in an endless cycle with a woman who's still living in the past. Who's constantly trying to turn me into her little doll. Whether it's dressing me up in clothes she thinks I should wear or nagging me about the kind of men I should date, she considers me her project. While we're all in Aruba for my father's wedding, she'll no doubt spend the week texting me incessantly about how awful my new stepmother is.

My phone buzzes again. This time the messages that appear have me shrinking into myself.

> Chrishell: Holy crap. TMZ just released pics of your father with Lake on the beach in Aruba. Are you going to the wedding?

> Taylor: Or did they elope without telling you?
>
> Chrishell: Is Daniel bringing a date? If you're going, bring Taylor as your plus-one, and I'll be Daniel's date.
>
> Taylor: She's probably not invited, Chrish. Drop it.

My "best friends" are awful. A petty part of me would love to send them a sneaky photo of Gavin right now and tell them exactly what I just did. They'd never believe it. But I feel oddly protective of this moment. If I told them, they'd figure out a way to make it about them, and for one night, I want something just for me.

"Ready?" Gavin asks, interrupting my downward spiral.

Am I ready? This is the moment to decide. I planned and schemed, and all the while I believed I was ready for tonight, but I can admit now that I could never have gone through with it if not for the man who's watching me right now, looking at me like he'll respect whatever decision I make. Like he's just happy that he got to spend time with me tonight. Content with the fact that he did what he did, with no expectation of anything in return.

But do I want our night to end here? For one night, I don't want to think about my family. I don't want to focus on my reality. How my father is marrying a woman half his age and how, once I return from his wedding, I'll still be living with my mother. I'll pick up where I left off, dealing with her daily tantrums and drama. I don't want to remember how awful Chrishell and Taylor are. How they masquerade their commentary on me and my life as something real friends do.

I take his proffered hand, and for a moment, all I can do is think about the way it engulfs mine. When I finally look up, he's smiling at me, his eyes warm and understanding.

"I'd like you to take me to your home," I say quietly, gauging his reaction.

There's no cocky smirk in response. Instead, his face lights up with genuine joy. Then he nods before pressing a soft kiss against my forehead. It's comforting and sweet and makes me feel safe.

He's absolutely the right person for me to do this with. Every cell in my body can sense it. He's the right man to give my virginity to. A man I trust to make it good.

Trust. That word is like a lead ball sinking in my stomach. Because while I know who he is, he's still oblivious to my real identity.

I second-guess my decision a thousand times during the five-minute ride to his place, but then we're pulling into the parking garage and he's ushering me into the elevator.

His home boasts beautiful views of the city and a gourmet kitchen. The artwork on the walls and candles and books on display make the space feel just as warm and comforting as Gavin himself.

Gavin's age and wealth and experience are evident in every crevice. With each step I take, I feel more unprepared. More inexperienced. More unsure that I can make him feel good. That last part has, for some reason, become paramount.

Used to messy dorms that smell like beer and boys whose clothes are wrinkled and whose sheets haven't been washed since god knows when, I'm completely out of my element when Gavin rounds the bar and offers me a glass of wine.

I do my best not to nod too eagerly, but a little liquid courage couldn't hurt. And the red he's poured for me is incredible.

"Thank you."

He taps his glass against mine. "We don't have to do anything, Peaches. If you want to just hang out on the couch and talk, I'd be more than happy with that."

I take a long sip of wine and then set the glass on the bar top.

Gavin watches me, expression thoughtful, as I take his glass and do the same. When I slip my hand in his and tug, his brows shoot up, and a pleased smile graces his face. Then I lead him down the hall to where I can only assume the bedrooms are, hoping like hell I'm not making a fool of myself.

Gavin hovers behind me, resting a warm hand on the small of my back. As we continue down the hall, he uses his free hand to push my hair to the side and kisses the space between my neck and shoulder.

"To the left," he directs.

I push open the door and step into his room. With a deep breath in, I allow myself a moment to find my bearings.

The space is simple. A television on one wall, a dresser, a door that likely leads to the master bath. The second door is open, and beyond it is a large walk-in closet.

Then there's the bed. A king-size bed covered in black bedding. Simple and masculine. The divine scent that envelops me—expensive cologne and man—makes me want to jump onto the bed, sink against the sheets, and just inhale.

Gavin slides his hands up and down my arms as he continues to press soft kisses along my neck. "Is this okay?" he whispers against my skin.

I nod, a little shaky at the sensation and the care with which he treats me, and suck in another breath. He's everywhere. In this room, against my body. My senses are in overdrive, though my nerves are settling.

"Can I take this off?" He slips one hand down to the hem of my dress.

"Yes. Please."

He lets out an unsteady breath against my shoulder, the warm air sending goose bumps skittering along my skin, and then he's lifting the dress.

I raise my arms to help him take it off, and then I'm standing before him in nothing but a pair of panties.

"Fuck. No bra," he murmurs, sliding his hands up my stomach. When he gets to my chest, he stops and takes his time palming my breasts, then tweaking and rubbing my already too sensitive nipples.

"Don't like them," I admit, dropping my head back against his shoulder.

"I want to turn you around so I can see your face, but damn if I don't love holding your tits like this. Fuck, Peaches, you are perfect."

Barely. My hips are wide, I'm short, and I've got a bit of a tummy that will never go away. My breasts are a good size, though they're not proportionate to my hips. I wouldn't consider my shape to be an hourglass, but it's dark in this room, the only light coming from the city outside the floor-to-ceiling window, and Gavin is hard against my back, so I don't think he's disappointed by my body.

I turn in his arms, because I want to see his face too, and he's on me, kissing my lips, my jaw, my neck, and running his hands up and down my body, moaning about how good I feel, how beautiful I am, and how lucky he is that I'm allowing him to touch me.

Legs shaky, I cling to him. I'm drunk on his words. Drunk on the taste of him. Desire pools low in my belly. The lust-filled haze makes me dizzy and giddy and excited.

"You're wearing too many clothes," I say, working the top button of his shirt. Despite my nerves, my fingers don't tremble and maintaining eye contact is the most natural sensation.

His smile sends not just heat but warmth coursing through me. "I need to taste you again," he murmurs. Then he's cupping me, sliding a finger under my panties and groaning when he finds me wet. "I can't wait to slide my cock in here. To feel how tight and warm you are."

I whimper at the images that hit me at his words and slide his shirt off his shoulders.

Taking a single step back, I drink him in. My breath catches in my throat as I catalog every ridge and dip along his chest and abdomen. His skin is tan and smooth, begging me to touch it. Hand splayed, I press it to his pec, then trail lower, lingering on his six-pack, rolling my fingers over each one.

Gavin undoes his belt and then his button and zipper, and then he's sliding down his pants and revealing his massively hard dick.

"Holy fuck," I whisper. On instinct, I palm him and work my hand up and down the length, imagining the way he'll feel inside me.

He's huge, and suddenly, I'm worried it won't fit.

My fears are pushed aside when he asks, "Are you on birth control?"

"Yes." The single word is all I can manage. Thank god too, because my thoughts are nothing but rambling nonsense. Certainly not sexy.

If he'd asked anything else, I may have stumbled through an incoherent sentence or two, but the birth control thing was easy. I've been on it for years to help with my horrible cramps.

"Fuck, Peaches, I'm losing my mind. You're squeezing my fingers so perfectly. I can't wait to get inside you. Tell me you'll let me have you. Tell me you're mine tonight."

"Yours, Gavin, I'm all yours," I promise.

I've never been anyone else's. Will he know? Should I tell him? Before I can consider, he sucks my nipple into his mouth and rolls his tongue over it, and all my thoughts blur.

"I'm going to make you come one more time on my tongue," he says, still worshipping my breasts.

"You've already made me come once," I breathe, dropping my head back and tugging at his hair. "I should take care of you."

Gavin nips at my nipple, pulling a squeal from me. "Letting me eat you out is taking care of me, Peaches. You're feeding me my goddamn favorite snack. Now please, can I eat?"

I smile through the haze of bliss surrounding me. "Who am I to argue with that logic?"

The chuckle that works its way out of him is dark. "You aren't. I'm older and therefore much wiser. You should listen to me."

So damn giddy, I giggle. "I wasn't going to point out how old you are."

"Brat," he teases as he picks me up. His mouth is on me the whole way to his bed, kissing and nipping at my shoulder. He only stops when he tosses me onto the mattress. "But a beautiful brat. Such a beautiful brat."

"Yeah, yeah," I breathe, relishing the soft bedding and the heat of his attention on me. "That's what you tell all the girls."

Gavin cages me in, a hand planted on the bed on either side of my head. "I really don't. And it's been a long time since I've wanted anything the way I want you right now."

God, this man.

With deft fingers, he slides my panties off. Then he presses soft kisses up my thighs and settles my legs on his shoulders. The feel of his skin beneath mine is surreal. His warmth seeps into me, and the heat is only compounded when his tongue hits me. The world goes even more hazy. When he flattens his tongue against my sex and then licks, I'm already dangerously close to the edge. "Oh fuck, that feels good."

His chuckle is a brush of air against me, making my whole body clench. "You're so damn tight. You might break my dick." With a groan, he slides two fingers inside me, stretching me.

"I—" I pant, unease suddenly battling with rapture. "I hope that's okay."

"Oh, Peaches." He curls his fingers inside me. "I'd gladly suffer for you. Break me, torture me with this perfect pussy, just promise you'll kiss it better."

My responding laugh quickly transforms into a moan.

I'm not sure what he does with those fingers and that tongue, but only seconds later, a wave crashes over me, rumbling through my body, dragging me under, leaving me breathless and wet and oh so desperate for him. "Please, Gav."

He drags himself up, peppering kisses along my hips, my abdomen, between my breasts, until his lips meet mine. I wrap my arm around his neck and my legs around his hips, pulling him closer and rubbing against his hard cock.

"Shit." The sensation makes my eyes roll back in my head. Why does everything this man does feel good?

He grinds down and lets out a low moan that sends tingles down my spine. It's deep and so fucking sexy. "Peaches, you keep doing that, and I'm going to come all over your stomach."

I roll my hips, relishing the zap of electricity that shoots through me, working myself over more fervently. This time, the head of his cock edges close to my entrance, dipping inside before he rubs it against my clit.

"Yes, that feels so good," I murmur, burying my face in the crook of his neck.

"I should get a condom."

"Yes," I say, even as I rub against him again and practically ignite when he sinks in just a little farther than before. My body is desperate for him, sucking him in, begging to be filled.

"Just a second." He kisses me, slow and deep, and this time, he lifts up a little farther, and now his cock aligns perfectly at my entrance as he grinds down.

"Yeah, let's just—" My words are cut off when he flexes his hips and slips inside again. Just the head of his cock breaches my entrance, but with another slight move, he sinks deeper. This time, the pain hits, and I squeeze my eyes shut.

"Breathe, baby. I got you." His words are a soft caress, and then his lips coax gentle kisses from me, relaxing me further. "I want to take this slow," he adds. "It's been forever for me, and I want to last."

He pulls back and holds my gaze, his brown irises infinite pools of desire and comfort as he presses in farther.

He's only saying that because he knows that it hurts. Despite his words, I see the care and concern etched into the lines on his face. If I had to bet, he knows precisely what I'm giving him right now, and he's taking it with a graciousness I never knew existed.

"Okay, I'm good," I say through another breath.

"Baby." Gavin dips in and pecks my lips. "I'm not even halfway. But we can stop if you want."

When he lifts up again, I dip my chin to get a good look at us. Holy shit, there's at least another four inches just hanging out there.

Deep breaths. I want this. I need this.

"Please don't stop."

With a hum, he licks at the seam of my lips, and when I open, he sweeps his tongue along mine while at the same time sinking deeper inside me, one inch, then another. With every heartbeat, I settle a bit more into the feeling.

"Okay, we're there," he says gently, holding himself above me, his face cast in shadow.

"God, I feel so full," I admit.

"Is it okay? Are you in pain?" He goes rigid with concern, his arms locked on either side of my head.

I dig my fingers into his tense shoulders and pull him closer. "I'm okay now. Can you—um—" I fumble for words. I actually don't know what to do now. He's inside me. Do I lift my hips? Can he move? Is it really possible I could break his dick if I'm not careful? The ridiculous thoughts swirling in my head make it impossible for me to focus.

"I'm going to move now. You're squeezing me so tight I might actually be a one-minute man," he says, lightening the mood.

"Okay." I exhale a shaky breath. "Just do what you do."

Gavin nuzzles his face into my hair and laughs. The vibrations work their way through me, making me needier, despite the humor of the moment.

Is it weird that we're laughing while he's buried inside me? It doesn't feel weird. I like his smile. I like having him this close to me. And I really like the way he feels when he slides out and then back in again.

"Oh, that feels good," I tell him.

"Good. Keep telling me how it feels, baby. I want to make this good for you."

With every thrust, my body relaxes, the initial pinch of pain a distant memory. Now the stretch of him is a sensation so all-consuming I can't help but rub against him, searching for more friction.

"So good," I pant.

"I want to see your tits bounce while you ride me," he says, his thrusts punishing and his rhythm steady. "Can we do that?"

He's the expert, and I'm eager to follow his lead. "Yes, okay, sure."

Without hesitation, he slides one arm under my back and flips me with ease. Straddling him like this, I'm even more full than I was before. After he gives me a moment to adjust, he works me over him, moving his hips in a way that hits the most perfect spot deep inside me.

Gavin leans up and sucks my nipple into his mouth, and I see fucking stars.

"Holy shit. Yes," I say as I grind against him.

He drops back to the mattress and then rubs my clit in time with his movements. That's all it takes to send me flying over the edge. This time as I come, I spasm around him, and he's the one crying out.

"Oh fuck, Peaches. Where do you want my cum?"

"Inside me," I pant, head thrown back. I want to feel everything. I want to know precisely what it feels like to have this man completely spent and losing control.

Maybe it's my words or maybe it's the way my orgasm squeezes him, because instantly, he's groaning and going stiff as he shoots inside me.

When his cock twitches, he drags an aftershock of another orgasm from me, sending sparks dancing along my nerve endings.

I fall against his chest, our heavy breaths matching, our hearts beating wildly against one another.

"That was incredible," I whisper.

For a long moment, Gavin is silent, just holding me tightly. Once our breathing has evened out and our hearts tap out steady rhythms, he presses a kiss against my forehead. "Be right back." He eases me to the bed beside him, then heads for the bathroom.

For the first time tonight, I feel awkward, and I don't know what to do.

When I hear water running, my heart sinks. Okay, I guess that's it. He's going to take a shower, and I should probably go.

Embarrassment swells and settles in my chest. Why do I want to cry? What is wrong with me? I grab a tissue from the nightstand and use it to clean myself up as best as I can. Then I toss it in the trash, ignoring the blood.

I'm grabbing my dress from the floor, ready to throw it on quickly and get out, when the door to the bathroom opens.

"Where are you going?"

"Um, I—" My heart seizes as I search the bed for my panties. *Where are my panties?*

"I ran a bath for you," he says, taking a step into the room.

"Oh, you don't need to do that. I get how this works." Keeping my head down, I continue my search. "We had sex. It was amazing. Thank you. I'll get out of your hair now."

With the bathroom light casting him in silhouette, he plants his hands on his hips and watches me. "I know it was your first time."

My skin heats with morbid embarrassment. "Is it that obvious how inexperienced I am?"

Gavin stalks toward me, completely naked. When he approaches, he brushes my hair from my face and slides his hand to my neck. Lowering his head, he forces me to meet his eye. "No, Peaches. You were perfect. And because I'm livid with myself for having taken that from you after only just meeting you, I'd really appreciate it if you'd let me take care of you. I ran a bath for you. You're probably sore."

"Cocky much." The humor I'm going for falls flat because of the tears clogging my throat. God, I didn't expect this to be so emotional.

"Maybe," he murmurs, though I think we both know he's just being kind. He sees I'm emotional, sees the tears welling in my eyes, and scoops me up and carries me into the bathroom.

The space is massive, all black marble and specks of gold. There's a shower big enough for at least two and an oversized jacuzzi tub filled with bubbles.

Gavin settles me on the edge of it and then leans in to feel the water. "Not too hot. You want to get in?"

I nod and almost cry out the second my body hits the water, the heat burning my sensitive bits.

"You okay?" The lines in his brow are deep with concern.

How many times is he going to ask that, and when will my answer actually be honest?

"I'm fine. You going to get in?"

With a smirk, he slides in behind me, and as soon as he wraps his arms around me, holding me against his chest, the first tear breaks loose. Like an avalanche that I can't possibly stop, another one falls, and then another until I'm silently crying in his arms.

"I'm sorry," I whisper. "I'm not sure why I'm so emotional."

"That's okay," he says far too gently for how this night began. "How old are you?"

"Twenty-two," I hiccup.

"Jesus." He sucks in a harsh breath and then squeezes me tighter.

"That bad?" I let out a trembling laugh.

"No, I just—Fuck, my best friend's kids are twenty-two. Makes me feel old is all."

I wince. Shit. He's talking about my brother and me and he has no idea. Swallowing back the guilt, I tip my head back and eye him above me. "Believe me, you can keep up."

His chest rumbles behind me. "You bet your ass I can. Why do you think I'm pampering you now? Gotta get you ready for another round."

I hum as he lathers me with soap and washes me gently.

"Will you tell me your name now?"

"I rather like Peaches."

This laugh is laced with a little resignation. "I happen to like you too."

I spin and drape my legs over his hips so we're face to face, and my heart trips over itself at the sight of him. His dark brown hair is mussed and his cheeks are flushed from the heat of the water. The gold flecks in his brown irises make his eyes sparkle.

"I didn't say I like *you*. I said I like the nickname."

His tongue slides against his bottom lip, and then he bites down on the same spot. "But you do." It isn't a question, so he doesn't wait for a response. Instead, he angles in and gives me a gentle kiss.

He's right. I really do. But it doesn't matter, because soon, he won't like me very much. I swallow that thought down and decide to enjoy what little time we have.

"If you could do anything in life, what would it be?" he asks.

The question surprises me, though the answer comes easily. If my father didn't own a wildly successful music label, and if he wasn't about to marry the biggest pop star in the world, I'd write music.

I'd planned to tell my father about my dream, but on the night we were set to have dinner together, he announced to the world in a fucking stupid display of lust that he was sleeping with my brother's ex-girlfriend.

A woman who is only four years older than me and the biggest musician on his label.

So fucking cliché.

I was mortified, but it was so much more than that.

On top of the embarrassment, it felt as though she'd taken my place. Because I'd dreamed of being involved in the music industry, working alongside my dad, who had seemed lonely. I thought I'd be enough.

But now he has her and little time for me.

Sure, he still invites me to meet him—or worse, them—for dinner, but I know they're pity invites. He'd rather be with her. He merely feels obligated to me.

He'd rather make music with her. *Spend time with her.*

For so long, I had no one but my father, and I always thought he only had me—which made me feel not so alone in this world. But now...

"Write music," I admit, because my mind is so jumbled there's no way I can come up with a credible lie.

Gavin gazes down at me warmly. "You have talent. Why don't you do that?"

"Because I played an old tune in a bar to a crowd of intoxicated people, you think I have the talent to write good music?" My tone is all humor. I enjoy sparring with this man.

He shrugs. "Yeah. Your voice was incredible. You're mesmerizing."

"He says while I'm naked and sprawled across his lap."

His laughter echoes off the bathroom walls as he shakes beneath me. "No. That was the first thought that came to me when I stepped into the bar. I'd barely seen you, and I was utterly bewitched. Besotted."

"Besotted?" I tease, relishing the joy dancing in the air between us.

"Besotted," he says, firmer, brown eyes glazing.

"And what about you? If you could do anything, what would it be?"

He arches one brow. "I see you're just going to ignore my question."

I press my lips together, silently imploring him to keep going, because yes, I'm doing just that.

He sighs and rubs circles against my back, the water sloshing around us. It's warm in the bath. Against his chest. I'm not quite sure I've ever felt so comfortable. Or so comforted. It's unexplainable, that a stranger could put me at ease this way. For now, I can't dissect the implications, so I push the thoughts away, determined to live in the moment.

"I'd coach hockey."

I try to hide my surprise, because I happen to know he *owns* a team. Not that *he* knows that *I* know that. Why would he prefer coaching a team when he can—and does—own the whole damn thing? If I asked him about what he does, maybe he'd explain, but if I ask, then I'm only adding another infraction to the list I've committed tonight. Now that I've gotten to know him, I want to lie as little as possible.

Because I like him.

A lot.

"Why hockey?"

"Oh god, why not?" he says with a laugh. "Best sport ever."

"So why aren't you coaching?"

He shrugs. "I was groomed to work in an office. I guess I never considered coaching as a real option for a profession."

The furrow in his brow makes it obvious that even now, he's thinking of all the reasons why he'd love to coach and all the reasons why he can't.

Like me, he can't go after what he wants, and I hate that for him.

I hate it for me too.

But I can't solve those problems for either of us. And soon, he won't care one bit about my opinion. For now, I just want to see him smile at me for a little while longer. And I want to bring him the kind of joy he's brought me for the last few hours.

"So tell me, Coach, how do you feel about blow jobs?"

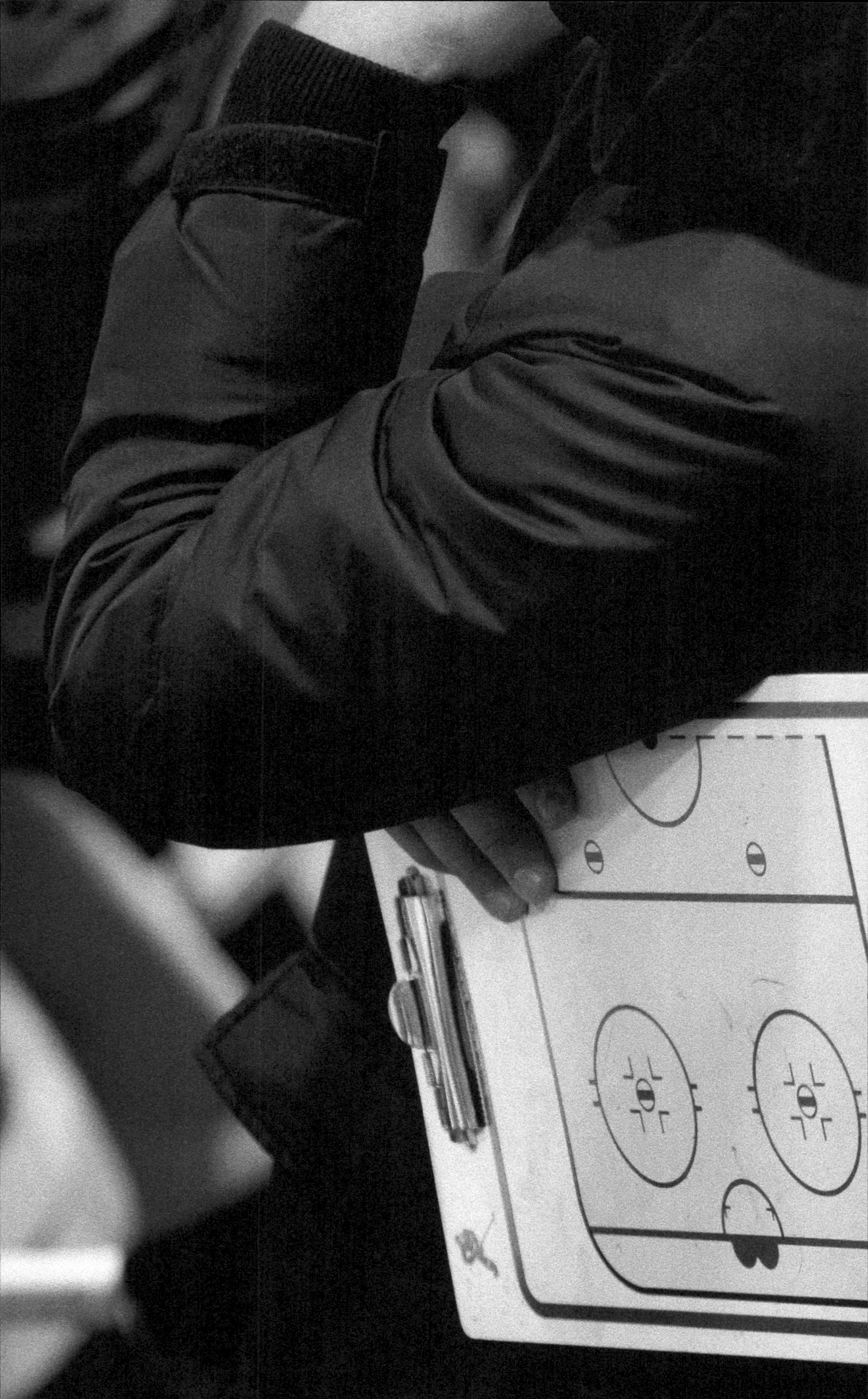

CHAPTER 5
Gavin

THERE'S no time to be disappointed when I wake up without her.

I have a plane to catch, and since we didn't go to sleep until sometime after four—after another three rounds or so—I'm running late. It was worth it, even if I almost fell asleep inside her.

But I knew she'd be gone when I woke up. She wouldn't even give me her name, so I was under no illusion that she'd stick around.

While I own the plane we're taking today, Beckett gets unreasonably annoyed by delays. If I don't haul ass and get to our private runway, I wouldn't put it past him to leave me in Boston while they all head off to Ford's wedding.

I plaster on a big smile when I step into the cabin, sunglasses on, Hawaiian shirt in place, and a bunch of leis in hand to gift to my brothers. Affecting my most obnoxious voice, I say, "I know, I know. I'm late, but I brought gifts. This way I'm not the only one who got laid this morning."

Beckett rolls his eyes as he folds his newspaper like the anal asshole he is and sets it down in front of him. The man is wearing a pair of navy-blue slacks and a button-down shirt. It's pink, I'll give him that, but still, we're going on vacation, not to a fucking board meeting.

I toss one at him, and the fucker surprises the hell out of me by putting it on without a fight. "I'll wear it for five minutes to make you happy, but only if you tell me the story behind the woman who's got you smiling so fucking big."

I grin. "It's a good one." Not that I'll tell him much, other than that I think I fell in love last night and that I'll probably never find her again. Even so, it's fun to play along.

In the back, Brooks and Aiden are sitting side by side. Daniel Hall—our newest recruit and Ford's son—is sitting with them too. I'd forgotten he was traveling with us. Beside him is a woman with her dark hair pulled into a ponytail. She's mostly hidden behind Brooks's massive frame, so all I can see is wavy brown curls.

I can't help but laugh. Kid has no shame bringing a woman along with him to his dad's wedding. Knowing him, he met her last night and Ford has no idea she's coming.

"Got leis for all of you boys. Don't worry," I say as I make my way down the aisle, winking at the flight attendant as I pass her. "Morning, Nicole. Would you like a lei?"

She holds up a hand, looking amused. "Pass."

I like Nicole. She's worked for my family for a few years, and she's been nothing but professional. We've gone through too many flight attendants over the years because many of the women take the job thinking they'll be joining the mile high club. But we don't operate like that. Especially Beckett. When we're working, he expects everyone to be professional. It's a good rule. Keeps my brothers from getting sued and keeps our turnover at the office almost nonexistent.

I throw a lei to Aiden, who catches it with ease, right around his neck.

"I'm telling you, Brooks," he says without missing a beat. "This girl might be the one."

I bite back a groan. I'd forgotten about his text last night. He met a girl. Again. And since the kid is nothing if not a romantic, I'm sure he'll be singing her praises for the next few days.

Hope she's worth it. Aiden deserves someone who loves hard just like he does.

"So you said," Brooks says as I hand him a lei. He nods a silent thank-you while giving me a look that tells me just how irritated he is with our baby brother.

Next up, Daniel. I pass a lei his way, and as he takes it, he turns to his seatmate.

"Want one, Mills?"

The woman looks up then, and I practically choke on my own saliva.

Peaches, *my fucking Peaches*, is sitting cozily next to Daniel Hall, the known playboy on my hockey team. As soon as her golden eyes meet mine, they double in size behind her oversized black glasses.

"Puck bunnies aren't allowed on the team plane," I grit out like an asshole. I'm speaking to Daniel, but I can't take my fucking eyes off her.

Her face is free of makeup and dotted with freckles. But beneath them, her cheeks go rosy as she blinks up at me.

"Gavin," Brooks warns.

I can barely hear him over the thundering of my heart. My focus is set on her and the anger brewing in my gut.

Daniel makes a choking sound beside her. "This isn't a puck bunny. This is Millie, my *twin sister*."

Holy. Fuck. A burst of air I didn't know I was holding whooshes out of me, and I inhale greedily, drowning in relief, because she isn't his. She's just his sister.

Thank fuck.

And now I know her name.

Millie.

I smile at her, even as she watches me like she's a deer and I'm a semi barreling straight for her. The flush that stained her cheeks for a moment is gone. Now she's pale and looks like she's on the verge of passing out.

"Millie," I say quietly, testing the name out on my tongue. "Fits." I clear my throat and hold out my hand to take hers. "I'm so sorry. I just—you caught me off guard. I wasn't expecting anybody but the guys."

Her palm is warm against my hand, and I swear to god sparks shoot between us.

"I was an asshole. I'm really sorry."

She runs her tongue across her lips and lets out the tiniest breath. Like she's accepting our new circumstances. Like maybe she doesn't hate our new circumstances. Like she doesn't hate that we've found ourselves thrown together again.

And then she smiles, and my heart fucking swells.

God, she has a gorgeous smile. Her lips are the prettiest shade of peach, naturally, and don't get me started on the freckles. I doubt there's a single thing I wouldn't like about her.

"Mr. Langfield, if you could take a seat, we're about to take off," Nicole says behind me.

Yeah, there's no way in hell I'm going to sit with Beckett when I could sit and talk to Millie. Fuck, what are the chances? This is incredible.

"Didn't my dad tell you Millie was coming with us?" Daniel asks, his eyes narrowed on me.

Frowning, I turn to him. "Why would your dad—"

That's when it hits me. Holy fuck, Millie *is* Millie Hall.

Peaches is Ford's daughter.

My stomach plummets, and every ounce of relief I felt only seconds ago is sucked from me like I've been tossed into a black hole.

I fucked Millie Hall.

I fucked my best friend's daughter.

So many times.

Fuck. I took my best friend's daughter's virginity.

Holy shit.

"Gavin," Beckett calls when I forget how to do anything but stare at Millie.

"Breathe," she mouths, her eyes begging me to keep my shit together.

Holy fuck, this poor girl gave her virginity to her dad's best friend. She must be freaking out right now.

And she's probably disgusted.

I want to assure her that I didn't know. I want to apologize a thousand different ways, but my throat has closed up and my vocal cords have been sliced. So I blink once, twice, and nod to the group. Then I force my feet to take me back to Beckett. As I drop into my usual seat, my mind races and the lead ball in my gut grows.

"What the hell is wrong with you?" Beckett growls.

Yeah, my brother growls. It's a daily occurrence. I really don't have time for his normal attitude, though. I'm in crisis right now.

"How old was the youngest girl you've ever fucked?" I hiss.

"What?" Beckett rears back, brows pulled low. "I didn't—I don't —what the fuck are you talking about?"

"Twenty-one? Twenty-two?"

"What the hell is happening to you?"

"Tell me."

Beckett runs a hand through his hair. "When I was younger, sure. But no, women that age don't really do it for me." He shrugs like that answers that.

Millie Hall is twenty-two. It threw me when she told me, but at the same time, it didn't. I knew she was young when she sat next to me in the bar. Knew she couldn't be over twenty-five, and while yeah, normally the women I sleep with are older than that, we clicked. She's mature and sophisticated. Or maybe I'm just an old pervert who is attracted to his best friend's daughter and I need my head examined.

More like your dick, asshole. Because both were involved in everything that happened last night, and they're both attracted to Millie.

And my heart. On cue, a sharp pain in my chest causes me to hunch over. Fuck. It wasn't just sex. I liked her.

A lot.

"You gonna tell me what's going on with you?" Beckett asks as the plane starts down the runway.

I'm gripping the seat so tightly my knuckles are turning white. Beckett notices and eyes me with nothing but concern on his face.

"I just—fuck, I called Millie Hall a puck bunny."

In an instant, that worried expression morphs into a smirk. "That's what has you all worked up?" He rubs at his jaw and chuckles. "She's probably used to idiots saying shit like that. Her brother's played hockey all his life."

Her brother. Daniel. Right. Because she's Millie Hall. Why can't I stop calling her that in my head?

She rests her elbow on her armrest and tilts to one side so she can see me.

"I'm so sorry," I mouth.

"She looks like she's forgiven you," Beckett says. "Calm down and tell me about your night."

She straightens, and I close my eyes, unable to stomach the thought of last night right now.

Somehow, someway, I need to forget every minute of it. I need to forget the way she tastes. The way she moans. The way she feels.

Like peaches and tequila, soft and needy and warm and tight.

Yeah, every single thing about her is imprinted in my mind. I'm not sure I could forget it if I tried, and considering I'm already actively trying to figure out how soon I can get her alone, I know I won't be trying.

But only because I need to talk to her. Explain that I had no clue who she was. And then...

Well, then I have no fucking idea what I'll do. The one thing I know I can't do is fuck my best friend's kid again, though.

She leans to one side and looks at me again, her lips pinched and her eyes swimming with dread. God, what I wouldn't do to sit beside her and pull her onto my lap. Remove that look from her face with a kiss.

No.

No, no, no.

There will be no kisses. No smiling. From here on out, she can be no one but Millie Hall: Ford's daughter.

And, somehow, I'll have to find a way to be okay with that.

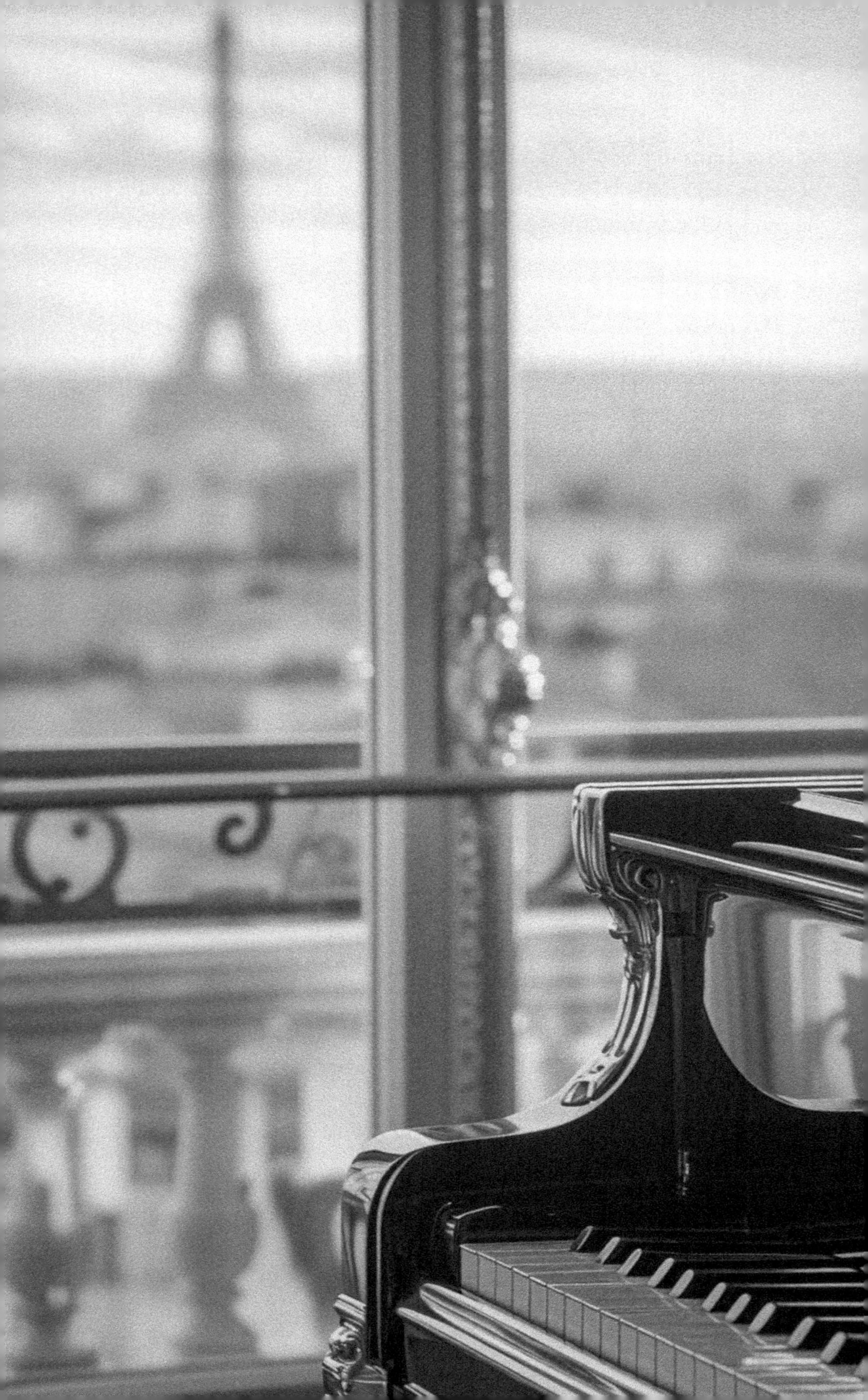

CHAPTER 6
Millie

MY BROTHER GETS comfortable in his seat, and for the whole trip, he doesn't leave my side other than to pee. Even then, I can't exactly get up and go talk to Gavin. Especially not when he's sitting next to *his* brother.

We aren't supposed to know one another. Hell, he called me a puck bunny, and then he looked utterly horrified when he found out who I really am.

I'd do just about anything to go back in time. To live in that bathtub with him. To just be the girl he opened up to, the woman he held so sweetly and kissed like he'd die if he didn't.

My heart nearly split in two when I snuck out this morning without saying goodbye, but nothing could have prepared me for seeing him again. And I *knew* I'd see him. I knew this was his plane. And I knew I'd be turning his world upside down. Yet I did it all anyway.

I'm an asshole.

"Want something to drink?" Daniel stands and nods at the bar.

This plane is sick. My father has money, obviously, but not Langfield money.

Actually, now that he's marrying Lake Paige, he probably does have Langfield money. She's a superstar. One of the wealthiest women in the world.

I wouldn't be surprised if her plane is even nicer than this one.

That thought has my stomach turning and my chest constricting.

I honestly don't understand what she's doing with my father. Yes, he's amazing. He's the best guy in the world—or at least he used to be.

I'm being an ass again. He's still the best guy in the world—he's just...God, I don't know what he's thinking marrying a woman who's young enough to be his daughter.

And there go the chest pains again.

Daniel doesn't have a problem with it, and Paul's all *I love my boyfriend, so whatever.* How Paul isn't at least half as angry as I am is beyond me. Lake was his *girlfriend.* Doesn't he care? Why am I the only one bothered by this? Though I suppose I'm not completely alone in my outrage. My mother carries enough of a grudge for all of us.

"Mills," Daniel says, hovering over me.

"Oh." I blink myself out of my spiraling thoughts and nod. "Sure, I'll take a margarita."

I need something to take the edge off.

Brooks and Aiden are on their feet too, and Brooks snickers. "Tequila at nine a.m. Impressive."

The second they're gone, I zero in on Gavin again. I can't stop looking at him.

Will he come over now that I'm alone?

In a bright Hawaiian shirt, he'd look like the relaxed, funny man my father has always described him as, but the tense jaw and aggressive typing on his phone are giving off the opposite vibe.

Fortunately, his other brother—the stuffy one who, while also ridiculously good-looking, did not even hit my radar when I considered who I'd fuck—is so focused on his newspaper he doesn't see me ogling his brother.

"Gavin," I whisper. When he doesn't react, I do it again, a little louder.

His brown eyes fly up and heat as soon as they land on me. I give a sharp nod of my head, summoning him over. With a few mumbled words to his brother, he's heading my way.

Though my stomach is in knots as he sits beside me and scans the cabin, posture rigid, my heart skips a beat at just the scent of him. How is it that we only spent a few hours together, and yet my heart seems to recognize his?

"I swear I didn't know," he rushes out.

"I know that."

His shoulders sag, and he blows out a breath. "I mean, what are the chances?" His lips lift in a hint of a small smile. "I wouldn't take it back," he says quickly. "I know that's wrong and fucked up, and I'm sure you're grossed out now that you know who I am. But I want you to know that I appreciate what last night was for you, and it meant something to me." He swallows audibly, searching my face, and then, in a softer tone, he repeats, "I wouldn't take it back. It's important to me that you know that, even if you wish you could."

I lick my lips and summon the courage to tell him the truth. I may be a lot of things, and we may have met under false pretenses, but I'm not a liar. "I wouldn't take it back either. And I'm not grossed out in the least because—" I wet my lips again, heart pounding. "I knew who you were."

Gavin's eyes, which have been warm and focused on my mouth, narrow, and he meets my gaze. "'Scuse me?"

"I knew who you were. Last night. It wasn't—" With a shake of my head, I blow out a slow breath, then launch myself right off the cliff. "I wanted to give my virginity to you. I planned it that way. I knew who you were. It wasn't kismet or fate or anything like that. I...I wanted it to be you."

His stare is piercing, penetrating, like he's trying to read my mind so he can make it make sense. I wish I could give him clarity. I wish I could explain it better. But we don't have the time. Not now. And I'm not sure I could explain it if I tried.

I'm horrified and disgusted with myself. Not because I had sex with him, but because I deceived him.

Because when I seduced him, I became the kind of person I hate.

It's the kind of thing my mother would do. It's almost as if she slipped into my head and plotted it herself. Which is gross on a completely different level.

"You knew I was friends with your father?" His voice is colder, and he's angled back. The move was almost imperceptible, but he might as well have put miles between us.

"Yes."

"And what?" He scoffs. "You're mad at him, so you decided to fuck me?" His teeth are clenched so hard his jaw ticks, and his voice is a little too loud.

Heart lodged in my throat. I press my hands against my armrests and crane my neck, hoping like hell the guys didn't hear him. As it turns out, we're completely alone. Even Beckett has disappeared to the bar.

"No. Well, yes," I stammer. "Originally. But I didn't go through with it."

He coughs out a laugh full of anger and incredulity. "Excuse me? If I remember correctly, you absolutely went through with it. Multiple times."

I suck in a breath and close my eyes. God, I'm not explaining this right.

"Yes. When I went into that bar, my plan was to seduce you. But I-I lost my nerve. I couldn't go through with it."

Gavin's jaw is locked so tight I worry he'll do real damage to his teeth.

"And then you made me laugh. And smile. And—"

"I get it. I was there." He closes his eyes and massages his temple. "Fuck. I—Whatever fucked up bullshit you have going on with your father," he bites out, eyes open and piercing me once more, "I don't want to be a part of it. His friendship means a lot to me, and if he finds out about us, it'll ruin that. So if you're being honest and you truly felt something for me, then you'll forget it happened. I know I will."

I nod quickly as my face grows hot and swallow back the tears that threaten to spill over. "Of course. I'm sorry. I swear I won't tell a soul."

His breathing is ragged, and his jaw pulses, but he doesn't say anything else, and when one tear escapes, I swipe it away quickly, but not before he notices. He closes his eyes and grimaces like he's in pain at the sight of it.

"I'm just gonna go to the bathroom," I say, my voice wobbly as I unbuckle myself. Head lowered, I rush off, unable to stomach another second of his disappointment.

I fucked up.

Majorly.

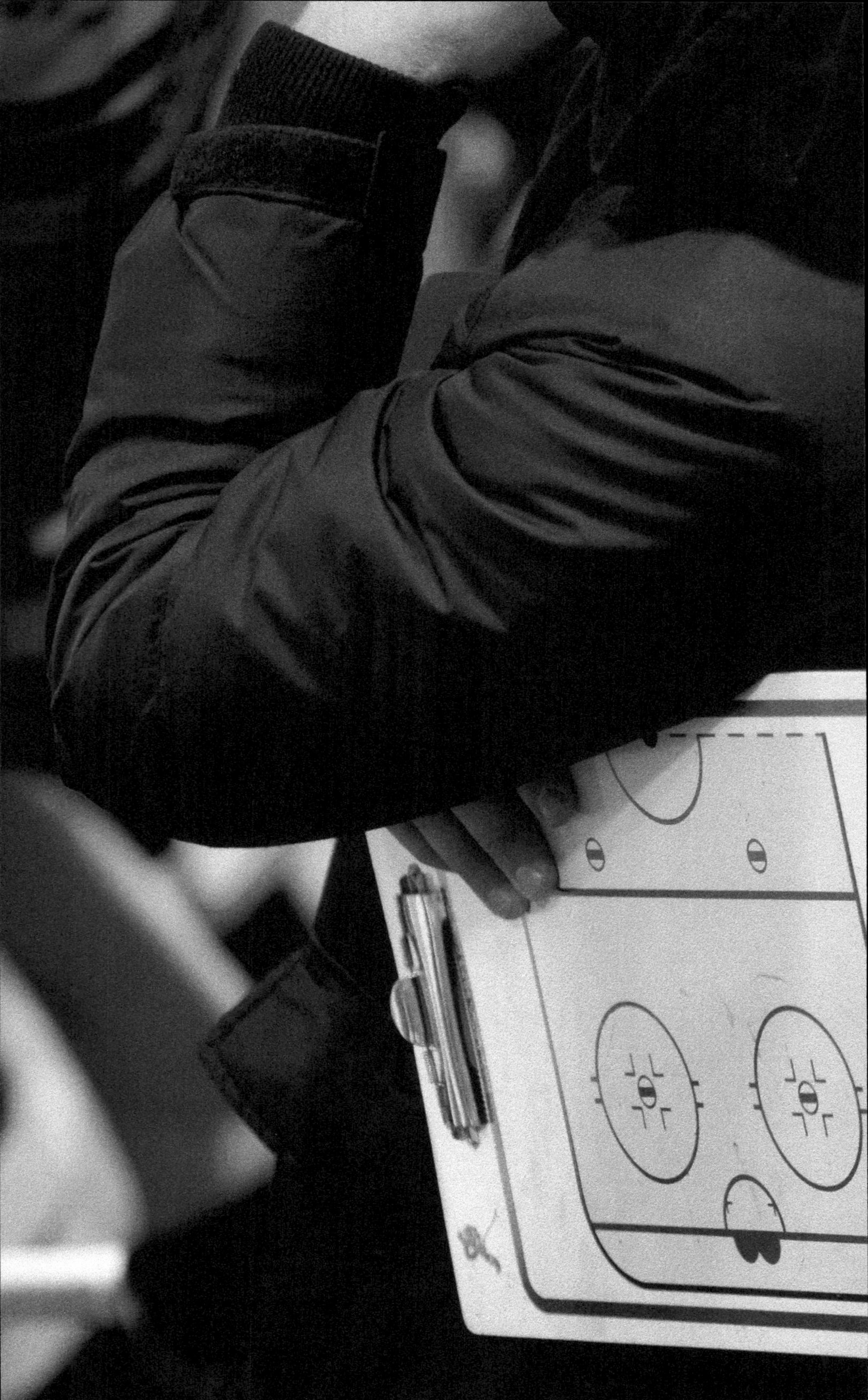

CHAPTER 7
Gavin

"I STILL DON'T UNDERSTAND why the two of you have your own rooms, but Brooks and I have to share," Aiden whines as we settle into the white chairs situated on the beach.

The wedding is set to start any minute, and it's taking all the self-control I possess to not look across the aisle to where Millie is sitting.

She looks lonely.

She looked lonely last night at the welcome dinner too. She barely glanced at Lake and said about two words to her father, and though Daniel tried to include her, she was also trying to avoid me. That left very few people for her to talk to.

Lake and Ford wanted a small wedding, though *small* isn't the word I'd use to describe the party gathered today. They know too many people to have the luxury of keeping it intimate. There are music industry officials and a handful of musicians. Melina, Lake's best friend and maid of honor, is a well-known singer, and Nate and

Amelia Pearson are famous musicians in their own right, but also good friends of Lake and Ford.

Then there's our crowd. Ford's group of friends includes my brothers and me, as well as Jay Hanson and his wife, Cat, whom I adore. Lake's family is here too.

Yet not one person other than Daniel is here for Millie, and he hasn't bothered to check on her, let alone talk to her.

It's difficult to watch.

I rub at the ache blooming in my chest but force myself to remain focused on my brother. The grown-ass adult who's acting like a child. "It's one more night. Also, you told us you 'fell in love,' so it's not like you need a room to bring a girl back to tonight."

He rolls his eyes. "Whatever. Maybe Brooks wants to."

Brooks arches a brow and smirks. "I'm fine. But if I walk into our room and you're FaceTiming your new girl with your dick out, we're going to have a problem."

I snort. Damn, Brooks is probably speaking from experience. The two of them share a room when they travel with the team and have for years. I can only imagine the stories.

"Whatever. Beckett, why can't you sleep with Brooks? Neither of you have a chance of getting laid tonight—on FaceTime or in real life."

Beckett leans forward, rigid as ever, and glares at Aiden. "Face the ceremony and shut your mouth before I staple it shut."

The laugh that rumbles out of me is deep this time, easing a little of the pain still tormenting me. Aiden crosses his arms and glares.

"Hey, I sign your paychecks," I say, using the sternest tone I can muster. I like to give him shit, even if my status as owner of the Bolts isn't really anything to brag about. Ownership was handed to me. This is the role I was always expected to play. Even if I'd rather be doing what he and Brooks do. Unfortunately, I was never as good as they are on the ice.

Truth be told, Aiden's talent is indescribable. I have no doubt he'll be in the hall of fame one day. The media will be talking about the Great Aiden Langfield for decades. I'm happy he's on my team and even happier he's my brother.

Not that I'd tell him that. The kid's head is way too big as it is, and he can't shut up. He'd never let me live it down.

Ford and Daniel head down the aisle, both wearing light gray herringbone suits and bright smiles. When he gets to the end of the aisle, Ford looks at Millie and winks.

In response, she gives him a tight smile.

Paul didn't show up, which is probably a good thing. If he were here, he'd be more of a distraction than anything. Half the people in attendance would be more focused on him and his potential reaction than on the wedding. Honestly, Ford and Lake are soulmates. Age doesn't matter. Circumstances don't matter. When they're together, it's easy to see how happy they are.

I rub my chest again and glance at Millie. She's sitting ramrod straight, focused on the ocean beyond the arch where her dad and brother are standing. What is she thinking? Does she really not see how happy her father is? Is she really so selfish that she'd rather he be lonely and unhappy than with a woman he adores who happens to be her age? And if she really felt something for me like she claims, wouldn't she understand, at least to some degree?

Or was it all fake?

Was it just a line, when she said she wouldn't take that night back?

Even as I think it, I know it isn't true.

She's broken.

Lost. Sad even.

Not evil.

And despite my anger over what she did—over how she seduced me—I can't help but feel for her.

Despite her loneliness, Millie is gorgeous. She's wearing a deep burgundy silk dress that falls to her calves. Her curly hair whips around her, and when she turns so I can see her face, I have trouble swallowing. As our eyes connect, my neck heats despite the cool breeze that comes off the ocean. The defeat in those golden irises, the weight pushing on her shoulders, and the clear shame that mars her pretty face nearly break me. I have no idea what I'm doing, but she can't sit by herself. Not in a moment like this.

Ford is beaming—rightfully so. He's about to marry the love of his life. Beside him, Daniel is laughing and joking, completely oblivious to his sister's heartbreak.

I don't know the true cause or why she's taking this so hard. But the woman I met on Friday night was kind. Determined. She didn't cower.

And then she sobbed after we had sex. If that doesn't tell me that she's struggling, that she's not devious, that she's not nearly the brat I made her out to be in my mind, then I'd have to be dead inside.

And even if she's in the wrong, I can't sit here while she's sad and alone.

"I'm going to go sit with Millie," I say to Beckett.

He glances across the aisle, and his eyes crease in understanding. "I'll watch Tweedledee and Tweedledum," he says. The small quirk of his lips is about as close to a smile as he gets.

I stand and head her way, garnering Ford's attention in the process. He tilts his head and watches me until I take the seat beside Millie. Then he shoots me an appreciative smile.

There's no way in hell he'd look at me like that if he knew the things I've done with his little girl, but I'm going to forget all about the way she tasted or felt beneath me and focus on being a friend to her when she needs one.

"What are you doing?" Her voice is quiet and filled with uncertainty.

I fiddle with the button on the front of my jacket and keep my attention trained on the altar. I can't look at her when she's this close. I'm liable to kiss her. "Shh, Peaches. Wedding's about to start."

In my periphery, she bites back a smile and ducks her head, her cheeks turning pink.

Up front, Daniel nods at me, then smiles at Millie. Her smile comes easier this time, filling me with an irrational sense of pride.

When the music starts and all eyes turn in the direction of the wedding party, I find that my focus is fixed on her.

As Melina comes down the aisle, Millie elbows me. "You're supposed to be focused on the wedding."

"Can't look away from the beautiful girl next to me."

She rolls her eyes as she continues to keep her gaze on the show before us.

In a deep red dress, Melina takes her spot opposite Daniel and winks at Ford. "Hey, Daddy Hall. Your girl looks gorgeous."

With a laugh, Ford shakes his head. "Mel, the nickname."

He hates being called Daddy. And for the first time, I really get that. The last thing I'd want is the girl next to me to call me daddy. And yet

I close my eyes, forcing the horrible thoughts—thoughts about the ways I could teach her, the ways I *did* teach her—from my mind.

The music switches to a soft melody, and the people around us stand and turn. Beside me, Millie sucks in a breath, almost like she's summoning her courage, and then she stands as well.

Every person here is focused on the bride, most of all my best friend, who is wiping at tears that fall despite his big smile. He's in love, and he's proud to show it. Nothing could tear his attention from Lake now, so I grasp Millie's left hand and step closer.

She snaps her head to the side and blinks at me, stunned, as the procession continues. We don't look away from one another. I hold her hand, stare into her eyes, and silently lead her through deep, even breaths as Lake makes her way down the aisle. When the wedding officiant asks us to be seated, she breaks eye contact, and I release her hand.

We sit side by side, not touching, through the ceremony. And the whole time, I can feel the warmth of her palm beneath mine. It's imprinted on my skin just like her body is from our night together.

This woman has stained me, changed me, and I'm not sure what to think about that.

Nor do I have any interest in reverting to the man I was before.

Fortunately, Daniel keeps Millie by his side for the reception. That means she's by my side too, since Daniel spends the night hanging with my brothers, and I'm a glutton for punishment who acts like I'm being forced to hang with them as well.

I could easily go and chat with a half dozen people right now. Instead, I stand beside Beckett at the bar, with Millie, Daniel, and my brothers to our left.

And I'm doing a terrible job of not staring at her.

"You might want to keep your eyes off his daughter. He's on his way over," Beckett says with a nod in Ford's direction.

I clear my throat and stand up straighter, avoiding my brother's knowing gaze. Fuck, I hope he thinks I'm feeling awkward about my puck bunny comment on the plane and he doesn't know what's really going on.

"Surprised you let go of her long enough to come say hello," Beckett teases, craning his neck like he's looking behind Ford for his bride.

The man just laughs, his eyes bright and his smile wide. He's never hidden his obsession with Lake. Pretty sure that only a few months ago, when we were teasing him about his fixation on his son's ex, his exact words were "you don't look away from perfection."

He was never ashamed of going after what he wanted, forbidden or not. Never hid how he felt. And now he looks like the happiest motherfucker I've ever seen.

"She went to the bathroom to freshen up since the dances are about to start."

"You probably should do the same. You've got evidence in your scruff," I tease, pointing at the red lipstick Lake is famous for on Ford's neck.

His grin is so wide it splits his face as he rubs at the spot. "What can I say? When he pronounced her my wife? Fuck, I needed her."

I roll my eyes, wondering if I'll ever feel possessive about someone like that.

And once again, I find myself seeking Millie out. Aiden's gesturing wildly like he's telling a hilarious story, and she's bright eyed and laughing. Damn. Just seeing her relaxed makes me feel lighter.

When Ford follows my gaze, his softens. "I'm glad she came."

"You didn't think she would?" Beckett asks.

Ford turns back to us, his lips tugging into a frown for the first time today. "Honestly, I wasn't sure. She's taking this hard. I don't know what to do to make it better for her. She dropped out of school."

My breath catches in my throat, and I dart another look at her. She didn't mention that. Though why would she have? Despite the connection between us, I really know little about her, and only the details she chose to share with me.

I know she likes peach margaritas, that she has one hell of a singing voice, and that if she could do anything, she'd write music.

Instantly, I'm studying her again.

She writes music.

Fuck, is that what this is about?

As if she can feel my attention on her, she meets my gaze, but a moment later, she breaks the contact and goes back to chatting with Aiden. All the while, my head continues to spin.

"Thanks for sitting with her." Ford grabs my shoulder and squeezes. "I wish she'd brought a date, or a friend. She seems so lost."

My stomach sinks at the same time my chest aches. For both of them. I wish they'd open up to one another. Ford is hurting and would do anything to make this easier for his daughter. And Millie is lost and unsure of how to be all right with it all.

I didn't before, but now that I know Millie, now that I've gotten to spend a little time with her, I see this is killing her. She doesn't want to be angry with Ford. But she doesn't know how not to be.

"She'll figure it out," I croak. "She's young."

Young. I'm not sure why that's the word I cling to but, nevertheless, it's the one I choose.

Ford nods.

"My bride is back." He leans forward, like he's being pulled by an invisible force, as Lake walks toward us.

Her dress is long and hugs all her curves, and beneath the beaded fabric that sparkles like a disco ball is a nude-colored layer that makes it look as though she's showing far more skin than she is. But we all know Ford would never allow any of us to walk out of here with our sight intact if she were bare beneath that dress.

"Hey, will you do me a favor?" Ford tears his gaze away from his wife for only a second and turns to me. "Will you ask Millie to dance tonight?"

"Me?" I ask, likely gaping like an idiot.

"Yeah," he urges. "She seems comfortable with you."

"Don't you think she'd rather dance with someone her own age?"

"Like one of your brothers?" Ford shudders. "Yeah, I'd prefer not to think about my daughter like that, so do me a solid and ask her to dance. I don't want her to be lonely, but I have zero interest in setting her up with one of the hockey guys. I know how Daniel is. I'm sure Aiden and Brooks are no different. Don't need her actually interested in anyone here."

A little wave of indignation runs through me in response to that last comment. My best friend is asking me to dance with his daughter because, in his mind, she'd never be attracted to me and I'd never touch her like that.

I should be offended. I *should* feel chastised. But he'd be singing a different tune if he had any idea that I've had her on almost every surface of my apartment.

Before I can formulate a response, Lake arrives, and Ford is already dragging her out to the dance floor, a glass of champagne in his hand. "Excuse me, everyone. I'd like to make a toast," he starts.

Once again, my attention is drawn to his daughter, who's watching, curious, like everyone else here.

Lake tilts her head back and gives Ford a dreamy look as he pulls her close.

"Thanks for traveling all this way for our wedding," Ford starts. "We appreciate it more than you know. I never expected that I'd be doing this again. Never thought I'd meet someone who'd make me risk my career, my reputation, and my heart. But then again, I don't think you can ever prepare for love." He holds Lake's gaze and smiles. "Falling in love with you was the easiest thing I've ever done. It wasn't a choice. It wasn't calculated. It took absolutely zero thought or effort on my part. Because you're you. The sweetheart who made me smile and reminded me that I still had a whole lot of life to live. You make me want to live a thousand more years, and you make me feel far younger than my knees would have you believe."

Chuckles ring out around us. Like me, the rest of the guests are captivated by my best friend as he pours his heart out.

"I love you, Lake. I'm proud to be your husband. Proud to call you my wife. I'm thankful that I get to spend my days with you by my side and thankful for the love of music we have in common. A connection that has created a true friendship between us on top of all we already share. Because of that shared love, I have one more wedding present for you."

Lake's lips twist as she beams at Ford, her eyes glassy and her cheeks flushed. "What are you talking about, Mr. Hall? You are my present."

A chorus of *awws* rings out as she pops up on her toes and kisses his jaw.

"Well, *Mrs. Hall*," Ford says, his tone full of teasing, "I sure hope you won't be disappointed with another present, since spoiling you is my favorite thing to do." He clears his throat and addresses the rest of us. "As you all know, Hall Records has had its best year yet, and that is in no small part because of my wife. Lake, you work your ass off day in and day out, speaking to the hearts of millions of fans, and my label has been the benefactor of that. Which is why I want it to now be *our* label."

Lake sucks in a breath and slaps a hand to her chest, the tears welling over now.

Hoots and hollers go up all around as Ford holds up his glass. "To my beautiful bride, the amazing and talented Lake Hall. Musician and now co-owner of Hall Records. I love you."

Glasses clink, and as the happy couple kisses, I turn to look for Millie. But her seat is empty, and I have a feeling I know why.

Shit.

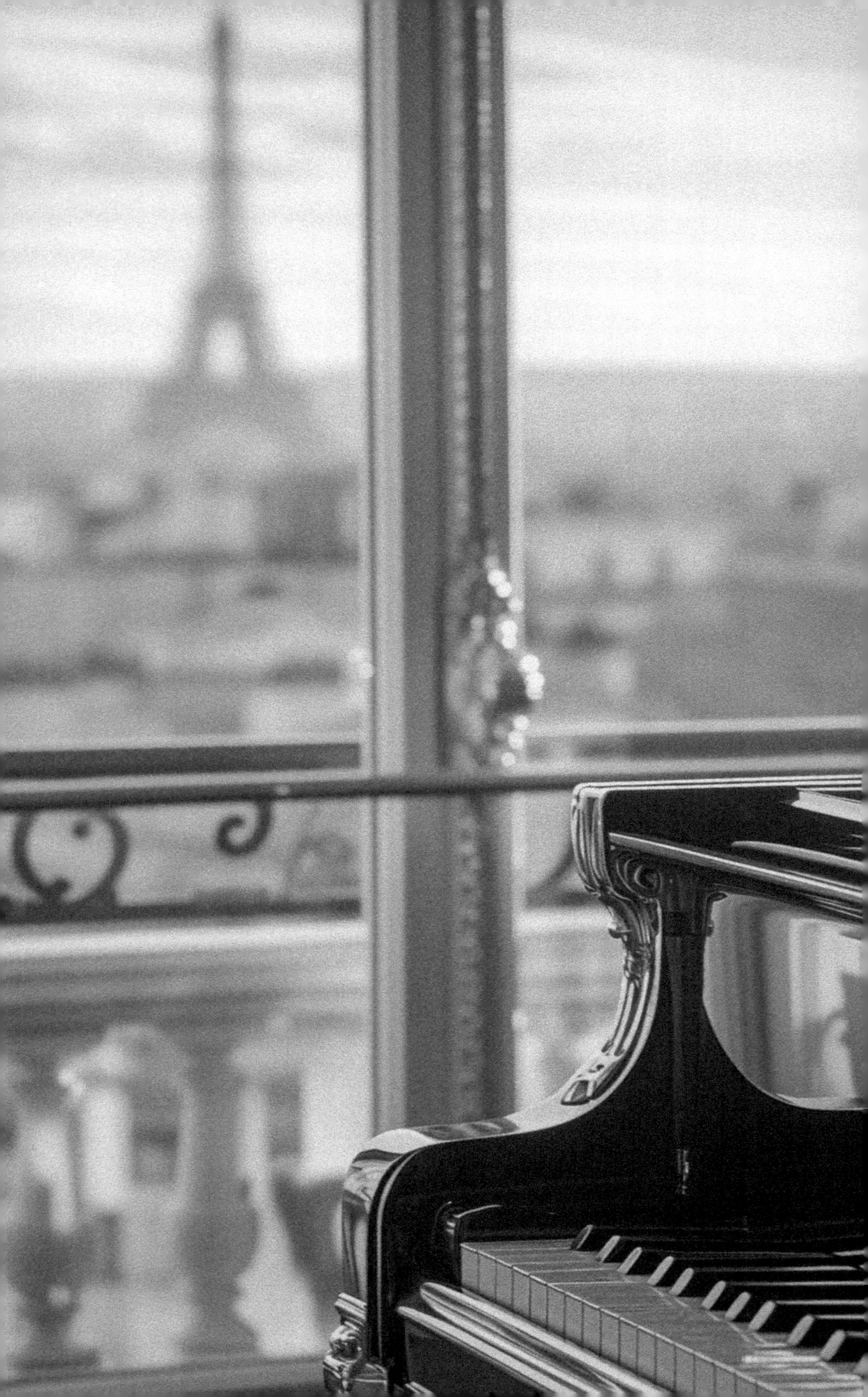

CHAPTER 8
Millie

DO NOT CRY. *Do not cry.* Despite the instructions, the tears are dangerously close to dropping. I've officially lost all hope of one day running the company with my dad.

Daniel has hockey, Paul—well, Paul doesn't seem to care about anything but spending money. Earning it has never interested him. Dad and I share a love for music and everything that entails.

That was my one escape.

Now though...now he shares that with Lake.

"Hey." The woman's voice, so close behind me, startles me enough to make me jump.

I'm in the bathroom hiding out after my father just gifted his business to Lake.

I thought I was alone. The last thing I want is a witness to my pity party.

Inhaling a fortifying breath, I choke back the tears and turn. The woman looks familiar, but I can't place her.

I offer her a tight smile. "Hi."

"Beautiful wedding. You're Millie, right? Ford's daughter?"

I nod, throat tight. "That's me."

She holds out her manicured hand. "I'm Cat. Your dad is one of my husband's best friends."

"Nice to meet you, Cat."

She gives me a genuine smile, and for a moment, the devastation that's taken over recedes, because damn, is this woman drop-dead gorgeous. Dark hair, whiskey eyes, and a big smile. The name doesn't ring a bell, but still, I know her from somewhere. "I'm sorry. I know everyone here today is someone, so I'm going to go out on a limb and guess you're in the music industry."

Her responding laugh is throaty and rich. "No. I own *Jolie* Magazine. My husband and I do. And I run Bouvier media. We're in the process of producing our first show. It will follow Sienna Langfield's spring collection in Paris."

"Oh my god, *yes*." For the first time today, a sense of true joy hits me. "I've been following that. So you flew in from Paris?"

Genuinely interested in the show and its production, I push away the despair eating at me. I can wallow over the loss of my father's company later.

"Yes, it's been a nice break. Jay and I never really get time alone. We have a daughter who keeps us busy, and with the new show, we've been going nonstop for months. So it's been nice to disconnect and focus on one another. And this resort is so gorgeous."

Cat leans against the sink and surveys me with genuine interest, as if chatting with me in here is about more than just being polite.

"So what do you do, Millie?"

I clasp my hands and lower my chin as a little of that defeat creeps back in. "I was in my last semester of college, but I—" I clear my throat. "I didn't know what I wanted to do with my life, so I'm taking a break while I figure it out."

With an approving hum, Cat nods. "I get that. College is a funny thing. You're supposed to know exactly what you want to do by the time you're twenty-two. And if you're not sure, then you're forced to waste hundreds of thousands of dollars trying to figure it out."

I laugh. "Yeah, something like that."

Her eyes brighten as she straightens. "We're in need of a production intern. Would you be interested while you're figuring things out? Sienna is amazing, don't get me wrong, but she kind of goes through interns like they're snacks."

The offer comes out of nowhere and hits me square in the chest, making it impossible to respond. For a moment, all I can do is blink at this stranger who just offered me a job in Europe.

"She wouldn't have the authority to fire you," Cat says with a devilish grin. "Oh my god, this is brilliant. Since your father and her brothers are so close, she absolutely wouldn't fire you. And that would mean we could make it through filming without getting further behind schedule. And without all the fires to put out, I could finally go back to working regular hours and having sex with my husband again." She slaps a hand over her mouth, eyes dancing. When she pulls her hand away, she gives me a sheepish grin. "Sorry, you should probably forget I said that."

I laugh and shake my head. "It's fine."

"Please tell me you might be even a little interested. The money is great, and the job comes with amazing perks, like a whole new wardrobe designed by Sienna. Everyone on set is required to wear Langfield designs, not that free designer clothing is a hardship."

Is this woman seriously trying to sell a position working on the set of the most anticipated show *to me*?

"And," she adds in an excited whisper, "it's Paris in the spring. Can you think of anything better?"

Honestly? No. Not a damn thing. And after my father's announcement, it might be the perfect distraction. "Do you have a card or something? Can I think about it?"

Cat reaches into her purse and pulls out her phone. "Here, input your number, and I'll text you so you have mine. Call me with any questions. Seriously, housing and transportation are all covered. You'd be saving me if you said yes."

A little of the ice that has formed around my heart these last few months melts away as I type in my information. As she slips her phone back into her purse, I wring my hands and take in a full breath for the first time tonight. "Thanks, Cat. I will definitely be in touch."

"I'll see you out there." With a wink, she's gone, leaving me alone to study my reflection and contemplate my life.

Accepting the job offer would be insane. Right? I've never even considered fashion as a career option. Then again, working in production isn't exclusive to fashion. It would certainly be interesting. And it would give me space from my mother and her constant commentary, as well as time to work through this issue I have with my father.

School is a nonissue. Dropping out might have been another knee-jerk reaction, but I can't imagine going back to the whispers and stares.

A few months away might be exactly what I need.

I leave the bathroom, stomach still in knots, scanning the reception space for my brother. The makeshift wooden dance floor on the beach is surrounded by string lights. And the burnt oranges and pinks of the sky as the sun hangs low above the turquoise ocean paints the most gorgeous backdrop. The tables set up in the sand are covered in sparkling gold fabric and surrounded by white and gold chairs. The bamboo bar is a popular spot tonight. It's crowded with wedding guests who are all laughing and smiling and enjoying the soft reggae music the live band is playing.

If it were anyone else's wedding, I'd be enamored.

I'm not blind. I can see that Lake makes my father happy.

That's all that should matter to me, but when I look at them swaying on the dance floor, it's like an anvil has been dropped onto my chest.

I finally spot Daniel, who's sporting a flirty smile while he talks to Melina. Dammit. I don't have a shot in hell at getting his attention right now. My brother is a man-whore, and while I now understand the appeal of sex, I'm still annoyed by him.

I head toward the bar but am stopped by a hand on my hip. A shiver works its way through me as Gavin leans in and presses himself so close I can feel his breath against my ear. "Dance with me?"

I turn and gape at him. "Uh—don't you think my father would kill you?"

The smirk he gives me is far too smug. "He asked me to. Apparently, he's nervous that one of my brothers will ask you, and he doesn't think you could possibly be attracted to me."

The laugh that bubbles out of me feels so damn good, but it's cut off quickly and replaced by a moan when his fingers tighten on my hips.

He inhales a deep breath, the sound so desperate my body ignites. "Please, Peaches," he murmurs.

Fuck me.

Ignoring every warning bell going off in my brain, I allow him to lead me to the dance floor. I also ignore the way my father smiles at me and nods at Gavin.

Is he doing this only because my father asked? Is he still mad at me? I don't blame him if he is, but I can't stop my brain from working overtime, and I can't shake the disappointment that swamps me at the idea that he's only doing it for my father.

It hits me then, that this is probably exactly how Gavin feels, thinking I only slept with him to get back at my father.

"I'm sorry." I pull back and frown.

Gavin holds me tight and continues to sway. "Hmm?"

"I'm sorry that I made you think I used you. I swear I didn't."

With his lips pressed together in a firm line, he nods. "What exactly was your plan, then?"

"I don't know. I just—I've been so angry for the last few months. I wanted to feel something other than anger. I don't want to be upset with my father. God, he's been my idol my entire life. He's always been my best friend, and now—" My voice cracks as I try to explain the unexplainable.

With the hand he has splayed on my lower back, he pulls me closer. There's barely an inch between us now. It's not right. I know how it looks, and yet I can't find it in me to create any distance. I crave his closeness. *Crave him.*

"I know it's wrong." I swallow back the emotion still thick in my throat. "I know I'm an asshole for doing what I did, and I'm sorry for putting you in this position. I swear I won't tell him what happened."

Gavin nods, his expression unreadable. "You mentioned the other night that if you could do anything, you'd write music." His eyes are so damn intense as he watches me. "Does your father know that?"

I look away, wishing he couldn't read me so well. It seems impossible. We barely know each other, yet he gets me already. I'm not sure anyone in my life has even tried to understand what I'm going through, and Gavin just zeroes in on the issue. No bullshit, no judgment, just understanding.

"No," I admit.

"Don't you think that if he knew, he'd have encouraged that?"

"I was going to tell him over Christmas break. We had plans—" I sigh. "We had plans to go to the Bolts game and dinner."

"Ah." Gavin nods. "And then he announced to the world that he was with Lake and brought her to the game instead."

"Yup. Maybe it's childish to be upset, but I was always his girl. Music was our thing. Daniel had hockey. Paul's obsessed with himself just like my mother, and Dad and I had music."

"It's not one or the other, you know," Gavin says softly, his gaze searching mine. "He hasn't replaced you by marrying Lake."

"Hasn't he, though? Now that he has her, it feels like there's no room for me." God, I'm whiny, but Gavin's gentleness, his demeanor, makes me think that I'm safe sharing these feelings with him.

"I think if you tell your father how you feel, if you open up about your dreams, you'd be surprised by how much he'd want them right along with you."

Focusing on the top button of his shirt to avoid his eye, I shrug. "Maybe."

"But you're not going to talk to him, are you?"

"Not tonight. We'll talk...eventually," I hedge.

Gavin pulls me close. "Then let's just dance for a bit, Peaches. No more tears, though, please."

How the hell does he know I was crying?

"Why?" I sigh, resting my cheek against his chest.

He brushes his thumb softly against my back, soothing me. "Because I can't stand to see you sad. Makes me want to make you smile, and I can't do the type of things I know would do that."

My thighs clench again. "Yeah, I know."

When the song comes to an end, I thank him for the dance and head to the bar. I need fresh air, distance, and a little tequila. Maybe then I can forget about all the ways that man could make me smile.

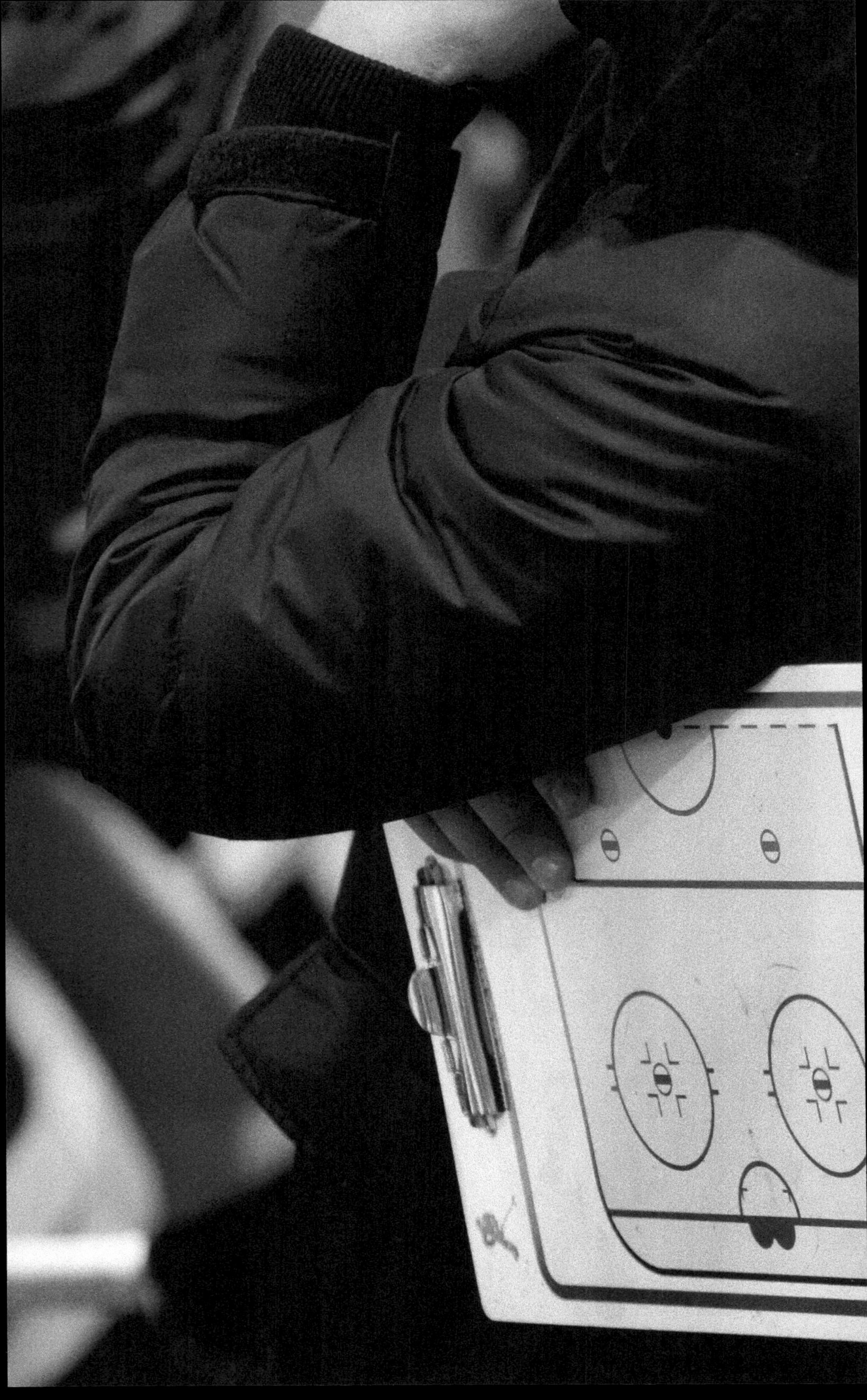

CHAPTER 9
Gavin

Beckett: Where'd you disappear to?

Me: Just hit the bathroom. We grabbing a drink at the bar?

Beckett: Nah, Aiden disappeared with his phone. Probably FaceTiming the new chick, and Brooks went to bed. I think I'll do the same. We have an early flight home.

Me: Okay, night.

WITH A SIGH, I pocket my phone. Millie's not at the bar where the last of the guests are now congregating. She probably went to bed too.

Ford and Lake disappeared about an hour ago. Naturally, he made a show of scooping her up and carrying her away bridal style.

Her loud laughter rang out over the crashing waves and the live band. I'm happy for him. Tonight was a perfect night. He even pulled Millie out onto the dance floor, and as they swayed to the music, they talked. I swore I even saw Millie smile.

That was the last time I laid eyes on her. It's for the best. I need to forget about her. I can't fix her problems, and it won't do me any good to continue watching after her. If I do, it'll only make me want to touch her, and that can't happen.

I rub at the ache that's formed in my chest again. Too much booze and not enough food, I guess. This heartburn is something else. That's the only reasonable explanation.

As I'm heading to my room, I take in the view of the ocean. This really is a beautiful place. Thousands of stars glitter against the cobalt-blue sky, and the way the moon illuminates the ocean makes it look mystical.

On the beach by the water's edge, I catch sight of a lone figure.

I know who it is before my feet start moving in her direction.

She's nothing but a shadow.

Her knees are pulled up to her chest, and she's got her arms wrapped tightly around them, keeping the fabric of her burgundy dress from blowing. Her hair is another story. It whips chaotically in the wind, making her look a little wild.

Beside her, wedged in the sand, is a bottle of tequila.

"You gonna drink that by yourself?"

Millie turns her head quickly at the sound of my voice, then gives me a half smile. "Haven't even opened it." She snatches the bottle of Jose and swings it back and forth, the liquid sloshing near the neck.

That makes me feel a modicum better.

"You going to?"

She shrugs. "Didn't have any limes or salt. And I didn't want to drink alone."

I glance back toward the bar. From here, the people still mingling are smudges of color. The music and sounds of conversation can barely be heard over the waves. We aren't alone, but there's no one even remotely close by.

Ford did tell me to watch out for Millie, right?

"Can I sit with you?"

She eyes the spot beside her in assent.

I put my jacket down on the sand and give her the same kind of look, silently offering it to her, but she merely shrugs. "I'm already sandy. No sense in us both being that way."

Once I'm settled beside her, legs bent and forearms resting on my knees, she hands me the bottle. Drinking tequila straight from the bottle has no appeal, but now that I'm beside her, I need something to keep my hands and mouth occupied. Because more than anything, I want to kiss her. I want to hold her.

Since I can't do either of those things, I unscrew the cap and swig. When I pull the bottle away, relishing the way the alcohol burns on its way down, she's holding out her thumb. Fuck, I'm an asshole. I'll use any excuse to get closer to her. So I don't hesitate. I grasp her wrist and suck on her thumb, all the while keeping my eyes locked with hers. Once I release it with a pop, I hum. "Perfect."

She smiles, her eyes a little hazy, like maybe she had a shot or two at the bar before she wandered out here. She takes the bottle from me, takes a swig, grabs my hand, and licks across my wrist.

The feel of her hot tongue against my skin is almost as incredible as the soft moan she makes.

"Fuck, Peaches," I curse, my body heating to levels I know it shouldn't. "We can't keep doing this."

Even as I say it, I snag the bottle from her grasp and take another swig, then I push her hair off her shoulder and lick a line right up her neck.

"Someone could catch us." Her voice is all sex. Breathy and teasing.

I hold her in place, push up her chin, and kiss the space beneath it. "I wouldn't be able to explain why I had my mouth on you."

She hums. "No, this is definitely not what my father had in mind when he asked you to spend time with me."

Now that I have my mouth on her, I can't stop. "Open," I say as I lift the tequila bottle.

She parts her lips and, focus fixed on me, sticks out her tongue.

My cock strains against my pants as I pour the liquid straight into her mouth. The second I pull it away, I dive forward and suck on her tongue. And a moment later, the bottle is in the sand, and I'm pulling her onto my lap.

"Oh shit," she murmurs against my mouth.

Fuck. I can't stop kissing her.

We're out in the open. The beach is empty, sure, but I have a dozen or more friends here. Her family and my family are all staying at this resort.

Any one of them could easily be out for a late-night walk. If they stumbled upon us, there would be absolutely no reasonable explanation for why I have Ford's daughter on my lap. His twenty-two-year-old daughter.

There's no innocent reason for her to be grinding against my erection. For our lips to be fused like this. For me to be grasping her tits like this.

I squeeze them, pulling a whimper from her.

"Gavin, god." She throws her head back. Then her lips are brushing mine again. "I need you."

"I can't fuck you now that I know who you are."

It's wrong. I *know* it's wrong.

"Can I fuck you? Can I just—"

I slam my lips to hers again before she can finish that question. There isn't a world where I'm not filling her up when she's begging for it. I slide my hands beneath her dress and pull her panties to the side.

"Take my cock out and ride me, Peaches. Make yourself come. Use me."

I won't come. I can't. But I can't say no to her either. Can't deny her.

With her lip caught between her teeth, she lifts a little so she can unbuckle my belt and unzip my pants. Then I'm helping her by lifting my hips so she can shimmy my pants and underwear down. Her hands are so damn warm and tempting, stroking up and down my shaft. I clench my jaw, staving off the almost uncontrollable need to possess her.

"Sit on me, Millie. Use my cock like you'd use a vibrator. It's not wrong when you fuck a toy, right? So just...use me to get off."

The web of lies I'm weaving is ridiculous. I could have earned a law degree with all the ways I'm bending the truth. But I'd do anything to make her come right now.

"I've never had a toy this large, and believe me, I have never made myself come the way you do."

She lines herself up and slides down, her warmth sucking me in, and god dammit, I can't help but grasp the hair at her nape and pull her down until her lips are on mine.

"I could never deny you," I say between desperate kisses.

Above me, she's fully sheathed and holding still so she can adjust to the feel of us finally together again.

She sighs into my mouth. "I love fucking you."

I laugh. "It is truly the best feeling. God, you're squeezing my dick so damn tight, Peaches."

The smile she gives me is slow and so fucking sexy. "I love when you call me that."

"I know. Now ride me before we get caught." I grasp her bare thighs beneath her dress and roll my hips.

It's torture at first. Slow and exquisite. She needs to get off, and god knows I shouldn't. I'm so goddamn depraved for doing this. But fuck, the way she's writhing above me, the way her pussy pulls me in, the way she flexes her inner muscles, squeezing me tighter, has me certain I won't be able to stop myself.

"Peaches, I'm gonna come so hard, and then you'll be walking through this resort with my cum dripping down your leg."

She grasps the front of my shirt and works herself over me faster. "Hold it, and I'll do ya one better."

Regardless of what she has in mind, I'd follow her to hell, so I do as she says. I grit my teeth and flex every muscle, holding back my release. Then I thumb her clit, stroking it until she unravels on top of me. "That's a good girl. Look at you riding my cock, taking what you want. So beautiful. So fucking perfect."

I pull her top down and suck one of her nipples into my mouth. After a couple of strokes with my tongue and another long pull, she shatters, crying out my name as she does. My vision goes dark, and I've barely recovered from the feel of her squeezing me when she lifts off me, then lowers down and sucks me into her perfect mouth.

"What the fuck are you doing?" I growl, tangling my hand in her hair and pulling her head back. Fucking her to make her come was one thing. Allowing her to blow me? That—fuck. "Millie, please, baby. That feels too good. I'm gonna come down your throat."

At my warning, she doubles down, moving faster and sucking harder, taking me all the way to the back of her throat until I'm fisting her hair and thrusting into her mouth and coming so hard I can barely breathe.

My vision is still mostly dark when I pull her up so she's lying on my chest, our hearts beating wildly against one another.

That's precisely how I feel about her. Wild and untamed.

"Fuck, baby. What are you doing to me?"

She breathes heavily against me. "God, that felt so good."

The husky note in her voice has me hauling her closer so I can kiss her again.

I wish I could keep her. I wish this night could go on forever.

"Let me walk you back to your room."

She shakes her head. "Daniel and I are neighbors. I don't want you to get caught."

I nod, even as my jaw hardens at the reminder that we can't be together. That even something as simple as walking her to her room would raise suspicions.

The dread that's weighed me down since the moment I realized she was Ford's daughter momentarily vanished when I was buried inside her, but now it comes rushing back with a vengeance. We shouldn't have done this. I should have stayed the fuck away. *Fuck.*

She presses one last kiss to my mouth, but I barely register it. I'm too busy spiraling.

She fixes her dress quickly and stands, but I take my time redressing, holding on to this moment for as long as I can.

"I hate this," I admit, rubbing a hand over the back of my neck.

She nods, her eyes downcast. "I really am sorry, you know. For putting us in this position."

I press a finger to her lips. "I'm not. Here," I say, holding my hand palm out. "Give me your phone."

Her eyes crease in question. "Why?"

"Text me when you get to your room. Let me know you're safe."

It's the least I can fucking do. I won't sleep until I know she's okay. But I'm also an asshole because by suggesting that I want to make sure she's safe, I'm also getting my best friend's daughter's number.

I'm already going to hell, though...

She rolls her eyes as she hands it to me, but she can't fight the smile that tips her lips. Yeah, she likes that I care.

Even if she didn't, now that I've met her, I don't see how I can't care about her. Even if she can't be mine.

Once I've programmed my number, I hand the phone back to her. "Be safe."

She swallows and then nods, gazing into my eyes. "You too, Gavin. Be happy."

I hate that this is goodbye, but I can't tell her that. It has to be.

I watch her make her way slowly back to the resort, my heart in my throat, pretty positive that I just let my soulmate walk away.

Then, with my hands shoved into my pockets and my head bowed, I walk back, in no hurry to get to my quiet room.

I'm just stepping into the building when my phone buzzes.

> **Peaches:** You programmed yourself as "Coach."

> **Me:** And you're Peaches. You back in your room?

> **Peaches:** Yes.

> **Me:** Good. Listen, use this number whenever you want. I'll always be here to talk.

> **Peaches:** Is that all I can use the number for?

> **Me:** I think that would be best. I'm pretty sure it's obvious how I feel, but in case you don't know, I'm crazy about you. If you weren't my best friend's daughter, I'd ask you on a date.

> **Peaches:** I'd say yes. Where would you take me?

> **Me:** Probably a fancy steak house. I'd want to impress you.

> **Peaches:** You could bring me to McDonald's, and I'd be impressed, Coach.

> **Me:** That's why I like you.

> **Me:** One of the many reasons, really.

> **Peaches:** I'd definitely sleep with you on the first date.

> **Me:** Ha. I wouldn't even try. I'd make you wait.

> Peaches: Now you'd make me wait?

> Me: True. I'd want to. I'd want to date you and wine and dine you and make you fall for me. But yeah, I'd probably give up on holding out after an hour because I can't say no to you.

> Peaches: Come to my room.

> Me: I can't. You know I can't.

> Peaches: I know. I'm sorry.

> Me: Don't apologize. I want you so much it's physical torture going to my room alone, but it wouldn't work. You have to work things out with your dad before you have a shot at a healthy relationship with anyone, and I can't get in the middle of that.

> Peaches: Maybe one day.

> Me: Maybe.

Inside my hotel room, I toss the phone onto the bed while I undress. The maybes and one days do me no good. She's too young, and she's got a lifetime ahead of her, but at forty, my one day is now.

I just have to accept the fact that what we had wasn't meant to last.

"Your sister coming?" I ask Daniel as I sidle up next to him beside the car waiting to take us to the airport.

He shakes his head and lowers his chin, his face mostly hidden beneath his blue Bolts baseball cap. "Nah. I guess some woman offered Millie a job, so she's staying here today to discuss details and then flying straight to Paris to start."

My stomach drops. "She's *what?*" I can't even hide the irritated shock in my voice. "She just met this woman, and now she's following her to Paris? You and your father are okay with that?"

Beckett appears at my side and squeezes my shoulder. "It's Cat James. I saw them at breakfast. She's going to be working on Sienna's show."

My lungs seize as my mind races. I'm really not going to see her again. I told her we couldn't keep talking. I pushed her away…

And apparently, I pushed her all the way to Paris.

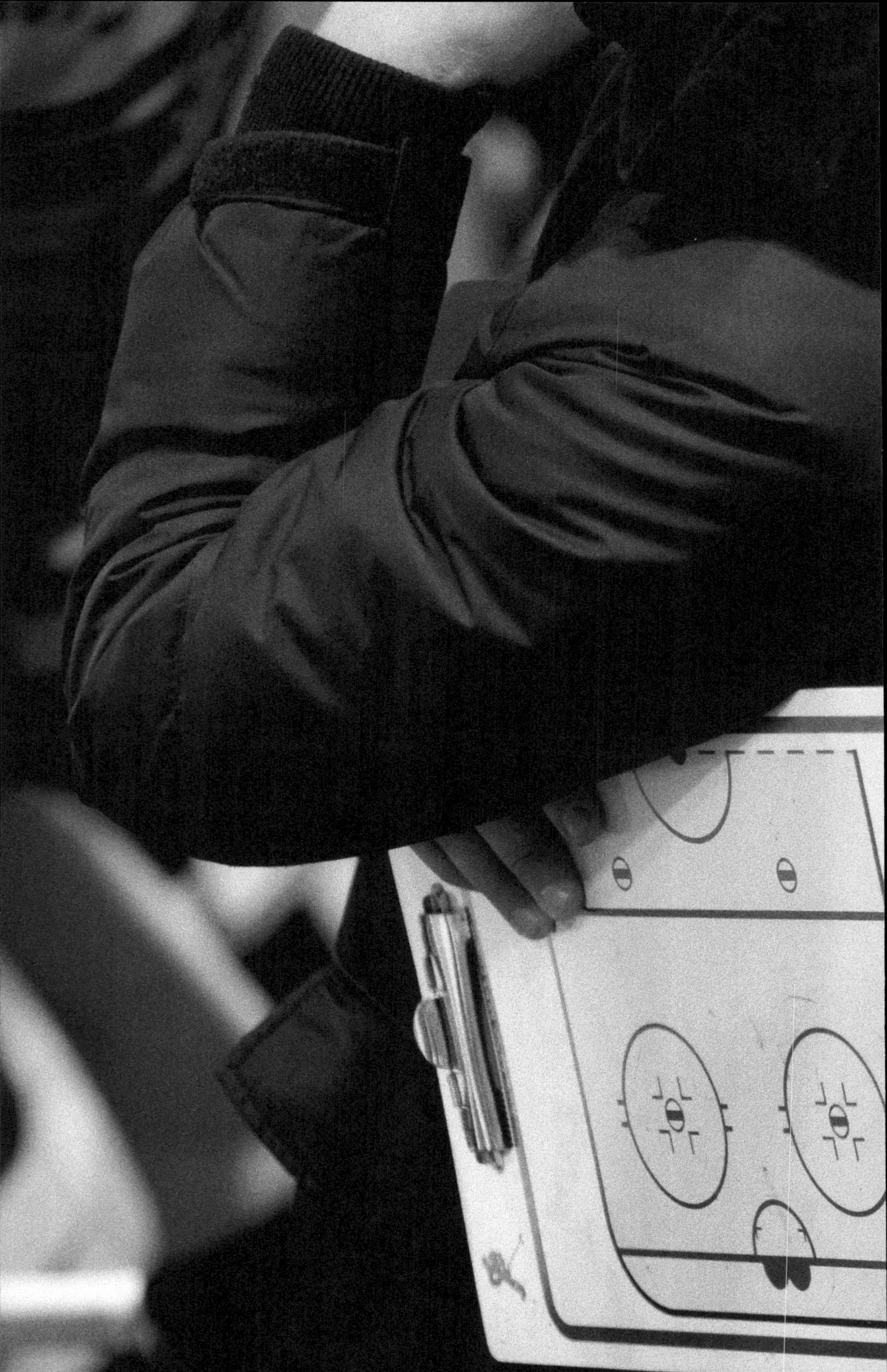

CHAPTER 10
Gavin

BESIDE ME, Henry—because after this much time together, we're on a first-name basis with one another—leans forward. "Then what happened?"

I shrug. "Nothing. We didn't speak for a year." I pause. "Well, that's not exactly true. She texted me a month after the wedding."

"What did she say?"

I chuckle. "Hi."

"Hi?" His voice is dubious.

I glance at him. "That was exactly how I felt. I'd been going out of my mind for this girl, and she sends me the shortest, most casual text."

Then again, I didn't have the balls to text her, period.

I pull out the phone and show him the text exchange.

> Me: Hey, how is Paris?

> Peaches: So good. Your sister is amazing. A little scary when she gets in the zone, but most of the time, she's great.

I can't help but grin at my phone. That tracks. Sienna has always been intense. She's the youngest in the family and the most successful. She's made a name for herself all on her own. It's impressive as fuck.

> Me: So you're happy?

I remember watching the dots dance waiting for a response. With every second that passed, my nerves frayed. Would she say yes, she's happy? That walking away was the right decision? That I did the right thing?

Or would she text that she was miserable? Would she admit to missing me as much as I missed her?

> Peaches: I am. This was a good decision for me. I know I was a mess when we met, and I just wanted to let you know I'm doing better now. Not that you probably care, but I wanted you to know that.

I shake my head as I reread that message. The fact that she thought I didn't care was insane. I'd been thinking about her nonstop, and she was off living her life in Paris. Happy. She probably is again. She's definitely not sitting on a park bench with a stranger, trying to work out the last two years of her life.

> Me: I care. And I'm glad you're happy.

> Peaches: Thanks. I hope you're doing well.

Henry nods, letting me know he's finished reading. "Sounds like Paris was a good idea for her. She seemed to grow up a bit."

He's not wrong. Millie needed Paris. Maybe she still does.

"When was this again?" he asks.

"Almost two years ago."

His white brows knit together. "And you're still talking about her?"

I look over at the jungle gym where Finn is playing with a few other kids. It's getting close to dinnertime. I should probably get him home soon. "It didn't end there," I say, giving Henry my full attention. I've had his for the last half hour.

"Okay, then what happened?"

I smile because this is a good memory. A great one actually. "We won the Stanley Cup."

Henry's face lights up. He's clearly a fan. "Ah, so this was just this past June?"

"Yup. Nine months ago."

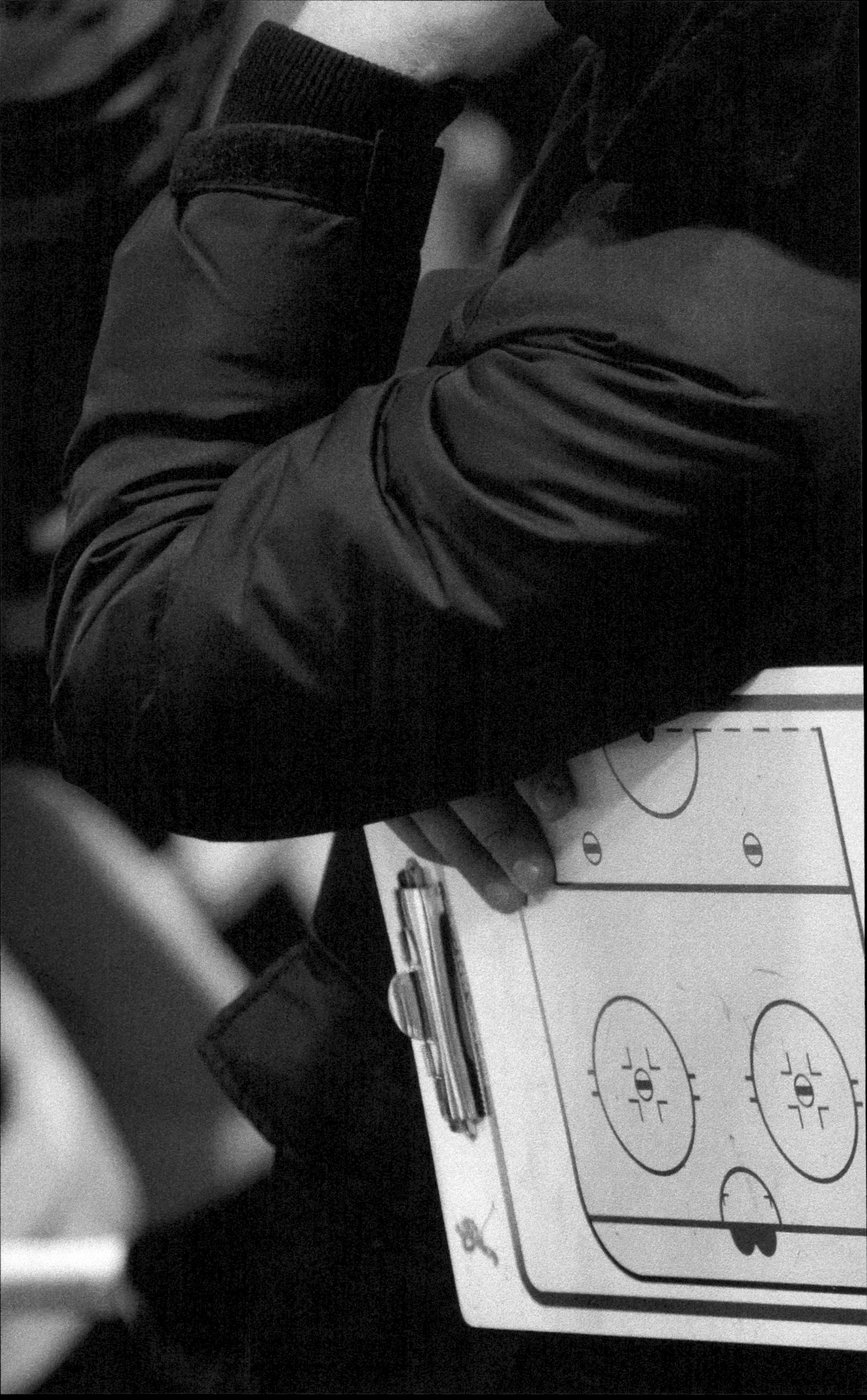

CHAPTER 11
Gavin

JUNE

Peaches: Congrats on the win! Stanley Cup champs! It's incredible. I'm sorry I missed you after the game.

Me: Thanks! Yeah, it got a little crazy around here. Are you still in Boston?

Peaches: No. Took the red-eye. I have to help Sienna prepare for her show in London.

Me: Sorry I missed you. Sienna has had nothing but good things to say about you.

Peaches: She's great.

> Peaches: I should be over you by now, right?

Fuck. I dig the heels of my hands into my eyes and groan. What the hell am I supposed to say to this girl? It's been over a year since I last saw her. And still, she haunts my thoughts day in and day out. My team just won the Stanley Cup. I should be on cloud nine. My brothers' first championship, the team's first ever cup, should be the only thing taking up space in my mind. But a simple text from Millie, and she's all I can think about.

I shouldn't want her. Definitely shouldn't still be thinking about her.

Every reason I have for staying away for the past year flits through my mind, one after another, on repeat, even as I grab my duffel bag and shove clothes and toiletries into it.

There are a million reasons to stay away.

A million reasons why we won't work.

I open the safe and snag my passport.

Then I text my driver.

Millie Hall is the last girl I should want.

But I'm tired of being reasonable.

Fuck it.

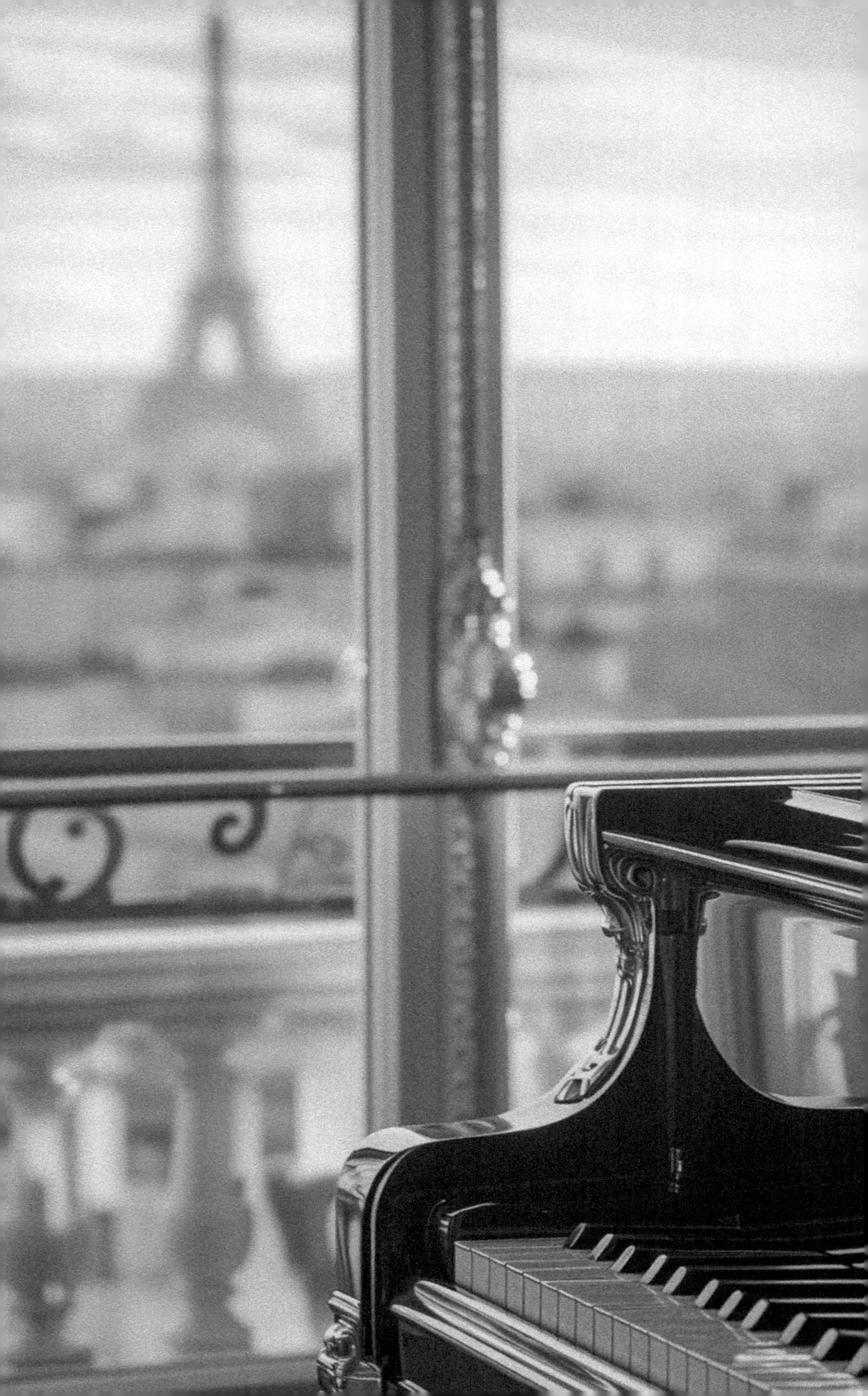

CHAPTER 12
Millie

Mom: Could you be any more selfish? You never call. You're always too busy for me.

🎹

Chrishell: Where are we going to celebrate your brother's huge win?

Taylor: This weekend is going to be EPIC!

Me: Sorry girls, I'm already back in Paris. Sienna needed me. But how are you both? I miss you!

Daniel: Please tell me you'll be back this summer so we can celebrate.

Daniel: Seriously. I miss you!

> Me: Come to Paris. It's amazing here.

Daniel: Will you introduce me to any of your hot friends?

> Me: No. My only friends are gay men and Sienna.

Daniel: I don't mind a little age gap.

> Me: Ha, pretty sure the owner of your team will mind if you sleep with his sister.

Daniel: Eh, true. Probably best not to mix business and pleasure. I'll come to Paris in a few weeks.

> Me: YAY! Okay, send me your flight info when you get it. Can't wait to see you.

Daniel: Same.

> Me: And I miss you too

"WHO HAS YOU SMILING?" Sienna asks as she looks up from her sketch. At any given time, the short brunette with the green eyes can be seen with a sketchbook in hand. That way, when inspiration strikes, she's ready. Kind of like how I'm always jotting down lyrics or tunes that pop into my head.

Lyrics that will never be read. Songs that will never be sung. At least her doodles are worth something.

"Just my brother."

My brother is the only person who's ever interested in talking *to* me. My mother likes to talk *at* me, my so-called friends only text when they think they can get something *from* me. And my father barely checks in anymore.

Pushing the negative thoughts out of my mind, I put the phone down and go back to checking the inventory list for Sienna's next show. We're in the warehouse, surrounded by clothing.

My life has been nonstop since I moved to Paris. Sienna doesn't take a breath. The woman is always plotting, always thinking, always marketing. She's got the next ten years mapped out, while I don't even know what I want for dinner tonight.

Once her show premiered, Sienna offered me a full-time position as her assistant. Since I had nothing to go home to, the answer was easy.

With the end of her pencil caught between her teeth, she studies the sketch she's working on, frowning. "Brothers are fun," she says, her tone dry.

"Yeah, he's going to come out in a few weeks. It will be nice to spend time with him. Daniel and I have always been close, so it's been hard being so far apart."

"Are you close with your other brother too?" She stands from the couch and wanders over to a table we've set up with a makeshift coffee station.

"Paul is..." I worry my lip, pondering a polite way to describe him. "Unmotivated."

Sienna smiles. "So nothing like you and Daniel."

I shrug. "Neither of us is like Daniel. Since the day he first put on a pair of skates, he's been driven to become a pro hockey player. And now he is."

Sienna laughs. "Oh, I get the hockey thing. And the sports thing. My family lives and breathes it."

I ignore the mention of her family because that will only send me down a tailspin thinking about her brother. And about the ridiculous text message I sent last night. God, what was I thinking?

I *can't* think about her brother. He's the only thing I've thought about for more than a year. Something must be wrong with me.

"You ever play any sports?"

She scrunches her nose. "Does this face look like it's ever been touched by sports?"

Of course not. Sienna's skin is porcelain white, all her features dainty.

"I miss my brothers too." She settles beside me again and hands me a cup of coffee. "I barely got to see them after the game, and I don't know when I'll make it back to Boston again."

"Do you regret moving to Paris?"

Sienna turns to face me, her eyes wide. "God, no. Do you?"

The answer should be easy. I should be ecstatic to be here, to be involved in what she's creating. But outside of work and Sienna, I don't have much tethering me to this city. And I can't get her brother off my mind, even if he's made it clear that there's no possibility of a future for us. "I don't regret it. But I do miss home."

Sienna nods. "That's the difference between you and me. This is my home." She pats me on the knee. "Come on, let's finish up here, and then I'll take you to my favorite restaurant. I'm making it my mission to get you to fall in love with this city just like I did."

It's after ten p.m. when I'm finally slogging my way up the steps to my apartment. The whole world has grand illusions about what it's like to live in Paris. Like every balcony has a beautiful view of the Eiffel tower and that fresh croissants and cappuccinos are hand delivered every morning. That has not been my experience. My apartment is tiny. It's furnished with a bed and a two-person table. Nothing more. There isn't room for more. The kitchenette isn't much bigger than the minuscule closet. There's no room for a couch or even an armchair for visitors.

Not that I'd have visitors. I work all day, then come home and crash, and that's how it's been for the past year.

Keeping up with Sienna is an impossible task. Even if I find the time to go out, I spend most of it on my phone working because Sienna never stops.

Tonight, all I can think about is crawling into bed and falling asleep. And maybe sleeping for the next twenty-four hours. She's giving me the weekend off now that we're finished setting up for next week. After flying back and forth from Boston to Paris in only two days, I need it.

And I need to sleep so I can stop thinking about Gavin and that damn text message from last night. I don't know what I was thinking.

You weren't, my mind taunts. I saw him in his suit out on the ice, holding up the Stanley Cup, smiling wide and looking beautiful, and I ached for him.

I'm sure he never even saw my last message. He was probably out celebrating and is sleeping off a hangover now. Maybe with someone else in his bed.

God, that thought makes my stomach turn.

It shouldn't. I shouldn't still want him.

It's been over a year.

But the moment I saw him, every emotion that plagued me for months after we met came rushing back.

At the top of the stairs, I stop short, and my heart races. Because there's a figure slumped against my door. The dim light of the hallway casts him in shadow, making it impossible to get a look at his face as I take a step back and dig my phone out of my pocket, prepared to call my landlord. The building door was locked when I came in, but this man found his way inside regardless. Shit.

"Peaches?"

The voice is scratchy, but I'd know it anywhere, and that one word sends my heart tumbling.

"Gavin?" I turn on my phone's flashlight and shine it in his direction.

With a hand shielding his eyes, he stumbles to his feet, but he doesn't move closer.

"What the hell are you doing here?"

As I get a good look at him, my stomach somersaults. He's wearing a pair of jeans and a black T-shirt that strains against his muscles. His hair is mussed and falling forward a bit, making it look longer than it did yesterday when it was slicked back and styled for the game. Disheveled or not, he looks hella sexy. And when he smiles at me, his eyes crinkling and his teeth showing, I know I'm screwed. He's just as gorgeous as always, maybe more so, and just as off-limits.

"I have no fucking idea."

A huff of a laugh escapes me, even as my heart pounds. "You flew all the way to Paris, tracked down my apartment, and waited outside my door for—"

"Three hours."

My breath catches. "*Three* hours?" I shake my head. "You did all that, and you don't know why you're here?"

Gavin shrugs as he steps closer.

I step back but hit the wall because the place is tiny. Might have mentioned that already.

"You're here," he says, coming another step closer, then another.

The lump in my throat threatens to cut off my air as I take him in up close. He's so much taller than me, and he's completely filled the space. His body, his scent, his heat, and that damn small smile.

"I am here," I admit.

"I couldn't stand being where you weren't." His words are a vise around my heart, squeezing so tight that I'm dizzy.

"What does that mean?"

Gavin shakes his head and licks his lips. "I don't know that either. I just—I wanted to see you, so I got on a plane, and here I am."

"Okay."

"Okay?" he asks, his head tilting in surprise.

I suck in a breath and take a step forward. I don't have the first clue where we go from here other than inside. "Yeah, okay."

Gavin steps to one side, allowing me to pass him. I watch him as I go, afraid he'll disappear if I look away. I only turn my focus forward when he follows me. And he follows me closely. Like maybe he's afraid I'm the one who'll disappear. He's so close as I unlock the door, I can feel the heat radiating off him.

The second I step inside, nerves swamp me. The last time we were together in a small space, it was his place, and honestly, *small* isn't an adjective I'd use to describe his penthouse. But when he squeezes my shoulder, his warmth seeps into me, assuaging some of my anxiety. For a moment, I close my eyes and just breathe. I don't care what he thinks of the place. I honestly don't give a fuck about anything other than the feel of Gavin Langfield's hand on me.

He flew here on a whim.

He's here.

I can't wrap my head around that thought.

But I open my eyes and force myself to move.

"Are you hungry?" I step away and flip on the light in the kitchenette. If I have any chance of surviving the next hour, or of not getting naked and begging him to fuck me, then I need some space.

"No. I'm okay. I'm sure you're tired."

I turn around and face him, finally getting my fill. He's so big in my space. Wide. Real. "The last thing I am is tired."

He smirks for the first time since he got here. It's the first time I've seen that expression in a year. God, I missed it—*I missed him.*

Sweet Gavin has always been my kryptonite, but cocky Gavin, *smirking Gavin?* He's my fucking undoing.

"Maybe a drink?" I pull open the fridge, forcing my attention away from that beautiful smirk. Even as I focus on anything but him, I can feel him watching me.

"Peaches." My name is like a sigh on his lips.

I suck in a deep breath and garner all the courage I have before I look his way. God, that nickname. "Yeah?"

"I haven't touched you in 461 days. Please get the fuck over here and let me hold you."

There is no hesitation. No second thoughts. My body knows it belongs in his arms. So I slam the fridge closed and practically barrel into him, settling my head against his chest. Breathing deep, I close my eyes and listen to his heart beat out a rhythm that matches mine.

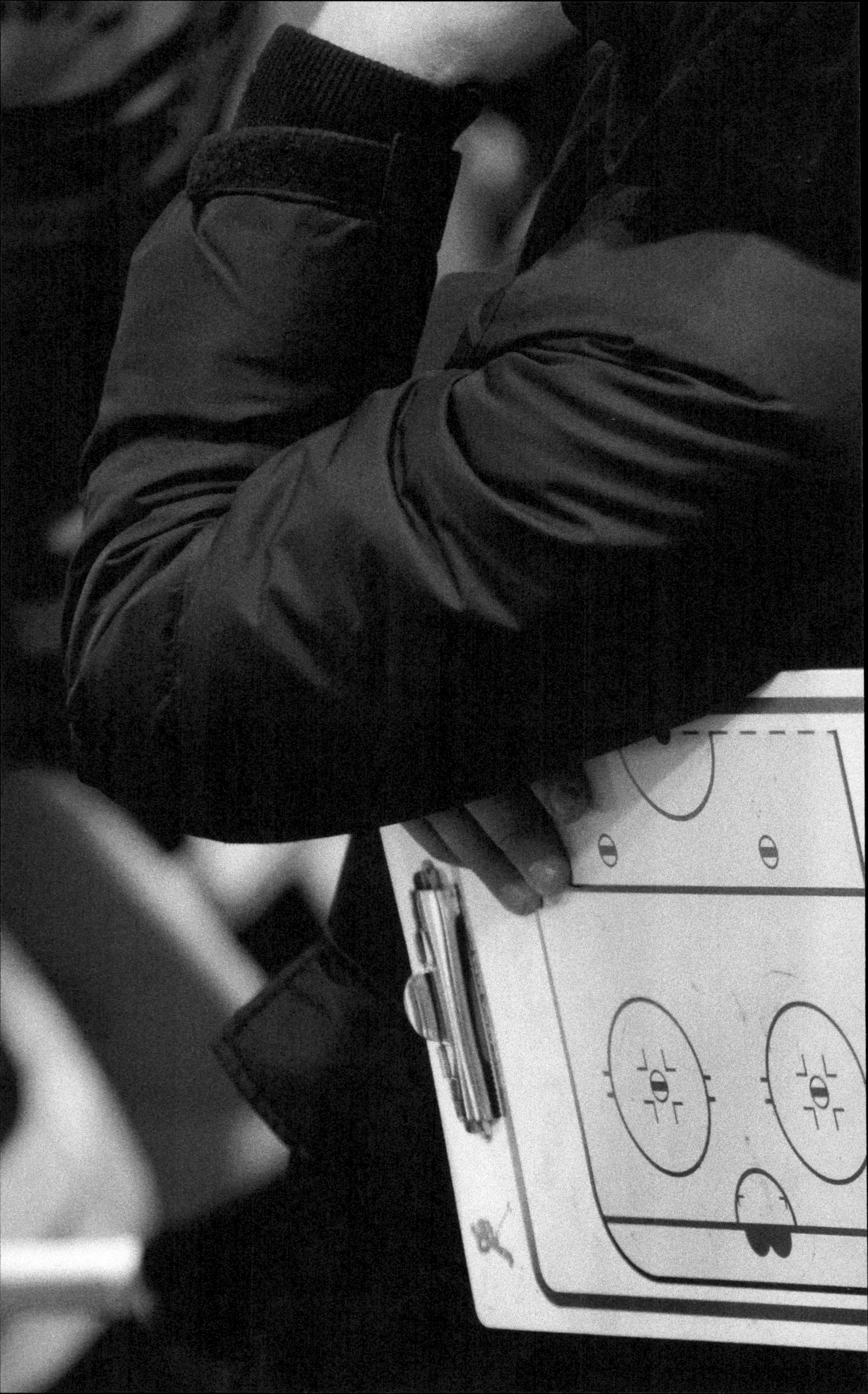

CHAPTER 13
Gavin

MILLIE'S APARTMENT IS SMALL. Minuscule, really. I want to ream out both my sister and her father for allowing her to live here. I entered the building behind a resident who didn't bother to make sure the door shut behind him. Then I sat on the floor outside her apartment for three hours.

Not a single person was concerned. That's a problem.

She tips her head up and gazes at me, her eyes slightly glassy.

"You been drinking, Peaches?"

The smile that spreads across her face quickly turns into a yawn. "Just a couple of glasses of wine with your sister."

I grasp her wrist and pull her toward her bed. "Come on. It's been a long two days."

With her lip caught between her teeth, she gives me a dreamy smile. "I still can't believe you're here. You won the cup yesterday!"

My responding laugh is too loud for such a small space. "I didn't win the cup. Believe me, Aiden has made sure I'm aware of exactly who won it."

She nuzzles her head into my chest. "Still..." She breathes in deep and sighs. "I can't believe you're here instead of celebrating with them."

"There's no one in this world I'd rather celebrate with more than you." And that's not an exaggeration. If I were anywhere else, I'd only be miserable and thinking about her, regardless of winning the cup. "We'll celebrate tomorrow, though. Right now, you need sleep."

The way her tongue darts out and wets her lips as she peers up at me through her lashes pulls a groan from deep inside my chest. It's been too fucking long since I kissed those lips.

"But what if I don't want to sleep?" she asks in that sexy rasp of hers.

Clutching her upper arms, I spin her and march her toward her bed. It's in her living room, along with everything else she owns. Fuck, this place is small.

"Come on, Peaches."

She sighs but doesn't put up a fight. Until we reach the bed, and then the little vixen spins around. With a devilish smirk, she crosses her arms, reaches for the fabric at her waist, and lifts it straight over her head, exposing the best set of tits I've ever seen.

I love the way this woman never wears a bra. I hate it at the same time.

I bite my fist to keep from touching her. But god, do I want to. She raises her brow at me, as if she's surprised, or maybe intrigued, by my silence.

I keep my focus fixed firmly on her face. I can't look at her nipples. Can't see how they pebble with need. How she arches for me.

But her face is just as tantalizing. And it's just as much trouble. Because I've been dreaming of her gorgeous face since the moment I met her, despite how wrong it is.

She's my best friend's daughter. I'm a terrible, terrible person for wanting her. Yet here I am. I flew halfway around the world just to see her.

She twists her lips, her expression teasing. "Look at you, Coach, holding strong."

I cough out a laugh. That goddamn nickname.

She arches those brows again. "Let's see how strong your resolve really is." With her thumbs hooked in her waistband, she shimmies out of her pants and underwear and kicks them across the room.

I curse softly under my breath and look away.

"Ouch," she mutters. "Not exactly the reaction I expected, but message received. You're not interested."

A low rumble works its way out of me as I stalk toward her. I barely find the willpower to stop myself when I'm a breath away, my chest heaving and my hands fisted so I don't reach for her. "The last thing I am is uninterested."

Gold eyes meet mine, holding me hostage. I'm her captive, under her control, just as I've been since the last time she stripped down and gave me everything.

I'm a goddamn hostage in my own mind. She owns me.

Her shoulders settle, and her expression evens out. "Okay, we'll sleep then."

Then she spins around, her peach of an ass swinging as she does, and slips beneath the covers. She scoots to the far side of the mattress, leans back against her pillows, and gives me a sweet smile.

"I'm just going to use the bathroom." Without waiting for a response, I snag my bag from where I dropped it by the door and hustle into the tiny space. Sure, a moment alone to brush my teeth is great, but really, I need a goddamn cold shower and to slap myself in the face a few times.

But more than anything, I need to not make another move with this girl until I figure out what the fuck my endgame is here. Because I can't fuck her again unless we can have more. I'm not willing to fuck up my friendship with Ford for anything less.

So I study myself in the mirror and make a promise. I will not fuck my best friend's daughter.

Not tonight, at least.

I wake up to an empty bed, a pounding head, and a throbbing dick. Spending the night next to a naked Millie, who rolled over and splayed her body across mine as soon as I got into bed, was the purist torture.

I blink up at the ceiling as I find my bearings. There's a strange noise filtering through her apartment. It's so low I can barely make it out, but it's a tune of some sort.

With a grimace, I sit up and scan the room, and when I spot Millie sitting at her kitchen table—if you could call it that—I'm hit with a wave of comfort. It's so good to have her this close. She has one knee pulled up to her chest, and she's bouncing her other foot on the floor as she taps out a tune on a small electric piano.

"Peaches," I rasp.

Her golden eyes find me, and her face lights up. "You're awake." She bounds out of her chair and launches herself onto the bed and into my arms.

Oh, to be in my twenties again.

I tangle a hand in her hair and angle her head so I can get a good look at her gorgeous face. Those pink cheeks, bright, excited eyes, and peach lips that smile so wide my chest aches.

"Hi, beautiful."

She licks her lips, her expression going a little wicked. "It's tomorrow."

I chuckle. "It is."

"And we've now slept." She walks her fingers up my torso idly.

"That we have." I tighten my hold on her hair just a little.

"So." She cocks a brow. "What are we going to do now?"

"Food would be good."

She makes a little growling sound that's so adorable my resolve weakens. "Food?"

"Yeah, I'm starving."

With a *hmph*, she rolls over and lounges against her pillow, taking her warmth and joy with her. With a loud, resigned sigh, she points to the bathroom. "Fine. I'm going to shower, and then I'll take you to my favorite café."

I press my lips together to keep from smiling at her frustration. What she doesn't know is that I'm frustrated too. But I have a plan, and I'm sticking to it.

We spend the day stopping in one café after another, along with all of her favorite spots in the city. While we're wandering through the Louvre, she mentions a small wine bar that sometimes has open mic nights, so I force her to take me there too.

While Millie is cozied up to me in a small velvet booth, entranced by a woman crooning a French song into the mic, I'm entranced by Millie.

I press my face against the crown of her head and breathe her in. "Are you going to sing?"

"No." She sighs, snuggling closer. "I like to come watch the locals do it."

"What were you playing when I woke up this morning?"

"Just a little something that came to me while lying in bed."

"A little something about me?" I angle back and smirk.

She lets out a soft laugh and rolls her eyes. "Possibly."

"Sing it for me, please."

Fuck, I'd do anything to hear this girl sing again.

She pulls back and studies me quietly, her mind working. "What do I get if I sing?"

Moving in so close my lips brush the shell of her ear, I ask, "What do you want?"

A shiver works its way through her. "I want you to kiss me."

I pull back and shake my head, even as my eyes drop to her lips again. They're glossy but still that same peach color.

Her shoulders fall.

The disappointment radiating from her just about breaks me. Fuck, do I want to give in. But I hold my ground. "Ask me for something else, anything."

"Tell me why you're here."

"I already have. I'm here because I couldn't stay away. I'm here because I want to be."

She sucks in a sober breath and nods. "Okay."

I blink at her, unsure of the meaning behind that one word. "Okay, you'll sing?"

A small smile curves her lips, highlighted by the glow of the spotlight on the stage. "Yeah, I'll sing."

"But I didn't give you anything."

"Not true, Coach." She presses a small kiss against my jaw and stands. "You came to see me." And then, in a voice so low her words are almost imperceptible, she says, "And that is giving me everything."

With a wink, she turns and saunters to the pianist. She leans in close as he's playing the last chords of the current song, and he nods in response to her words.

I don't speak a word of French, so when he speaks into the mic and the crowd breaks into a round of applause, I follow suit.

As he stands, every person in the room seems to press forward in their seat, almost in anticipation. Electricity sparks in the air, making it clear the crowd is excited about whatever he said.

Millie replaces him at the piano, adjusts the mic, and says something in French, her voice so damn sexy I have to clench my fists to control the possessiveness that overtakes me.

She looks right at me and smiles. "This one's for you, Coach."

And then she sings the most heartbreakingly beautiful tune in a language I don't understand but vow to become fluent in so that I can go home and find out exactly how this girl really feels.

When we get back to her apartment, I take in the inexpensive piano sitting on her table. She deserves the real thing. She deserves a real apartment, with more than one room and an actual kitchen table. I want to promise her all these things. Want to tell her I'll give her everything.

But something holds me back.

Someone holds me back.

"Will you play the song for me again? But this time in English?"

She drops her focus to the floor and shakes her head. "You still haven't kissed me."

My chest goes tight as I study her lips for the hundredth time today. "Believe me, I fucking know."

She sighs and motions at the space between us. "What is this? You slept in my bed and held me all night. Then you took me from café to café, smiling at me, holding my hand." Her face is etched with worry as she considers me. "I can tell you're attracted to me." She steps closer. "I can tell you *want* to kiss me. So why haven't you?"

"Have you talked to your father?"

A small gasp escapes her, and she steps back, almost as if I slapped her. "What?"

I grasp her wrist and brush my thumb across the smooth skin there, hoping she knows my questions come from a place of genuine care. "Have you spoken to your father about music? Did you tell him you were upset when he gave half the company to Lake? Have you talked to him at all?"

She tucks her chin, avoiding my gaze, and shakes her head.

My heart sinks. Dammit. For months I've hoped she'd worked to heal those wounds, but nothing has changed.

"You're upset with me," she says slowly, like the pieces of a puzzle are slotting together, her version of it, at least.

"No. I'm realistic. I wanted to see if what we had was real. Wanted to know if, outside the sex, this was something more."

Her lips turn down, and disappointment flashes in her eyes. "And it isn't?" Her voice is a sad whisper.

I reach for her hand again, and this time, I hold it against my chest and press a kiss to her forehead. With a deep breath in, then back out, I grasp her chin and tilt her face up so I can look into those big golden eyes that captured me the very first day I met her.

"No, Peaches. It's not more. It's *everything*. Being with you this weekend, *without the sex*, has shown me that I'd rather sit in a room and do absolutely nothing with you than spend an hour living it up with anyone else. This isn't about sex. It's not about the forbidden. It's not a game or a mid-life crisis. I like you. *A lot*."

"Then why won't you kiss me?"

"Because you're not ready."

Her brows furrow in an adorable, annoyed expression. "What? How can you say that?"

"Because you're living in a city you don't love and spending your days doing work you couldn't care less about because you refuse to have a conversation with your father. My best friend." I grasp her chin a little harder, hoping she sees my sincerity and how much I desperately want her to have it all. "You're not ready for us, and I can't force you to get there."

"What are you talking about?" She takes a step back. "I like my job."

"You want to write music. But you're hiding in your apartment, and when my sister isn't working you to death, you're writing music on a piano fit for a toddler."

Her eyes go hard and her nostrils flare. Dammit, she's gorgeous when she's angry. "Last time I checked, you're not actually a coach either, Gavin." She takes another step back, but I follow, cupping her cheek this time.

"I'm not saying this to hurt you, Millie." I rub my thumb over her smooth skin. "I'm saying this because I care about you. I care about you so fucking much it doesn't make sense. I've been friends with your father for years, and he'd fucking kill me if he knew what I was doing, but I'm doing it anyway because I. Care. About. You." I annunciate each word, hoping I can get through to her.

She lets out a defeated sigh and crosses her arms. "I'll talk to him."

I shake my head. "Don't do it for me. Do it for you. I want you to do it when you're ready."

Her eyes are glassy as she surveys me. "That's not fair."

I smile, despite the ache in my chest. "Don't I know it. Talk to me about fair. The girl I'm crazy about is half my age and my best friend's daughter. Plus she lives three thousand miles away."

"How do you even know you're still crazy about me? You haven't even kissed me in more than a year."

I drop my forehead to hers for a breath, then pull back. "You're working hard for that kiss."

"Maybe I just need proof of your feelings. And a little motivation."

With a dark chuckle, I brush my lips against hers, and fuck, do I want to own these lips. I want to shove her back onto her bed, strip off her clothes, and take my time with her. But she's not ready, and I can't force it.

"You have my phone number. You know where I live. Figure out what you want in life, Peaches. Until then, I'll be your friend."

Darting forward, she clutches my shirt and nips at my lip.

The sensation pulls a groan from me, and my forehead falls to hers. I hold still, our eyes locked on one another, letting her sink those teeth into my flesh, wishing I could give in. But if I do, if I sleep with her again, we'll end in nothing but devastation.

She needs this time, and she needs to fix things with her father.

And if I'm lucky, one day, she'll be ready. And I hope like hell that when that day comes, I'm still single.

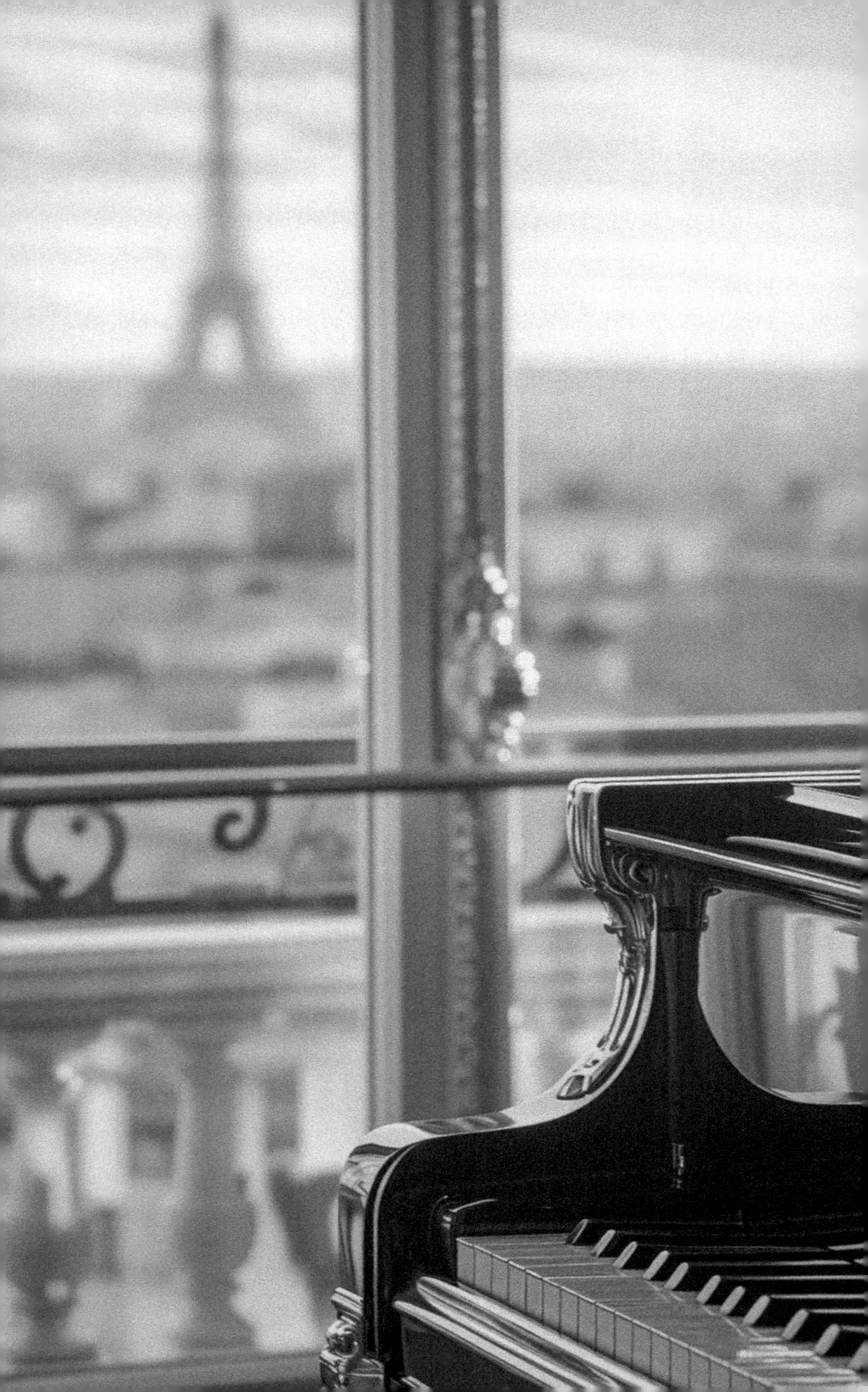

CHAPTER 14
Millie

Me: Text me when you land, please.

Coach: Just touched down.

Me: Is it pathetic to say I miss you?

Coach: If it is, then I am too.

Me: Pathetic?

Coach: Missing you like crazy.

Me: And yet you refused to kiss me.

Coach: You damn well know it isn't because I didn't want to.

Me: That's what you tell all the girls.

Coach: There are no other girls, Peaches.

Coach: How was work today?

Me: Your sister was amazing. She got a standing ovation. It was incredible.

Coach: You're incredible.

Me: Ha. Flattery will get you everywhere.

Coach: Oh yeah? Like where?

Coach: You're just going to leave me hanging?

Me: LOL sorry. Gabe stopped by and I got distracted. We're going to grab dinner. TTYL

Coach: Who is Gabe?

Coach: Millie.

Coach: Who the fuck is Gabe?

Me: Aw, are you jealous?

Coach: You went radio silent for hours. I've gotten absolutely zero work done, and that's your response?

Coach: I don't play games, Millie, so if that's what this is, count me out.

Coach: Yes, I'm fucking jealous. I'm jealous of anyone who gets to spend time with you. I'm jealous of my own goddamn sister because she gets to see your beautiful face every damn day. I'm jealous of your shadow because it gets to be where you are. So yeah, I'm jealous of whoever this Gabe is because he just got to have dinner with you.

HOLY SHIT. I reread Gavin's message at least five times. Then I decide I'm done with texting. So, with a glass of wine in hand, I head for my bed and click on Gavin's name.

Two rings later, he appears on my screen. His face is etched with frustration and his hair is wild, like he's been pulling on it. His brown eyes dart from side to side, like he's scanning my surroundings. Then he sighs and all but deflates.

"It's just me, handsome." I give him what I hope is a sexy smile and hold up my glass of wine.

"Where's *Gabe*?" He says Gabe's name like it's a disease. It's hard to contain my giddiness over seeing him this way. Maybe I should feel bad, but jealous Gavin is hot. Like scorching-level hot.

I run my tongue over the rim of my glass and then take a sip.

His eyes go molten as he watches me.

"He left."

Then that jaw ticks. "Are you going to tell me who he is?"

I set my glass on the nightstand next to my bed, then I prop my phone up against a candle and shimmy back a few inches. "Figured you'd prefer doing something other than talking about my gay best friend slash coworker." Without waiting for his response, I pull my shirt over my head, exposing my breasts.

"Jesus." Gavin roughs a hand down his face. "Please tell me you wore a bra to dinner with your friend."

I slide a finger over my nipple and circle it until it pebbles. "I don't like to lie."

"Fuck, Mills, what are you doing?"

The rough timbre of his voice lights a fire inside me. I nibble on my bottom lip and duck my chin innocently. "I *was* in the mood to play, but then you said you don't play games."

Gavin stands, his leather chair squeaking, and disappears from view. "You are in so much trouble." A door clicks shut on his end, and then he's back, dropping into his seat with a scowl. "I'm in my fucking office."

"Shame. I'm naked in my bed."

He angles forward like if he does, he can see my lower half. But the screen cuts off at my belly, so he can't tell if I'm completely naked. The vein throbbing in his forehead has me worrying he'll hurt himself trying to figure it out, so I put him out of his misery and go up on my knees so he can see that I'm still in my leggings.

"The way I want to lick those tits, Peaches." He groans as he settles back in his chair.

"Give me a tour of your office."

The smirk he gives me is pure mischief. "That really what you want to do while we're alone and you're topless?"

"Show me your office, and then maybe I'll show you something of mine."

"Right." He snatches his phone off the desk and flips the screen. Then he pans the space slowly, pointing out one thing after another. Bookshelves, a couch, visitor chairs, a couple of things hanging on the walls. He rattles them all off quickly, rushing so we can get to the good stuff.

His impatience makes me grin, but I like seeing this part of his life. The CEO at work. Now when I think about what he's doing, I can paint more accurate pictures of how he spends his days. Makes him feel more real. And as I see this Gavin, one I'm unfamiliar with, I can't help but wonder if I could ever really fit into his world.

It's a healthy dose of reality. A reality I'll think about later.

"Do me a favor, Coach," I say, pushing away the concern beginning to niggle at the back of my mind. "Lean back in your chair and show me what you'd do if I were actually there."

The screen goes dark for an instant, and then Gavin's there again. "Uh-uh. I gave you your little tour, now I want one of my own."

"What is it you want to see?" With both hands, I circle my nipples again and give them both a little tug.

He closes his eyes and groans as if he's in pain. "Millie Hall, please, baby, you are killing me."

"Oh, the full name. I must have done something really bad if you're pulling that out." I hold both hands out, then, still on my knees, I slide my palms down my stomach and to my hips until my thumbs have dipped beneath the fabric of my leggings.

"Don't do it, baby. Please."

Heart pounding wildly in my chest, I give him a saucy smile. "But I miss you, and since you aren't here to take care of me, I need to take care of myself." I slide my pants down, revealing that I'm also not wearing panties.

He puts his fist over his mouth and growls. "Fuck, you're so pretty. Grab the phone and lay down."

There he is.

Liquid heat pools in my core as I settle against my pillows and plant my feet on the mattress, knees wide. "What should I do next?"

"Slide your fingers inside your pussy. Tell me if you're wet."

I obey, first sliding a finger against my clit, then dipping into my heat. The moan that works its way out of me as I arch my back is loud and long. "So wet."

"Show me."

My breath catches, and I meet Gavin's gaze. With a shudder, I pull back slowly, then hold a finger up to the screen so he can see the way it glistens.

"Oh, Peaches, do you have any idea how good you taste? If I were there, I'd be licking that finger clean."

I whimper at the memory that confession conjures, and the heat low in my belly ignites. "It's been so long," I whine.

"I know, baby. Let me ease that ache. Circle that needy clit for me."

"Do you want me to move my phone so you can see?"

Gavin shakes his head quickly, jaw pulsing. "No. I want to watch your face flush. I want to see the way your lips part and how you sink your teeth into that peach flesh when it becomes too much. I want to memorize every glorious expression, because you are so beautiful, Millie."

I'm already working small circles over my clit, his words edging me closer and closer to orgasm. "I know what you mean," I pant. "That's how I felt when you let me suck your cock."

Gavin makes a throaty noise and runs his tongue along his lower lip. "When I taught you how to deep-throat me."

I nod. "Yeah. I loved having your cock in my mouth."

"Fuck," he hisses, pushing back in his seat.

"I loved how you pulled my hair back for me, how you fisted it and tugged just a little, then told me to stick out my tongue."

"Millie," he pleads, the muscles in his neck taut like he's gripping his armrests to keep himself in check.

"Come on, Gavin. Take out your cock and fist it. Pretend I'm sucking on it. Remember how good it felt when you slid inside my hot mouth and then told me to hollow my cheeks and lick. God, I can still feel the vein that throbbed as I did it. You were so hard, and I loved every minute of it."

His image goes shaky, like his hands are unsteady. Then he props his phone up on his desk again, and metal clinks against metal as he undoes his belt. Next, he quickly unzips his pants. "I can't believe I'm going to fucking jack off in my office right now. You are such a bad influence."

I let out a satisfied hum as I continue to work my clit.

"If you were here, I'd force you onto your knees for getting me to do this, and I'd fuck your throat."

"Oh my god. I would love that."

"I know you would. You're filthy and perfect."

"For you I am. Roll your thumb over your head. Let me see if you're wet."

Gavin gives me a dark look. "That's my line."

A thrill races through me at his wicked tone. "I learned from the best."

"Damn right you did." He slides his thumb over the crown of his cock and then holds it up to the phone, confirming my suspicion. He's dripping just like me. "Now what, Peaches? You going to lick it?"

His dirty words send a zap of desire through me, pushing me closer to the edge and pulling a loud moan from deep within me.

"Don't you dare fucking come yet," he grits out. "Pinch that fucking clit and hold on for me."

With a deep breath to steady myself, I do what he says. I don't want this to end yet, and the pain puts me right on the edge again. "Now what?"

"Start slowly." He slides his hand up and down his shaft. He's still in a white button-down shirt, but the sleeves are rolled, giving me an incredible view of the bulging veins in his forearms as he works himself over.

"You're CEO porn right now," I murmur.

He pauses his movements and barks out a laugh. "Fuck, Peaches. You're..." He shakes his head and smiles, looking away.

"Don't stop now."

Gavin focuses on the screen again, his brown eyes molten. I want to sink inside them. I want to drizzle myself in this feeling that only he can provoke in me. I'd bottle it up and keep it. Keep him.

"Oh, we're not stopping until I see those pretty little lips fall open and you're crying my name."

"Deal."

"Prop the phone up with a pillow so I can see you, baby. Then I want you to do everything I say."

"Yes," I pant, ready to lose myself in him. No more overthinking. No more second-guessing. I want this man, and I want to come.

Behind Gavin, through the large window, the sky has turned every shade of orange and pink as the sun sinks low. He's a world away, and yet I feel so close to him as we moan and writhe and encourage one another.

"That's my good girl," he urges. "Fill that greedy cunt with two fingers just like I would and circle that clit. If I were there right now, I'd flip you over and force you to ride my face while you sucked my cock. I'd have to remind you to breathe because you'd be so caught up in rubbing that needy pussy all over me, begging to come."

"Yes," I murmur as my legs tremble and I gasp for air.

"But you wouldn't listen. You'd keep sucking because you love having my cock in your mouth. You love bringing it all the way to the back of your throat and showing me how fucking incredible you are at taking all of me."

My fingers are a mess as I rub and fuck myself, all the while watching Gavin slide his hand up and down until he's cursing that he's going to come. The deep rumble that emanates from him as he slams his eyes shut pushes me over the edge. Then I'm screaming his name and coming so hard my body arches off the bed and I grip the sheets, wishing like hell that it was him between my legs.

When coherent thought returns and I open my eyes, Gavin is watching me, his eyes glassy.

"You're beautiful." The words come out so soft and yet gruff at the same time. Like he's annoyed at just how much I affect him. Like the words tumbled from his mouth without his permission in the same way his body gives and gives and gives when I'm around.

I hate that he's a sticky mess on the other side of the world and I'm naked and exposed on the bed without him. I hate that our conversation is probably over before it even began, because once again, I seduced him.

It's painful trying to swallow past the lump in my throat, but with a long breath, I dig deep, garnering the strength to say good night. But Gavin speaks before I can form the words.

"Give me twenty minutes to get cleaned up and head home. If you're still up when I get there, maybe we could just..."

"Just what?" I ask, unable to hide the hopefulness from my tone.

"Talk."

The smile that splits my face makes my cheeks ache, and a laugh bubbles out of me. "You want to talk to me?"

Gavin leans forward and reaches for something out of the frame. Then he's sitting back again and cleaning himself up with tissues. When he looks up again, his hair still mussed, he hits me with that gorgeous smile of his. "Yeah, Peaches. I wanna talk to you until you fall asleep. I want to know everything about you. Fight sleep for a little longer?"

God, I love the way he smiles at me. The way he speaks to me. The names he calls me.

"Okay, Coach. I'll be waiting for you."

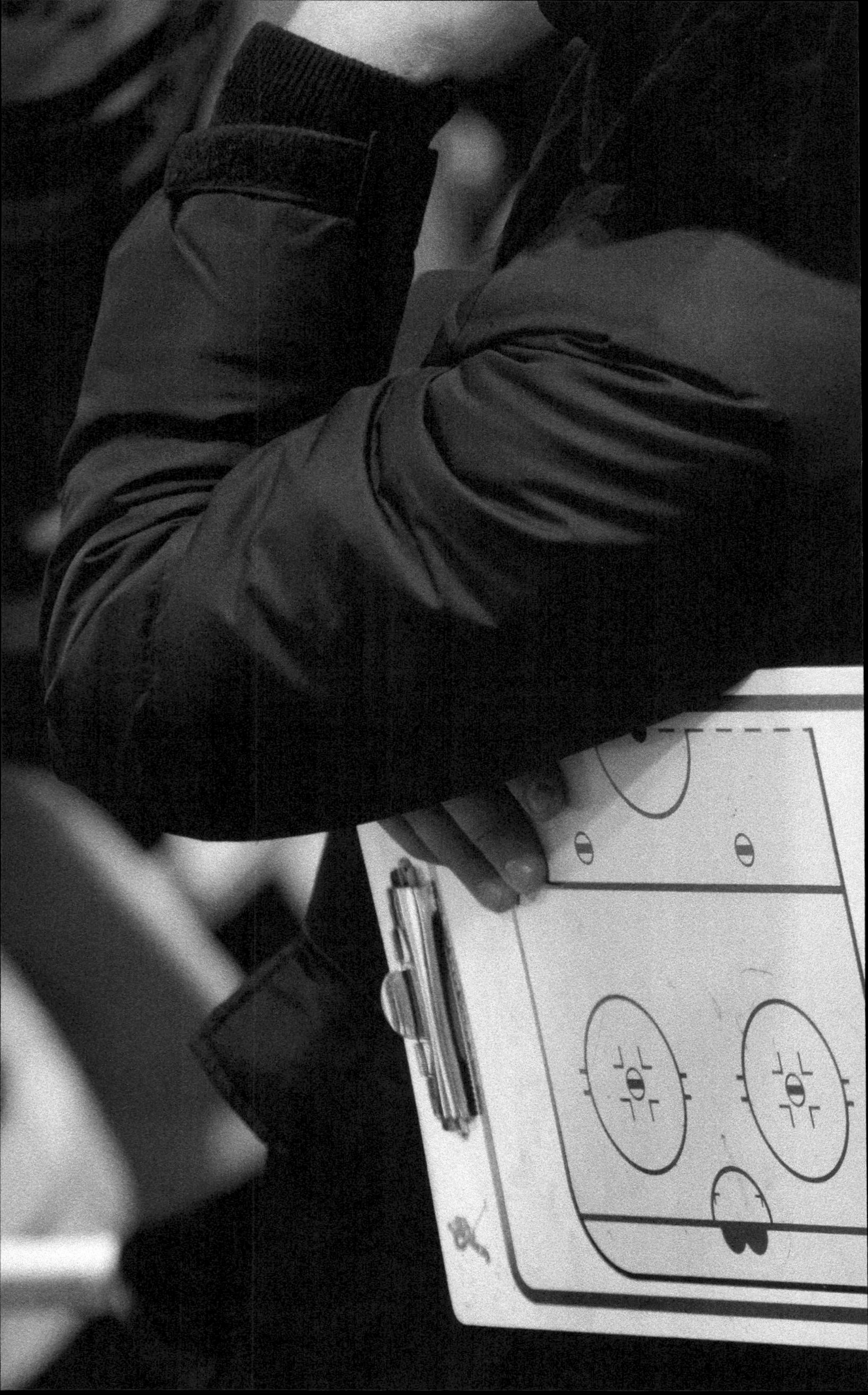

CHAPTER 15
Gavin

> Beckett: Why the duck am I in a car with Aiden and you're riding with Brooks?
>
> Aiden: Duck you! I'm in this chat, you know.
>
> Beckett: I'm aware. I was hoping you'd see it and stop singing for one ducking second.
>
> Aiden: Finn happens to like my singing.
>
> Beckett: Oh, because my five-year-old likes when you sing Disney songs at the top of your lungs in the car, you think that means the rest of the world isn't suffering?

BROOKS CHUCKLES beside me as the computer in his truck reads us the text messages between my brothers in a monochromatic voice.

"You going to reply to them?" he asks as he pulls off the highway.

All four of us are headed to Ford's house in Bristol for Daniel's graduation party. Kid finally finished classes while playing for my hockey team and helping us win the cup. I'm proud of him.

"Nah. They can keep each other occupied."

"So," Brooks says, taking his eyes off the road for a moment, "last weekend..."

Affecting a placid expression, I meet his eye. "What about it?"

"We didn't see you at any of the celebrations. It was like you vanished. What was that about?"

Every one of my brothers has asked, and I've been vague thus far. I'm not going to change tactics now, despite how much I hate lying to them. "Just needed to get away."

Brooks sighs. "You okay?"

I turn to my window and scan the scenery as we pass. It doesn't matter whether I'm focused on the ocean dotted with boats or the lighthouse in the distance, because all I see is her. In the week since I returned from Paris, I've spent every waking moment thinking about her, texting her, listening to her sleepy, raspy, sexy voices while she FaceTimes me from her bed after she gets home from work.

Not kissing her before I left Paris might have been the hardest thing I've ever done, but I kept that promise to myself. I can't have only a part of her. A relationship based on sex alone would never be enough.

I hum, assuring Brooks that yes, I'm fine, and we continue the trip in silence.

As we pull up to the oversized white stone fortress that Ford calls his home, Brooks ducks low and takes it all in. "Place is sick."

Again, I hum a response.

"Dude, seriously. Are you okay?"

Brooks has always been the most observant of my brothers. The most sensitive. Why did I think he wouldn't pick up on this?

The truth is, I am okay. I get to spend the day with my brothers, celebrating my best friend's son graduating from college. A kid who now plays for my team. A kid I watched grow up. For years, I've watched him playing hockey and listened to Ford go on about his talent and his drive. I scouted and *drafted* him.

But Millie? She's a completely separate entity.

I didn't watch her grow up. I saw Daniel at games in New Hampshire or Massachusetts when he was in high school, but I'd never met Millie before that fateful night. Sure, I'd ask Ford how his kids were doing, but the conversation was typically superficial, obligatory.

And now…fuck, now she's the only thing I can think about.

I take a deep breath and climb out of Brooks's truck. "I'm fine. Now let's go get a drink in us before Aiden gets here and starts singing *Moana* songs."

Brooks's deep laugh has me smiling. It's all going to be fine.

Everything is fine.

"Ah, the boys are here!" Ford croons as we step into the backyard.

The space is mostly covered by a large white tent and dotted with tables. Each one is decorated in Bolts blue and surrounded by gold chairs.

The crowd is already a decent size, though I don't recognize many of them.

"Daniel has half the team in on a game of flip cup right now, Brooks," Ford says, holding out his hand to shake my brother's.

"Congrats." Brooks slips his hands into his pockets. "I'll go grab a drink and find the man of the hour."

As my brother disappears, Ford tilts his head toward the bar. "Whiskey?"

"Place looks gorgeous," I tell him as I follow him toward the bar. "I'm guessing Lake is due all the credit."

Ford laughs and eyes me over his shoulder. "She and Kyla actually planned it together."

I suck in a breath. Of course Daniel's mom is here today. It's a big day. But I never would have expected Ford's ex-wife to get so chummy with his current one.

"Glad everyone is getting along." Though I wonder what Millie must think of it all. According to her, Kyla is always grumbling about

Lake and Ford. And she's far from the most supportive mother, which is unsurprising. Ford has never had the best things to say about her.

"Thank god for that. Even if Kyla wasn't on her best behavior, she couldn't put me in a mood today. My youngest son finally graduated, my oldest son finally got a job, and my baby girl is home."

My heart stops at his words, and as if on cue, Millie steps out of the house, a platter of food in her hands and a sundress hugging her frame.

When her golden eyes meet mine and light up as bright as this beautiful June day, I know that everything is so not fucking fine.

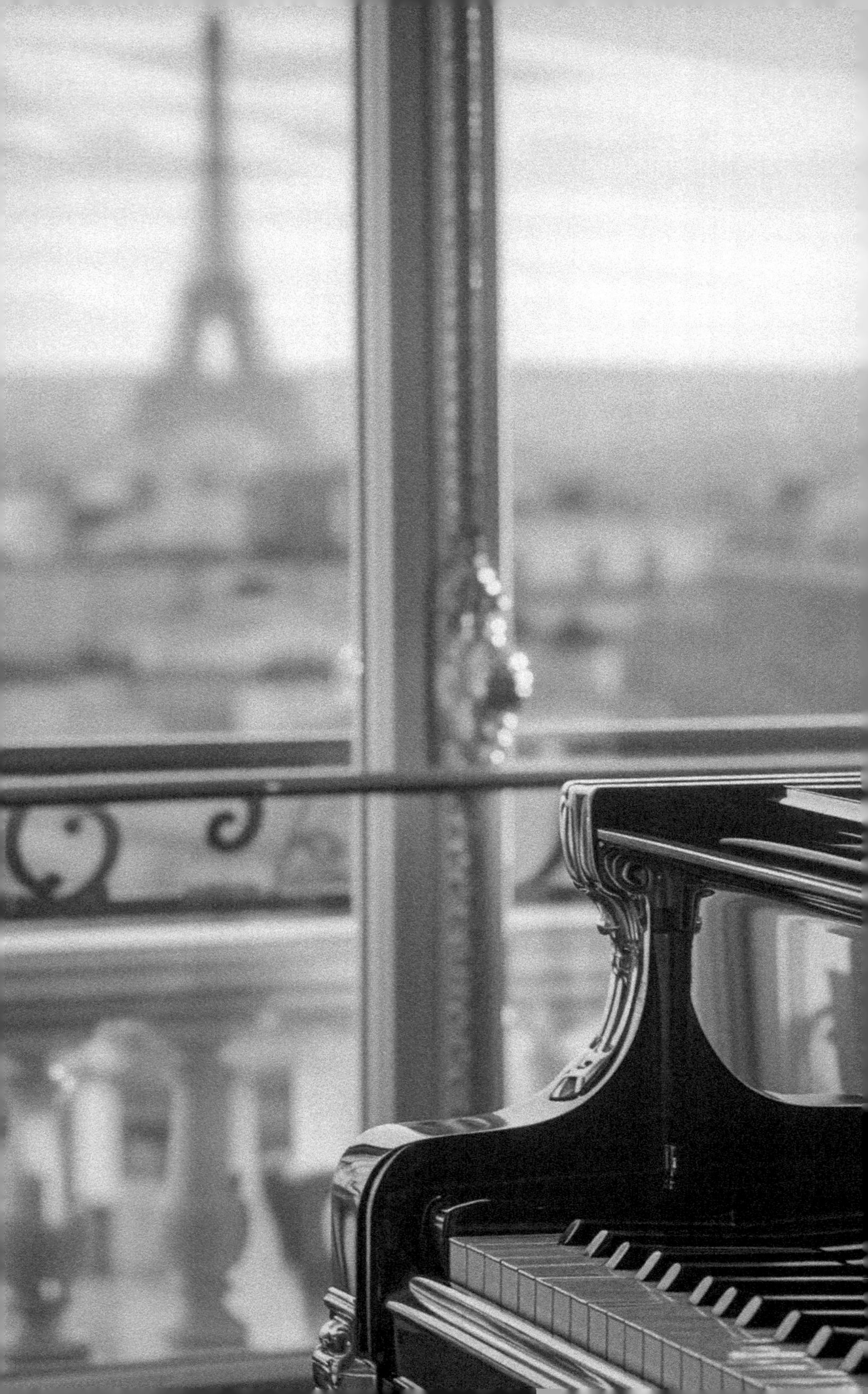

CHAPTER 16
Millie

I CAN'T STOP the smile that tugs at my lips when I see Gavin. It's only been a week. A week of phone calls, of texts, of staying up too late so I can talk to him before bed. A week since he held me while I slept and told me we were everything. Told me he wanted this. Me.

If I could just get my shit together and talk to my dad.

A much easier decision than I thought it would be. I miss my dad. Stupid pride, too much distance, and an embarrassing amount of time clouded my ability to see what was right in front of me. My father with a proud smile on his face every time he looks at me. He's not upset about how I handled his wedding, and he's not angry at me for leaving. No, he's nothing but thrilled that I'm here.

I called him the second I said goodbye to Gavin at the airport, and he jumped into a full conversation without hesitation. And when I asked if I could stay at the house for Daniel's graduation weekend, his response couldn't have been more perfect. "This is your home, Millie. Wherever I am is your home. You're always welcome."

Sure, it was awkward seeing Lake when I walked into the house —her home now—but I replayed Dad's words, reminding myself that her presence doesn't diminish the love my dad has for me.

The reunion with my mother wasn't quite so smooth. She showed up here pretending to want to help. All day, she's plastered on smiles, pretending to be thrilled for my father and Lake, but when she gets me alone, her underhanded comments are back.

My so-called friends are here too, and they've paid me zero attention. They made no secret of their priority today: meeting my brother's NHL friends. Whatever. I couldn't care less about my brother's friends. It's my dad's best friend that I'm salivating over right now.

"You remember my daughter, Millie," my father says as the two of them approach me.

My smile only grows as the grown man whose dirty words ripped an orgasm from me during our video call just a few nights ago squirms.

In a pair of navy shorts and a light blue polo shirt, the man is beautiful. It doesn't hurt that his toned arms are on full display and that, with every inhale, his shirt strains against his chest. Or that he's so hung that even when he's not hard, I can still see the shape of him beneath his shorts. I probably shouldn't be staring at my father's best friend's dick while I stand next to my father, but seriously, he's sex on a stick. I have to lick my lips to hold back the drool.

"Uh yeah. Sure, of course. Hi, Millie. Right, you look. You're—" he stutters, his eyes wild with panic.

My father frowns and gapes at him.

"Relax," I mouth while Dad is distracted by Gavin's insanity.

Gavin clears his throat and ducks his head. When he looks up again, he's schooled his expression. "You look lovely."

"Thank you, Mr. Langfield," I say in a voice sweet enough to make his teeth ache.

My father laughs and rocks back on his heels. "Oh god, has anyone ever called you that?"

Gavin huffs. "I run a fucking hockey team. Of course people have called me that."

His brother appears—the married one—with a kid clinging to one leg as he walks. "Called you what?"

Gavin scowls, but the expression melts almost immediately, then he's crouching and holding out a fist to the little boy. "Bump it."

The kid immediately releases Beckett and pounds his knuckles against Gavin's.

The bright smile on Gavin's face and the look of adoration on the little boy's makes my heart melt.

"Mr. Langfield," my father says.

Beckett laughs. "Yeah, no one calls you that."

"'Scuse me?" Gavin croaks from his spot beside the kid.

"You's Uncle Gav. Not Mr. Langfield. Sometimes Mommy calls Bossman that, and then he turns red. I think he's allergic to it."

Beckett presses a fist to his mouth and coughs.

I have to press my lips together to hold back a laugh. Obviously, the kid has overheard his parents' sexy talk.

Gavin's grin is so wide it's hard to look at. "I'm going to take this guy to play with the other kids."

"Don't you want that drink?" Ford asks.

"I can bring him one, Daddy," I offer. "What would you like, Mr. Langfield?"

My father points at me, wearing a faux stern expression. "Don't you get smart over there."

I shrug. "Who, me? Never."

Gavin's cheeks have gone pink when he stammers, "A—a water is fine."

"You sure? I make a great peach margarita. I could whip one up for you."

Gavin's eyes bulge, and he just about swallows his tongue. "Water's good. I'll uh—I'll just be over there." Almost woodenly, he turns and heads straight for Beckett's wife and other kids.

My father drapes an arm over my shoulders. "Let's put this food down, and then we can make a batch. I haven't had a peach margarita in years. Sounds good."

Biting back a smile, I sneak a peek at Gavin, who is now on the grass, wrestling with the little boy. The joy radiating from him only magnifies when a smaller girl wanders close and squeezes his face between her palms. It's so strange to see him in this environment. To picture him as a family man.

But god is it good to see him.

I look back at my father. "Yeah, peach margaritas are my favorite."

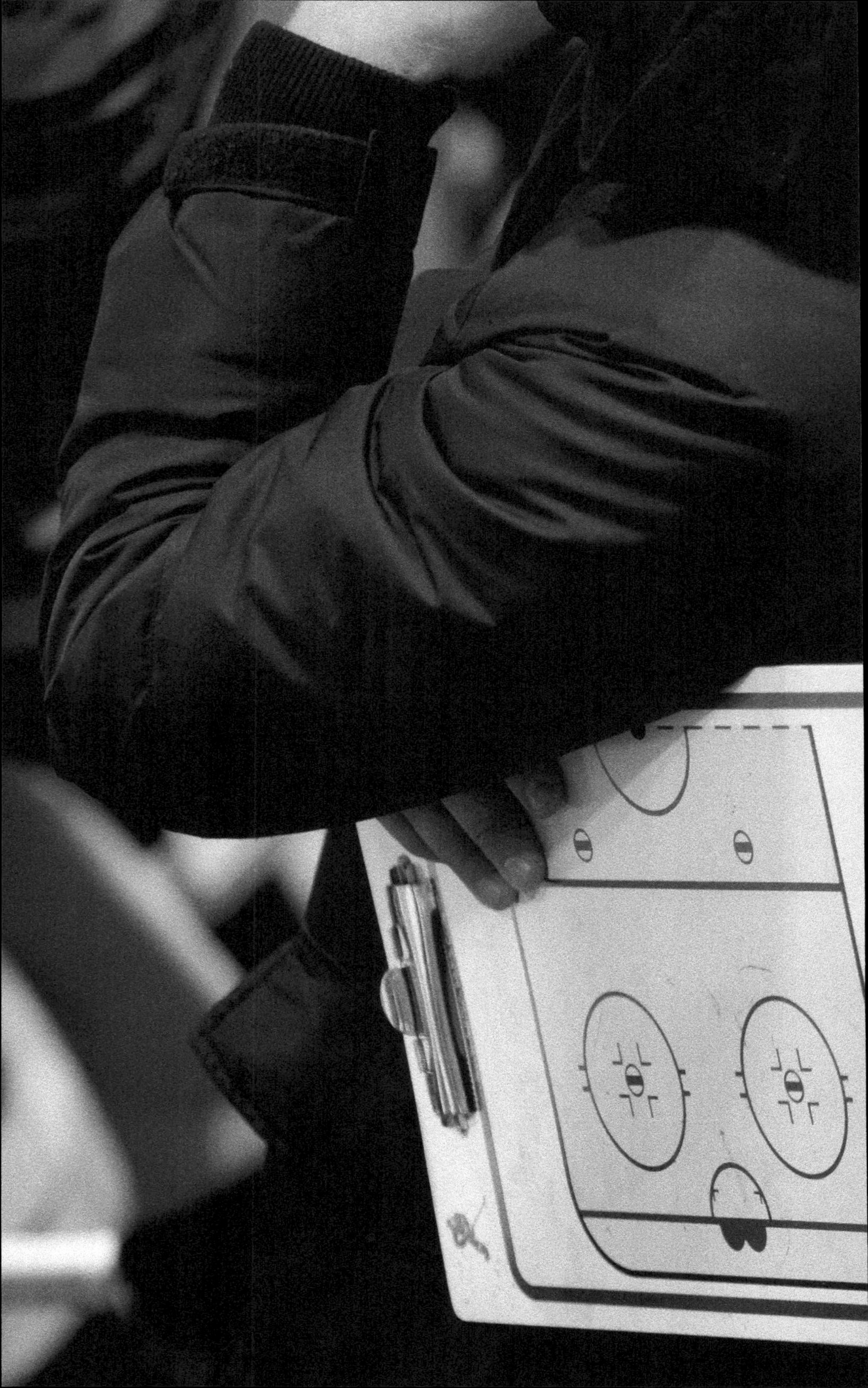

CHAPTER 17
Gavin

WITH MILLIE HERE, I do the only thing I can. I drink. Copious amounts of liquor. And I avoid her. Avoid looking at her, avoid talking to her, and definitely avoid thinking about how good she looks.

Okay, the last one is a complete lie.

I do a really good job of avoiding her. I can't go near her, not with the way my emotions are bubbling up to the surface. Like they're written all over my face. Like "I fucked your daughter and I plan to do it again," has been tattooed on my forehead.

Because yeah. Now that Millie is here, my thoughts and feelings are out of control. Despite the rules I've created for myself, the hold I have on my willpower is slipping.

But I can try. I can sit back and watch her play beer pong with Daniel and the other guys on my team. Guys who make me millions. Guys I cheer for, guys I bet on, and guys I genuinely like.

Today, though, I hate every last one of them. Even Brooks. When he's paired up with Millie for a round of beer pong, I hate him with a passion.

I would actually consider murdering my own brother if he laid a hand on her.

I'm so unbelievably fucked.

"The guys would let you play if you wanted," Ford cajoles beside me at the firepit.

I grunt. "I'd wipe the floor with them."

Beckett, on my other side, sighs and brings a cigar to his lips. He hasn't lit it all night. He just holds it, sniffs it, fondles it.

Guess he doesn't want to smell like it, or maybe he's worried about setting a bad example in front of Finn.

I'm abstaining too, because if I partake, there's no way I won't get sick. I've had far too much whiskey today while avoiding the peach margaritas Millie doled out to the whole crowd.

"I think I've hit my limit for fun." Lake snuggles against Ford's chest, her legs covered in a soft blanket.

He drops a kiss to her forehead. "Close your eyes here. I'll carry you in."

Damn. Guy's so desperate for his wife's company he won't even let her go to bed when she's half-asleep.

She gives him a secretive smile and murmurs an *okay*. Then her eyes fall shut almost instantly.

"You can go play, ya know. Don't have to keep us old married men company," Ford teases.

"Speak for yourself," Beckett grouses. "I'm not old."

Liv appears at his side with a sleeping Addie in her arms. "Yes, you are, baby. As am I, so if you could take Little One before I fall over, I'd appreciate it."

Before she's finished her request, Beckett's up and grabbing their daughter, who's fast asleep. With more care than seems possible for a man so cranky most of the time, he shifts her in his arms and murmurs into her hair. Once the little girl is clinging to his neck with her head nestled beneath his chin, he looks up at his wife. "Ready to head out, Livy?"

"Yeah, I think this part of the party is for the graduate and the kids his age. You want to ride back with us, Gav?"

Ouch. Her words hit me like a slap. Because she's right. I'm too damn old to be hanging out with the kids still partying. I glance over at the table where Millie is still playing games, hoping my expression gives nothing away. There's no way I can leave without having a minute alone with her.

"Um, I'll wait for Brooks."

"Wait for me for what?" Brooks asks, suddenly appearing at Liv's side.

"We're heading out," Beckett explains.

"Yeah, I'm going to head back too." He dips his chin, a few strands of hair that have escaped his man bun swaying. "Aiden is going out with some of the guys, but I'm beat. I told Sar I'd watch a movie with her when I get back."

It's no surprise that my brother would rather go home and hang with his "best friend" than go out prowling for girls with the hockey team. His life revolves around two things: hockey and Sara Case.

"You ready, Gav?"

A commotion from the other side of the yard has us all turning to the group at the beer pong table. Every guy in the crowd is tearing off his shirt and stepping out of his shoes. Millie's there too, pulling her dress over her head. Beneath, she's in nothing but a minuscule bikini.

I can't look away as she takes off for the pool and launches herself into the air. She pulls her knees up and cannonballs into the pool with a loud splash. Then, one by one, the guys on the team follow her in, including Daniel.

I turn to Ford, expecting him to throw a fit about the gang of NHL players in the pool with his drunk twenty-three-year-old daughter.

The air whooshes from my lungs when, instead of launching to his feet and going on a tirade, the man fucking laughs.

"Ah, it's good to see those two here together again." He looks back at me with a big smile on his face. "Why don't you spend the night? Let me get Lake upstairs, and then you and I can have drinks by the fire." With a kiss to his wife's head, he shifts forward in his seat. "I've obviously lost any shot of hanging with my kids for the rest of the night."

The *yes* is out of my mouth before I even think about it. Hanging out with my best friend would be great, sure, but I'm staying because there is no way in hell I could go anywhere while Millie is practically naked in the pool with all of these men around.

I'm irrationally angry and have no right to be.

We're not together. She has every right to do whatever she wants.

Except that's bullshit. She's been mine since the night she seduced me and gave me her virginity. If anyone gets to put his hands on that naked body tonight, it's going to be me. Even if I go to hell for it.

Two hours later, most of the guests have filtered out. When Ford finally calls it, he shows me to my room. I hang tight for a solid ten minutes before I sneak out and head back outside to find his daughter.

I'm a fucking asshole.

The moment I step outside and the warm, musty June air hits me like a fog, Millie comes into view, and I sag in relief. She's in the hot tub—alone, thank Christ—with her head tilted back and her face lifted to the sky.

She's in an emerald-green bikini, and her curly dark-auburn hair is in a messy knot on the top of her head. The lights of the tub highlight the water on her skin, making her glisten, and as her chest rises and falls, so does the swell of her breasts.

"Are you gonna come in?" she asks, her eyes still closed and her head still tilted back.

My pulse takes off at a sprint. I clear my throat. "No. I'm gonna head to bed."

She finally sits up and blinks her eyes open. "I did what you asked, and you're still standing all the way over there." She waves a hand up and down my body.

I take a step closer and lower my voice, hoping like hell there's no one within earshot. "What I asked?"

"I talked to my dad."

This is news to me. Welcome news, though. But I'm still cautious. This entire day has been a mindfuck.

"You told him how you felt when he gifted half of the company to Lake? How did he take it?"

She shakes her head. "I just mended things—you saw me hanging out with Lake tonight. We're good."

She did spend time with Lake, and they seemed to get on well. Still... "Really? But your music—"

"I like my job, Gavin. Please, let's not talk in circles. Are you getting in?" She sits up now and gives me a long, unforgiving perusal. The intensity in her expression makes my heart pound and my dick throb.

Fuck. The woman merely has to look at me, and I'm hard. Scratch that—her sheer existence leaves my cock weeping.

Lips pressed together, I scan the empty yard. "That's not a good idea."

"Why?"

"You know why."

"You either get in with me, or I take off my clothes right now."

My blood heats despite my apprehension. "*Millie.*"

"You're not my dad, Gavin. Don't use that tone with me."

I rest my hands on my head and tug at my hair, groaning. "You're right, but your dad is five fucking feet away."

"Don't be dramatic. It's at least thirty feet, and he's asleep."

Jaw locked tight, I stare her down. Dammit. She's not bluffing, and I'm so goddamn weak. With a huff, I pull my shirt over my head. Then I shuck off my shorts. "Happy?"

The grin that spreads across her face is wicked and hot as fuck. "I'll be happier riding your cock, but this is a start."

I drop my head back and curse at the sky. *This fucking girl.* "Don't start. I'm getting in, but nothing is happening."

She hums as if she doesn't believe my protests and sinks lower.

Boxers on—and staying that way—I put one foot into the water, then the other. "Shit, do we have towels?"

She sighs and tips her head back against the cushion. "Are you always so practical while women are throwing themselves at you?"

I bark out a laugh, even as my chest constricts. "Millie, you don't have to throw yourself at me. You know how I feel. But nothing is happening while we're in your dad's hot tub."

One brow raised as if she's unamused, she points to a cabinet behind us. "Towels are in there. Don't worry, my dad is as uptight as you are, so he thinks of everything."

Before I'm even fully seated, she swims toward me and climbs into my lap.

Of their own volition, my palms settle on the smooth skin of her thighs. "New rule. No talking about your dad while you're on top of me."

Her responding smirk sends a frisson of need through me, dammit. "Finally, we agree on something."

"Enough out of you," I chide, squeezing her generous thighs.

For a moment, we sit silently, taking one another in. "Hi, Peaches," I whisper. It's impossible not to feel at ease when this woman is in my arms.

She smiles. "Are you going to kiss me now? I've been a good girl."

"You are *anything* but a good girl."

"Mmm. True, but don't lie; you like it."

The growl that slips from my throat makes it clear how much I like every little thing she does. Especially the way she licks at her lips, teasing me.

She's too fucking good at tormenting me. That one move is all it takes for me to snap. With one hand still on her thigh, I grasp her neck with the other and pull her close.

"You're a tease, Millie Hall. A brat. I'm not supposed to want you or crave every little fucking thing about you, but I can't stop myself." My heart pangs in my chest at the admission. "I can't force myself to put my friendship with your father first. It's impossible to think of you as his daughter when the only thing you'll ever really be now that I've been inside you is *mine*."

The pulse in her neck beats wildly beneath my thumb, and her eyes widen. "I may not know what I want to do with my life. Hell, I don't know what I'm doing, period. But I know if you don't kiss me right now, I may die. I'm yours, Gavin. All yours if you'll have me."

She is mine. Wrong or not. What we're doing will fuck up both of our lives. Her father won't understand, and he'll never believe I'm good enough for her. But what I told him when he met Lake applies here too. I can't put others first. Not in this aspect of my life.

Truth be told, the only person I need to put first is Millie. So that's what I'm doing. Right here. With her perched on my lap and wearing a smile so big it's obvious she knows precisely what I'm thinking.

Yes, Millie Hall's happiness is all I give a fuck about.

"Don't die, Peaches. I'll kiss you." Squeezing the back of her neck, I pull her in and tease her lips with my tongue.

She whimpers as I finally take exactly what's mine, sucking on her bottom lip, relishing the taste of her, then kissing her slowly, taking my time, owning her.

With another needy, throaty sound, she presses into me and loops her arms around my neck. She rakes her fingers through my hair, scratching at my scalp and tugging at the strands.

I groan into her mouth. "Fuck, Mill. I need one taste."

Pulling back, she focuses on me, eyes dancing and lips turned up seductively, as if she knew all along she'd get what she wanted. Dipping back in, she grinds against my hard cock.

"Please, Peaches," I beg against her lips. "Let me taste you."

"Only if you'll make me come when you do."

I run my tongue down her neck, licking up the salty-sweet taste of her skin. "This is a terrible idea."

She moans and swivels her hips, sending a tingling sensation through me. "Terrible. Truly."

"But you need my tongue on your clit?"

Humming, she grinds down, working us both up, unraveling all my control. As if I've had even an ounce of it since the minute I first saw her today.

This was the only way tonight was going to end. Me licking her until she cries my name. Her sinking down onto my cock. Us together. Finally. Again.

With both hands beneath the warm water, I grasp her hips and lift her so her feet are planted on either side of my thighs and her core is inches from my face.

She hovers above me, chin tucked and watching with hooded eyes, dripping and gorgeous.

"Slide that scrap of fabric over. Let me see what you've been keeping from me for over a year."

The dirty smirk she gives me has me digging my fingers into her calves. "I haven't been keeping anything from you, Coach. You did this all to yourself." She hooks one finger beneath the edge of the wet green fabric and pulls it to the side.

Fuck. She's so damn close. Leaning in an inch, I inhale her. Her scent lights me up inside and pulls a moan from deep within.

"Don't tease me," she whimpers, bucking closer. "Lick me. Please."

Finally giving in, I do what she asks. We both groan as I finally taste her. I slide my hands up her calves, then around to the backs of her knees, holding in her place.

"Oh my god, Gavin," she cries far too loudly as I work her over. "This feels so fucking good."

"Shh, Peaches. Unless you want to get caught, you need to stay quiet." The words are a tease, but guilt hits me like a punch to the gut even as I say them.

She swivels her head around toward the house, but a heartbeat later, she's watching me again and gripping my hair. Then she shoves me face-first into her pussy. "Suck."

Without argument, I follow her command, sucking on her clit while she rides my face.

"Oh fuck. I need you." She babbles incoherent curses and tosses her head back.

My mind is a whirling, chaotic mess as I devour her. Her hands are in my hair, tugging and scraping. And then she's gone. I'm gasping for air, confused as fuck, when she straddles my lap and captures my mouth with hers. With quick work, she slides my cock out of my briefs and impales herself on me, sucking me inside her hot body.

"Holy fuck, Millie," I grit out, going rigid.

"Still on birth control," she murmurs, "and I haven't been with anyone else. I'm safe."

"Millie—"

She shuts me up with a kiss. "I know you are too. You would never put me at risk, right?"

Hand in her hair again, I pull her back just an inch so I can look into her golden eyes. "Never, Millie. You're the only person I've ever had bare—"

"And the only one you ever will."

The statement is so confident, so final. She knows. She doesn't need me to tell her. I wouldn't do this if she wasn't it for me. Wouldn't risk it.

But Millie isn't a risk; she's my future.

She shifts her hips and sinks down again, setting a languid pace, tits bouncing perfectly in my face.

"Look at how perfect you are riding my cock." I grip her hips hard and thrust up, meeting her, welcoming the heat that rushes through me. "I love that I was the first to ever have you."

Golden eyes glisten as she watches our bodies moving together. "The only person, Gavin. You. You're it."

Something calms inside me. The inferno that's been burning me alive, eating at me, scorching in all the worst ways, pulls back. It's replaced by a completely different kind of flame. As much as I hate myself for it, I've been beside myself worrying she'd been with someone else during our time apart. That she'd gifted another man with her time, her attention, her body.

She's been my obsession, the unattainable, for the last year. Yet right now she's mine.

"I can't tell you how many nights I thought about this." I lift her up and then slam her back down. "Thought about fucking you. Thought about tasting you."

"Same. I touched myself so many times, thinking about our night together."

"Which one?"

"The one on the beach." She nips at my lip and tugs. "God," she moans when she releases me. "There was something so hot about the potential to get caught."

"You like that?" Keeping a steady pace, I palm one breast, then tug at her nipple through the fabric of her suit. "You like knowing that at any moment, someone could walk into the backyard and catch you riding my cock in this hot tub? Catch you seducing your dad's best friend?"

"I'm just sitting on your lap," she reasons, grinding over me in a way that brings me dangerously close to detonating. "You're keeping me warm."

"And you're keeping my cock warm."

"See?" Water sloshing, she picks up her pace. "Totally reasonable explanation. But if I did this," she slips her fingers beneath the inner edge of one triangle of fabric of her top and pulls it to the side, "maybe you could use your mouth to keep this warm too."

Hands trembling, I dig my fingers into the flesh of her hips and suck her breast into my mouth, teasing the perfect peach nipple with nibbles and bites, then licking away the sting. God damn, I missed these tits.

"Yes, just like that." She clutches at my shoulders, her nails no doubt leaving crescent-shaped indentations. "If someone walks out, I'll take the blame. I threw myself at you, forced myself onto you. Needed to have you. How could I not when you take care of me so well? You make me feel so good. Better than anyone has ever made me feel."

I chuckle against her soft flesh. "Your father and brother would still kick my ass." Tilting my head back, I grasp her chin, stroking it softly. She's so goddamn beautiful. "But it's all worth it. I'd lose it all for you. Now be a bad girl and fuck me until you come so I can fill you up."

With her tits thrust in my face again, she picks up her pace. I match her, frenzied. Hot water sloshes as she rides me, grinding her pussy against me while I suck on her nipple until she's pulsing around me, then gripping me tight and crying out.

"Come now, Gavin. Fill me up. Make me yours."

Her sounds, her cries, her warmth overwhelm me, and when she clamps around me, I come so hard from the feel of her vise-like grip, from the way she milks me, squeezing every ounce of my pleasure into her body, filling her completely, just like she asked. She collapses on top of me, her chest heaving just as frantically as mine.

Pulling in one deep breath, then another, I rub slow circles on her back. "Thank you."

With a satisfied hum, she sits up and presses her palms to my pecs. "Come on, Coach. Take me to bed."

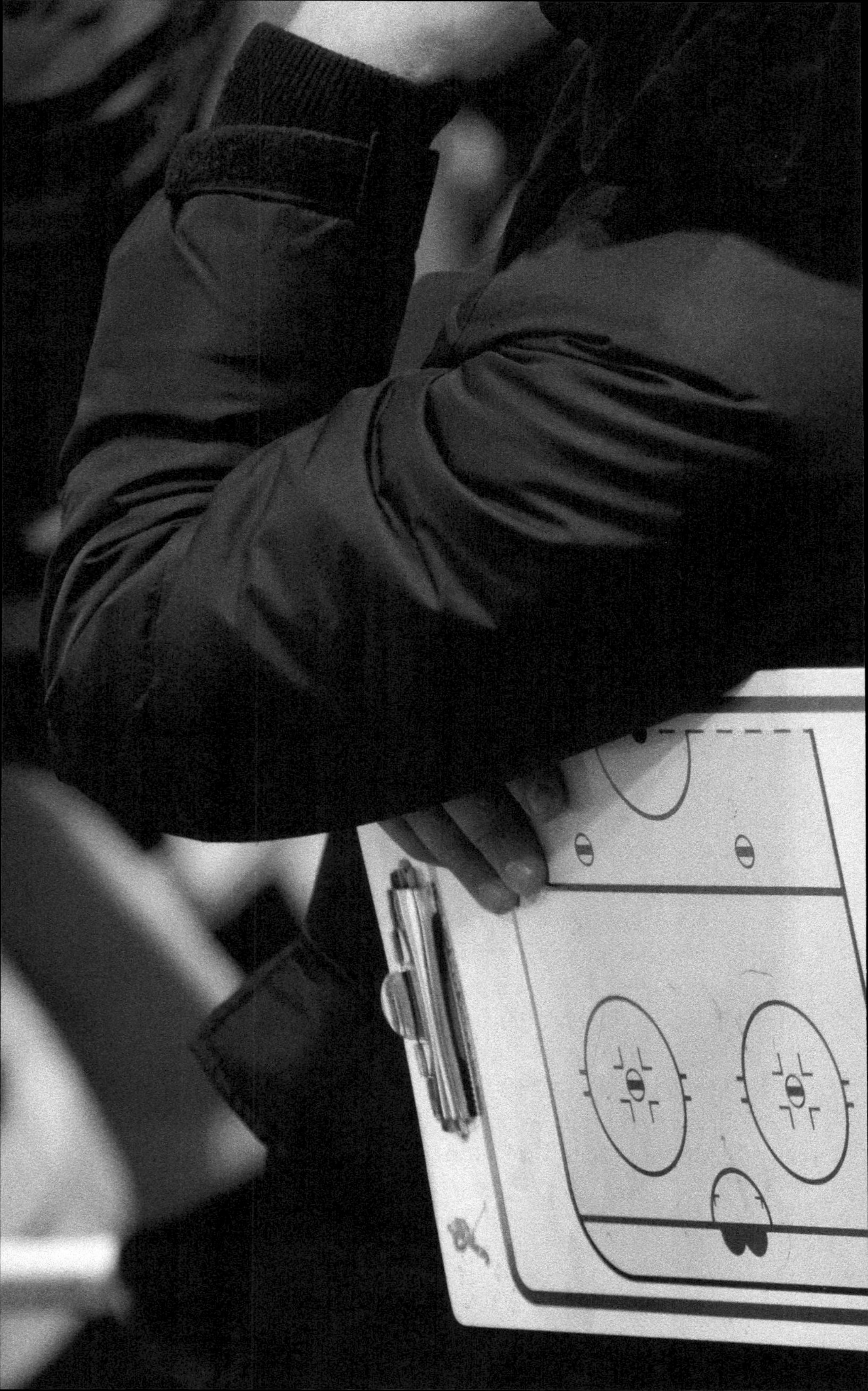

CHAPTER 18
Gavin

"YOU NEED to go back to your room, Peaches." I press a kiss to her lips.

The sun is barely up, and I've already made her come twice this morning. Once on my tongue and then on my cock. Being inside Millie bare is an obsession that could never get old.

Keeping her quiet is another one.

I held my hand over her mouth as I moved over her languidly, and fuck if the way she nipped at my palm didn't send zaps of need straight to my cock as she writhed and spasmed and milked my orgasm from me.

The image of her golden eyes wide and lust filled is burned in my memory.

"Fine. But don't leave before I come down. I'm not ready to say goodbye."

That glimmer of vulnerability pulls at my heart. I slide off her but keep one palm pressed to her skin until she's out of bed and wrapping herself in a blanket.

This setup couldn't be more convenient. The guest bedroom shares a Jack and Jill bathroom with Millie's bedroom, so there's no risk of being caught as she slips back into her own space.

After I'm showered, I head downstairs and find Ford sitting at the table alone.

"Looks like it's just us old guys up right now," Ford says with a nod to the coffeepot. "Cups are in the cabinet, and if you want creamer, you're shit out of luck. I drink it black, and Lake doesn't drink it at all."

"Black is fine." I pull a mug down and lift my chin. "The bride sleeping?"

"Yeah. My kids are too." He lifts a brow at me over his newspaper. "I guess Daniel had a late night."

I fill my cup, then head back to the table, sipping slowly. "Oh yeah? Why do you say that?"

With a low laugh, he sets the newspaper down on the table. Then he glances toward the stairs before angling closer. "I think he had company in the hot tub," he says, voice low. "Gonna have to empty the damn thing."

Panic clutches at me, making it hard to breathe. "Hmm?"

"Noises from outside woke me up. When I got up to check, Lake was stepping back in from the deck off our bedroom. Apparently, Daniel was in the hot tub with a girl." He drops his head and shakes it. "That's the last thing I want to see, so I went back to bed."

Palm pressed over my mouth, I hide my horrified expression and force out a noise that I hope resembles a laugh. "Guess that's why they call him Playboy."

Ford grins and holds his coffee cup aloft. "Just like you."

That comment is like a punch to the gut. Shit. I shake my head. "I'm not like that anymore." There's no way I can admit to what I'm doing with his daughter, but I need him to know that's not who I am anymore. The father of the woman I'm dating has to know he can trust me when he finally finds out the truth.

"Oh?" He arches his brows. "You meet someone?"

For once, I don't give him my canned answer, that I've met several someones, because the one and only someone I've met is shuffling into the kitchen, legs bare, smile sleepy and eyes soft.

"Hey, Daddy. Gavin," she says, zeroing in on me.

"Morning, baby girl," Ford says.

Lowering my head, I make a mental note to never call her that. With a Herculean effort, I remain focused on my cup of coffee and not the beautiful woman that is now pressing a kiss to her father's cheek.

"Daniel just texted that he headed back to Boston already, but I was thinking of heading into the city to see some friends and then have dinner with him tonight. Could I take one of the cars?"

"I have a car coming in an hour," I offer. "Want to ride with me?"

"Thanks, man. Appreciate that." Ford smiles up at Millie. "I'd take you if I could, baby girl, but I want to help Lake clean this place up, and honestly, I'm wiped. My age must be getting to me. I can't hang like I used to."

"That's okay, Daddy. I'm sure Gavin will take care of me." She gives him an innocent smile, then turns it on me.

Teeth gritted, I narrow my eyes on her. Girl loves playing with fire.

"Of course he will. He knows you're my pride and joy. I want to see you before your flight leaves tomorrow. Think you'll be coming back this way tonight?"

"It probably makes the most sense to stay in Boston. Want to meet up for lunch there tomorrow?"

Ford slides his phone out and taps at the screen. "I'll have my assistant make a reservation. Gav, you want to come?"

I swallow down my nerves. How is it possible that seeing Millie could be this easy? Phone out, I pull up my calendar and pretend I'm actually checking it. It wouldn't matter what my plans are. Even if I was meeting with the commissioner of the NHL tomorrow, I'd cancel it. "Sure. I've got nothing else going on."

He nods and focuses on his phone again. Millie drops into the seat across from us and gives me a seductive smile.

It's not until I'm mimicking the gesture that I realize Lake has been standing at the sink with a cup of tea in her hand, watching us. And the look on her face makes it clear that while Millie's father may not have a clue what's going on, she definitely does.

Fuck.

"So who do you have plans with today?" I ask Millie as I usher her into my apartment. Regardless of her plans, I'm stealing a little more of her time, whether she likes it or not.

With a hum, she turns in a slow circle, taking in the space. "It's weird being back here."

I step up closer and pull her against my chest, and with one hand in her wild curls, I angle her head so she's forced to look at me. "Why?"

Her golden eyes are alight with humor as they search mine. "I did lose my virginity to a strange man in this apartment."

I laugh. "I'm strange now?"

"You were a stranger that night."

An ache forms behind my ribs. "Feels like a lifetime ago."

She nods.

"I hope I was gentle enough with you." I loosen my hold on her hair but don't remove my hand. Part of me still hates the way our story began. That I was her revenge. But the trepidation that hits every time I think about it is soothed, because we're so much more than that now.

"You were perfect." Her voice and expression are soft, genuine. "I'm happy it was you."

I press my lips to hers, sweeping my tongue into her mouth and groaning. "If it had been anyone else, I'd kill them."

Pulling back, she sinks her teeth into her bottom lip. "You're a little possessive, huh?"

And now I'm back to gripping her hair tight. "Terribly when it comes to you."

"That's kind of hot." She slips a finger between the buttons of my shirt and tugs, teasing.

"Oh yeah? What else do you find hot?" I want to know her every desire. Want to give her every first.

"Your bathtub was pretty hot."

Silently telling my cock to stand down, I press a kiss to her jaw, then straighten. "I think you liked sucking my cock in my bathtub."

She licks her lips. "Oh, I really liked that."

Images of that night pummel me as I fixate on her mouth. Memories of teaching her how to deep-throat me. Praising her, encouraging her, rewarding her. Fuck, everything about that night was perfect. How is it that every time I'm with her, it's more perfect than the last time?

"So, your plans?"

She bites down on her bottom lip. "I lied. Just needed an excuse to get you to bring me back here."

Tugging her close, I squeeze her to my chest and plant a kiss on the top of her head. "You know I wasn't leaving that house without you."

She sighs and pulls away. Then she spins on her heel and wanders out to the living room. Fuck, do I like seeing her in my space. She fits here.

"I was nervous that you'd get weird after having breakfast with my dad."

Dipping my head, I take my wallet out of my pocket and drop it onto the black marble island, then pull two bottles of water from the fridge. With a nod, I head to the couch, silently inviting her to join me. "I know this makes me an asshole, but it's like I've somehow disassociated you from him. Like I know you're his daughter, his Millie, the one I've heard about nonstop for the past ten years."

She saunters over and settles her legs on either side of my hips, straddling me.

I set our waters on the cushion beside me and grasp her thighs. "But now you're *my* Millie too."

She grinds against me and brings her lips to mine. "I am your Millie, Gavin. I'm all yours—"

My phone rings, interrupting her, and she straightens.

I drop my head back against the couch, annoyed by the interruption, and lift my hips while clutching her with one hand so she can't move. Then I dig the device out of my pocket.

Aiden's name flashes on the display, which means I've got no choice but to answer. If I don't, he'll just keep calling. "Hello."

"We're going out tonight."

I grunt. "No we're not."

"Come on. You didn't celebrate with us last week, and you didn't come out with us last night either. You get a girlfriend or something?"

Millie grins, obviously catching Aiden's side of the conversation.

"Leave him be," Brooks says in the background. "If he doesn't want to come, we don't have to go out."

There's a muffled feminine laugh, then Sara says, "Come on, Brookie baby. We're going out!"

I grit my teeth. "I'm not coming."

Millie pulls her phone out of her back pocket, holds it up, then turns it so I can see the text on the screen.

> Daniel: Dad said we're going to dinner? If you're going to use me as a cover for whoever you're hanging out with, you best be meeting me out for drinks later. And bring the guy. Need to see if he's good enough for my little sister.

I raise my eyes to her, and she shrugs before typing and then showing me her message.

> Millie: There's no guy to meet. Just didn't want to hang with Lake and Dad. <Throwing up emoji> Where are we going tonight?

At this point, Aiden is rapping about how I won't come out to the tune of "Locked Up" by Akon.

"Locked down, he won't come out
The new girl won't let him out
Brothers, he's locked down,
The girl won't let him out, no...she won't let him out."

"If I come out, will you stop singing?" I snarl.

If Millie's going out, then I am too, even if it means spending another night in her proximity without being able to touch her.

"Don't let him fool you," Brooks says, though the last few words are muffled. "Sar, quit it." There's a scuffle, and knowing him and his best friend, she's trying to muffle him. "Aiden will never stop singing."

I laugh, and Millie presses her lips together, trying her best not to join in. I sit up and cover her mouth to make sure her giggles don't break free.

"Just text me where I'm meeting you later. I gotta go." I hang up before Millie gives us away, and then I cup her face and pull her closer. "This is a terrible idea."

She shrugs, her eyes dancing. "It could be fun."

"Fun?"

"Yeah, fun. Trying not to get caught."

I let out a long breath. "You are such a bad girl, you know that?"

"Come on, we could have sex in a club somewhere—" Her eyes widen. "Or on a roof."

"Sex in public really does it for ya, huh?"

She smiles down at me softly. "No, you really do it for me."

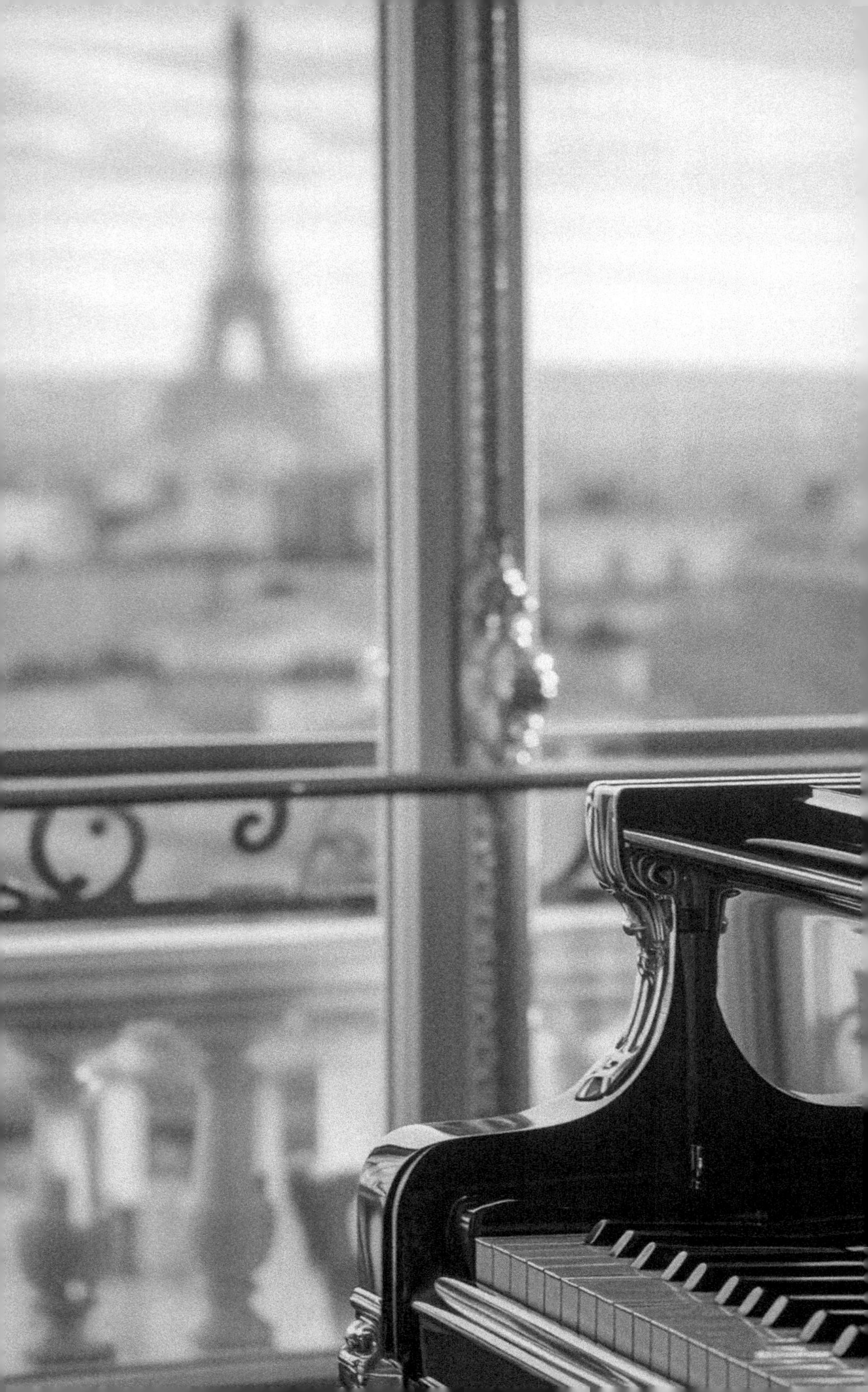

CHAPTER 19
Millie

AUGUST

The next few months are a blur of red-eyes and late-night FaceTime calls. When Gavin doesn't have a game or an event to attend with the team or the Langfields, he flies to Paris. The first time he visited again, he begged me to let him move me into a nicer place. With security and an actual bedroom. But I like my place, and there's no way in hell I'll let him pay for my apartment. He growled, so I gave him a blow job. That stopped the conversation. Until the next time he visited and tried again.

We haven't had that argument yet tonight, though our current situation is much, much worse.

Coach: Get him out of here.

I clench my phone in my hand and eye my father, then glance at the closed bathroom door.

Currently, Gavin is hiding in the shower.

Thank god it's got a curtain rather than a glass door. Even if the tiny space and lack of luxuries is one of the many reasons Gavin lists when urging me to move to a nicer apartment.

The man is bougie, and that's saying something coming from me.

"This is the best surprise," I say, plastering a smile to my face. "I should shower before we go to dinner. Why don't you head to the hotel? I'll meet you there for a drink before dinner. Sound good?"

My dad shrugs. "Nah. I'm happy to hang here until you're ready. I'd rather not have you wandering this area alone."

I cough out a laugh and have to choke back the impulse to say *okay Dad,* like I do when Gavin makes the same kind of comments. That kind of response would be a little too on the nose, since this man is actually my father.

"Daddy, I walk everywhere alone every day. I'll be fine."

He grumbles and crosses his arms. "I don't know why you won't let me help you get a nicer place."

"I like this place. My favorite café is on the corner, and the wine bar Sienna and I love is only a few blocks away. And the weatherman who hangs out at the bottom of the stairs lets me know if it's going to rain every day so long as I give him a euro or two."

Dad drops his arms to his sides and groans. "He's homeless, Millie. Not a weatherman. We sheltered you too much."

Of course he's not a weatherman, but it's fun to push Dad's buttons. "Aw, don't say that around Pierre. He only smells that way because the French don't shower as much as we do in the US."

"Millie." The vein in my dad's temple is now pulsing. Oops. Maybe I've pushed him a little too far.

My phone buzzes in my hand, distracting me from the conversation.

> Coach: Have you lost your goddamn mind? Stop teasing your father and get him out of here.

I snort and pocket my phone again. "I'm just teasing. Seriously, I'll be fine."

He shakes his head and settles himself in a chair at my tiny table. "Just go get ready. Pretend I'm not here."

Dammit. With a defeated sigh, I grab an outfit from the world's tiniest closet and head for the bathroom. Once the door is locked behind me, I pull open the curtain and am met with the most gorgeous angry face I've ever seen and an equally gorgeous naked body.

"What part of get him out of here did you not understand?" Gavin hisses, his fists clenched against his bare thighs.

When my dad knocked and called out from the other side of my door, Gavin had my hair wrapped around his fist while he was fucking me from behind. Panicked, I shoved him into the bathroom. It wasn't until I was scrambling to pull my clothes back on that I realized his were scattered across my floor. Heart pounding right out of my chest, all I could think was to toss them onto my messy bed and throw a blanket over them. So yeah, my dad is hanging in my sex bedroom right now. Getting him out of here ASAP is all I can do at the moment.

I turn on the water, and Gavin hisses again as the freezing spray hits him.

I can't hold back my giggle. "You're lucky my phone is on the sink, or we'd really have a problem," he says as he pulls me beneath the cold water, clothes and all.

"Ass."

With a sigh, he pulls out of the spray and holds me, waiting for it to warm up. "I'll text him."

"My father?" I ask as I pull my soaked shirt over my head.

"Yes. And then I'll text Sienna. I'll tell her I'm in town and I want to have dinner." Gavin gets a faraway look, as if he's thinking.

"Won't that be weird? Your sister, my father, and us?"

He sighs. "It's the only way I can spend the evening with you. Got a better idea?"

"I don't know," I panic. "I'll call Gabe too."

"Oh great, your best friend who never stops talking."

That comment breaks through my spiraling, and I can't help but smile. Outside of Sienna, Gabe is my only real friend. But Gavin's right. He never shuts up.

"I'll make it up to you," I offer, sliding my hands down my boyfriend's abs until I'm cupping his balls and squeezing lightly just the way he likes it.

"Millie Rosemarie Hall, don't you fucking dare." Gavin's voice is like ice.

"Oh," I purr. "Bringing out the full name. I wonder what you'll do when I put your cock in my mouth."

"Your father is on the other side of the door."

"Hmm." I tilt my head and give him an impish grin. "Looks like you have two options. Either fuck me—though we both know I'm not quiet—or let me suck your cock."

"Millie."

I drop to my knees, the warm water hitting my back, and look up at Gavin. Already, I can tell he's losing the fight. His brown eyes are hooded as he looms over me, water running over his shoulders and dripping down his black lashes.

"You're going to get us both in so much trouble, Peaches."

"What are the odds that we'd both end up in Paris?" my father says to Gavin for the second time tonight.

Gavin nods and runs a hand down the front of his shirt, smoothing the fabric. "Should have coordinated better, minimized our carbon footprint."

Sienna snorts. "Since when do either of you care about that?"

Whiskey in hand, Dad shakes his head.

Gavin laughs a little defensively. "I do care."

"Right." Sienna hums. "Tell me again, dear brother. Why are you here?" She eyes him over the rim of her martini glass, one brow raised in suspicion.

She and Cat, the owner of *Jolie* who originally hired me, both insist I drink dirty martinis along with them, but I still prefer my peach margaritas. I'm not sure what they like about the drink. Tastes like dirty water to me.

With a shrug, Gavin settles back in his chair and sips from his own whiskey glass.

Nerves skitter through me and, eager to find a safer topic, I look at Gabe. For a guy who never shuts up, he's being ridiculously mute tonight.

"Gabe, didn't you want to tell Sienna about the new color you saw Hermes using?"

Gabe has an elbow planted on the table and his chin in his hand, watching Gavin. "We shouldn't talk about work, Millie."

Ass. He's loving watching me squirm. I kick him beneath the table and shoot him a look when he finally glares at me.

Sienna hums. "Yeah, we can talk about that tomorrow. Tell me, Gav, what are you doing here?"

"Can't a guy come visit his sister?"

"Considering you visited me just last month, I'm surprised." Her gaze turns to me. "Does your brother visit you that much, Millie?"

I shrug. "Um, sure. Maybe."

My father laughs. "Has your brother been here once?"

"Yeah, of course," I say. Once. Last summer. But who's counting?

The pianist returns from his break and launches right into a song. I try to relax and enjoy it, but I can't quite get comfortable.

While sneaking around has been exciting, and I enjoyed our little shower game, this is not fun. I don't actually want to get caught. Especially like this. I'm not sure when I'll be ready to tell my dad about Gavin, but it isn't tonight. Dinner went smoothly, but now that we've each had a couple of drinks, looser lips are making everyone more daring. What exactly does Sienna know?

"You going to sing for us?" Gabe asks, probably thinking he's being helpful by diverting the focus of our conversation. Of course, when he finally decides to step up, he makes everything so much worse. Because if I have another secret as big as my relationship with Gavin, it's my singing.

"Oh, Millie girl doesn't sing anymore," my dad says when I don't respond. "Though you did have a beautiful voice when you were a kid." He smiles at me, his eyes going soft. "I used to love when you'd play the piano and make up songs. Not so sure her brothers loved it, though," he adds.

Gavin frowns, sitting forward again. "You don't sing anymore?"

I sigh. "Here and there I do, I guess."

Gabe laughs. "If 'here and there' means every night we're not working late."

Sienna raises her brows. "Really? You been hiding a talent from us?"

More like hiding the real me from everyone except Gavin and possibly Gabe.

My father watches me with his eyes narrowed, as if he's finally putting the pieces together. That's the last thing I want. I'm not interested in having a heart-to-heart over what I'm doing with my life. I just want to get through this awkward night, go back to my apartment, and curl up with Gavin. He's my safe place. Everything else just feels daunting.

"It's nothing, really."

Gavin's brow furrows deeper, and he frowns. His scrutiny makes the back of my neck heat. His brain is working, putting together just how much I'm hiding from my father. I can already hear the comments he'll make later.

"You never talked to your father, did you? You're using our relationship as a Band-Aid. You're not really okay."

Desperate to break the tension, though I'll invariably make it worse, I'm sure, I force a smile. "I can do a number, I suppose." My heart pounds wildly in my chest, but when Gavin's shoulders ease, I feel like I can breathe.

I can do this. I can prove to him that I'm okay. I can show my father that this isn't a big deal. Hell, I can show myself this isn't a big deal.

My music is for me.

Even with that mantra in my head, my hands shake as I stand and walk to the edge of the stage.

The hostess smiles as I approach, already knowing what I'm going to ask. I sing here weekly, so this is nothing new.

It's my therapy. My escape.

Yes, running to Paris was just that—running from my problems. But it was what I needed. A break from that life. Fresh scenery, where I could figure out who I was without my mother's influence or commentary from the toxic girls in my music program.

But suddenly, as I wait for my turn, wringing my hands in front of me, the weight of all of their whispers sits on my chest like an anvil.

Can you believe she sang that song?

Millie, you should wear a little more lipstick.

Would you want to come out with us tonight? Don't forget to bring your brother.

When the hostess tells me I'm up next, I focus on my breathing, working to quiet the insecurities that so often take the shape of the bullies of my past.

Though perhaps focusing on past hurts would be easier than considering the opinions of the very real people who mean the most to me and are currently watching me from a table only ten feet away.

When I step up to the piano, Gavin's attention is the most potent. I keep my eyes averted, but I imagine he's probably looking back and forth from me to my father, gauging his reactions and my mannerisms.

He's always seen more of me than anyone else in my life.

Almost like he sees the person I hope to one day be. The woman beneath the girl. The woman who possesses a strength I've yet to master and knows precisely what she wants and how to get it.

The woman he fell for the night we met, the façade I put on before I realized he was more than I'd ever hoped he'd be.

I settle my hands on the keys, and as the first notes fill the space, the song I wrote for him bleeds out of me.

Every word is an explanation to my father. The words are in a language he doesn't understand, but they're a confession. The truth about how I fell in love with the person sitting beside him.

It's freeing, baring my truth in this way. Telling it exactly as it happened. With each line, the weight I've carried all night diminishes until, as I finish, I feel lighter than I have in years. When I look up, finally brave enough to meet the eyes of the people I care about, I'm smiling.

Until I see Sienna's face.

My stomach plummets as I remember that she speaks French. The expression she wears tells me she understood every single word of my confession.

On shaky legs, I walk back to the table, keeping my focus locked on Gavin. He wears a look that might give us away, if I haven't already. Hearts in his eyes and a smile so big it's blinding. As I approach, he pulls me in for a suffocating hug.

"That was incredible," he murmurs.

Though I expect my father to question the gesture when he snatches me from his best friend's arms, he spins me around, and when he sets me on my feet, his smile is almost as big as Gavin's. "Millie Rosemarie Hall, what the hell was that?"

I shrug. "Just a little something I've been working on."

"That's not a little something, Mills," he gushes. "That was incredible."

My chest expands under his praise. Maybe now is the time to tell him more about my music. Maybe now I should—

"You should talk to Lake. She'd love to hear your music. Maybe she'd even help you polish it or buy one of your songs." My dad lights up as he talks, brows lifted like he's waiting for my excitement to match his.

I bite my lip to keep from giving away precisely how his words gut me. "Yeah. Uh, maybe." My voice is hoarse, so I run with the excuse and point to my water, then shuffle back to my seat.

Once I'm settled, Gavin squeezes my thigh beneath the table, reassuring me. He sees me. He knows exactly how clueless my dad is. The daggers he throws at my father for the rest of the night are the only things that keep me from crying.

Later, when we're in bed and snuggled close, he presses soft kisses to my forehead, telling me how proud he is of me. How beautifully I sang. But it's not until he believes I've fallen asleep that he says the words that break me. "I'm so sorry, Peaches. Never thought I'd say this, but I kind of hate my best friend right now."

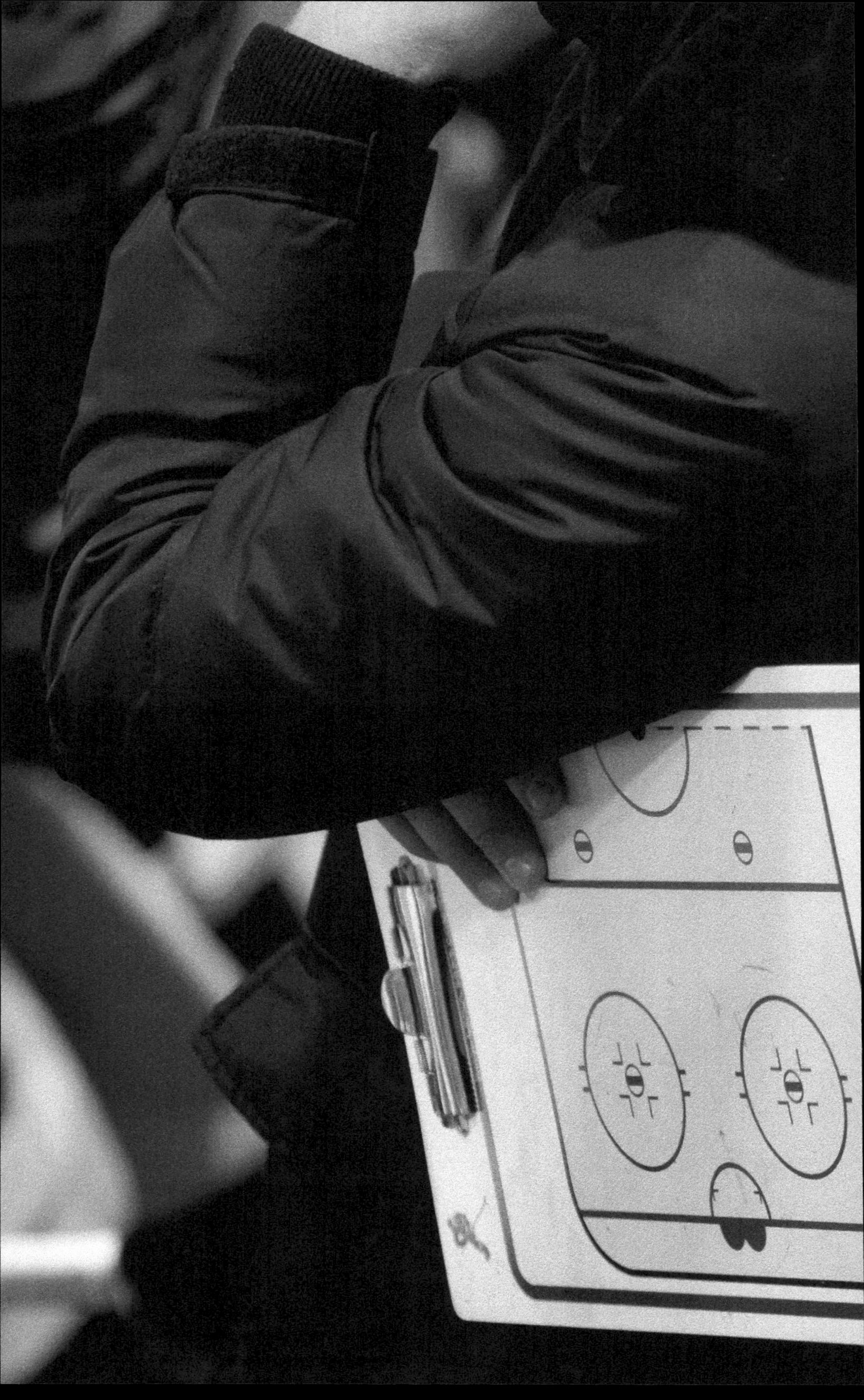

CHAPTER 20
Gavin

PRESENT

"Uncle Gavin, can I get an ice cream cone?" Finn interrupts us, his hand already out, waiting for money. The kid knows I never say no to him.

"Your father is going to kill me," I mutter, grabbing a couple of bills out of my wallet.

Finn counts them three times before holding out his hand again.

"What now?"

"I need to buy our friend one," he says, motioning to Henry beside me.

The old man nods at him. "Listen to the boy. He's much smarter than you."

I scowl and prepare to stand. "If you don't want to hear the rest of the story—"

He reaches out and squeezes my arm. "You aren't leaving me hanging here. I can guess where things went wrong, but I can't help you if you don't tell me everything."

I grab a twenty from my wallet and push it toward Finn. "One ice cream for you and one for him."

Finn grins and runs off toward the ice cream truck.

"And no candy!"

I watch him as he gets in line behind a few other kids.

"So let me guess, her father caught you?"

If only it was that simple.

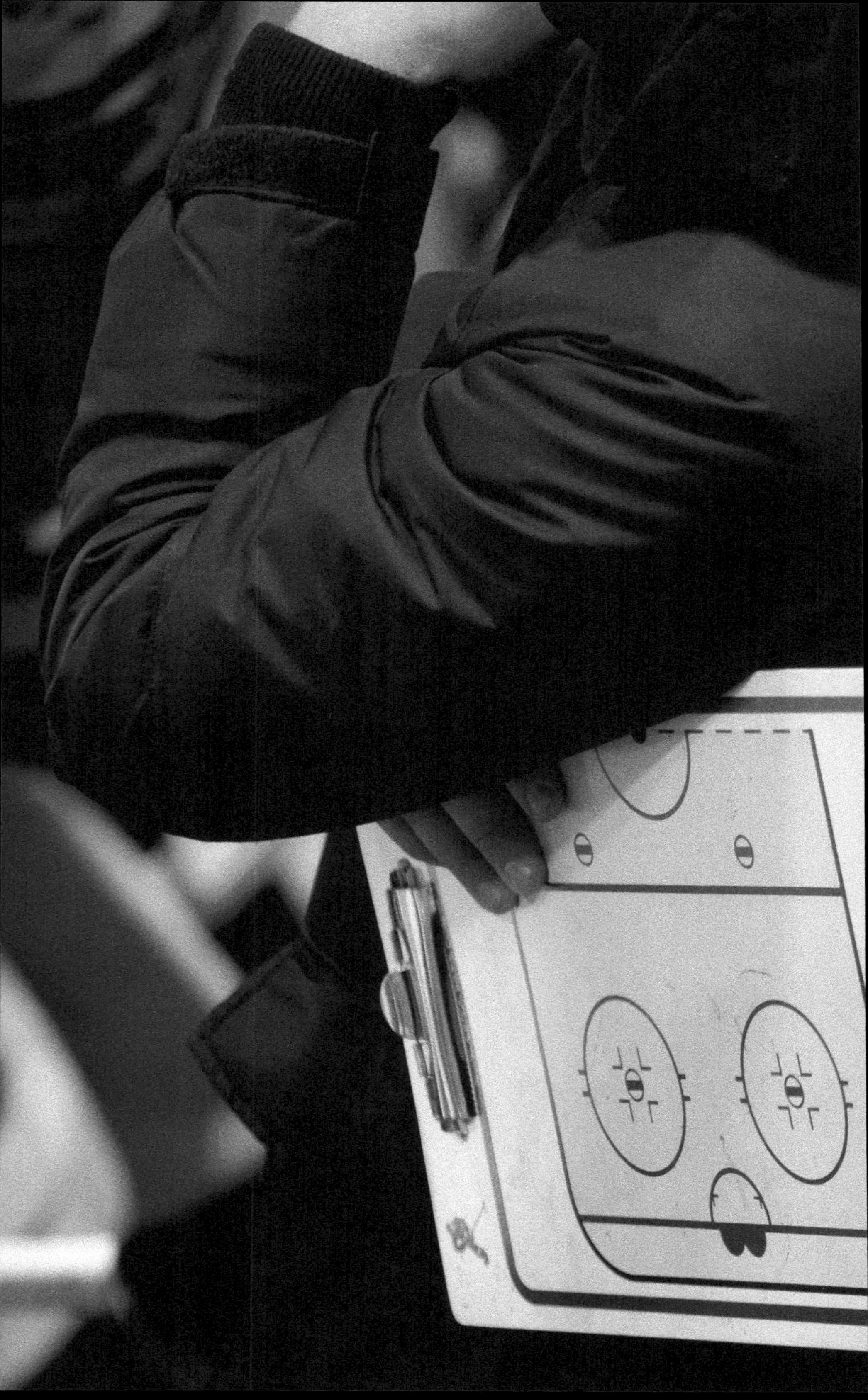

CHAPTER 21
Gavin

DECEMBER

The fall was filled with almost weekly trips. Any time I could get away between games, I'd fly to Paris. Half the time, I didn't know whether I was coming or going. I only truly felt like myself when I was lying in bed with Millie. Whether that was in Paris, which was quite often, or when I was on the road and she'd fly in under the guise of wanting to see her brother play.

We met up in Vegas once when Lake and Ford came along to watch the Bolts play the Vices. Ford, thank fuck, was the one to invite her along, so there was no reason for him to be suspicious. Though we came dangerously close to getting caught during that trip. For months, I'd been agonizing over coming clean with Ford, and that trip only made the desire to do so more urgent. I just hoped that Ford would forgive me when I finally told him the truth.

Or at a minimum, not castrate me.

Ford's blessing was a wish too far for even the brightest of shooting stars, but after that scare, I knew we couldn't keep lying. It was only a matter of time before we got caught. And the fallout from that would be so much worse.

Even still, Millie had become my obsession—her smiles, the sound of her voice, the feel of her beneath me. I'd come to crave her thoughts on almost every topic, and I looked for her in every space.

There's no world in which I'd choose anything or anyone over her. Which means it's time to tell our friends and family that we're together.

Though I have no plans to do it tonight.

Or at least not while I'm lying in bed holding Millie, who's just come so hard I'm still panting into her shoulder.

"Having a heart attack, old man?"

The ribbing she gives me is because of the way my whole body goes rigid at the image on my Ring app. "Don't tell me you forgot we ordered dinner before you started going down on me, asking for an appetizer. The poor delivery boy has probably been waiting for five minutes while you fucked me into next Tuesday."

While the smile Millie has directed at me is usually all I need to be put at ease, tonight, it won't cut it. Not in this situation. I put a palm over her mouth as I talk into the app. "Be right down."

"No rush," her father says through the speaker.

Beside me, Millie goes as rigid as I am, and her eyes grow wide. "What is he doing here?"

I hop out of bed and snag the shorts I tossed onto the floor when I decided I couldn't wait a second longer to be inside my girlfriend. I slide a palm down my face and suck in a painful breath. "No fucking idea."

She pulls the sheets up to her chin, hiding her naked body like her dad could walk into the bedroom at any moment. "Does he normally just show up like this?"

My heart races so wildly I can barely hear, let alone think straight. "No."

"Shit," she mutters.

Trying a little trick I've seen Liv use a hundred times when she's losing her shit with my brother, I pull in a long breath, count to four, and let it out. Then I kneel on the bed and press a kiss to Millie's lips. "It's going to be okay. Just stay in here. I'll get rid of him."

As I walk out of the room, I text my brother.

> Me: Call Ford and ask him to come over. Now.

> Beckett: What? Why?

> Me: Please don't ask me to explain. Just do it.

> Beckett: This is about Millie, isn't it?

> Me: Don't ask questions you don't want me to answer.

> Beckett: Fuck, Gav. What were you thinking?

> Me: Are you calling him?

> Beckett: Yes. He said to come by your place. He wants to talk to both of us.

At the bottom of the stairs, I groan and pound my fist against my forehead. Fuck.

> Beckett: Seriously, what the fuck were you thinking?

> Me: I love her.

> Beckett: I'll be right there.

At the door, I give myself two more seconds to breathe. Then I force myself to face the music. I swallow down the trepidation swamping me and open the door. Under the harsh hallway lights on the other side, my girlfriend's father—my best friend—is standing before me, wearing a nervous smile.

Fuck, what the hell does he have to be nervous about?

"H-hey," he says, clearing his throat. "Sorry for just showing up."

I wave him in, then offer the most awkward man hug, cringing when I realize it puts us too damn close since, two minutes ago, I was balls deep in his daughter. Fuck, I hope he can't smell her on me.

"Anytime." I head to the bar to put some space between us. "Can I grab you a drink?"

Ford follows me, almost in a daze. Unlike me, he's dressed like he's ready for dinner, in a pair of black slacks, a gray shirt, and a suit jacket. "Big event today?" I ask, picking up the whiskey bottle.

"Had a meeting with Crystal Stewart today. She's thinking about leaving Kennedy Records."

I pause, bottle in one hand and the cap in the other. "Shit, that's huge."

Ford picks up one whiskey, and when I do the same, we clink glasses. "Tell me about it. But it was all Lake. I'll tell you, bringing her on as part owner was the best decision I ever made. Artists love the idea that they can work with her, and she's so passionate about giving more power back to them. It's really a win-win."

That part of Ford's decision made sense, sure, and I'm happy for him, but even so, it's hard not to get angry. The situation was devastating for Millie, and this man is so goddamn clueless about it. It feels almost like a betrayal to congratulate him, so I take a long sip of my whiskey—a Hanson specialty bottle that Garreth had sent over—and nod noncommittally. "So you came over here to celebrate?"

Ford smiles but shakes his head.

Smiling is good, right? A father who's just discovered that his best friend is fucking his daughter wouldn't smile. So it stands to reason that he isn't here to beat the shit out of me. Though that gives me little comfort when his naked daughter is upstairs.

"We should wait for Beckett to get here," Ford says as he settles on the barstool beside me. "What's new with you?"

"Oh, uh, just lots of travel. Hockey"—*not fucking your daughter anytime I have a free moment*—"the usual."

Ford's practically glowing as he takes another sip of whiskey, and the smile he was wearing when he walked in is still firmly in place.

When the Ring app alerts me to Beckett's arrival, I sigh in relief.

"That was quick," Ford says, mirroring my thoughts.

I can't get away from Ford fast enough, so I hustle to the door and throw it open. When Beckett barrels in, he's breathing heavy. Fuck, I've never loved him more.

"You run here?" Ford jokes.

My brother eyes me as he shakes his head, though his breathlessness gives him away. "I was across the street at the stadium."

"Working late?" Ford, completely unaware of the silent conversation my brother and I are having, just sips his whiskey with a dreamy look on his face.

Beckett's eyes ask *Where is she?*

With a tilt of my head toward my bedroom, I tell him *Down the hall.*

His wince is a sharp *fuck*.

"Yeah, Livy had dinner with her friends tonight, and Brooks and Aiden offered to babysit, so I figured I'd get caught up on some work before meeting you for drinks," he says to Ford.

I grit my teeth and shoot another silent look at my brother. One that says *Why the fuck didn't you warn me that our best friend was coming into town tonight?* If I'd known, I would have taken Millie to the Four Seasons to ensure we didn't have any run-ins.

As it was, I planned to drive down to Bristol to see him tomorrow. I want everything out in the open before Christmas, and the clock is ticking down. There's no way I'm spending the holidays without Millie by my side.

With any luck, the holidays will have my friend in a better mood and less likely to murder me.

"Why don't you two head to the restaurant, and I'll meet you there?" Whiskey in hand, I motion to my T-shirt and shorts. "I'm not really dressed to go out."

Much to my dismay, Ford shakes his head. "I need to tell you something before we go." He sets his whiskey glass down on the bar beside him and rubs his hands together. The smile he's worn all night suddenly disappears as he rubs the back of his neck.

For a second, I worry he really does know the truth. My heart takes off again as I brace myself for the implosion of our friendship.

Instead, his smile returns, even bigger this time. "Lake is pregnant," he says, his voice full of awe. "I'm going to be a dad again."

"Holy shit, congrats." My brother pulls Ford in for a hug.

I should be congratulating him too, but all I can do is blink as I try to wrap my head around what this means for my relationship.

Fuck, there is no way in the world Millie is going to handle this well.

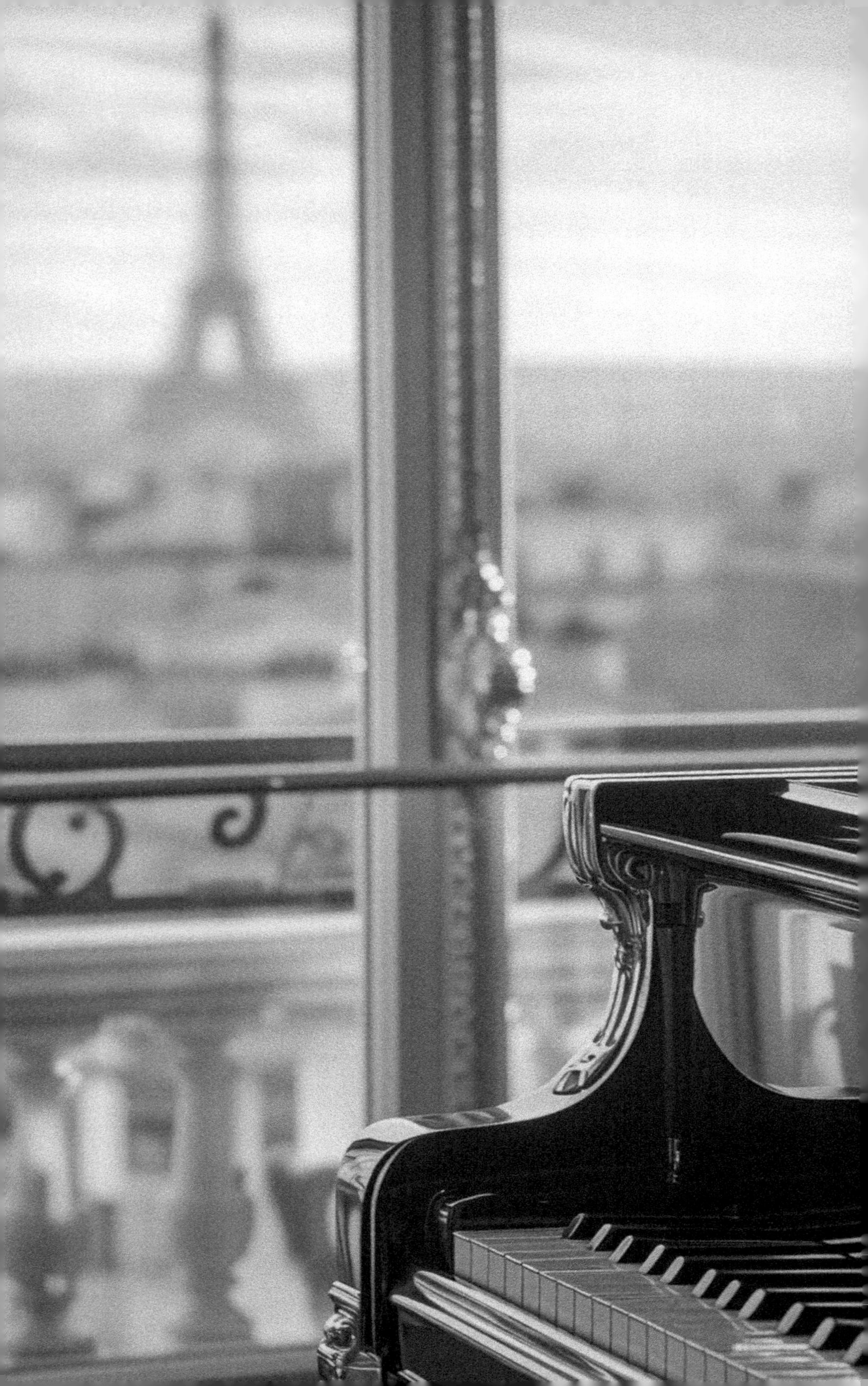

CHAPTER 22
Millie

I LIE IN BED, terrified to move. Does the floor creak? I can't remember if the floor creaks. If I get out of bed, will my father know there's a woman in Gavin's room? Dammit. This is the worst possible way to get caught. He cannot find out about us while I'm naked and in Gavin's bed. All arguments for why we work and how age shouldn't matter go right out the window when it looks like we're doing nothing but sneaking around and having sex.

Gavin and I are so much more than sneaking around and sex. Sure, the forbidden thing was fun, and yes, the sex is phenomenal, but so are our conversations and the feel of his arms holding me tight. His smiles and his forehead kisses and his encouragements. He makes me happy every day, even when we aren't together. Though we're together more often than seems possible now thanks to Gavin's private jet.

When the season started, I was at the game, cheering on my brother, and then I spent the night in my boyfriend's bed, lost in him, in us. So much so that we were both late to brunch the next day with my father and Lake. Lake definitely knows the truth, even if she hasn't said it in so many words, but my father is completely oblivious. Hell, he's the one who invites Gavin along every time we meet up in Boston.

Despite how adamant Gavin is about coming clean with my dad, it's the last thing I want to do.

If Gavin and I date out in the open, then it'll send a message to them that I'm okay with my dad's relationship with Lake. And though I'm better at keeping it to myself, I'm still struggling on that front.

Not because I don't believe that my father loves her. Or that she loves my father.

The root of the issue lies in my relationship with my dad. Since Lake came into the picture, things have not been the same between us. Maybe it's unfair to put that on her, but it's easier than admitting the truth: that my father broke my heart.

He broke my heart when he gave her half the company without considering that I may have interest in working with him. Yes, I told Gavin that I'm happy with my job, and while it's not a complete lie, I've become stagnant.

But so long as I have Gavin, I can push all those concerns away. He's like a bandage, covering all my ugly, broken pieces and keeping me stitched together. It's not until I'm alone that the anger starts to bleed out of me again.

And if my father isn't okay with us dating—if he makes Gavin choose—I worry that he may not choose me. And regardless of the disconnect between us, I don't want to lose my dad either.

But time is barreling forward whether I want it to or not. And now my father is down the hall while I'm here, naked in his best friend's bed.

Fuck.

Could this get any worse?

I've spiraled for a solid thirty minutes when the main door opens and closes again. Two minutes later, the bedroom door swings open, and Gavin walks in.

At the sight of him, I blow out a breath of relief. "Is he gone?"

Gavin nods slowly, but the movement is robotic, like his mind is somewhere else.

"Everything okay?" I ask, finally sitting up.

Without responding, Gavin snags my robe from the back of his bathroom door. Little by little, my things have migrated here and found homes in his space. I don't hate the way he smiles every time he finds something else of mine.

He holds it up, silently signaling that it's time to get out of bed. Once he's wrapped me in it, he presses a kiss to my neck. "Yeah, we should talk."

Tying the sash, I spin so I can see his face. "That doesn't sound good."

Head shaking, he rubs at his chin, blinking again. "It's not bad. He doesn't know."

He leaves it at that. It's a reassurance, though his words fill be with dread instead of relief.

"What's going on, Gav?"

He drops to the mattress, then pulls me onto his lap. "Your father really should be telling you this, and he plans to. Tomorrow, I guess. But I can't know and not tell you."

Anxiety races through me as I clutch his shoulders and search his face.

Is my dad sick? Is he—

"Lake is pregnant."

For a moment, my brain goes blank, and I hold my breath. There's a humming in my ear, maybe a buzzing, a warning, perhaps, that I'm being starved of oxygen.

"I know it's probably not what you want to hear," Gavin continues, pulling me into his chest, "but maybe it will work to our advantage. He's happy. And yeah, it will be a little weird when our kids are close in age to your sibling, but stranger things have happened, right?"

He pulls back, his lips quirked in a hopeful smile, as if he's waiting for me to agree, but his words are still ricocheting through my brain.

"Did—did you just say *our kids?*" I latch on to that one thing as my heart hammers painfully in my chest.

His smile fades slowly, and the light in his eyes snuffs out. "Millie, I'm not getting any younger."

"I'm twenty-three," I deadpan.

"Believe me, I'm aware." He runs a hand through my hair, frowning. "Do you not want kids?"

He swallows audibly, studying me as if he's trying to read my mind. One of the things I love most about him—how well he understands me—makes me feel itchy all of a sudden.

God, please don't let him read these thoughts.

Trembling, I turn the question around on him. "Do you?"

His expression is thoughtful as he nods. "I never used to think I did…"

I breathe out a sigh of relief. Okay. He's just having a moment. "Then where is this coming from?"

"My brother is such a good dad to Liv's kids, and now he's having twins and he's so excited about it. And then your dad—"

I groan. "Please stop reminding me that my father is having a baby with someone my age."

"She's older than you, and their age difference is the same as ours," he argues.

"No, they're twenty-one years apart." I smile. "We're eighteen."

He laughs. "Do you hear yourself?"

I close my eyes and bow my head. "I know. I know I sound ridiculous, but give me a minute with this. A couple of hours ago, we were talking about telling my dad that we're seeing each other. Now you're talking about kids, and I've got a new brother or sister coming. This is insane."

"My hope to have a family with you is not insane. And I wouldn't be telling your father about us if I didn't want you in my life forever, Millie. I wouldn't have risked my friendship with him months ago. I want to marry you. I want to have kids with you. And I want my best friend to be okay with that."

This is so not how I thought today would go. I sit there, dumbfounded. Shocked. "You haven't even said I love you, but you want to marry me?"

"Millie—"

I cover his mouth. *"Don't.* Not like this." I shake my head and suck in a breath, suddenly feeling slightly claustrophobic. "I think I need to go for a walk. Get some fresh air."

"It's seven already. It's dark and it's freezing out. Don't do this. Don't run."

My breaths come in ragged, uneven gasps, my lungs burning. "I'm not. I'm just—" I can't look at him. Can't see his face when I say this. "I can't do this. I think..." I swallow and take in another breath, searching for words that make sense. "I should go back to Paris. We'll be fine. This just isn't the right time to tell my dad. I think maybe... maybe later." I nod. Yes. That's exactly what needs to happen. We need to slow down. Things have been so perfect between us, and I want to go back to that. We just need to hit pause for a little bit.

"You're going back to Paris?"

I stand and snag my clothes. Then I spin in a circle, searching for my other belongings. My suitcase is still full and open on the floor. I've only been here for a few hours. "Yes. Then my father can't tell me about Lake, and I—we'll—things can stay the way they were. Nothing has to change." I turn around, clutching my clothes to my chest, and plead with him. "Please, Gavin. I can't tell him. I can't hear it. I can't do that." I point to him, then to myself. "I can do this. We're perfect. Come back to Paris with me. We can spend Christmas together in my apartment. We'll get a little tree and go to that café you like. I'll even sing that song you love." My heart starts to settle the more I think about being with him there, away from all this. Yes, this is what we need. To spend the holidays, just us two. No talk of kids or the future. No Lake or my father.

No pressure. Just us.

"No."

"Fine. I'll sing it in English," I say with a smile.

His frown only deepens. "I tell you I want to marry you, and you start packing your bags?"

"That's not—" I shake my head and look away. The pain in his eyes makes my heart feel like it's cracking in two. "I'm not ready to tell my father."

"Millie, I'm saying this because I lo—"

I whip around and glare at him.

He swallows and huffs out a breath. "Because I *care* about you. I do. I care about you so much." He steps closer and grasps my hand.

My stomach twists at the wariness in his expression. He's watching me like he's trying to weigh his words, as if I might break. "I've risked my friendship with your father for you, and I wouldn't take it back. Not for anything. But we can't have a healthy relationship if you don't talk to him. I won't be a dirty secret, and I won't be an act of revenge."

Pain blooms in my chest, so acute I have to fight not to double over. *Revenge.* That might have been my motive that night, but he has to know that changed the moment I went home with him. Lungs burning, I heave in a breath, but when I speak, my words are barely audible. "You know you aren't."

For several long seconds, we stare at one another. In the silence that stretches between us, I will him to remember every moment we've shared. Every word. Every touch. To hold on to the connection we have. But then he blinks, and the deep brown of his irises goes dull. That's when I know we're not on the same page. Hell, we're not even reading from the same book.

"Then prove it to me." He sighs and releases my hand. "I've got to go. I told your father I'd meet him at the restaurant."

"What?"

He shuffles to his closet and removes a pair of dress pants from a hanger. He steps into them, then slips a button-down shirt on. Once his shirt is buttoned, he turns around and looks at me, his face a mask of calm determination. "I can't keep playing these games, Peaches. The sneaking around isn't fun anymore. Not when I feel the way I do for you." He steps up to me and presses a kiss to my lips. It's so quick I don't have time to return the gesture. "I'll always be here for you. Always." His forehead falls to mine, but he doesn't hold my hands, clasp my arms, touch me anywhere else. "But this isn't healthy."

My heart splits in two, and a tear slides down my cheek. "Are you breaking up with me?"

When he steps back and a rush of cool air hits me, the loss of him is palpable. "How could I break up with you? We're—" He shakes his head and takes another step back.

"I can't lose you," I whisper. The world is upside down right now, but that's the one thing I know for certain.

Gavin presses his lips together and gives me a pitying smile. "Can't lose something you never truly had," he says. "Take care, Millie."

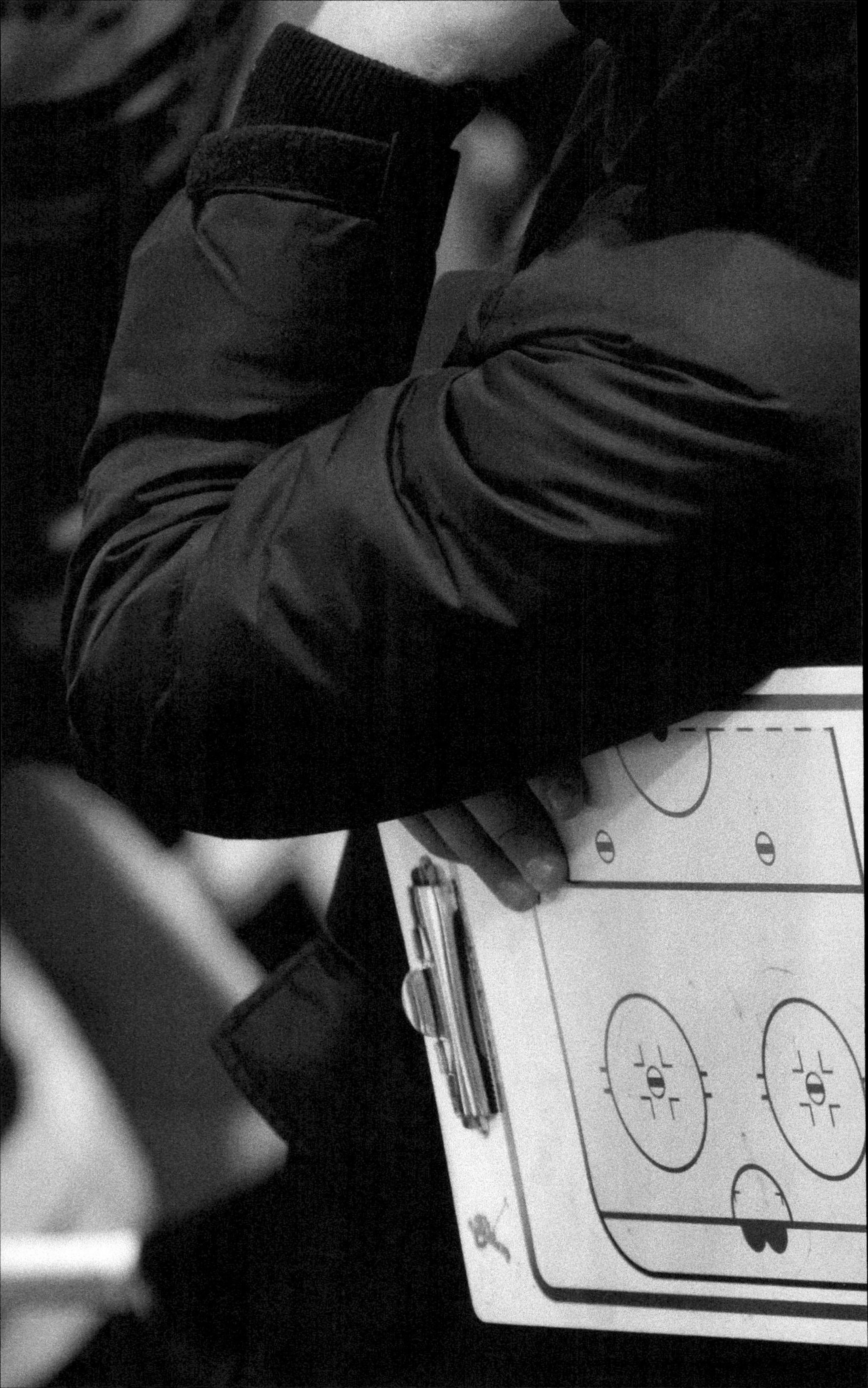

CHAPTER 23
Gavin

PRESENT DAY

"And then what happened?" Henry says, swiping at his eyes.

I scrub a hand against mine as well. Fuck, this is sad. "Nothing. I haven't spoken a damn word to her since."

"That'll be a thousand dollars, Uncle Gav," Finn sings as he appears from behind me.

Dammit, the kid is sneaky.

Henry leans forward, elbows on his knees. "You didn't go after her?" He sounds affronted. Like he's the one who got his heart broken.

I stand up and point to Finn. "Come on, buddy. We gotta get you home." Then I turn to Henry. "She didn't want what I wanted. *Should* I have gone after her?"

The old man clucks. "Come back tomorrow with a burger and

fries from Wendy's for me. I need to think this one through tonight. Figure out how you can make this right."

I snort out a laugh. "McDonald's not good enough for you?"

He smiles. "There's no real competition. The fries and chocolate Frosties from Wendy's are far superior."

I shrug. "You got a deal." I pull out my wallet and dig out a couple hundreds. "Thanks for listening. Make sure you stay somewhere warm tonight."

The man stares at my outstretched hand, but he doesn't take the money, so with a sigh, I push it into the breast pocket of his shirt.

"I'm not homeless," he grumps. "I was just sitting on a bench, enjoying the afternoon sun."

Finn giggles beside me.

Frowning, I hold out my hand to the man. "Well, you can give me that back, then."

"Lesson number one. You don't take back gifts. Maybe you don't deserve to get Princess Peaches back after all." The man pats his pocket and grins. "Don't forget my Frosty tomorrow. Same time." With that, he stands and walks away, whistling a tune.

"I think you just got swindled, Uncle Gav," Finn sings.

I laugh, feeling lighter now that I've finally told someone the whole truth. "I think you're right."

Hours later, I'm in my new apartment at a long dining room table with half the guys from my team. I moved in a couple of weeks ago, right after I added *head coach of the Boston Bolts* to my résumé. It's my dream job, even if the way I got it was more like a nightmare.

I had to fire the head coach, Sebastian Lukov, after it was discovered that he'd had an affair with the head of PR, Sara Case, without disclosing to her that he was married to my aunt. It was a shit show, as expected, and worse, the woman at the center of the scandal, Sara, is my brother Brooks's best friend.

During the fallout of the affair, Sara and Brooks began fake dating and somehow managed to fall in love. Now, they're happier than ever.

When Sara came to me about the affair in hopes of saving her job and Brooks's, I did some digging. Apparently, my uncle had been cheating on my aunt for years. But I've kept that information to myself. Aunt Zoe was devastated as it was, and I have no interest in rubbing salt in her wounds.

I lost no sleep over firing his ass, but finding a coach mid-season—one the guys and I could trust implicitly after what the team had been through—proved more difficult.

Okay. Maybe I didn't look all that hard. Because this is the job I've always wanted.

And it came at the perfect time. When my uncle's indiscretions were blasted all over the media, I'd already lost Millie. Honestly, the job saved me from a depression I was easily sinking into. Now I'm just on the left side of grumpy.

Moving into the building where my hockey players lived seemed like a no-brainer. A fresh start. Langfield Corp owns the whole place, and we encourage our guys to live here—i.e. we offer them apartments rent-free—to build comradery.

My hope is that by moving in here these guys will come to trust me. For all they know, I don't have the first clue about how to coach an NHL team. I sign their paychecks and I wooed them when I was drafting them to my team, but they have no idea that I know what I'm doing when it comes to the game. They're probably under the impression that I think my last name makes me entitled to this position.

That's definitely what the media is saying.

I'm determined to prove everyone wrong.

Grinding my teeth, I read the most recent text message from my asshole uncle.

> Sebastian: I'm not signing the divorce papers until you agree to abide by the terms in my contract.

Fuck this man. He's holding my aunt hostage in their sham of a marriage because I refuse to agree that if the team makes it to the playoffs, he'll still get his contract bonus. Yes, he held the position of head coach for more than half the season, which is what the contract stipulates, but he's a scumbag, and I refuse to pay him another dime.

I turn the phone over and blow out a breath. I won't allow him to ruin another thing for my hockey team.

"I have to sing for my food." Aiden, my youngest brother, stands and does his vocal warm-ups. "Do, re, me—"

"No. You really, really don't." I grasp his arm so I can force him to sit and shut up, but he pulls away.

Not only is Aiden my little brother, he's also the best center in the NHL. Commentators even argue that he's one of the best to ever set foot on the ice. He's also the biggest pain in my ass, and he loves to sing to get the team amped up. I get it. It's good for morale. And before I took over as coach, I even liked it. But now that he's constantly singing his own versions of Ariana Grande songs and inserting my name into the lyrics, I want to kill him.

The doorbell rings, and I jump up to get it, happy to have the attention off me and the long list of Aiden's past coaches that, according to his song, aren't as great as me.

"Sar, if this is another one of your packages, I'm going to start charging you delivery fees."

As this is the only apartment in the building with three bedrooms, I took it, despite the fact that it once was my uncle's.

The only issue? During her epic revenge tour against him, Sara set up regular shipments to be delivered to Sebastian in hopes of pissing him off. The number of dildos and lingerie sets she's sent to him—and me, since I now live here—is insane.

Sara laughs from beside Brooks, and his face flames. My brother is so in love with her it's not even funny. A grown man blushing.

"The last time I called, they swore the deliveries would stop," she says as I open the door and look out into the hall.

The elevator is just closing, probably taking the delivery person back down to the ground floor.

That sends a bolt of annoyance through me. They couldn't even wait for me to get to the door before running off? With a huff, I shake my head and turn to the floor in front of me to see what the latest delivery will be.

What I don't expect, what I don't think anyone could ever really prepare for, is to come face to face with a baby. It's wrapped up tight in a big peach contraption—a jacket maybe?—and strapped into a car seat.

My heart stops. For a beat, I just look at her, then I holler at Sara over my shoulder. "Sar, seriously!"

Heart pounding, I catalog the child. While my brother and Liv just had twins, there's no way this is one of them. June and Maggie are a month old, and they're still tiny. This little girl is all round cheeks. They're tinged pink from the cold, as is her button nose. The hair that peeks out from beneath her hood is dark. Definitely not one of the twins. They barely have any hair. Poor girls are bald little things that Finn says look like aliens.

They do, sort of.

My mind is a mess of questions. Who is this child? Why is she here? Where are her parents? But an arm on my shoulder forces me to focus.

"Aw, it's a baby!" Sara coos, leaning forward.

"I see that. Why in the hell would you have a baby delivered to my apartment? Your kinks are getting out of control," I growl.

Fuck, I'm not a growler. I've totally become my brother.

Sara's eyes bug out, and she chokes on a laugh. "I did not deliver this beautiful little girl to you." Seemingly unbothered by my anger, she bends at the waist and scoops the baby up, car seat and all.

The little thing doesn't so much as make a sound. She just blinks her big brown eyes at Sara like she's not sure what to make of the situation.

"Aren't you beautiful, and what a good little girl too," Sara happily chatters with the baby while she pulls her out of the car seat.

Me? I'm ready to lose my mind. This prank has gone way too far.

For the first time, I realize Brooks is here too. He scoots past Sara, picks up a diaper bag from the hallway floor, and pulls at the card that's sticking out. "Looks like there's a note."

"Well, fucking open it," I demand.

"Gavin, has Finn taught you nothing?" Sara chides. She turns to Brooks and arches a brow. "What he means is *ducking* open it."

I let out an annoyed breath. "Ducking A."

Brooks slides the card out, and his eyes go comically wide as he reads it to himself.

"Out loud," I grumble.

Brooks pushes it toward me. "No way am I being the bearer of that news. Read it yourself."

"This family and their inability to talk. Fine, I'll do it. *Coach*," I start, pointing to myself. "Guess that's me. *I can't do this. I know you said it's over and we couldn't be more—but she's more.*" My heart stumbles, making it hard to speak, but I power through anyway. "*Too much for me. Meet Viviane, your daughter. You have more than enough resources to help her. So keep her or put her up for adoption. Either way, I can't do this.*"

Keep her. My daughter. Can't do this.

The words are all a jumbled mess, but as they swirl through my mind, all the air escapes my lungs. When they form a coherent thought, I suck in a harsh breath.

The letter falls to the floor as a drum pounds loudly in my ears.

I think it's my heart.

"Gavin," Sara says softly, almost nervously, like I maybe look the way I feel.

I swallow down my shock. Swallow down my anger. Swallow

down the complete and utter sense of loss washing over me. Then I do what any person would do. I look at the little girl in Sara's arms and I take a deep breath, knowing this is bigger than me.

Knowing that every moment in my life is insignificant in comparison to this one, I push away the confusion and the hurt and reach for the little girl, needing to hold her. Needing to know she's real. Just, quite frankly, needing her.

This stranger. This piece of me I didn't know existed until this moment.

"Viviane," I say softly, swiping my thumb gently against the fabric of her peach outfit. My mind is at war with my heart, because what are the fucking chances...? "Hi, baby girl. I—" I clear the emotion from my throat. "I'm your—*dad*."

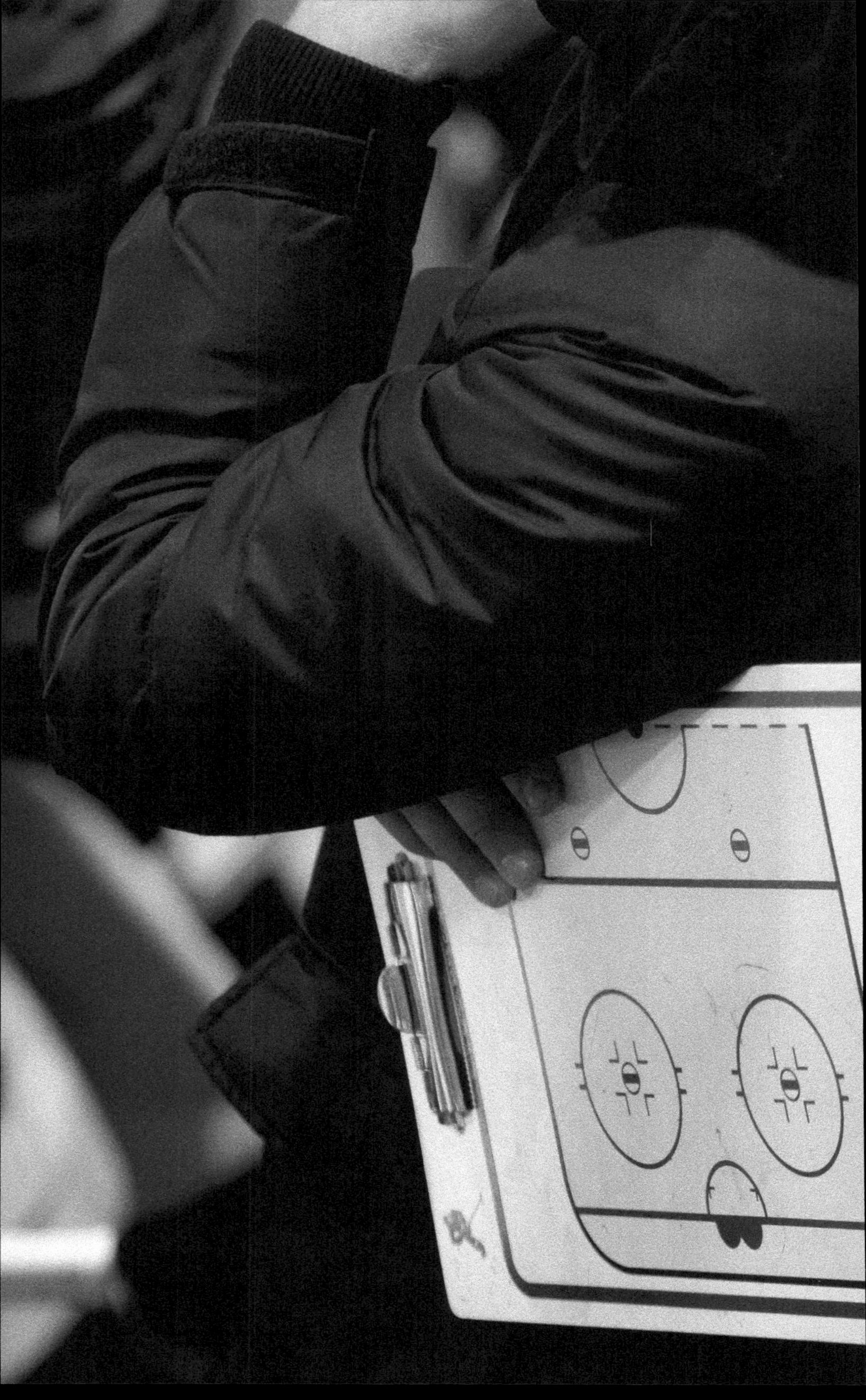

CHAPTER 24
Gavin

"IS THAT A BABY?" Aiden peers into the hall.

I can't speak. I can't look away from the little girl in my arms.

Brooks squeezes my shoulder. "Yeah, man," he says to Aiden. "It's a baby."

"Her name is Viviane," Sara adds. "She's...she's Gavin's daughter."

"She's *what*?" he shouts.

Vivi startles in my arms. Then her face scrunches up and turns red. For the span of two heartbeats, she doesn't move, doesn't breathe. And then she screams. The sound is ear-piercing and heartbreaking all at once.

Shit. Shit. "What do I do?" I look at Sara. "How do we make it stop?"

She shrugs and cringes a little. "Um, try a soothing voice. It's okay, baby girl," she coos, rubbing the baby's arm.

I bounce her, bending at the knees. "Daddy's got you. It's okay." I pull her to my chest, rocking her like I've seen Beckett do with the twins. "I've got you. Don't worry, I'll rip your uncle's vocal cords out. I've been planning on it since he started singing Ariana Grande songs." I continue talking to her even after her cries turn to little whimpers and fade off completely. "That's my girl."

Without stopping the motion, I eye Brooks. "Text Beckett. Tell him I'm on my way."

"What do you want me to do about all the guys?" Aiden hitches a thumb over his shoulder. "Am I in charge?"

Already more overwhelmed than I was the day I took over as head coach, I snap, though I keep my tone low. "I have a kid, Aiden. An actual living child who belongs to me. You are no longer the kid in my life. So I'm going to need you to grow up and handle this. Can you do that for me?"

Aiden's lips turn down in a frown. "I just asked if I was in charge."

I sigh, and Brooks adds, "I told Beckett you're on the way. Didn't tell him what was up. Figured I'd let you handle that."

"Like I have a ducking clue what the heck to tell him. I have a kid, guys. A kid."

Sara steps up close and rubs Vivi's back. "You want us to come with you?"

"No, just get everyone out of my apartment so when I come home, they don't make her cry again."

Aiden whines. "It was one time. It was a shock. You gotta give me that."

"*You're* shocked?" I deadpan.

Aiden scratches his head. "I'm gonna head back to the dining room and take care of the guys."

"You do that." I stare down at the car seat and the note that her mother left when she abandoned her here. I can't believe she did this. Just left her. Who does that?

"What do I do with this thing?" I ask Sara, tapping the seat with my toe.

She shakes her head. "Having a vagina does not automatically mean I know how that works."

Brooks nudges her. "Crazy girl, no saying vagina in front of my brothers."

Sara sighs and slumps dramatically. "No anal, no vagina. You take away all my fun."

I snort, though the humor that usually comes so easy is absent. "You two are strange."

"Hey, neither of us had a random baby dropped off at our door," Sara defends.

Brooks nudges her again and shakes his head. "Too soon."

"Yeah, too ducking soon."

Aiden reappears, grinning far too wide for my liking. "Aw, he's a dad now. Ducking. That's too ducking great. Can I record you saying it and send it to Beckett?"

I glare at him. "You, get out of my sight. You"—I point at Brooks—"follow me down and help me figure this thing out."

Brooks grabs the seat with one hand and tosses the diaper bag over his shoulder, and I head toward the elevator, clutching my daughter a little tighter.

My daughter. How the duck did this happen?

In the end, Brooks and I didn't have a clue how to buckle the car seat in, so we wrapped the seat belt around it as many times as it would go while the Uber driver stared at us. Then I looped an arm through the handle and held on with all my strength, all while trying not to freak the fuck out over my reality.

I have a driver that probably could have helped with all this, but the thought didn't cross my mind until after the fact because my brain isn't working on all cylinders. I have a fucking child.

How do I have a fucking child?

By the time I reach Beckett's house, my thoughts are spinning on overdrive and I'm running through a list of things she'll need. In order to get into the best colleges, she probably needs to be put in a good day care. I know from Beckett's musings that the lists for those are years long. I'll get him to add Vivi to the lists he put the twins on. What's one more kid? He can tell them they have triplets but he must have messed up the paperwork.

Yes, that should work.

When the Uber stops outside Beckett's brownstone, I unbuckle the seat belt and sigh, feeling a modicum better now that I have a preschool plan.

Halfway up the steps, though, Vivi turns bright red in her seat, and when she lets out the loudest screech, all the dread returns. I don't have the first fucking clue what caused the issue or how to fix it, and this time, I don't have Sara to help.

I put the seat down on the steps and pick her up. "Holy duck, kid. You've got some pipes on you." Holding her close again, I rub her back and bounce. She seemed to like that before.

There are a lot of things I've learned from my brother, but honestly, I've never been so happy that he's done this before me. He'll help me figure it out. We've got this.

I ring the doorbell, and a second later, Vivi isn't the only one screaming. "That would be your cousins," I tell her, doubling down on my bouncing. "Apparently, you have a lot in common."

She doesn't laugh at my one-liner like people normally do, and that only fills me with another wave of panic. What if she doesn't think I'm funny? What if—

"What part of *don't ring the doorbell* do you not understand?" my brother says as he swings open the door. He's bouncing a screaming baby just like I am.

When he and Liv were first married and she lived with her mom friends, Beckett called the twins in the house the Shining Twins. Then he went and had a set himself. And they do *a lot* of crying. I'd give him shit about it, but seeing as how we both have a screaming kid in our arms, I'm not gonna lead with that.

"Shh, it's okay, Maggie Mae. Your idiot uncle is going to take all the other kids for the night, and we'll have a quiet house so you can sleep." Jaw locked tight, he looks up from his daughter, glare already in place. When he spots the screaming child in my arms, his eyes go wide and he takes a step back. "No. Nope. Not going to happen. No more babies. Liv!" he shouts over his shoulder. "What did you do? No. We have enough kids here. Liv!"

My brother is full-on ready to go into a crying fit over what he apparently believes to be another child that Liv what, preordered? I'd laugh if it wasn't actually my kid.

"Not your kid. Calm down." I push past him. Finn is standing just outside the entryway, decked out in denim and watching us, so I wave a hand at the open door. "Can you grab Vivi's car seat for me, bud?"

While he darts outside, I walk in circles around the foyer, bouncing as I go, silently begging Vivi to stop screaming. "It's okay, Vivi girl. We got this. We just need Liv to tell us what to do."

"Why are you holding a baby?" Beckett, the lucky bastard, has silenced his baby, and now he's guiding Finn back into the house by his shoulder.

"How'd you do that?" I ask, jutting my chin at his now silent daughter.

"Whose baby is that?"

"Answer me first," I demand over Vivi's cries.

"You have to take that thing off her head," Liv says as she appears in the foyer with the other twin in her arms. This twin is the quieter one, I think.

"What thing?"

Liv pushes June into Beckett's other arm, and he balances both of his girls easily while scrutinizing me.

"Here," she says, tilting Vivi back and pulling at a strap under her chin I haven't noticed. When Liv releases it and pulls the hat from her head, I can see the deep indentation beneath her chin.

I pull her close again, rubbing her back, and finally, her cries level out. As she hiccups against me, rubbing at her eyes and her flushed cheeks, I see red.

What the hell kind of person leaves a baby with a death trap of a hat on her head?

"Whose baby is that?" Beckett grinds out again.

I readjust my daughter and rub at her dark hair. "Mine."

Liv coughs out a laugh. "Excuse me?"

"No fucking way," Beckett hisses.

"Thousand dollars, Bossman!" Finn hollers far too loudly in this small space.

Liv breathes in deep, lets it out again, and points down the hall. "Go watch TV in the other room. We're having an adult conversation."

"But he cursed, Mommy." Finn plants his hands on his denim-covered hips. "He needs to pay up."

Beckett sighs. "I'll put it in your college fund. Go watch TV." Then he heads to the living room. "Let's talk in here. I have a feeling this is going to be a *very* adult conversation."

I follow my brother and settle in one of the chairs while he and Liv take a seat on the couch, each with a twin in their arms.

"Does Ford know?" Beckett asks.

Beside him, Liv gasps, and her eyes go wide.

"What? Why would Ford know?"

"It's safe to assume Millie's the mom, right?"

"Wait, you slept with Millie Hall?" Liv asks, leaning forward. Then she whips her head to the side and glares at her husband. "And you knew and didn't tell me?"

Beckett shrugs. "The fewer people who knew, the better."

Liv smiles. "Proud of you, Bossman. Normally you can't keep anything to yourself."

"You know that's not true. I kept this house a surprise for months.

As well as my plans to make all your friends fall in love. Let's not forget how I kept my feelings for you to myself for twelve years."

She snorts. "Actually, when you put it that way—"

"Can we focus?" I grind out. "This is not Millie's kid."

"Whose is it, then?" Beckett asks.

I clench my jaw and push back on the anger bubbling up in me. "I don't know."

"Where did she come from?" Liv tilts her head, frowning.

"She was left at my front door."

"What?" Beckett shouts, going ramrod straight.

That sets Vivi off again. The kid is definitely not big on loud noises. Bouncing her in my lap, I press my cheek to her head. "Shh. Can you stop making my kid cry?"

"Hang on." Liv hops up and disappears. When she returns a moment later, she's holding a binky like the ones the twins take. This one has a cow clipped to the end of it. "It's brand new," she says, holding it out to me. "I just washed a bunch. See if she likes it."

Blowing out a breath, I take it. I'll try anything. The second I hold it in front of her, Vivi reaches for it and pulls it to her mouth, quieting almost immediately.

My shoulders sag in relief, and so does my heart.

"Now start at the beginning. Where did you find her?" Liv asks.

"I hosted team dinner tonight, so most of the guys were over."

Beckett nods. He and I talked about this earlier. Taking over midseason as head coach hasn't been easy, but I want the guys to trust that I know what I'm doing. That starts with making sure they trust *me*, and hosting team dinners will hopefully nurture that trust.

"The doorbell rang. I assumed it was another one of the ridiculous packages that Sara set up to be shipped to Seb—" I shake my head. If I never see another pink dildo or flavored underwear, it will be too soon. "Anyway, it wasn't. It was her."

Vivi tilts her head back, spits her binky out, and gives me a gummy smile that hits me right in the heart. I can't help the way my lips tip up in response to her. I'm not sure if a single smile has come to me this easily since I last held Millie. If memory serves me, the last time a smile came to me unbidden, it was as Millie launched herself into my arms at the airport when I picked her up on her last trip home. The trip that ended everything.

"So there was a baby sitting at your door, and you just assumed she's yours? The fuck is wrong with you?" My brother scowls.

"Nothing is ducking wrong with me," I correct him, rubbing Vivi's silky head, soothing her in case Beckett's tone sets her off again. "She's mine. There was a note explaining everything."

Liv eyes me. "What did the note say?"

"That her mother couldn't do it and that she's mine. That's basically it."

"So if Millie isn't her mother, then who is?" Beckett asks.

I look down at my daughter as if she could tell us who brought her into this world. "No ducking clue."

"I don't get it." Beckett grits out. "Give me a list of women you've slept with. I'll find the mother."

"What does it matter? She's here. She's mine. I wouldn't let whoever the woman is near my child again anyway. Not after the way she left her at my freaking door." Dread swirls in my gut at the what-ifs. "What if I hadn't been there? Who knows how long she would have sat there alone."

"Gavin," Liv says softly. "We need to find her mother."

"No."

Liv and my brother share a look, but I'm not interested in their opinions on the matter. Honestly, I haven't put much thought into who her mother could be. While Millie was in my life, she was all I cared about. And before her? Fuck, I couldn't tell you the last time I had a one-night stand.

That first night, the connection between us was so strong. I was certain it was the start of something real, and then I found out she was Ford's daughter and she moved to Paris. For over a year, I did my best to forget her.

Then she came back into my life in June, and she was all that mattered. Until she broke me.

Until I told her I wanted a family, and she told me she wanted to continue hiding our relationship from everyone we knew. At that moment, I thought I'd never have a child. That I was destined to be the fun uncle and nothing more. And now I have Vivi.

I honestly don't have the answers Beckett and Liv think are so crucial, and I'm not going to concern myself with finding them either. Like me, Vivi was all alone in this world, and now we have each other. As far as I'm concerned, we're better off without her mother.

"How old is she?" Beckett asks.

I tilt to one side, studying her, then I lift her foot. "I don't know. Is there, like, a marking that would tell us that?"

Liv chokes out a laugh. "Gavin, she's not a tree. We can't count rings or wrinkles."

I shrug. "Can't a doctor tell? She needs a birthday. Is there a registry somewhere?"

"Oh my god. He can't be serious," she mutters.

I frown at my brother, who is looking back at me, equally thoughtful. "He's got a point. The vet could determine how old Deogi was, and we didn't have any paperwork for him."

"Oh my god. I'm dealing with Dumb and Dumber. Beckett, no. Gavin, think. Who was the last woman you slept with before Millie?" She shakes her head. "I can't believe I'm even saying those words. If Ford finds out you slept with his daughter—"

"Focus, Liv," Beckett says. "Ford won't find out. But seriously, Gav. You have no idea?"

I sigh. "It doesn't matter."

"It does if we want to know how old she is." Liv slaps her knee with a huff. "I can't do this alone. I'm calling Dylan." She pops up, deposits June in Beckett's lap beside her sister, and with a disgusted look at both of us, she strides out of the room.

"So you have a kid," Beckett says slowly, like he's really absorbing the fact.

I smile. It's another real one. "She's cute, right?"

"Of course she's cute. She's a Langfield." He grins. "Mom is going to lose it, though."

I sigh. "Everyone is going to lose it."

"And Millie?"

My heart aches like it does every time I hear her name. "Why do you keep asking about her? And why did you mention her in front of Liv?"

Beckett grunts. "Because last I checked, you were in love with her, so it was easy to assume this was her kid."

"Millie would never leave her kid on my doorstep. Even if she wasn't ready." I know in my bones that Millie would be an excellent mother. But she's twenty-three. I understand her reasoning now, even if it hurt to hear it at the time. "Things worked out as they should have. Millie's off living her life, and I'm here, with Vivi."

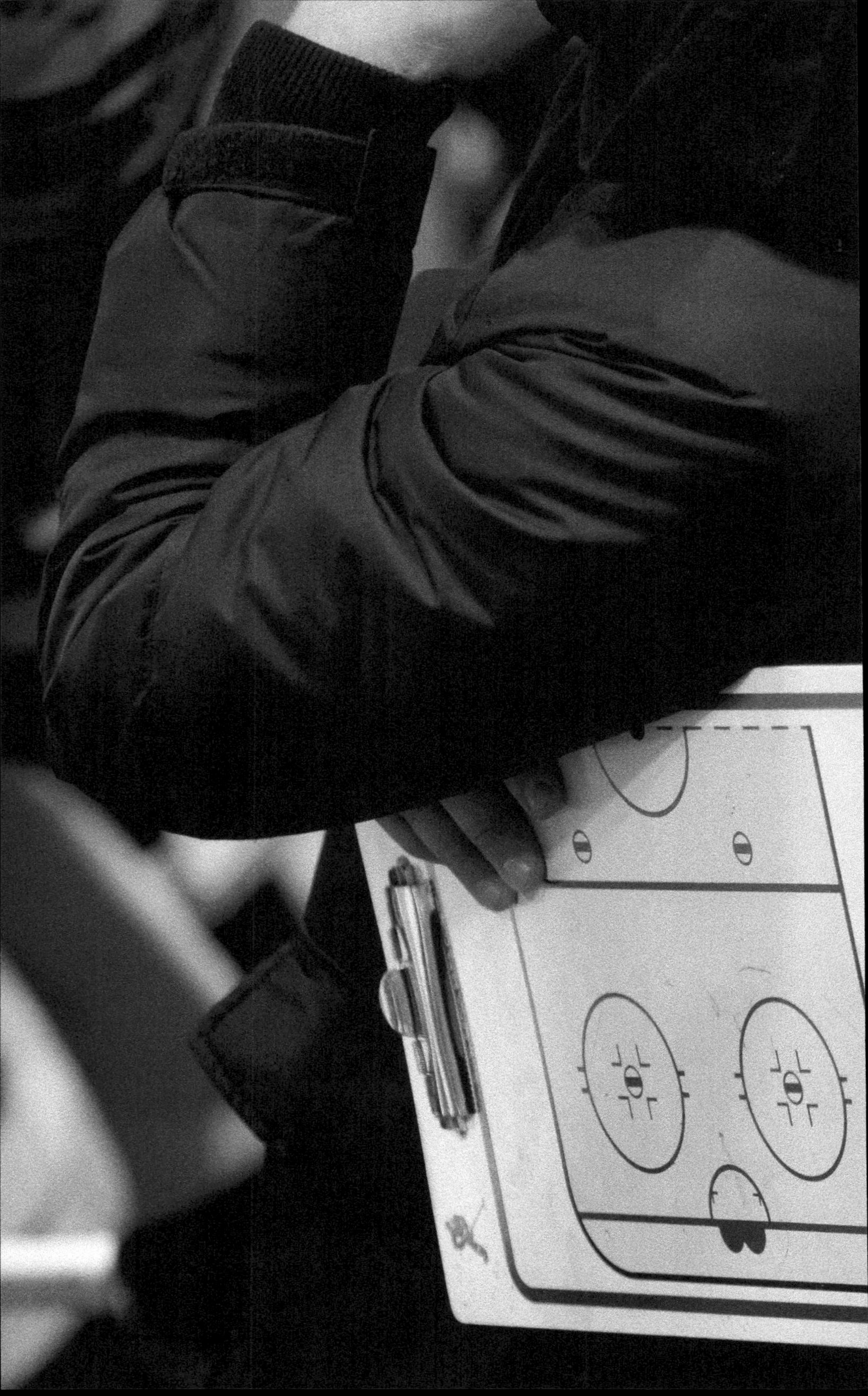

CHAPTER 25
Gavin

"I HEAR THERE'S A NEW BABY." Liv's friend Dylan appears in the entryway, her curly red hair a mess on top of her head, a dark glob of something on her shoulder, and a bright smile on her face.

"Yes, we're trying to figure out how old she is," Beckett says.

As Dylan steps closer, I get a whiff of the substance on her shoulder. Chocolate. She smells like cupcakes. My mouth waters at the thought. I never did end up eating dinner.

"May I?" she asks, holding out her hands and smiling at Vivi.

I nod and hand her over.

She hums and holds Vivi close, studying her. "Oh, she's six months old. First week of October. If I had to give a specific date, I'd say the sixth."

I smile, strangely feeling better about this already. "Thank you, Dylan."

Liv scowls and steps up beside her. "How the hell do you know that?"

"She's a Libra," Dylan says, grasping the pendant she always wears and sliding it along its chain. "It's her energy. Very calm and balanced. Aren't you, pretty girl? Not like those Aquarius twins of yours, Becks."

My brother growls and squeezes his daughters a little tighter. "My girls are perfect."

"Of course they are," Dylan assures him, her smile serene. "But they're going to be a handful, and Vivi won't be."

I grin at Beckett. "I got the better one."

"This isn't like crayons, Gavin."

"Right, but if it was, you'd totally want to steal mine, because I got the best one."

Liv laughs. "Oh, lord help us. How in God's name did they give you a baby?"

I snort. "I really have no idea. So if she's born in October, that makes conception...?" I trail off and look from Liv to Dylan.

Liv sighs and presses the heel of her hand to her forehead. "Nine months earlier, Gavin."

"Why are you looking at my brother like he's an idiot?" Beckett huffs. "You were only pregnant for like seven months."

"Felt like a century," Liv mutters.

They're all talking, and I'm over here doing math. "So February of last year," I say.

Dylan's golden eyes warm as she studies me. "Possibly late January."

"So you know who the mom is now?" Beckett peers at me.

I scratch at my face and let out a low hum. "Nope, not a clue." It's not a lie. I have no fucking clue who Vivi's mother is because now that we've got a timeline, I know without a doubt I'm not the father. Before I hooked up with Millie at Ford's wedding, I may have been a scoundrel.

But since then?

Since I met Millie, I haven't so much as thought about another woman, let alone touched one. There was a fuzzy night or two the year Millie and I didn't speak, but I'd bet my fortune nothing happened on those nights either. And even if they did, they were during the late summer, before hockey season started.

Which means Vivi isn't mine.

Yet I'm all she has. It's a two-way street, though, because she's all I have as well. Instinctively, I pluck Vivi out of Dylan's hold and settle her in the crook of my arm, rocking her. I'm pretty sure the movement is more of a comfort to me than her.

Her big brown eyes settle on me, and my heart is done for.

This little girl may not be mine, but there is no fucking way I'll be telling any of them that.

Mind made up, I move onto the next issue facing us. "So, what am I supposed to do with her?"

Dylan is watching my little girl with hearts in her eyes and her hands clutched to her chest.

Immediately, an idea forms in my head. "You can take care of her." Yes, this will be perfect. Dylan helped raise all her friends' children when they lived together, and she runs a daycare at Langfield Corp. This will be perfect.

She doesn't take her eyes off Vivi as she replies. "Um no."

"What?"

Even as she continues to deny me, she does it with a big, bright smile on her face. "No. I'll help you get set up tonight, and I can pop over tomorrow to check in too, but you're this little one's daddy. Taking care of her is your job." She peers over her shoulder. "It's best to learn on the go, right, Becks?"

My brother smiles down at his girls. "Yeah, if this was a crayon box, I'd definitely be the blue one."

Liv snorts. "What does that even mean?"

"We always fought over the blue crayon," I grumble. "Ya know, Langfield blue."

Dylan giggles. "They're so spoiled they thought their family owned the color. That's adorable. We're not going to let you grow up like that, right, Vivi? You'll be smarter than these fools."

My girl smiles up at Dylan, her dark eyes depthless and her cheeks pink. That one look makes me fucking melt. Damn. My chest aches with an emotion I've only ever felt for one other person. How is it that I've fallen in love with Vivi in a matter of an hour?

One twin is squirming in Beckett's arm, getting restless, and a moment later, the other joins in.

Just the thought of them being uncomfortable sends a shudder of worry through me. "What's wrong with them?"

Liv laughs and steps up beside Beckett. "They're hungry. I'm going to go feed them."

"Can I watch?"

Beckett growls low in his throat. "You will not watch my wife feed my daughters."

Scratching my head, I look up at Dylan. "Why is he growling at me?"

She smiles that soothing smile of hers. "She breastfeeds the twins."

I cringe, and that prickle of worry turns to dread.

Dylan snorts, misreading my response. "It's completely natural."

"I know it's natural." I frown at her and eye my chest with a frown. "But I don't have breasts."

Liv cups her mouth, hiding a smile. "And with that, I'm out. Beckett, give me a minute to get settled, then bring the girls upstairs for me, please."

My brother watches his wife with so much love in his eyes I feel sick. For months and months, I've been jealous as fuck of what he has. And now I'm envious of him not only because he gets to be with the love of his life, but because he has a partner to do this with. A woman who wants to raise their children alongside him. And poor Vivi just has me.

Maybe it's selfish to keep her. Just about any person out there would be a better parent than me.

Dylan squeezes my arm. "Okay, let's figure out what you need.

She'll need to eat soon, so we should place an Instacart order and have it delivered."

Beckett stands, wearing a cocky smirk. "I duplicated the order we made for the twins and had it sent to his apartment."

My heart squeezes in my chest at my grumpy brother's thoughtfulness. "Thanks, Beck."

Liv scrunches up her nose. "Um, Beckett, we ordered two of almost everything."

"Fuck," I mutter.

"Duck," Beckett reminds me. "You're a dad now. Act like it."

My gut clenches. Dammit, he's right. How the hell am I going to do this without totally screwing this child up?

"I'll text Brooks and Aiden. Have them hang out at your place and wait for the order," Beckett offers. "They can separate it all and return what you don't need."

Since the moment I opened that door and found Vivi, my body has been strung tight, but for the first time tonight, a little of that tension ebbs. Because my brothers are the fucking best. "Thanks. Seriously, I don't know what I'd do without you guys."

"Okay, I'll put in a grocery order too. Do you have a car seat?" Dylan peers around, and her eyes light up when she sees it in the corner. "You do! Oh, good boy, Gavin."

Beckett laughs as he heads for the stairs. "Don't think he has a base, though."

"Hmm." Dylan frowns, her brow furrowed.

"What's a base?"

"It's the piece you buckle into the car so that the seat doesn't go flying."

"Huh. So that's why Brooks and I couldn't make that thing stay."

"How did you get here?" Dylan asks, crossing her arms over her chest.

"Um, I wrapped the seatbelt around it like five times and then held it in place."

Dylan covers her mouth and giggles. "Oh no." Then she takes a deep breath and schools her expression. "Let me run next door really quick. We have an extra for when Willow rides to the stadium with Cortney and Beckett."

"That's a thing? They carpool?"

"Your brother is very needy," Dylan says as she heads for the door.

I peer down at Vivi, who's still watching me, curious. "Tell me something I don't know."

The car seat base is a genius invention. Once Dylan installed it, Vivi's seat popped right in. But as soon as we make it back to my place, Vivi becomes inconsolable.

"Why won't she stop crying?" I hold her out in front of me and turn her from side to side, searching for another offending item that could be cutting off her air supply like that damn hat. The rest of her clothes seem loose fitting.

"She's probably hungry," Dylan says. "I'll heat up a bottle."

My brother settles on my couch and rests an ankle on a knee, as if he's enjoying the show.

"You could help, you know," I grumble.

He laces his fingers behind his head and laughs. "I have five kids. I'm pretty sure you could handle one."

"And you have Livy at your side, doing it all with you. You didn't have to figure this shit out yourself." I've never been so angry that I live alone as I am right now. "Can you believe there's no test I need to take in order to keep a baby? You can't drive a car without passing a driver's test, but they just trust you to know how to keep another human alive? To go to college, you have to take the fucking SATs, but here, take this baby. Figure it out. What the fuck?"

Beckett wears a lazy smirk. "I seem to remember a certain

someone betting I wouldn't make it a weekend in the brownstone with Livy."

"You weren't left to care for an infant *by yourself*. You were living with four women who all had parenting experience. I'd have helped you if someone gave you a freaking child to raise on your own."

With a sigh, he hauls himself to his feet and takes the screaming baby from me. With Vivi in his arms, he sits on one end of the couch and lays her on her back on the cushion. "Go grab the diaper bag."

How he handles a screaming child so calmly is beyond me. My heart is being pummeled, and I want to pull my fucking hair out.

I find the diaper bag by the door, unzip it, and rifle through its contents, feeling helpless.

For the thousandth time since I first held Vivi, I wonder how the hell I'm going to do this, all the while knowing I have no choice. Vivi needs me. She's got no one else.

My brother waves me over and points to the other end of the couch, near Vivi's head. "Sit and hold her belly still. I'll grab what we need and show you how it's done." He snatches the bag from me, and once I've got both hands on Vivi, he digs through it. "I'm only doing this once, Gav. So pay attention."

Damn, I think he might be my hero. He may only be two years older than me, and truthfully, I haven't looked at him like he's my big brother since we were kids, but right now, I feel small. And I'm downright awestruck by the way he talks in a soothing voice to me—clearly for Vivi's benefit—and tells me exactly what he's doing while he pulls out a diaper, some kind of cream, a package of wipes, and powder. The whole time, he alternates between watching what he's doing and checking in with me to make sure I understand.

She's changed and he's holding her out to me when Dylan steps into the room holding a bottle.

"Make sure to test the temperature before you give it to her," she instructs.

With a roll of my eyes, I snatch it out of her hands, bring it to my mouth, and suck. The second the flavor registers, my stomach revolts.

"Holy shit," I cough out between gags. "What the fuck are you feeding my child?"

"You don't drink the formula," Dylan says, yanking the bottle from my hand.

I rub my tongue over the roof of my mouth and stick it out, desperate to get rid of the flavor. "You said to test the temperature."

"With your *wrist*. Have you never been around babies before?"

"Only the twins, and as you so aptly pointed out, they don't take bottles." I swipe it back and hold it up in front of me, inspecting the off-white liquid. "Fuck, we can't feed this horrible stuff to her."

My brother is clutching his stomach and flopped back against the cushions, laughing so hard tears pour down his face.

"You ducking try it." I toss the bottle at him, panic rushing through me as my daughter screams in my arms once again.

"I don't know what the universe was thinking," Dylan mutters. She takes Vivi from my arms and the bottle from Beckett and disappears into the kitchen.

"Tell me about it," I mutter, focusing on the city skyline and rubbing at the pain in my chest.

"It can't be that bad," Beckett muses.

I stick my tongue out and wipe my sleeve across my mouth, then head to my bedroom so I can brush my teeth. When I return, Dylan is on the couch, holding Vivi, whose eyes are heavy, like she's almost asleep.

"Poor thing has had a long day," she says softly to the baby. She looks up at me, her eyes full of tears. "Who could leave this beautiful girl alone?"

The weight returns to my shoulders as I settle beside her. "No one worth thinking about." I sigh. "Can you show me how to make the bottles before you leave?"

"Yes. Beckett, go set up the playpen in Gavin's room." She pats my leg. "I know this is overwhelming, but just take it one day at a time."

One day at a time. Ha. I blink down at Vivi. It's only been a few hours, and I'm wiped out. Yet I have to do this again tomorrow. All day. For the next eighteen years, at least.

"What would happen to her?" I whisper, my heart twisting.

"If what?" Dylan asks, studying me with those keen golden eyes.

"If I hadn't been here today? If she didn't have a father? Who would have taken her?"

Dylan brushes her thumb over Vivi's cheek. "Social services would get involved, and she'd be placed with a foster family. They have emergency placements, but without either parent, she'd probably be in the system for a while. They'd try to find them first. Then there would be hoops to jump through before she could be adopted."

I swallow past the lump in my throat, silently promising this baby girl that I won't let that happen to her. No matter how hard this is. No matter how unprepared I am. I've got to be a better alternative than that. Right?

Fuck, I hope I am.

"How do people do it?" My words are barely audible, but Dylan smiles in response.

"With help and a lot of alcohol."

That moment of levity lifts my mood a little, though I'm still overwhelmed with fear when Beckett returns.

"All right, Dippy Do," he says to Dylan. "I gotta get home to relieve Livy. Gavin, seriously, if you need help, call Brooks."

I glare at my brother. Was I just thinking of him as my hero? And now he's taking off and telling me to call someone else when I need help?

"Don't give me that look. I set up her playpen next to your bed. She'll probably need a bottle in the middle of the night. You'll need to change her then as well. The delivery guys should be here in the morning."

"That's it? You're just going to leave me alone with her?"

Dylan stands with a yawn. "Sorry, Gavin. I have a baby to get home to as well."

As she places Vivi in my arms, genuine terror hits me. "What happened to getting through this with a lot of help? Where's my freaking help?"

Beckett leans down and kisses Vivi's forehead, then cups the back of my head and presses one to mine. "You'll be fine, Daddy."

I tamp down on my fear and roll my eyes. "No thanks to you."

He cuffs the back of my neck and jostles me gently. "You're welcome."

"What if I forget how to change her?" I ask as I follow them to the door. I don't think I can do this on my own. "What if I forget how to make the bottle? Are there instructions somewhere? Even freaking McDonald's toys come with manuals, but you're leaving me alone with a baby and no instructions?" My voice is panicked as they open the door, making Vivi whimper in my arms.

"I stuck a list of instructions to the fridge," Dylan calls. "You'll be fine."

The moment the door closes, I eye Vivi. Her chubby cheeks, the little wisps of dark hair.

They really left me alone.

An hour later, I'm sitting on the edge of my mattress. In the middle of the bed, surrounded by pillows, Vivi sleeps soundly. I couldn't put her in the crib. She was too far away. There's no chance I'll close my eyes tonight. What if she stops breathing? What if I fall asleep and don't hear her cry and she's all alone again? Nope, I'll lie here and keep an eye on her. I don't have the first fucking clue what I'm doing, but I do know I won't abandon her.

I ease onto my back so as not to disturb her and slide off the stack of friendship bracelets I wear on my wrist. All but one. Never have been able to take it off. Then I take out my phone and do the same thing I do every night.

I open to our text chain and start at the beginning.

> Peaches: You programmed yourself as "Coach."

Me: And you're Peaches. You back in your room?

Peaches: Yes.

Me: Good. Listen, use this number whenever you want. I'll always be here to talk.

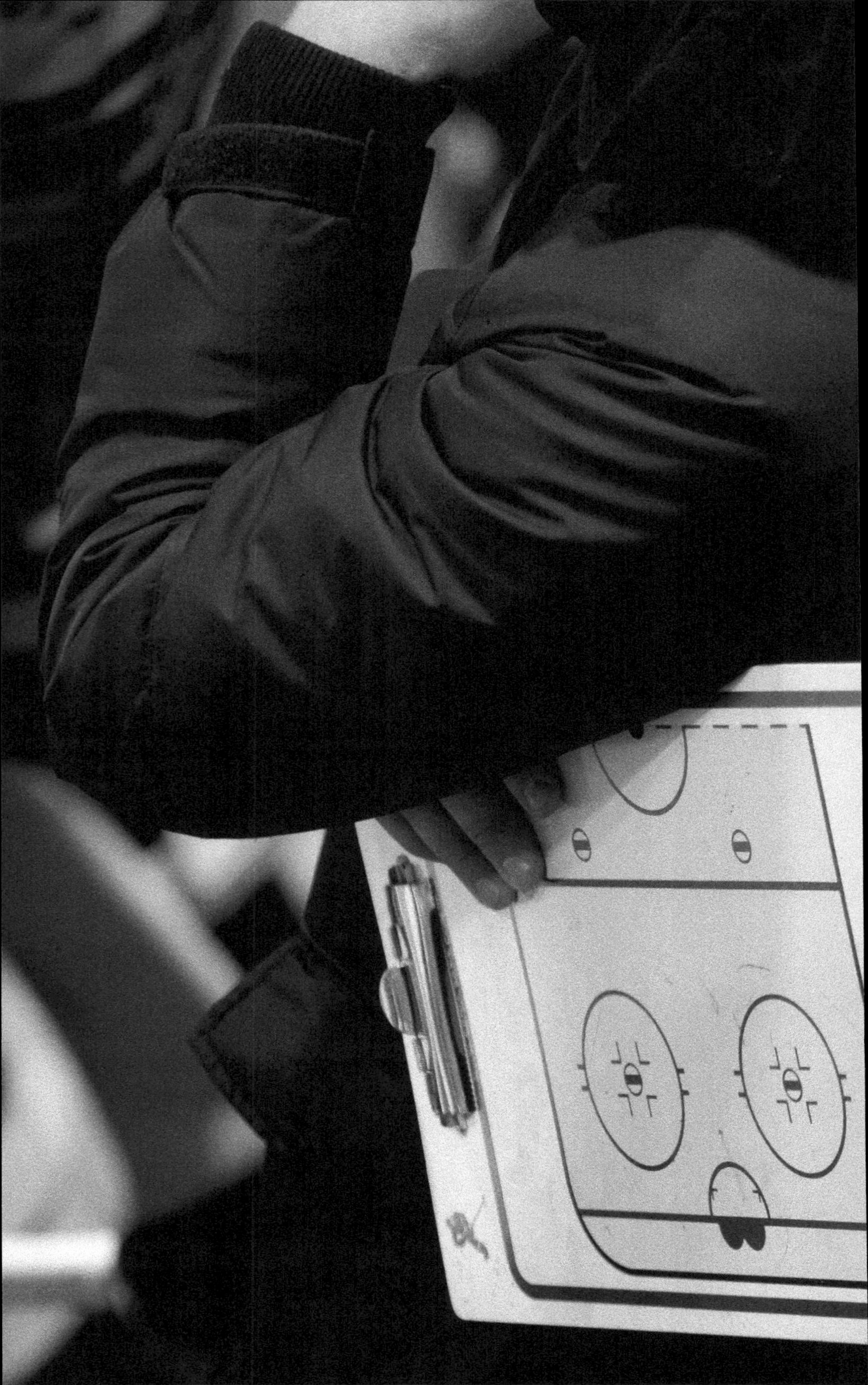

CHAPTER 26
Gavin

Brooks: How are you holding up?

Aiden: Are we having practice today?

Beckett: He's got one ducking kid, and I have five. How come you never ask how I'm doing?

Aiden: How are you doing, Beckett?

Brooks: LOL. Sara's grabbing coffee, then we'll be by to help.

Beckett: That's so nice of you. The kids would love donuts.

Brooks: Obviously I was talking to Gavin.

Aiden: Gavin?

Beckett: Gav, you okay?

Brooks: I'm coming in.

. . .

I GROAN at the text chain from my brothers. My phone battery is at 2 percent. I fell asleep while obsessing over Millie's photos like an insane person. Then Vivi was up three times. I feel like a zombie. How do people with babies function daily? It's torture.

Footsteps sound in the hall, and then I hear Brooks. "I haven't found him yet. He's probably still sleeping." He's silent for a second. "I don't know. Black, probably." Ah, he must be on the phone. "Okay, and get me a protein bar, please. Thanks, crazy girl. I love you."

I let out a heavy sigh and breathe through the tightness in my chest. Is everyone in love?

I roll to my left side and come face to face with Vivi. She's still on her back, head turned and brown eyes wide, sucking on her hand.

"You really are a happy baby, aren't you, Vivi girl?"

She breaks into a gummy smile.

"Oh, you like that name, huh?"

My bedroom door swings open, catching Vivi's attention, her chubby little body shifting.

"Sleeping in?" Brooks asks.

I heave out a breath and fight the urge to throw a pillow at him. "Make yourself useful and go fix a bottle for her."

Brooks frowns, running a hand against his cheek. "How do I do that?"

"Ugh, are you really that useless? Mix the powder with warm water, then shake it."

It only took me two tries to figure it out last night. I tested the temperature on my wrist like Dylan showed me, then stupidly licked at the liquid to make sure it wasn't too hot. Then I accidentally inhaled the formula powder while I was putting the lid on the container. The powdery taste is still haunting me. But Brooks doesn't need to know how difficult it's all been.

"How about I watch the baby and you do that?" Brooks offers, stepping into the room.

"You think I'd trust you to watch my daughter?"

"Considering that you only met her yesterday and you've known me my whole life—"

I growl at him to shut him up, sounding way too much like Beckett for my liking.

He holds up his hands and backs out the door. "Fine. I'll make a bottle." Then he's gone, and a moment later, he's talking again, probably to Sara. Good, maybe she can talk him through it and keep him from screwing it up.

"Come on, Vivi girl. Let's get dressed and go to practice."

"Is that a baby?"

Vivi's bundled up in her car seat, seemingly soothed by the rocking motion as I lug the thing into the rink.

Fitz, the goalie coach, has been my saving grace since I took over as head coach for the Bolts. He's been running practices with me and guiding me through this transition. It's been a month, though, and it's time to start showing the guys that I can handle this.

"It's not a puppy," I retort as War slides to a stop in front of me. I set Vivi down on the bench, keeping my hand on her carrier to keep it from tipping.

"You can't bring a baby to practice," Fitz says, giving me a confused frown.

"What would you like me to do with my daughter, then? Can't leave her at home by herself."

"You have a daughter?" Fitz pulls the Bolts hat off his head and runs his hands through his hair. "Since when?"

War rests his elbows on the gate and angles over her. "Hey, Vivi. Your uncles haven't stopped talking about you." The star left winger grins and straightens. "How you feeling, Coach?"

"Tired," I mumble. "Hall, come over here and watch Vivi for me while we practice."

Daniel skates over and leans against the boards. "You don't want me to watch your kid, I promise."

I look down at Vivi. She's all wide eyes as she takes in the guys around her. "And why not?"

"Millie's the one who's good with kids. I've never even held one."

The sound of her name in such a casual tone hits me like a slap and steals the breath from my lungs. I blink slowly to keep from wincing, but Daniel gives me a puzzled frown, like maybe I'm not hiding my reaction well.

"Didn't ask you to hold her, Hall," I grit out. "Sit your ass down on the bench and don't take your eyes off her. If you can't handle that, then I'll put you in the net and let War take shots at you for the next hour."

"That would be awesome," War crows, clapping his gloved hands.

"Hey." I point at him. "You're watching her next. You'll all take ten-minute shifts while I run practice."

Fitz steps up close and ducks his head. "We're trying to build trust and respect here, remember?"

I take a step back and holler for the guys to gather around. Most of them have migrated this way, clearly curious about the baby by my side. "Let me make a quick introduction. Guys, this is Vivi, my daughter. Her mother left her on my doorstep last night. Anyone have a problem with me bringing her to practice while I figure shit out? No?" I ask without waiting for a response. "Great. Now let's play some hockey."

The guys all nod, and Fitz lets out a heavy sigh and skates off toward Brooks, who's still at the net.

"'Kay, Vivi girl. Be good for Daniel. I'll be back in a few minutes." I bend at the waist and press a kiss to her forehead. When I pull back, she gives me that big gummy smile again. Fuck, she's cute.

Aiden moves closer to me, his expression more stoic than I think I've ever seen. "I can watch her."

I pat my brother on the shoulder. "As much as I love you for offering, you're our center. If I sat you on that bench right now, I'd actually *not* be doing my job."

War pokes at my brother with his stick. "Yeah, Lep. We need our good luck charm on the ice at all times."

I head for the ice and blow my whistle. "Line up, boys. I don't have all day."

My phone rings just as practice wraps up. When Beckett's name appears on the screen, I answer quickly. Maybe he's got news on when all Vivi's stuff will arrive. Or maybe he wants me to come over and hang out while we stare at our babies. Maybe take turns napping.

"Hey, Beck."

"Finn is freaking out. He says you promised to take him to the park."

Wow. No *hello*. No *how are you?* He didn't even ask about Vivi. It's nice to see Beckett is his usual self today. After that forehead kiss last night, I was concerned he'd been possessed.

"Fuck." I scoop up Vivi's seat and hit the light on my way out of my office.

"When he was adamant about it this morning, I told him you were busy," he says. "But as soon as he got home from school, he brought it up again."

Standing in the empty hall, I survey Vivi. Could I handle taking her to the park? The old man on the bench yesterday was more than happy to offer advice. Maybe he knows a thing or two about babies. Or maybe some fresh air and time with Finn will do me good.

"Nah, tell him I'll be there shortly. Any update on Vivi's stuff?"

"I'll have Brooks and Aiden go to your apartment to wait for the delivery guys. Once the girls are down for the night, I'll bring pizza over."

"Thanks, Beck. I'll see you shortly."

With a Wendy's bag in one hand, my other arm looped through the handle of Vivi's seat, and Finn at my side, I scan the park for our bench mate from yesterday.

Yesterday.

It feels like I've lived an entire life in the twenty-four hours that have passed since we were last here.

"You added another child to the brood. Weren't getting enough advice from this one?" a voice says from behind us.

I spin and chuckle at the old man shuffling our way. "Shut it. This is—" I take a deep breath; this is going to take some getting used to. "This is Viviane, my daughter."

He smiles warmly at her. "She's beautiful."

My heart expands with pride. She really is a beautiful child. Her cheeks are rosy from the cold, and she's taking in the scene quietly, as always. I set her seat on the bench and press a kiss to one cheek, making sure her blanket is tucked in around her. "Here," I say to our friend. "I brought you your burger."

"All right," he says, snagging the bag from me with a chuckle. "Let me get settled, and then you can explain how you ended up a dad between today and yesterday."

I snort. "That obvious I'm new to this?"

He shakes his head. "You told me yesterday Peaches didn't want kids and you did. I imagine if you already had one, that would have been a discussion long before you broke up."

I shake my head, ready to brush off the topic. Millie is the last thing I should be talking about. While Finn chases squirrels, I spill every detail of the last twenty-four hours.

"And Peaches isn't the baby's mother?" he asks, his tone a little too judgmental for my liking.

I don't know who the baby's mother is, but it's not Millie. Fuck, do I wish she were. Hell, I wish we were both this little girl's parents. Not that she'd want that. She made it abundantly clear the last time we talked that she was nowhere near ready for that. "No."

"Seems like you have a lot more on your plate than you did yesterday, huh?"

I rub at my little girl's foot through the blanket, and when her big brown eyes hold mine, I nod. Before today, I would have told this man that without Millie, the likelihood of me becoming a father was nonexistent. Now this little girl owns my heart.

"Yeah, I think I have to let Peaches go." I force a deep breath of fresh air into my lungs, willing it to clear my mind. "So tell me, Henry. What do you know about babies?"

THE HOCKEY REPORT

"Good Morning, Boston. Colton and Eliza here, and this is the Hockey Report."

"It's certainly a strange day in Boston," Eliza says. "Not so sure it's a good one, though. Not if the reports are true and Sebastian Lukov has been hired by New York."

"It appears they are. New York has gone through several coaches over the past two years, and not one of them has been able to keep owner Ben Jones happy. Given the circumstances surrounding Sebastian's leave from Boston, it's hard to believe he'll be a good fit for the team."

"He didn't leave, Colton. Gavin Langfield gave him a swift kick in the butt when he fired him."

Colton's responding laugh is weak. "Well, Brooks Langfield certainly kicked his butt. As for Gavin, the current owner and coach of the Boston Bolts seems to have a bit more on his plate these days too, so I doubt he's too worried about where Sebastian landed."

"Yeah, there are reports that Coach Langfield was seen wearing a baby at practice."

"Any news about whose baby it is?"

Eliza sighs. "Nope, but let me tell you, after seeing the pictures floating around on the internet of Gavin wearing an adorable chubby baby girl out on the ice, I'm pretty sure there will be a line of women hanging around the rink at all hours if someone doesn't claim them soon."

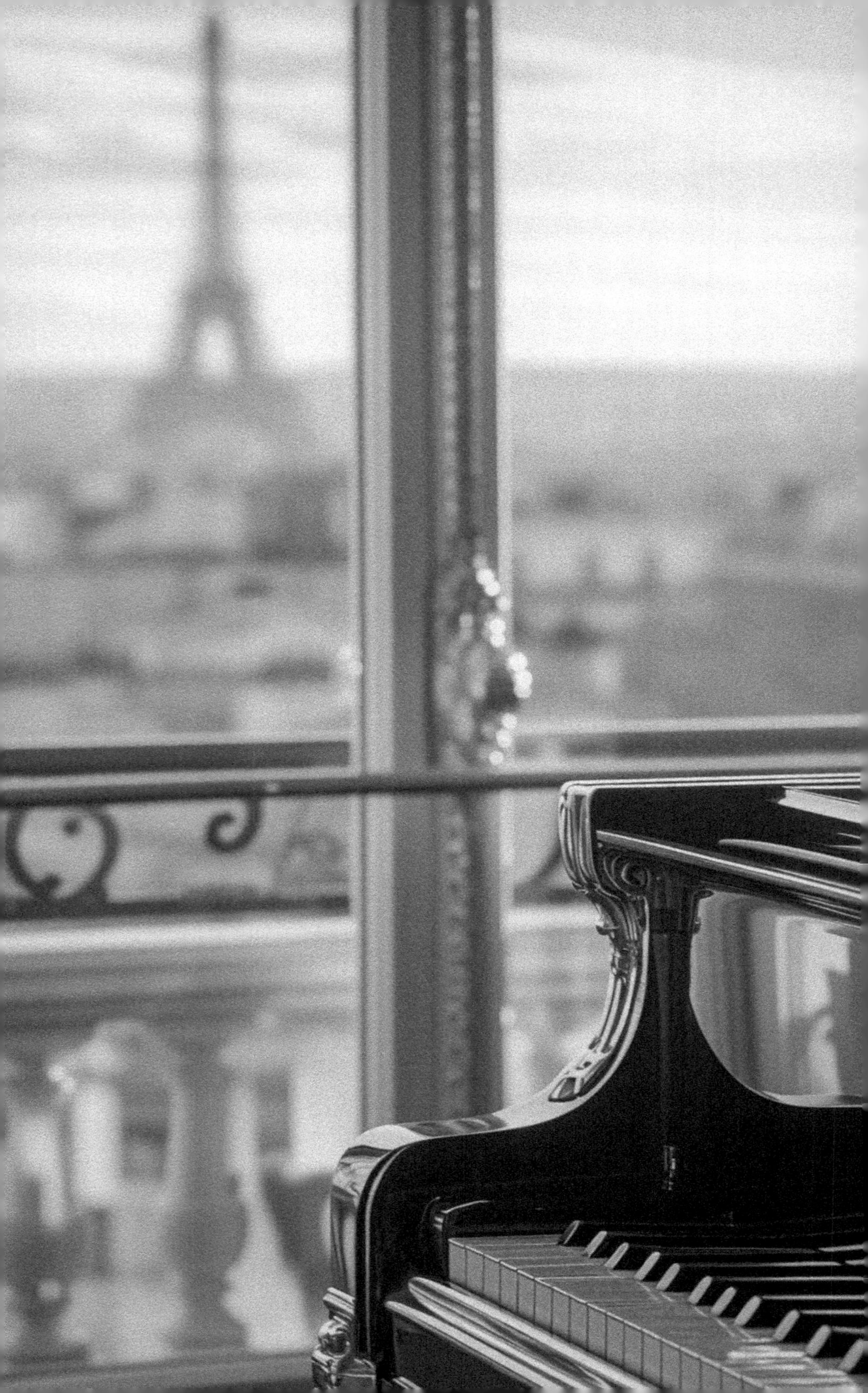

CHAPTER 27
Millie

STILL MARCH

Everyone knows the five stages of grief: denial, anger, bargaining, depression, and acceptance.

I've run the gambit of them over the last few months. The moment Gavin walked out of his apartment, leaving me there with my mouth on the floor, I entered my first stage: denial.

There was no way he'd actually ended things. That was a certainty in my mind. So I did what any rational person would do. I packed up my stuff, drove to my mother's house, and waited for him to call.

The phone never rang.

Christmas passed without a word. Without a single text. Then I saw photos of him circulating online. He was out and about with his brothers, smiling and laughing and looking as if he'd already moved on.

That's when anger set in. If he could be out and about having a grand ole time, then so could I. Pissed off, I called Chrishell and Taylor and made plans to fuck him out of my system. Fortunately—or unfortunately, depending on how one looks at it—Chrishell and Taylor continued to disappointment me. They were nothing if not predictable, I suppose. When I was adamant about not attending my father's New Year's Eve party, they were conveniently too busy to hang out.

Apparently, I was only worth their time if it meant hanging out with my brother and his NHL friends at my dad's party.

The truth hit me hard then. There wasn't a single person in my life who was willing to show up just for me.

I wasn't enough.

So I got on a plane back to Paris and entered my bargaining stage. Depression slid in quickly from there. I told myself that I'd do anything to stop feeling so empty, so morose. I drank too much, ate absurd amounts of chocolate, ignored calls from my parents and Daniel, dedicated all my attention to work, and got my nipples pierced.

That last one was drastic, yes, but since Gavin had always been obsessed with my tits, I suddenly hated them and knew only changing them would solve that problem.

Then my father showed up at my door in February, suitcase in hand, eyes weary and arms open.

"Daddy, what are you doing here?"

"You don't return my calls, and you didn't come home for Christmas. I miss you." My father stood in the hallway, his face etched in lines of desperation and sadness. But he was here. Present. He'd shown up for me. And it was in that moment that I knew it was time.

Time to grow up. Time to admit to my father what Gavin had begged me to tell him almost two years ago. How music had been my dream. How I'd wanted to work with him but had been devastated when he gave half the company to Lake. How it wasn't so much their relationship that caused the rift between us, but how he'd stopped seeing me when he met her.

Not in the real sense, but in the figurative sense. He'd stopped being my person.

It had taken me a long time to come to terms with the fact that my father had simply fallen in love.

He hadn't done those things intentionally. He wasn't Chrishell or Taylor. He wasn't even like my mother. He'd gotten swept up in his own love story—something I finally understood, because I'd lost mine.

I rushed into my father's arms, and then over dinner, I opened up. About all of it. Except Gavin.

"I never knew." He shook his head, his face a mask of shock.

I shrugged. "I didn't know how to say it." My face heated in embarrassment. "I felt like a whiney teenager who just wanted her dad's attention."

"The company is yours, Millie. I want it to be. I'll turn over my shares to you right now. Hell, I'll talk to Lake. We'll figure something out—"

I held up my hand as a wave of painful relief hit me. Somehow, just having my dad finally see me—having him recognize that I was lost—freed me.

It was in that moment that I realized that the dream I'd been clinging to was no longer what I wanted. Like my dad, I wanted to build my own life. For almost two years, I'd watched Sienna run her company on her own terms. Even though fashion wasn't my passion, standing on my own two feet was.

So after my father and I spent the weekend reconnecting, I gave Sienna my notice and started working at the bar in Paris where Gavin and I had gone that first time he came to visit me, singing when I could and tending bar to pay my bills.

Most of my songs are written while there are tears in my eyes and snot running down my face because even though I'm finally doing what I love, I miss the man who opened my eyes to the truth about why I was unhappy. The man I buried myself in to hide from all the hurt. The man I used as a Band-Aid to cover my emotional wounds. Gavin was right to break up with me. I just wish it hadn't taken losing him to realize how wrong everything else in my life was.

I like to think I'm now living between the depression stage and acceptance.

That realization, unfortunately, doesn't change my circumstances. And that's why I'm currently sitting at the piano in the club, crooning another sad love song, much to the crowd's dismay.

As I finish my set, with tears streaming down my face, I look up and find Sienna and Gabe watching from the crowd. My neck goes hot, and I suck in a breath. Then I scramble to my feet and rush off the stage, swiping at my eyes with the backs of my hands, knowing I must look like a wreck.

"Bonjour." I kiss Gabe on both cheeks, then Sienna. Then, wringing my hands, I clear my throat. "What brings you here?"

Sienna gives me a pitying frown.

Gabe's expression is one of pure guilt, making it clear who I should blame for this unexpected visit.

"It had to be done," he says in his thick French accent. "You don't even brush your hair anymore."

I pat at my head and scowl. "I do too."

Sienna studies me in her quiet way, her head tilted to one side. "No, I don't think you do."

I sigh and drop into a seat at their table. There's no avoiding this little intervention. That's obvious. When they sit too, I wave to the bartender, silently signaling that I need a drink.

With a cocktail in hand, I'm feeling only a modicum better, but I force myself to meet Sienna's green eyes. "I know this looks bad, but seriously, I'm fine. This is what I want to do. Write music. Do this on my own. Just like you did with the fashion industry."

She arches a brow and sips her dirty martini. "Like I did?"

"Yeah. How you bucked your family's plan for you and paved your own way."

"My family wasn't in the fashion industry." She takes another long sip, her eyes locked on me, warning me not to interrupt. Then she sets her drink on the table. "I didn't do it all on my own. Beckett lent me the money for the start-up because my parents refused. Gavin set me up with the company jet without my parents' knowledge every time I had a meeting. Brooks sat with me in the back of a limo with his arm around me while I cried and hyperventilated into his jacket because I was so afraid of failing. Aiden posted almost daily on every social media outlet he could find about how proud he was of me and how everyone needed to see my designs." She presses her lips together, her expression pitying again. "If my family hadn't offered to help, and if I hadn't accepted it, I would not be sitting across from you wearing my own design, in a room filled with people whose outfits are in some small part influenced by me, chiding you for being so obtuse."

Heat creeps up my neck and into my cheeks so quickly I drop my head in an effort to hide. "But you had people who believed in you. I don't have that."

Sienna's face softens. "Yes, I have four brothers who would do anything for me. Maybe Daniel and Paul have been too busy to notice you floundering, but I know for certain that, at one point, you had the full support of one of my brothers."

My breath catches in my throat, and I sputter, searching for a denial.

"Please," she tuts, picking up her glass. "I've never seen my brother so taken by someone. Anyone with eyes could tell he'd bend over backward for you."

I swallow down my nerves and breathe deeply, trying to keep a straight face. "I-I'm not sure I know what you're talking about."

She smiles. "Oh, Gavin may love me, but I've never seen him more in my life than I did last year. I don't believe for a second it was because he's got some hockey thing going in Paris. The man was here to see you. And the song you sang that night, the one about forbidden love, that was about him, right?"

I flatten my lips and pull my shoulders back, refusing to give an inch.

"Listen, I'm twenty-six and alone. I've never had a love like that. But I have an amazing career. And that's thanks to my family. I may not have gone into the family business, but I definitely used my family connections to get where I am.

"Yes, our last names come with certain expectations, and sometimes they weigh us down and make us feel like we need to run in the opposite direction of our parents to be taken seriously, but if you really want to make a career of writing music, then you have to take all the help you can get.

"And if you find a love like you so clearly had with my brother, you don't walk away from it."

Her words hang between us as my already shattered heart disintegrates further.

Gavin tried to tell me he loved me, but I wouldn't hear it. He begged me to tell my family about my music, and I kept my mouth shut.

"What if it's too late?" I whisper, barely able to breathe past the weight pressing down on my chest.

A pleased smile forms on Sienna's lips. "What if it's not?"

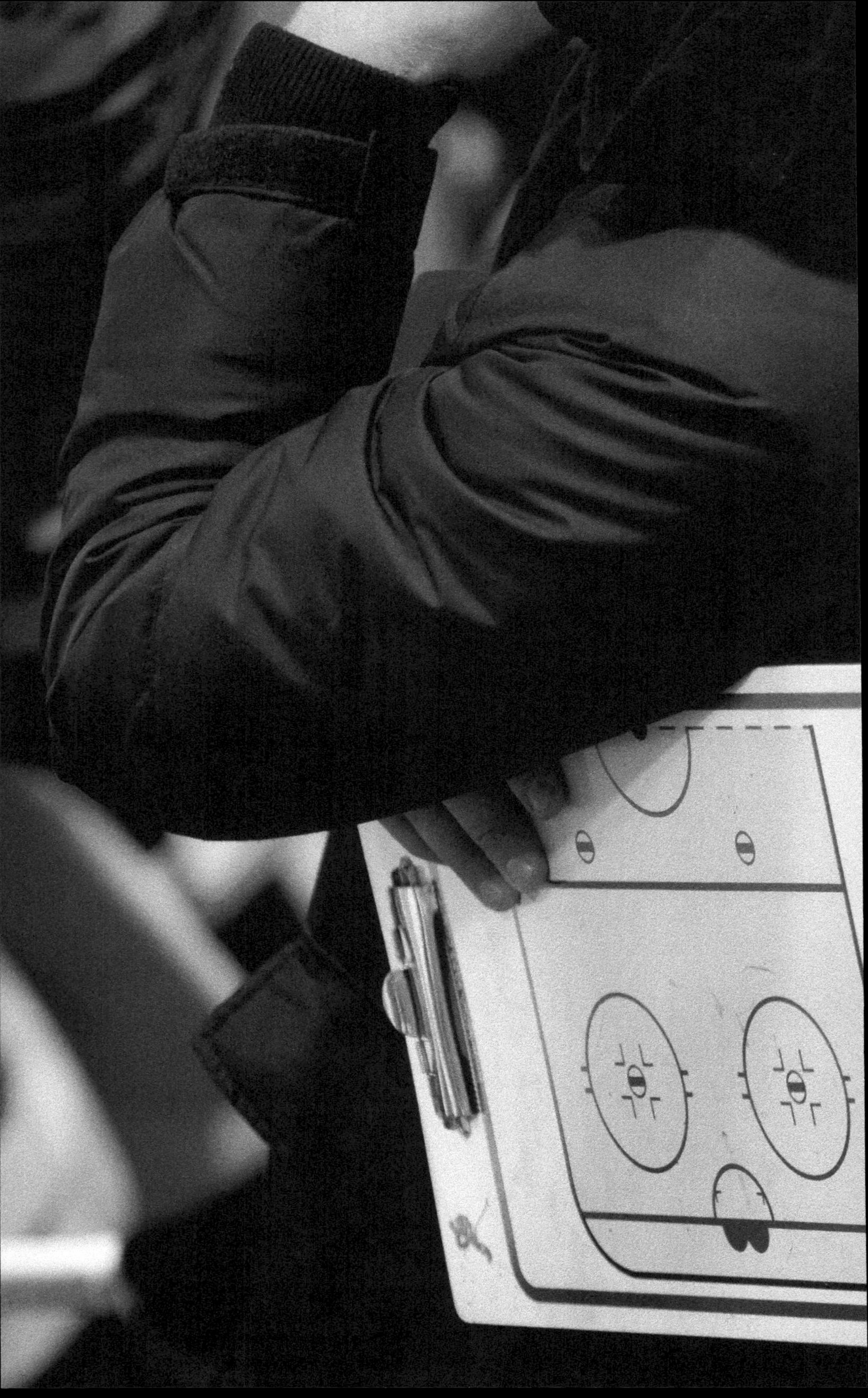

CHAPTER 28
Gavin

APRIL

In the two weeks since I became a dad, my life has become unrecognizable. The living room, which I've always kept free of clutter, is now littered with a baby mat—for tummy time; it's important according to all the books—toys, washcloths, diapers, and a playpen.

Brooks and Sara come over most nights so I can shower and make dinner without having to wear Vivi.

The baby carrier Beckett ordered has been a lifesaver. Both Vivi and I prefer when I hold her, and I do it as often as I can, but I draw the line at using the stove with a baby strapped to my chest.

One time I had the preheated oven all the way open before I realized I was wearing her. For days after that, I had visions of what would have happened if I'd dropped her.

How the hell do people do this alone? Yes, I'm a single dad, but I've got all three brothers, Sara, and an entire hockey team helping me. Thank god I moved into this building when I did. If it wasn't Brooks and Sara stopping by, it was one of my players. None of them have much experience with babies, yet they're a hell of a lot better with her than I am.

Tonight, Sara and Ava—the head of charitable relations for Langfield Corp—disappeared with Vivi, and then the team showed up with pizza and beer and a couple of cans of paint. Apparently, they decided we should paint Vivi's room.

When I brought Vivi to a game, Sara lost her mind, saying she shouldn't be out so late.

I get it, but what else was I supposed to do with her? I won't leave Vivi with just anyone.

Since then, I've been paying Ava a ridiculous amount of overtime to travel with the team and help me take care of Vivi.

I hate every minute that I'm not with her. The memory of finding her all alone, knowing her mother left her there, will forever haunt me. No child should ever feel abandoned, and I'll spend the rest of my life making sure she knows she's wanted. Fuck, she's wanted so much I can hardly breathe when I look at her.

It isn't until Daniel cracks the lid and pours the paint into a roller tray that I get a look at the color they picked out. "Blue? Don't tell me you guys think I'm going to decorate her room in Bolts colors."

Aiden laughs and picks up a paintbrush. "Nah, it's *1989* themed. If we want Vivi to be a Taylor and Lake girl, we gotta start now."

With a grunt, I pick up my own paintbrush. "1980-what?"

"Taylor's *1989* album? Come on, man," Aiden groans.

I look at Daniel and mouth, "What the fuck?"

With a paint roller in one hand, he shrugs. "My dad owns a record label. I'd be disowned if I didn't know my music. And Taylor is one of Lake's friends."

"Taylor who?" I'm totally teasing them at this point.

Brooks snorts, rolling out a long strip of blue painters tape. "Don't let Sara hear you ask that question."

"Taylor Swift," Aiden says, eyes wide like I'm the idiot here. "Come on, Heartbreak Prince."

"Heartbreak who?"

I'm totally goading my brother. He's been singing Taylor songs at practice every day this week. "Ms. Americana and the Heartbreak Prince" is his go-to when Vivi is around.

Obviously dedicated to helping me understand, he breaks into his rendition.

"Gav and Vivi, that's his whole world,
Ms. Viviane Langfield, she's the team's little girl
The whole team will paint this room blue
Gav's Vivi girl, we really love you."

With his hands on his hips, Aiden stares me down. "Recognize it now?"

It takes a lot of effort, but I keep my expression blank and dip my brush into the paint. "No idea what you're going on about, but fine, let's paint."

War nudges my arm. "You know all the lyrics, don't you?"

"Who do you think got Lake Paige to play for the team on New Year's Eve two years ago? And Taylor last year? Of course I know every word," I mutter.

War throws his head back and laughs.

For two hours, Aiden sings one Taylor song after another. After each one, he looks at me, brows raised expectantly. "You really don't know this one?"

Every time I play dumb and shake my head, he gets more exasperated.

By the time we're done, I've learned that War is not only aggressive on the ice, but he can draw the shit out of birds. I was lost about the meaning of the birds until Aiden pulled up an image of the *1989* album cover—Taylor's version, of course. War painted his birds in varying shades of purple and light pink, making the room look perfect for Vivi girl.

"Ready to hit the road again next week?" Hall asks as he leans against my counter, beer bottle in hand and clothes speckled blue.

"Are you?" I counter. "You're the one playing."

He smirks and lifts his beer. "You know what I mean."

I sigh, my chest tightening. "I hate dragging her from place to place, but what choice do I have?"

"You should look into a nanny." He waggles his brows. "Isn't that a thing? Single dad and the nanny?"

Just the idea of a woman who isn't Millie makes my skin crawl. And bringing a strange woman around my child? "Pass." It's hard enough leaving her with Ava.

"Come on, take one for the team. You don't have to hook up with her, but I could."

I give him my best disapproving look. "You do not need any help finding a woman."

He grins. "True. But seriously, think about it. You need full-time help, and Ava has a job to do."

I take a sip of my beer and check on Vivi. Brooks is holding her while he and Sara make silly faces. The house is filled with laughter and loud voices, just like I envisioned it one day would be. Even Vivi fits perfectly. There's just one thing missing...

"I'll think about it."

Daniel grins. "Not trying to push my luck here, but my father should be calling any minute. He's going to invite you and Vivi down for the weekend. Say yes. Lake can help with the baby, and you can have a little time to yourself."

I shake my head. "Um, that's okay. It's—"

"He thinks you're mad at him." Daniel scratches his head, grimacing in discomfort, but he continues on. "He says he hasn't seen you since the day he told you Lake was pregnant. He's worried that maybe the idea of him having a kid has you feeling, like, left behind or some crazy shit like that."

Damn. I give the kid credit. Speaking up like this, to not only the owner of his team but his head coach, takes balls.

But fuck if what he said doesn't send a wave of shame barreling through me. I could see why Ford would think I'm upset with him. I've been avoiding him because I haven't felt like I could look him in the eye after his bombshell led to the discussion that destroyed my relationship with his daughter. I've been too afraid I'd blurt it out.

"You need friends, and you need help. And if I'm being honest, he needs you. You were the only one to talk sense into him when he tried to walk away from Lake."

"How do you know that?"

He hits me with a grin. "My dad and I talk."

I love that. I've always been big on being honest and just communicating. "Fine. I'll say yes if he asks."

Daniel nods and heads toward the living room, leaving me by myself in the kitchen, hoping like hell his father doesn't actually call. Five minutes later, though, my phone rings and Ford's number flashes across the screen.

Guess I'll be spending the weekend in Bristol.

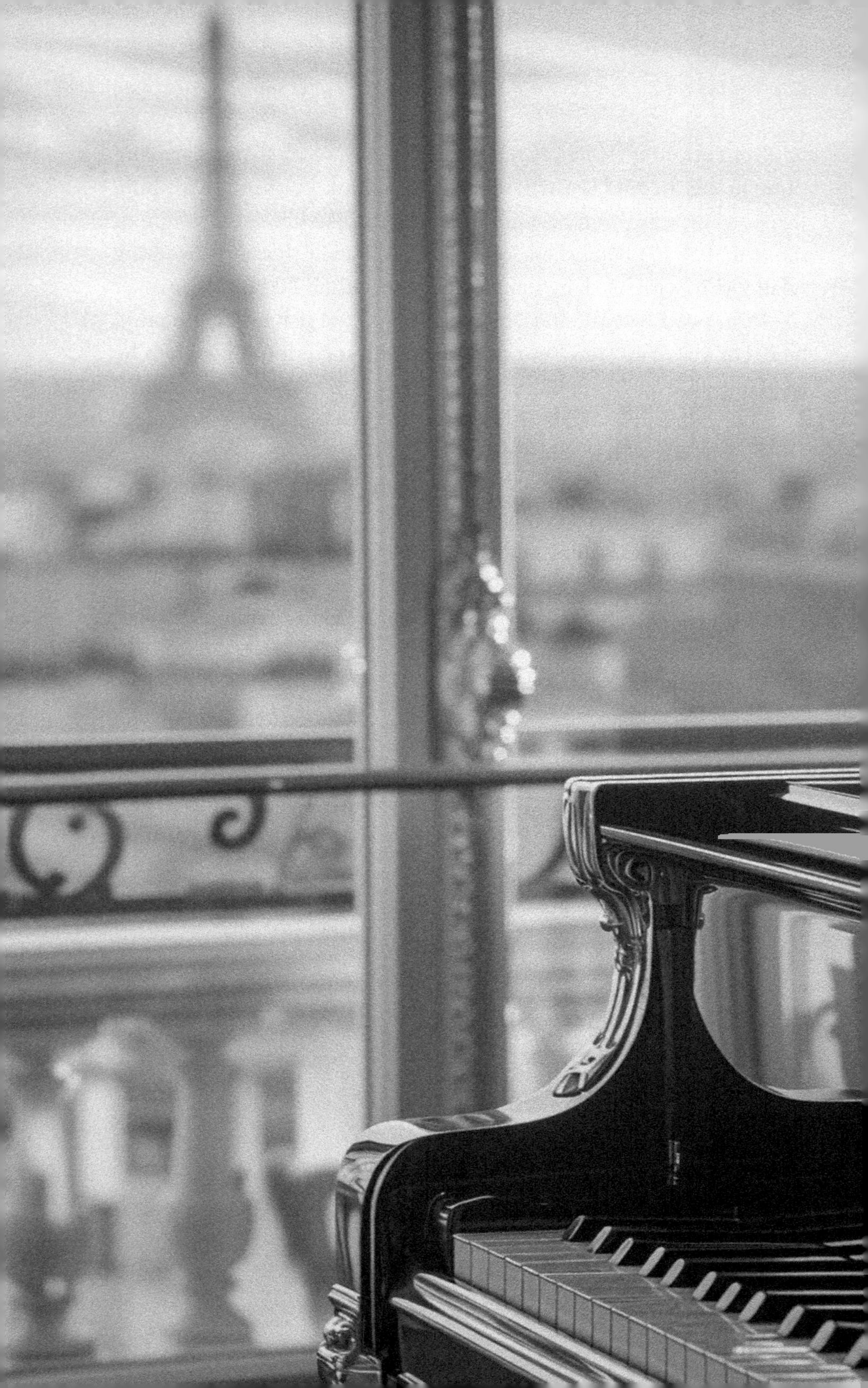

CHAPTER 29
Millie

APRIL

I climb out of the Uber, desperate for a shower, a strong drink, and another ten hours of sleep.

If I'm going to make things right with Gavin, this is where I need to start. With Lake. With admitting to my father that maybe his idea that I work with her isn't the worst idea. Why didn't I see it sooner? What kind of person would pass up working with Lake Paige, international popstar and musical prodigy, to write and sell music?

Being stubborn has cost me everything I ever wanted, and now I'm determined to make a change. Accept help, be vulnerable, open up. New year, new me, or maybe new country, new me. Whatever it is, I'm done getting in my own way.

Of course, when Lake is the one who opens the door, I lose a little of my determination. She looks perfectly put together, big smile affixed to her face, brown hair hanging in waves, makeup perfect and dressed in a pair of dark jeans and a white sweater that shows off her tiny bump. Her pink feathered earrings sway when she steps forward, and when sunlight reflects off her big diamond ring, it practically blinds me.

"Millie!" Her tone is far too loud and full of exaggerated excitement. Clearly, she's not only surprised to see me, but she's hoping that single word will draw my father's attention. "We weren't expecting you. Come in." She holds open the door.

With a big sigh and my new *I can do this attitude* in place, I smile back. "Surprise! Sorry I didn't call first."

"Please don't apologize." Lake shakes her head and gives me a rueful smile. "This is your home. Your father will be thrilled you're here. You just caught me off guard. I thought you were Gavin and Vivi. I'm sorry."

I nearly choke on my own spit as my heart sinks to my feet. "Gavin and who?"

She smiles. "Oh, Vivi. I'm so happy for him. Sure, it all happened so fast, but the way he just moved her right in without blinking is so sweet. And from what Daniel has told us, it's like she's been part of his life since day one. It's crazy, right?"

I nod, that fake smile souring. "Yeah. Crazy. And they're coming here?" I ask, hoping the dread pressing down on me isn't obvious.

I'm going to die. Gavin met someone, and he's already moved her into his apartment? And she's coming here?

Now?

Holy shit.

Holy *fucking* shit.

Maybe I should have called.

"Yup. I'm so excited to meet her. I've only seen pictures, but she's absolutely gorgeous. And the way he holds her?" She presses a hand to her chest and all but melts. *What the hell?* "Sounds like he'll barely let anyone come near her. We'll have to stop that tonight, right? I want my time with her."

Yeah, you can take whoever this Vivi is, and I'll take my time ringing Gavin's neck. Sure, it's been four months since I last spoke to him, but what the hell? It has *only* been four months since I last spoke to him, *and he's already moved on?*

And what's with Lake's obsession with this chick? What's so great about her?

God, if she sings too, I'm going to scream.

"Right," I say slowly, fighting the urge to turn and head straight back to Paris.

"Millie!" My father jogs down the stairs wearing a bright smile.

He's got me wrapped in his arms a heartbeat later, and for a moment, I forget everything else and just sink against him. Before all the drama of these past two years, I was a daddy's girl. He was my favorite person in the world.

God, I missed him.

I wrap my arms around his waist and squeeze, hoping the pressure will ease the ache in my chest. "Hi, Daddy."

"What are you doing here?" He grasps my shoulders and holds me at arm's length, beaming as he gives me a once-over. "Did you just fly in? I would have picked you up. Your brother didn't say anything." He takes my carry-on from me and hefts it over his shoulder, then guides me into the living room, eyeing my two suitcases as he does. "How long are you home for?"

"Um." I look from him to Lake, who's followed us into the room, and back again.

She steps up beside him, giving me a genuine smile, and he wraps an arm around her waist. In the past, that would have bothered me. But she's part of his family. She's having his baby. My brother or sister. Which means she's officially my family too.

"I—um. I'm back for good."

My dad frowns and drops his arm from Lake's waist. "Why?"

With an awkward laugh, I lower my gaze to the floor and will myself not to get teary at that reaction. "Thanks, Dad. Tell me how you really feel."

He steps close so we're toe to toe and stands silently until I look up at him. "I'm happy you're home. I'm just hoping it's because you're running toward something and not away from something. When I saw you in Paris—"

Lake clears her throat and rests a hand on his back. "I'll give you guys some privacy. I have to get things ready for dinner anyway." She smiles and squeezes my arm as she passes. "I'm really glad you're home."

I swallow down my emotions as we watch her leave. When she's out of earshot, he clears his throat and starts again, this time in a lower voice. "Last time we spoke, you seemed lost."

I nod. "I was running then. I'm not anymore. I know what I want, and I think this is where I'll find it."

He pulls me in for another hug and presses his cheek to the crown of my head like he did when I was a little girl. "If there's anything I can do to help—"

"I know, Dad." I release him and step back.

"And I promise I won't push Lake on you. I know—"

I squeeze his arm, stopping him again. "You were right about that. And honestly, if she's willing to help..."

The smile that splits his face is so big it hurts to look at. "I'll let you handle talking to her. But I can't imagine she'd say no."

He's right. Lake is one of the kindest people I know. I'm not sure why I didn't give her the benefit of the doubt before. Feeling lost and jealous made it hard to think straight for a long, long time.

"Lake mentioned that Gavin is coming over," I hedge, going for nonchalant, even as my stomach twists itself into knots.

"Yeah, he and Vivi are staying for the weekend. I hope that's okay. I could put you in Daniel's room if you want. That way they don't keep you up all night."

I have to fight back a shudder at my dad's insinuation. Gross. Would Gavin really fuck a girl while he's visiting my dad?

What am I thinking? The man fucked *me* while he was visiting my dad, so it's probably not the right question to be asking myself.

That's highly unlikely anyway, because the minute he sees me here, he'll probably book it out of this place. God, could this be more awkward?

"I'm sure I'll be fine." I wander back to the foyer with my dad on my heels, ready to take my suitcases upstairs and take some time to collect myself. "I think I'm going to shower. It was a long flight."

"Of course, baby girl. Let me help you carry up your luggage."

The moment my dad shuts the door to my room and I'm alone, I fall back against the bed and squeeze my eyes shut. In the quietest scream known to man, I release my aggravation, my disappointment, my devastation. How the fuck did I let this happen? Truly. How?

And what's so great about this Vivi?

I pull out my phone. Do I have the balls to google Gavin? My heart rate picks up just thinking about it. I stopped following the Bolts and actively avoided asking my brother about anything team related the day Gavin left me standing alone in his bedroom.

Right about now, talking to Daniel would be the smart thing to do. As far as twins go, he's a pretty good one, and I know he would help if I told him everything.

But god, how do I even broach the subject? And if Gavin is in love with this Vivi, would it even do me any good?

If there's no chance for us, then the last thing I want is for my father to find out about our relationship. What would be the point? A lot of people would be hurt for no reason. No. I'm done being selfish. I'll show Gavin that I've changed. I'm going to shower, get dressed, go downstairs, and smile. I'll be the best damn ex in the history of exes. And maybe, just maybe, he'll realize what a mistake it was to move on so quickly.

Or maybe I'll stay up here and kill a little time by googling ways to make an ex wish he'd never said goodbye ...

At the sound of the doorbell, my spine goes rigid and my heart flips over. With a deep breath, I force my body to relax, and then I finish applying my lipstick.

For a few seconds, I don't move away from the mirror. I take this moment to let myself live in denial and pretend that this Vivi chick doesn't exist. That Gavin is still mine to have.

Closing my eyes, I let the memories of the time when he was still mine play out and soak up the love and the pain that come with each one. I visualize his smile. His loud, carefree laugh. The way his brown eyes would turn almost molten when I'd walk into the room. How he'd track me with his gaze. How being near him was never enough. We had to find a way to touch. Even if we shouldn't. Whether it was out with our brothers, his hand on my knee beneath the table, or in my father's hot tub.

With a hand pressed against the ache in my chest, I zero in on the bed where he held me so many months ago. The longer I look, the more acute the pain gets, and the bigger the Gavin-shaped hole inside me grows.

I've been frozen for months. Stuck in a cycle on repeat.

But that ended today when I got on the plane. When I decided to take my life back.

Fuck this insane situation. I won't let him move on from us. I'll remind him of who I was to him. I'll put in the damn work.

I'm not going anywhere. This Vivi better be ready, because I'm taking back my man.

With a deep exhale, I open the door and trudge down the stairs.

"Oh my gosh. She's so perfect," Lake coos, her voice carrying from the kitchen.

Oh my god. I truly was trying to give her the benefit of the doubt, but is she high? Who talks *about* another woman, *in front* of that woman, no less, like she's a fucking child?

"She really is perfect, Gavin," my dad says. "Couldn't be happier for you. Can I hold her?"

My mouth falls open, and I miss a step. What the hell have they been smoking? I have to clutch the banister as I continue, because at this point, my knees are a wobbly mess.

"Of course. She loves everyone, and my arm could probably use the break. Right, Vivi girl? Daddy could also use a whiskey."

My stomach rolls. *Gross.* He calls himself Daddy?

"I'll get you one," Lake says. "Ford, you want a whiskey, too? I'll see if Millie wants a margarita. I think we have the peach mix she likes."

My timing couldn't be any better. I'm just crossing the threshold into the kitchen when Lake says my name.

Gavin's back is turned, but he goes ramrod straight then. "Millie?" he says, his voice hoarse. And then, as if he can sense my presence, he spins. When he zeroes in on me, his gaze narrows, almost in accusation. I barely spare him a glance, though. Not once I catch sight of the most adorable baby girl cradled in his arms.

My stomach does a bit of a somersault as I scan the kitchen. Lake is in front of the sink, her bright smile slipping with every second I remain stunned and silent. Beside her, my father, dressed in a black shirt and jeans, looks even more joyful than he did when I arrived.

Okay, two people accounted for.

The only other adult in the vicinity is Gavin. I continue my perusal, though, searching for another woman—perhaps this child's mother. I only stop when Lake clears her throat.

"We were just gushing about Vivi. It's hard to handle how beautiful his daughter is, don't you think?"

I'm pretty sure my eyes do one of those cartoon things where they get really wide, and I kind of feel like my entire body falls forward in shock. I'm actually surprised when I don't hit the ground. No one seems to notice my out-of-body experience, though, so maybe it's just that I've actually lost my mind. Because surely Lake didn't just say that Gavin has a daughter.

"Y—" I clear the disbelief from my throat. "Your daughter?" The words somehow find their way out of my mouth, but if I'm acting like a lunatic, Gavin has joined me in the mental ward, because he's yet to say a word. He's staring at me, mouth ajar, like I'm the one who just handed him the damn kid in his arms.

"Here," my father interrupts, reaching for Gavin's *daughter* —okay, I'm not sure when that word will come out easily, but right now, I feel like there's cement in my mouth. "Hi, Vivi girl. I'm your Uncle Ford. It's good to meet you."

Gavin blinks twice, and his eyes clear. Then he turns to my dad, and his expression softens. The shift is probably imperceptible to anyone but me, but I know that smile. Those crinkles, the joy that radiates, the love. It's the way Gavin looked at me for all those months.

"I'll take that whiskey now," he mumbles as he leans against the counter, his gaze decidedly roving in any direction but mine.

"Margarita, Mills?" Lake asks, shaking me from my stupor.

When I turn to her, the look on her face is pure pity.

She knows. She's known for a while.

And now it's probably obvious to her that I had no idea who Vivi was. That things with Gavin and I are so over that he went and had a baby with someone else, and I had no idea.

My nod is barely a bob of my head.

"She sleeping at night?" my father asks.

"She sleeps great. It's me who needs to get a grip."

"I remember those days. Wondering if they're breathing, if the sound they made is going to result in a cry. Certain you shouldn't even bother closing your eyes, because as soon as you do, they'll need you." My dad chuckles. "Shit, I can't believe I'm doing this again."

"Duck," Gavin mutters, pinching the bridge of his nose.

My dad throws his head back and laughs, making Vivi startle, but she doesn't fuss. "Oh, I see you're like your brother now, huh?"

Gavin shrugs. "Figure since I'm all Vivi's got, I better do as many things right as I can."

My swallow is heavy. So there is no mother? I take a step farther into the kitchen, shuffling through all I've learned in the last few minutes. But as I ease closer to Gavin, the smell of him and his proximity steal all the thoughts from my brain, and somehow, everything else just fades away.

It's just him...and her.

Vivi. I like that.

As I come close, she turns and focuses those deep brown eyes on me. Her cheeks—so rosy and pudgy it's an effort not to pinch them—lift, and she claps her hands twice and squeals. She's wearing a purple onesie, and her wavy brown hair is disheveled.

With a smile on my face, I keep my gaze on her and ask, "How old is she?"

Gavin still hasn't answered my first question, and if he doesn't stop acting like a complete asshole, my father is going to question why he hasn't even said hello to me.

When Lake pushes a whiskey glass into his hand, he takes a long, slow sip. Then he clears his throat. "About six months."

Six months. So she was born in the fall. I count back nine months and quickly determine that Gavin must have hooked up with her mother during the year we didn't speak.

It shouldn't bother me. We aren't together now, and we certainly weren't together then, but my stomach sours just the same.

Then again, the idea of Gavin with anyone but me makes my stomach roll.

"Ford, can you help me find the good tequila?" Lake interrupts.

My father spins Vivi in his arms and pushes her toward me. "Want to hold her?"

I reach for her before Gavin can object, swallowing down the painful thoughts. I'm the reason we're not together. I'm the reason we weren't together back then too. *My immaturity. My problems.*

I seduced the man and then left the country. I can't fault him for any of it. And now there's this sweet little girl...

In awe, I coo at her, brushing a hand over her soft hair. "Well, hello, beautiful."

Lake practically drags my father to the bar, yammering on about the ingredients she needs like she's doing her best to keep him distracted.

The sweet little girl in my arms tips her head back, studying me.

"Did you steal this baby?" I whisper.

Gavin's eyes bulge and he chokes on his drink. "Excuse me?"

I scoff and hold her close to my chest. "Come on, Gavin. Where's her mother?"

His gaze sharpens. "That's hardly your business."

I smile. I can't help but rile him up. This isn't the way I wanted to go about it, but if I can get under his skin, maybe we can get somewhere. "Gavin Langfield, where did you get this baby?"

A sound that could almost be categorized as a laugh comes from his throat. But then he clears it again. "What the hell are you doing here?"

"Me? You have *a baby*?" I whisper. "Last time I saw you, which was only four months ago, if you remember, you said you wanted to have kids. Now listen, I know I didn't handle the conversation well, but this is..." I hold up Vivi and smile at her. "Well, I mean, it's certainly one way to go about it."

Gavin's brown eyes narrow on me, his annoyance palpable.

I lean in closer to him, my voice a teasing whisper. "You can be honest. I won't tell anyone that you stole her."

"Are you high?" He grunts and holds his arms out. "Give me back my daughter."

Oh my god, the way he says *my daughter* has parts of me tingling that have no business being affected. Why is that so hot? I know I should be all sorts of things right now—upset that he had a child with someone else, annoyed that he isn't at least a little happy to see me, worried that he'll never forgive me—but I can be nothing but happy right now, because Vivi is a baby. *Not his girlfriend.* She's the daughter who now lives with him, not a woman he moved into his apartment.

"No. She likes me." I spin her away from him and rest my cheek on the top of her head. "Don't you, Viv? We're going to be best friends."

"You're delusional." He sets his whiskey glass on the counter and steps up to me, holding his arms out again.

I pull Vivi back. "Now, now. I'm spending time with my new bestie. Give us time to bond." I press my lips to her cheek and blow a raspberry, causing the sweetest giggle to escape her.

"You are not bonding with my baby," Gavin practically growls.

I hold her up so we're cheek to cheek and smile, hoping she's doing the same. "Come on now. Tell me this wasn't your plan all along."

"I have no idea what the—"

"Aw, Millie." My father suddenly materializes by my side and squeezes my shoulder. "Look at you. You were always so good with babies."

I tip my head back and smile up at him, happy he's interrupted grumpy Gavin. "Thanks, Daddy. She's adorable."

"Want to help me with the margarita? I got the ingredients." Lake motions toward the bar.

"Sure, Viv and I will help out."

"Vivi." This time the sound that leaves Gavin's mouth is a full-blown growl.

I shrug and focus on Vivi. "Maybe. But I think she likes when her bestie Millie calls her Viv."

As if in confirmation, Vivi presses a chubby palm against my cheek and squeezes. Her sharp nails dig in a little painfully. Even so, I can't stop the laugh that bubbles out of me.

With one more grin at Gavin, I follow Lake out of the room,

knowing full well that Gavin is tracking my every move. Maybe it's a bit devious and calculated that I've stolen his daughter to keep his attention on me, but now that I know Gavin is still single, I don't plan to go easy on him.

I will get Gavin back, and my new bestie, Vivi, is going to help me do it.

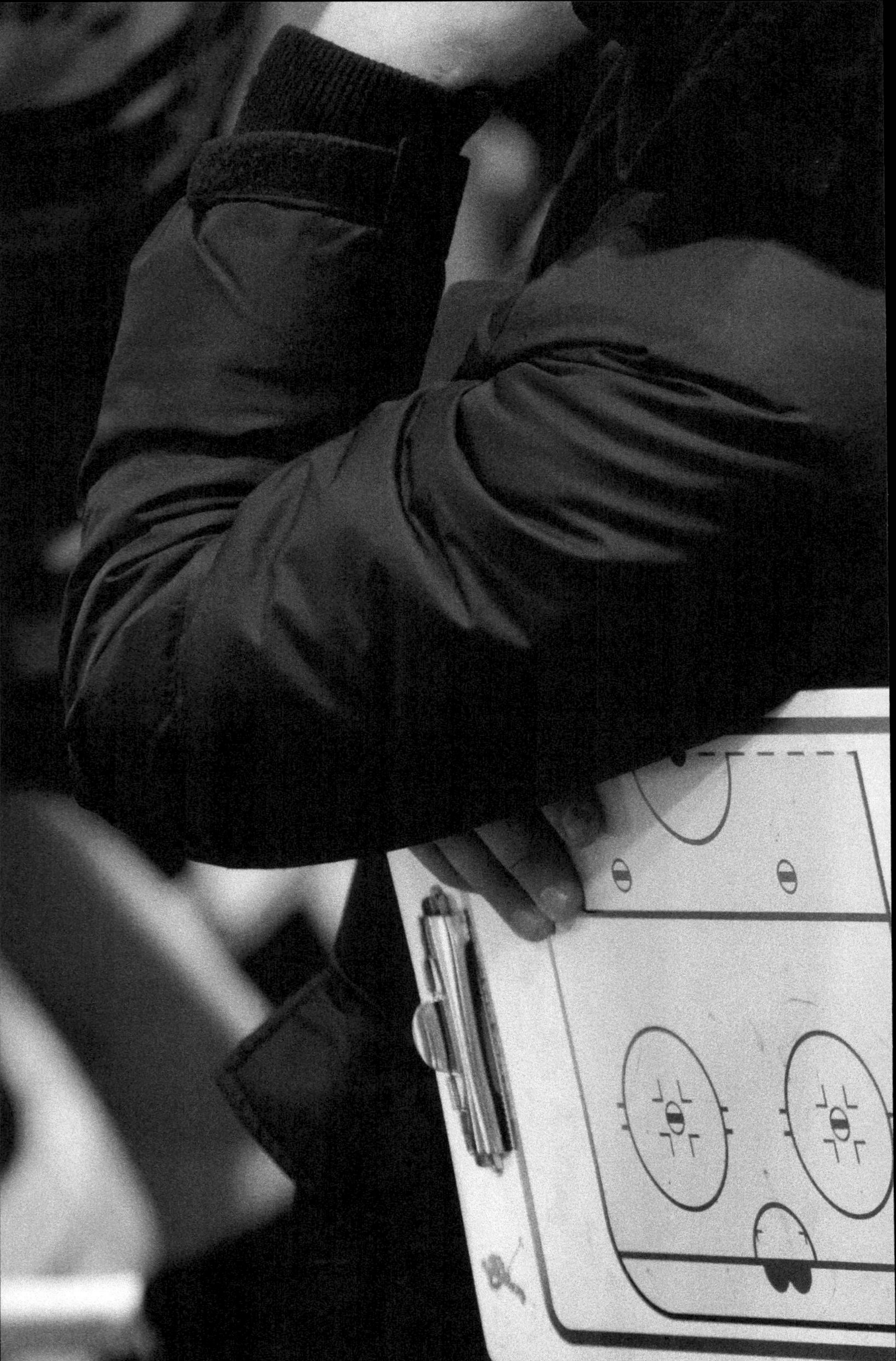

CHAPTER 30
Gavin

WHAT THE FUCK is Millie doing here, smiling at me like she didn't break me months ago? And what the hell is she doing holding my child and cooing at her like she's enamored and acting like she didn't force me to walk away because she didn't want a child with me?

And how the hell does she know Vivi's not mine?

Shouldn't she be angry? The Millie I know would be throwing a hissy fit, demanding to know who I slept with and when.

Jealous that I'd have the audacity to touch another woman.

I didn't, of course, but she doesn't know that.

No. She's already figured out that I couldn't possibly be Vivi's dad. Fuck. I need to get her away from Vivi before she ruins everything.

"Don't worry. Millie is great with kids." Ford eyes me, his content expression falling a little. "You doing okay?"

I don't even know how to answer that. Before I arrived, I'd have said sure. Obviously, that would have been a lie, since who the fuck is really okay on any given day while parenting a six-month-old? Especially since I became a dad overnight and have absolutely no idea what the fuck I'm doing.

But now? With Millie less than ten feet away, shocking the shit out of me with her reappearance and acting all…friendly? Yeah, I'm nowhere near okay.

I pull my phone out of my pocket and study the screen like I've just received a text. "Give me a sec. I need to check this."

He nods, and then he's heading out of the room, his focus fixed on his little girl and mine.

> Me: I need one of you to call me with an emergency.

> Aiden: Okay. What kind?

> Me: I don't care. Make something up!

> Aiden: I need better acting directions than that. What is my motivation? Am I constipated? Did Jill and I have a fight? Does it have to do with the way my wrist has been hurting since the game the other night?

> Brooks: Dude, is this two truths and a lie? If so, you def aren't constipated.

> Beckett: What did Jill do now?

> Brooks: Seriously, dump her.

> Aiden: It was actually three truths. I need Miralax. Beckett, can I come over? I need someone to talk me through this.

> Beckett: Talk you through shitting?

> Aiden: No, Jill.

> Beckett: Ducking A. You do realize it's Friday, right?

> Brooks: Anal Friday.
>
> Beckett: What the duck is wrong with you?
>
> Me: Can someone freaking pay attention here? I need help!
>
> Brooks: Want Sara to call? She can come up with a work emergency.

Heaving out a breath, I glance at Ford. He's smiling so big now it leaves me feeling like complete shit. I've been avoiding my best friend for months because I fucked his daughter and then she broke my heart. I swore to myself that I'd spend time with him, make sure he understands he did nothing wrong.

Fuck.

> Me: No. Just. Fuck. Forget it.

My phone buzzes with another text, but this time it's from Beckett only in a separate thread.

> Beckett: I can come to you with the twins. We can hang and watch a game or something. Livy will understand. I can't imagine how hard it is doing this alone, and if I haven't told you before, I'm proud of you.

Fuck. Who the hell is this man and what has he done with my grumpy, stoic big brother? Ignoring the tightness in my chest, I respond.

> Me: Millie's here.
>
> Beckett: At your ducking apartment?

> Me: No. Worse. At Ford's. He invited me for the weekend. What the hell do I do?

> Beckett: How is she acting?

> Me: She asked if I stole Vivi.

> Beckett: Who steals a child?

Sighing, I run a palm down my face. Me, apparently.

> Me: Who the fuck knows? She's…I don't know…different.

> Beckett: I can say Dad needs us.

> Me: No. I can do this. It's over. Vivi is all that matters, and Ford looks so fucking happy holding her with his daughter here. I'm the ass in this situation. I'll just ignore her. We both know this has to have her skin itching with the need to run.

> Beckett: Just text duck if you need me.

> Me: Not quack?

My phone buzzes again, this time with a message in the other thread.

> Aiden: So can I come over?

> Brooks: Aiden, Sara said to come over to our place. Let Beckett and Liv have their date night.

> Beckett: Thanks, Brooks. Tell Sara she can choose where we order breakfast from next week when we're in the office.

> Me: Sara is the best.

> Brooks: Damn straight. Crazy girl says donuts from the place on Thayer Street, Beck. Aiden, don't you dare take Miralax before you get here. Gav, you got this. Whatever this is.
>
> Brooks: But is it safe to guess that "this" has something to do with Millie holding your daughter?

My stomach drops, along with my jaw, as I gape at my phone. How the hell?

Before I can make my thumbs work to ask how the fuck he knows that, an image appears in the thread. And now my heart is dropping too. The photo is of the woman who is currently the bane of my existence. And sure enough, in it, she's holding my Vivi girl in her arms. Even as my jaw hardens in anger, I save it to my camera roll.

> Brooks: Lake just posted this on Instagram. Sara is still squealing about it.

I can actually picture that happening, and I surprise even myself by laughing at the way the moment plays out in my head.

Millie peers over at me. Her curious expression has me clamping my mouth shut. She doesn't get my smiles. Not anymore.

But dammit, the only woman I have time for is currently looking at Millie like she hung the moon.

Quack.

"What are you doing with Vivi when you travel?" Lake's question is expected. Everyone, including sports commentators, is interested in how I'm handling being a new single dad as well as the coach of the Bolts.

The table in the kitchen is situated under a large window with a perfect view of their gorgeous backyard. I'm glad we're not sitting in the formal dining room. Fancy chairs and babies don't mix.

And bringing a highchair didn't even cross my mind. Lake, of course, was prepared, though it's awfully convenient that she just so happened to pick one up while she was out this morning.

She's part of a growing club full of people who are prepared for me to screw up.

Yes, she's pregnant, but she's still got months before the baby comes, and it's highly suspicious that she'd be out stocking up the day I arrive.

"I've been paying the woman who handles our charity work to help. She's sweet, but it isn't a long-term solution. I just—" My words dry up when I catch Millie watching me with what looks like pity in her eyes.

The last thing I want is to pour out all my issues in front of my ex.

My ex who's got her hand on Vivi's tray. Each time we set something on it, she picks it up with one chubby hand and tosses it over the side, and Millie's apparently taken on the task of holding her hand to keep her from throwing food while we eat.

The way their hands twine together makes my heart clench, but I curse the stupid organ and push the feeling away. "It'll take some time to find someone permanent."

"I could help you." The words are barely audible, and when I zero in on Millie again, her eyes are wide, like even she is surprised that the suggestion left her lips.

For the first time today, I turn my full focus on her. Now that she's made an offer like that in front of her father, it'd be suspicious for me to avoid looking at her like I've done my best to so far. Her freckled cheeks heat under my gaze, but she holds her chin up, almost daring me to say no.

Fuck, she's pretty.

Her curly auburn hair is down and hangs to her shoulders, framing a face so gorgeous it's painful to look at after all the shit we've been through. She's wearing a simple black sweater, but even from here, I can tell she's not wearing a bra. It was a habit of hers I loved when we were dating. Now I have to actively remind myself to keep my eyes off her chest before my mouth starts to water.

With a heavy swallow, I shake my head. "That's very kind, but no."

"I've got nothing else going on right now," she counters. "And it would give me a chance to spend more time with Daniel. I've barely seen him play this year."

Ford clears his throat. "Don't you have a job lined up?"

I expect Millie to wince and for pain to flash in those golden eyes. Instead, she merely smiles at her father. "That's actually why I came home." She takes a deep breath and turns to Lake. "I was hoping that you would be willing to look over some of the music I've written. Dad mentioned that I'd have a place at Hall Studios if that's what I want, but to be honest, I don't want to do it that way. I'd really like to work on my music and then present it to you, and maybe to others if you aren't interested."

Lake nods, her eyes alight. "Absolutely. Just let me know when you're ready. I'd love to listen."

I've been holding my breath so long stars dance in my vision, so I force myself to inhale. Despite everything, I want Millie to have this. And I can't help the pride that swells in me as she asks for what she wants.

But then she turns those golden eyes on me again, and I swallow my tongue. "So since I have some time on my hands, and you need help, let me watch Vivi for you."

I narrow my eyes, silently conveying to her that she's playing a dangerous game. And in return, I swear hers say *game on*.

But what fucking game is she playing?

"Your apartment has three bedrooms, doesn't it?" Ford says.

Millie's lips quirk while I squirm. "One room is for Vivi, obviously, and the other is set up with bunk beds for Beck's kids."

"Oh, Daniel and I had bunk beds for years," Millie chirps unhelpfully.

Ford's chuckle is deep and full of fondness. "Yeah, they did. Even though they each had their own room. I forgot about that." He shakes his head and picks up his wineglass. "This would be great for you, Gav. Millie's excellent with kids, and it would give her plenty of time to work on her music. You'd have someone who could travel with the team until you find someone more permanent."

My best friend smiles like moving his daughter into my home and encouraging her to travel the country with me is genius rather than what should be his literal nightmare. And likely would be if he had any clue what I did with her for months behind his back.

"As much as I appreciate it, I'm looking for someone with a bit more experience."

Millie grins. "I double majored in college. Music and early childhood education, in case I decided to teach music, instead of writing it."

"Though your father would love if you'd come work for Hall Studios," Ford reminds her.

She glances at him, and I'm pleased to note that she doesn't have the same disdain for the offer as I would have expected. "It's important to me to do it this way, but I appreciate the offer immensely."

"Just want you to know you always have a place with me. Whether it's in this house or in my business. You're a Hall, Millie. Remember that."

I look to Vivi, wishing for the first time that she was a baby that cried. Then I'd at least have an excuse to disappear from this table. But after that first night, she's barely fussed. So I'm stuck here trying like hell to figure out a way to get out of hiring Millie Hall as my daughter's nanny and moving her into my home.

"So what do you say?" Ford looks at me again. God, I've never wanted to muzzle a guy so badly, and that's saying a lot, considering Aiden Langfield is my brother.

Millie's lips twist like she's trying to school her expression, but there's no hiding her glee.

Jaw locked tight, I nod once. "I guess we can give it a try."

With a squeal, Millie lifts Vivi's hand. "Hear that, bestie? We're going to be roomies."

My daughter's gummy grin cracks the ice hardened around my heart. Every day, she busts through a little more. She's changed my life in a hundred ways since that fateful night.

And with my ex-girlfriend back in the country and moving into my apartment, I have a feeling my life is about to be flipped upside down.

When it comes to Millie Hall, I should be used to it by now.

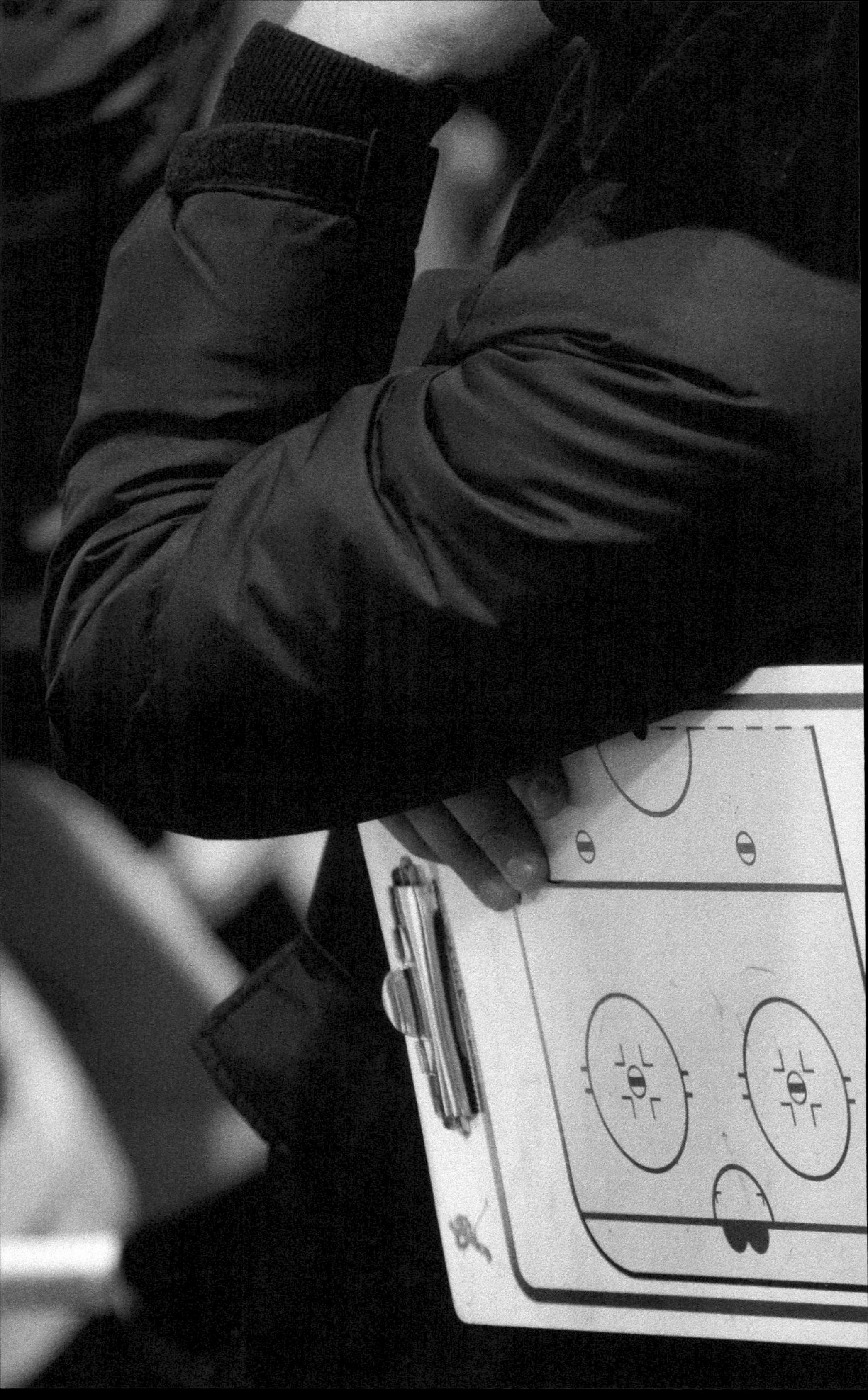

CHAPTER 31
Gavin

"JUST GIVE ME A MINUTE," I say as I survey Vivi's car seat and beg my exhausted brain to remember which way the base goes.

"Need help?" Millie stands behind me with my daughter in her arms.

Lake and Ford are behind her, and they're all waiting for me to figure out how the fuck to make this work.

With all of Millie's luggage, the Pack 'n' Play, and the four bags I packed full of her stuff because I had no idea what she'd need, I had to shift the car seat to the other side to make it all fit.

"It snaps here, right?" I glower at it, drenched in sweat and anxious to no longer be the subject of scrutiny. "It's a children's item. Shouldn't it be childproof?" I grumble.

"Lake, will you take Vivi?" Millie says. A second later, there's a gentle hand on my back. "Can I help?"

Wiping at the sweat forming on my brow, I sigh and back up. She might think it's a simple task, but it's complicated as fuck. But if she insists, I'll just sit back and watch her lose her mind. Maybe then I'll feel a little better about myself and my ability to raise a child.

All weekend, she's been stepping in, helping make bottles, rocking Vivi to sleep, attending to her every need before she can even make a sound. Proving with her every move that I have no fucking idea what I'm doing.

But even she can't—

"All set." Millie pops up and brushes her hands off.

All set? Is she ducking kidding me?

"How did you do that?" I hiss.

Ford has given me more than my fair share of looks this weekend. I think he's giving me grace because he knows I'm stressed, but I've barely been more than cordial to Millie since Friday night. He's likely regretting encouraging me to hire his daughter and move her into my home.

Please reconsider it. I wish I could just tell him why it's the worst idea he's ever had.

"Like I've told you every time you've asked, I used to babysit a lot. Not much has changed." She reaches for Vivi, but I'm quicker.

"Thank you for having us," I say to Lake as I settle Vivi against my chest.

When Ford pulls his daughter into his arms, I turn away so I don't have to watch them together. The less I see Millie behaving like a well-rounded adult, the better. Latching on to my anger is my only form of defense at this point.

"When do you find out the baby's sex?" Millie asks as Lake envelops her in a hug.

As they pull apart, Lake rests her hands on her stomach and turns to Ford. "This one over here doesn't want to know."

"Dad! We need to be able to plan."

Ford drapes an arm over Lake's shoulder. "It's a baby. He or she needs very few things in the beginning. Besides, I'm not a huge fan of pink. Look at Vivi, here. She looks perfect rocking the blue."

I huff out a laugh. "It's all from Aiden. If he had it his way, Langfields would only wear blue."

"I, for one, would love to know what we're having," Lake says. "So work on your father."

Ford drops a kiss to the top of her head. "You know it's almost impossible for me to say no to you. Don't add Millie's puppy dog eyes in. I'll never survive."

Millie pouts and bats her lashes. "Please, Daddy?"

Ford groans, and Lake shakes with laughter beneath his arms.

"I'll call you when he's set up the appointment," she says with a wink.

I'm struck stupid by the easy way they've interacted this weekend. What happened between December and now to facilitate such a monumental change?

When Millie turns to get in the car, she bumps into me because I'm frozen in place, staring like an idiot as I try to figure out what her endgame is.

"Gonna get in the car, Coach?" That nickname in her sexy lilt is the kick in the gut I need.

I nod another goodbye to Ford, and with my resolve strengthened, I place my hands at ten and two on the wheel and drive the fuck away.

Ten seconds down the road, the chatter starts. "How do you like living in the hockey building?"

"Fine."

One-word answers. I can do this.

"Did you move in there before or after you stole Vivi?"

I shoot her a quick scowl before I focus on the road again. In my periphery, she's beaming.

"Before."

"Should I call you Coach, or should I go with something more appropriate?" She taps on her plump lips.

Fuck, even with my eyes on the road, I can't help but fixate on her every move. "Oh, I know, baby daddy?"

"No."

"Are you going to give me more than one-word answers?"

"No."

"Fine, then Vivi and I will just have to do all the talking, right, bestie?" She spins in her seat and smiles at Vivi's reflection in the mirror installed above the baby seat so I can keep an eye on her in my rearview mirror.

As soon as Vivi spots Millie, she smiles.

Fuck my life.

"How about we order dinner from that Italian place in Chelsea you love?" Millie asks, settling back in her seat.

"No."

"Chinese?"

"No."

"Fine, we'll do the Thai place, but only if you order extra Pad Thai. You always eat the peanuts off mine, and that's my favorite part."

"Ms. Hall, we will not be eating together. We are not friends. You are here to take care of my daughter. That's it. I have to leave for the arena by seven a.m. most days. Normally Vivi comes with me, but I've been told wearing my daughter while coaching grown men on the ice isn't the most responsible thing, so I'm trusting you to take care of her until I get home. Then you'll be relieved of your duties, and you can go hang out with friends or your brother. Really anyone but *me*."

I merge onto the highway, white-knuckling the steering wheel as my heart beats out of my chest and refusing to look in her direction.

"It's been four months, Gavin," she says softly, lifting her hand like she might settle it on my arm, or maybe my leg.

I shift closer to the door. I can't let her touch me.

"Exactly. Four months since you told me you didn't want kids. Since you told me you couldn't do *this*. I'm a father now. The only parent that little girl has. She's my only thought. My only concern. If you can get on board with that—if she can become your priority, rather than a pawn in whatever twisted game you've come up with—then fine." I swallow back the rage that's threatening to bubble over and grit my teeth. "I can tell she likes you, and since I want to give her everything, I can deal with having you around. But that's as far as this goes. Can you handle that?"

I keep my focus on the road. As long as I don't look at her, I can do this.

"You used to like me, you know? I was once your favorite person." The words are laced with a desperate sadness that claws at me, leaving me raw.

I don't dare say another word, and I don't look at her.

Finally, she lets out a resigned sigh. Her voice is stronger when she replies. "I can handle it."

I'm not sure whether the heaviness that settles in my chest is a permanent thing now, or if this is as close to relief as I'll ever get when it comes to her.

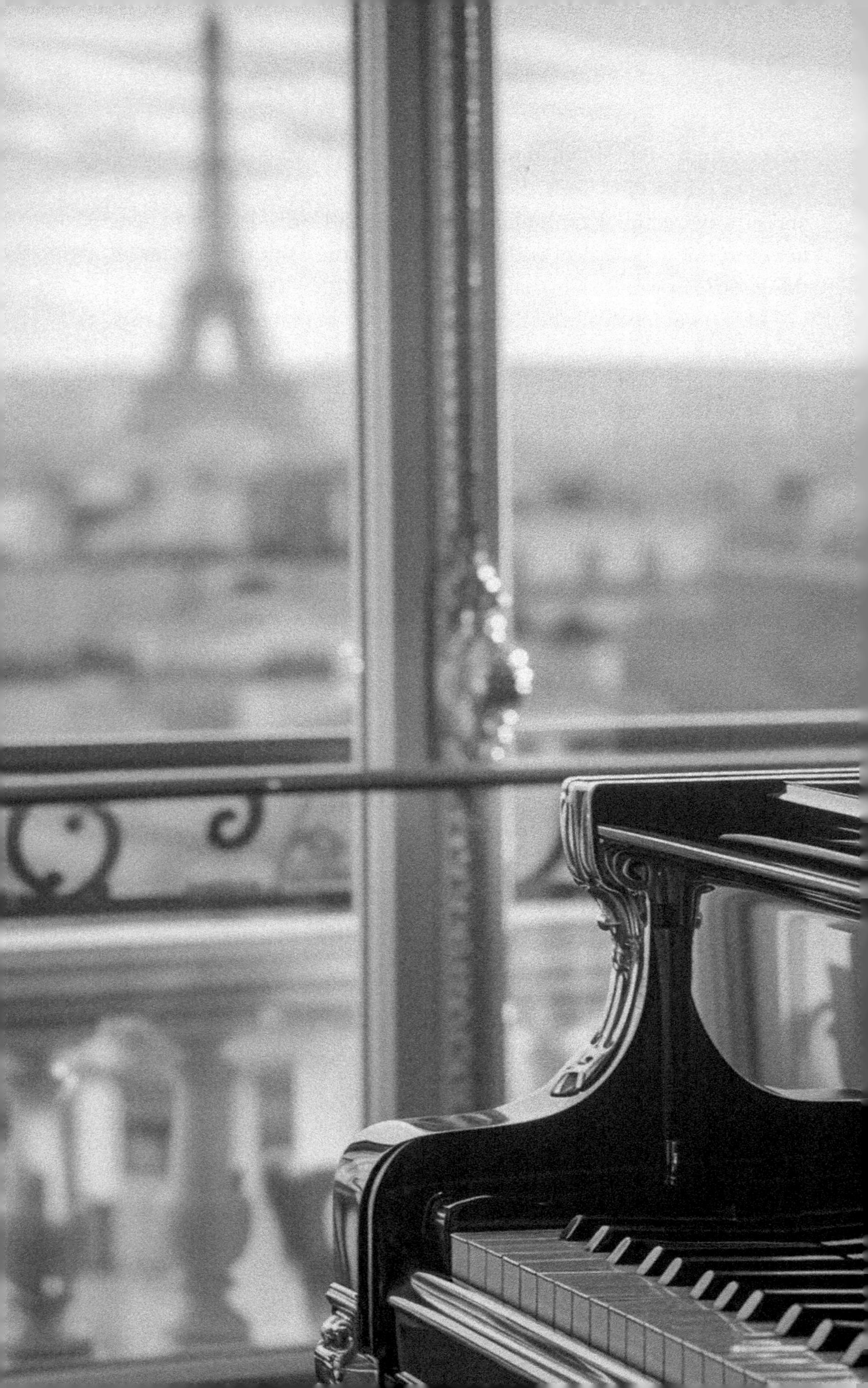

CHAPTER 32
Millie

AS MUCH AS I've always loved Gavin's penthouse, I couldn't be happier that he's moved since the last time I saw him. The fact that his new apartment is only a couple of floors away from my brother may be my only saving grace in this situation. At least I'll have somewhere to sneak off to when Gavin lashes out.

A weaker woman would be sad right now. Maybe even angry.

But I've decided to ignore this Gavin. This Gavin is overwhelmed and slightly unhinged.

But my Gavin is somewhere beneath the prickly exterior. He's been trapped, and I'm determined to set him free.

Is my plan slightly delusional? Possibly. But honestly, it's better than letting his words get to me. What we had was real and so, so good. I fucked it up, but I refuse to believe I can't fix what I broke. I'll start by being here for him in every way I can be. I'll put him and Vivi first. Already, despite his cold demeanor, it's easy to do, because I haven't felt this at home in months.

"Leave it," Gavin says as I reach for my bags. He's already got Vivi. He's always got her. It's clear to me after less than forty-eight hours that he's most comfortable when she's in his arms. "I'll send the guys down to grab everything."

"Little abuse of power, Coach?"

His responding growl starts low in his chest and works its way up to his throat. Before I have a chance to tease him about it, he's striding away. I scurry after him, and when we reach the elevator, he steps to the side, silently urging me in first. His jaw is rigid as he follows me in and hits the button for the fourteenth floor.

"Oh, the top. Fancy!"

At the sound of my voice, Vivi squirms until she can see me. Then she gives me a sweet smile. Her daddy just gives me a bored expression. I make faces at her, and the little brown-eyed cutie squeals and kicks her feet.

When the elevator door opens, I let him step out first so I can follow.

"Baby Hall!"

I turn and find a group of guys sitting in an open space set up with couches and beanbags and a couple of TVs. It's minimalistic and modern, with sports memorabilia hung on the walls.

Hit with a wave of relief that not everyone here is annoyed by my presence, I start in their direction.

Gavin's growly again when he calls my name. "Where are you going?"

Over my shoulder, I give him a wink. "Saying hi to my brother and his friends. Give me a minute."

Daniel hops up and meets me halfway, wrapping me in a bear hug and lifting me off the ground. "Mills! What are you doing here?"

I squeeze him back. "Have you gotten bigger?"

He's been taller than me since he shot up when he hit puberty, but he was still pretty lanky through high school. Now he's nothing but muscle and pure strength.

My cocky brother doesn't disappoint. "Sure have." He sets me down and takes a step back, his shaggy brown hair falling into his face as he studies me. "You look good, Mills."

"Thanks." I peer over his shoulder. "What are you boys up to?"

One of my brother's teammates gives me a flirty smile, and it's met with not one but two growls.

"Don't even think about it," Daniel says.

"Eyes off my nanny" comes from behind me.

I turn around and glare at Gavin, but he's laser focused on the guys and misses the figurative daggers I'm launching at him.

"Nanny?" Daniel asks.

"Ah, Vivi's got a hot babysitter!" Aiden teases. He's decked out in his typical blue Bolts attire and kicked back on the couch.

"Baby Hall," Tyler Warren adds from beside him with a wink. Talk about a hot hockey player. The man has dark hair and piercing blue eyes, and with the ink peeking through wherever skin shows, he has bad boy written all over him.

Daniel drops his head back and groans. "Seriously, dudes. No talking about my sister like that. Remember," he says, pointing to Aiden, "you have one too."

"Who happens to be my bestie and a total hottie," I remind them all.

Gavin lets out a heavy sigh. "Can we go now?"

"Wait. Not until you explain what this is about." My brother stands taller, his gaze bobbing between Gavin and me.

Gavin may not be a ripped hockey player, but he's just as formidable. He takes a step closer, and then the men are zeroed in on each other, eyes narrowed.

With a huff, I take the baby from Gavin's arms. "Viv and I are going to be spending some time together."

"Which means she's off-limits." Gavin crosses his arms over his chest, the move punctuating his decree.

Laughter threatens to spill out of me at the display, but I bury my head in Vivi's neck to stifle it, making her giggle. Yeah, my ex is totally over me and not possessive at all.

Ha.

"Does that mean she'll be living here?" Daniel looks at us both dubiously.

Camden Snow, who's a close friend of Daniel's, tosses his Xbox controller onto the coffee table and stands up. "Need help moving in?"

Physically, Camden is the polar opposite of Tyler Warren. He's all blond hair, blue eyes, and a dimple that pops when he smiles. And that dimple is on full display right now as he stares at me like I'm the best thing he's seen in months.

I don't exactly hate it, especially when the tension radiating off Gavin ratchets way up.

"You can all help." Gavin folds his arms across his chest. "Millie and Vivi are coming with me. The rest of you go down to my car and bring up their stuff."

"On it, Coach," Tyler says, heaving himself off the couch.

As they pass, Aiden presses a kiss to the top of Vivi's head, and she makes googly eyes at him. He has that effect on women. Most of them do. These hockey boys are something else. Before he steps away, he presses a kiss to my cheek. "Happy you're home. I'm sure your dad is thrilled." He juts his chin in Gavin's direction. "Maybe he'll even start smiling again now." With those words, he heads off.

I blink as I watch him stride toward the elevator with the rest of the guys, dissecting the comment. Does he think my presence is what will make Gavin smile? Or the help with Vivi? I suppose it doesn't matter. For now, my only concern is this little one. I have to prove to him that I want to be part of his life, and this is the best way to do it. Lucky for us all, this sweet girl has already carved out a place for herself in my heart.

"We're not done discussing this," Daniel says with a squeeze of my arm. Then he's hightailing it after the guys.

Gavin lets out a long breath. "Are you ready now?" His voice is a fraction kinder than it has been.

In a matter of seconds, the guys are gone, leaving the common area eerily quiet and an absolute mess. Empty bags of chips, Powerades, video controllers, and straight-up porn are strewn about. "It's like Daniel's college dorm all over again."

The noise Gavin makes is somewhere between a laugh and a growl.

My heart floats in my chest at the sound. I'm wearing him down already.

Vivi squirms and rubs her face against my chest, and for the first time since I met her, starts to cry. "Hey, bestie. What's going on?" I bounce her gently, patting her on her back.

"She's probably hungry. And needs a diaper change." Gavin plucks her out of my arms and settles her against his chest. "Come on, Vivi girl. Let's show Millie her room, and you and I can relax."

I follow him down the hall, pushing away the throbbing ache that hits me every time I observe the two of them like this. His soft, comforting words to her make me want to lie against his chest and beg him to love me again.

He guides me through the door at the end of the hall, and as I step inside, I'm hit by how very real this all is. The floor is littered with toys, and the kitchen is cluttered with bottles and a can of formula. A highchair is set beside a stool at the kitchen counter. The visual of Gavin and Vivi sitting here nightly, having dinner, leaves me smiling. It's all so domesticated, and I kind of love it.

His penthouse was the definition of a bachelor pad, decorated impeccably, if not a little sterile, with beautiful views of the city. This place is just as beautiful, but more lived-in, with an open floor plan and a gorgeous view of the seaport. As my gaze sweeps the space, cataloging every inch of my new "home," my heart thrums in my chest wildly.

This will either be the beginning of every dream I've ever had, or it will be a heartbreaking disaster.

Gavin stands in the middle of the open room, bouncing a crying Vivi, watching me. Almost like he's holding his breath, waiting for my reaction.

I spin dramatically and inhale, ready to tell him how beautiful it all is. I'll have to tease him a little too, add some levity to the moment. But mid-twirl, I come to an abrupt stop, and my heart lodges itself in my throat. In the farthest corner, beside the door, sits a beautiful black and gold grand piano with a black cushioned bench in front of it.

Slapping a hand to my chest, I pull in a sharp breath. "Did you—"

The words die on my tongue when the front door swings open and the guys barrel in.

"Where should we put Baby Hall's bags?" Tyler winks at me, then grins at Gavin, obviously relishing how easy it is to piss Gavin off.

"Try the one that isn't Gavin's bedroom," Daniel says, knocking Tyler with a shoulder so hard the guy stumbles.

I'd laugh at the insanity of the situation if I wasn't still fixated on the piano.

Why does Gavin have a piano? Was it here when he moved in?

He certainly didn't have one in the penthouse.

Around me, the guys continue to rib Gavin, chatting loudly as they carry in the bags and then settle around the counter.

Of their own accord, my feet shuffle to the piano, and one hand gently brushes over the smooth, lacquered surface. It's stunning.

My fingers ache to slide against the ivories, but I squeeze them tightly, swallow thickly—willing my heart to return to its rightful place—and take a deep breath. When I've found a modicum of composure, I turn and join what has become a party.

"You ready for your first road trip with us?" Camden asks as I join them in the kitchen.

Daniel is the one who answers. "You're going to travel with us?"

Tyler nudges him. "Looks like you'll have to keep it in your pants for the rest of the season."

I roll my eyes. "Please, I've been watching him parade his flavors of the night around for years. Don't go changing for me, Danny."

"Danny!" Aiden crows.

"Oh no," Gavin grumbles.

The rest of the room falls eerily silent.

"What?" I frown and scan the guys, who are all side-eyeing Aiden.

Aiden steps forward. "Summer lovin'," he croons.

"What's happening?" I whisper, eyes wide.

Tyler leans in close. "Aiden lives in song, and you just brought up his favorite musical. I guess this road trip will be *Grease* inspired."

My brother's face is fixed in a murderous expression, and he's directing it right at me.

I hold up my hands and mouth, "I didn't know."

Vivi is still fussing, but when Aiden takes her from Gavin and bounces, she goes quiet, and when he breaks into a rendition of the *Grease* song, she shoves a finger into her mouth and watches him with rapt attention.

"Vivi girl, got a new nanny,
Vivi girl, she's pretty fancy,
She's Hall's twin, and she calls him Danny
Don't call her baby, or my brother will flip
Vivi girl, you're going to be
Oh ah, the happiest girl"

I lean closer to Tyler. "Does he not know the words?"

He shakes with silent laughter. "The kid remembers the day he lost his first tooth like it happened yesterday—and he'll tell the story in detail—this is just *his thing*." He wraps an arm around my shoulders and sways along to the beat. "By the way, everyone calls me War. Welcome to the team, Baby Hall."

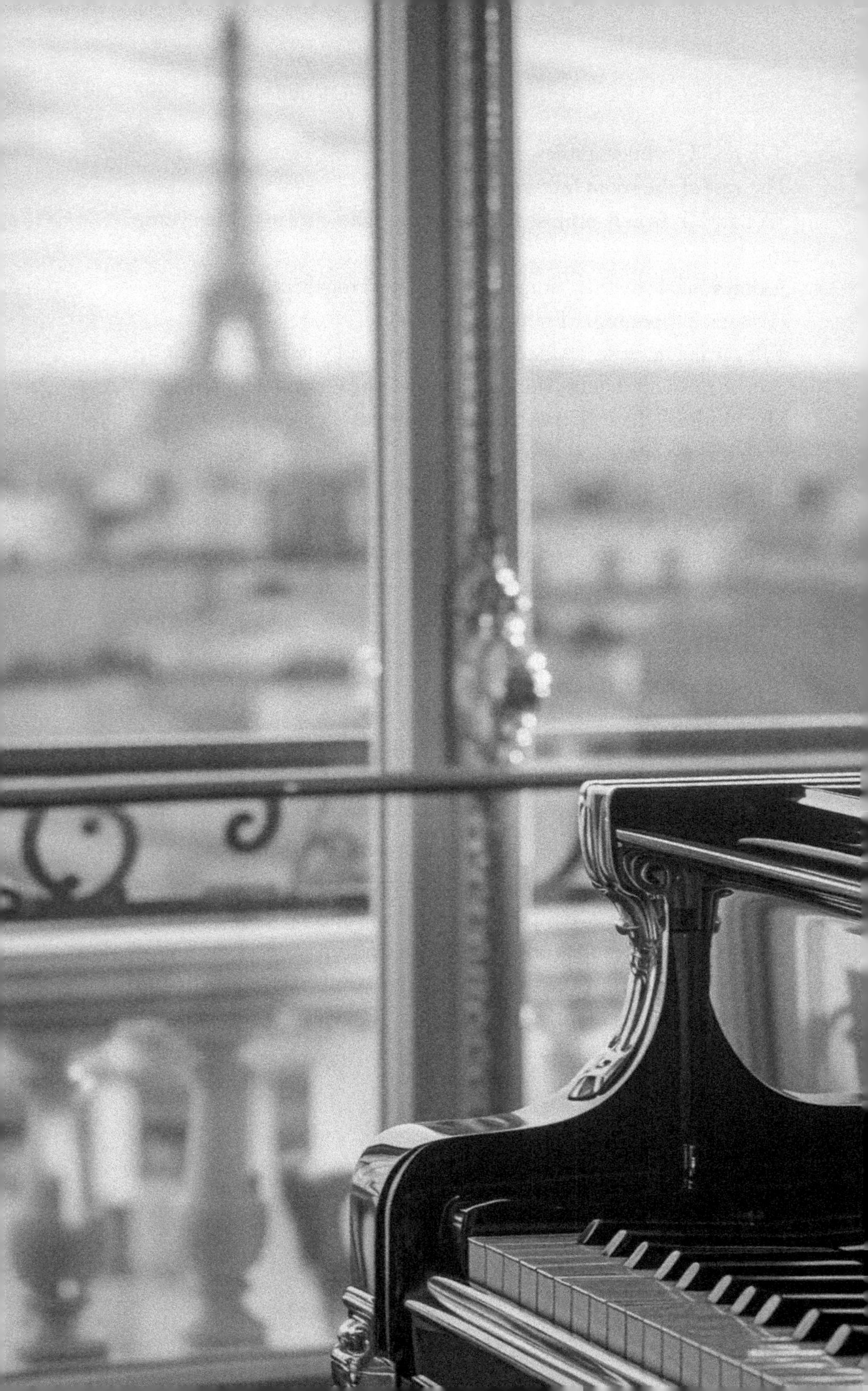

CHAPTER 33
Millie

GAVIN LEFT EARLY FOR PRACTICE, kissing Vivi goodbye before reminding me of her schedule for the sixth time. The only interactions we've had since he kicked the guys out last night and disappeared into his room with Vivi have revolved around that schedule.

I took my time organizing my clothes—which basically took me no time at all because there is only a small dresser that's already half-full of kids' stuff. No way was I going to move it and risk getting yelled at by Gavin again. I'd rather live out of my suitcase.

As promised, there's a bunk bed in the room, but fortunately, the bottom bunk is a double mattress and surprisingly comfortable.

Though when Vivi woke in the middle of the night, I did hit my head on the top bunk. I rushed into her room, only to find Gavin already changing her. Without a word, I tiptoed to the kitchen and made a bottle. When I offered to give it to her so he could go back to sleep, he just turned away and settled in the cream-colored rocking chair, his eyes trained on Vivi and Vivi alone.

It's how it should be. He's a devoted dad. I saw that within moments of meeting Vivi, though being so easily dismissed stung. It's not that I even wanted his attention all on me. I just wanted to stand in that room and watch him rock her and talk to her in that soothing voice.

But I'm not a creeper, and his body language made it clear my presence was unwanted, so I went back to bed. Or more like I lay in bed and listened to every little sound, every creak of his movements, until he closed his bedroom door softly. Then I snuck in to check on Vivi, who was fast asleep.

It seemed I needed them more than they needed me in that moment, so I crept back to bed and tossed and turned for the rest of the night.

"What should we do today, bestie?"

From her Boppy chair on the floor, Vivi watches me, curious as ever.

"Maybe we should go for a walk. Get some fresh air?"

She babbles excitedly, kicking her feet, as if she actually understands me.

"I agree, baby girl. Fresh air will make everything better."

Once I've got Vivi bundled up in a cozy little outfit with lightning bolts that I imagine came from one of her uncles, I strap her into her car seat and clip it onto the stroller next to the door.

I can't help but chuckle, wondering if Gavin has figured out this contraption yet. I'm cooing at Vivi as I maneuver the fancy set of wheels out into the hallway. But when there's a flash of pink, I stop and do a double take. A tall woman with pink hair quickly disappears into an apartment, and the door slams shut behind her. A heartbeat later, though, it swings open again.

"Oh my gosh. Is that a baby?" The woman pokes her head out into the hall and looks one way, then the other. Then she motions me over. "Come here, but shh. Don't let anyone know I'm here."

My heart takes off at a sprint as I wheel Vivi's stroller back and step in front of it. I was under the impression that Gavin had this building on lockdown, but if that's the case, then how did this insane person get in here?

"No, that's okay. I'm just going to head back into my apartment."

She tilts her head, her brow furrowing in concern. "Are you okay?"

"Um, sure."

"Oh my gosh. You think I'm a stranger." Her face splits into a bright smile.

"Um, yeah. I don't know you. That makes you a stranger."

"True, but I'm not strange. Promise." She tosses her head back and laughs, her pink hair flying. "Okay, I'm a little strange." She holds up her hands. "Okay, I can be *a lot* strange. I admit it. But I'm not a stranger. I'm Sara's best friend."

That response does nothing to ease the trepidation running through me. "Who's Sara?"

"Oh my god," she shouts. "Maybe *you're* the stranger." She puts her hands on her hips. "How do you not know who Sara is?"

I shrug, still keeping Vivi behind me.

"She's head of PR for the team, and Brooks Langfield's girlfriend."

Oh, that Sara. "Right."

"Is that Gavin Langfield's kid? Oh my gosh." She slaps a hand to her mouth. "Are you the mom? How could you just leave her on his doorstep all alone like that?" Her blue eyes go hard, and her face flushes with anger. "Why are you here? So you can steal her back?"

Both my jaw and my stomach drop. "Oh my gosh. That's what happened?"

She pulls out her phone and unlocks it, all the while glaring at me. Her pink-tipped finger does a little circle as she points. "Who are you?"

I sigh, my heart aching for the sweet baby girl behind me. "I'm Viviane's nanny. And I'm Daniel Hall's twin sister."

Her scowl quickly morphs into a megawatt smile. Then she scampers out, grasps my hand, and gives it a tug. "Why didn't you start with that? Come in, come in."

The way she says it—as if I'm the one with something to prove and not her—puts me at ease while also making me laugh. I'm not sure how Vivi and I end up in her apartment, but for a minute, I hover at the open door and take in our surroundings. The place is much smaller than Gavin's, but it's warm and cozy. All light creams and coffee-colored everything. Serial killers don't have serene apartments like this. We should be good.

Pink girl saunters to the kitchen, her hips swaying. The woman has curves as big as her personality. It's slightly infectious. "Can I get you something to drink?"

"Um." I glance down at Vivi in her seat. She's totally chill, doing what she always does and silently taking in the world around her. Babies can sense danger, right? Or maybe that's animals. Either way, I get the sense that this girl might be delusional, but she's harmless. "I'm sorry, what's your name?"

"Oh, right. That would be helpful, huh?" She giggles as she grabs two bottles of water and returns with both of them. "I'm Lennox Kennedy," she says as she holds one bottle out to me.

The water bottle tumbles to the floor between us as I snap my attention to her face. "As in Kennedy Records?" My dad's label may be the most prestigious at the moment, but her family is rock royalty. American royalty, really. They own a little piece of every industry known to man.

She smiles, but her blue eyes dull a fraction. "The one and only."

"Wow. Do you work for the Revs?"

She shakes her head, her lips pressed together.

"The Bolts?"

Her pink hair sways as she shakes it again.

I frown, confused. "Then why do you live here?"

Her lips twist, and she hums. "About that..."

My heart stops, and my fingers go numb. Shit, she doesn't live here. She's probably a psycho off her meds who snuck in.

Slowly, hoping not to startle her, I take a step back, being sure to stay between her and the baby.

"Oh my god, will you relax?" She waves a manicured hand. "I'm just kinda sorta squatting in my best friend's apartment."

"But you're a Kennedy." I can't hide the judgment in my tone.

"And you're a Hall, yet you're nannying for the man next door," she counters.

I sigh, shoulders slumping. She has a point there.

With a nod at the couch, she asks, "Can we sit?"

I look over my shoulder, checking on Vivi. "I promised her I'd take her for a walk and some fresh air."

"Oh!" Lennox clasps her hands in front of her chest. "I love that idea. Let me grab a scarf, and I'll join you." Then she's gone, scurrying into the bedroom without waiting for a response.

Leaning over the stroller, I run a finger gently over Vivi's cheek, checking to make sure she isn't overheating. "Looks like we've got a new friend, Viv. What do you think?"

The sweetie rubs her eyes in response.

"You'll be asleep in minutes, won't you? Guess it's good I've got someone to talk to, then." I stroke her cheek again.

She grasps my hand, her tiny fingers wrapping around my thumb.

"Oh, Vivi girl," I whisper, my heart cracking open. "I'm sorry your mommy left you."

I've known this little girl for forty-eight hours, and already, I dread the day when Gavin finds a real nanny. If I can't convince him to forgive me, if I can't get him to see that I'm ready for this—to be his partner, to help him raise his little girl—then I'll have to walk away too.

And I have absolutely no idea how I'd ever do that.

I fell a little in love with Gavin the night we met, and I've been *in love* with him for almost a year. Viviane must have inherited her daddy's bewitching powers, because I'm already head over heels for her.

Lennox appears again, wrapping a black scarf around her neck.

She pulls a leather jacket from a hook near the door and slides it on over a light pink shirt that dips low, emphasizing her ample chest. I'm pretty sure each of her breasts is bigger than my head. "How long have you been banging Hockey Daddy?"

My breath gets caught in my lungs, and I have to pound a fist to my chest before I can breathe again. "Excuse me?"

"You and Hockey Daddy. How long has it been going on?"

"Is that what people are calling him?" Despite the shock she's just put me through, I giggle at the thought of Gavin's reaction to that. Old Gavin would find it hysterical. I'm not sure about this new guy, though.

She shrugs. "I don't know about people, but I am. So spill. When did you start doing the nasty?" She holds the door open wide.

This time she doesn't just get a giggle from me. It's a full-blown belly laugh. "Is this how you talk to everyone?"

Brows arched, she nods, serious. "Yes, so spill."

"I barely know you. Five minutes ago, I was trying to decide whether you were a serial killer or a harmless delusional person."

She shrugs, a big smile on her face, and leads me toward the elevator. "Jury's still out. Now tell me, is he pierced? His brother is, and let me tell you, my friend is *very satisfied*."

"Wait." I gape as she presses the call button. "Brooks Langfield is pierced?"

"Oh, was I not supposed to tell people that?" She taps a finger against her pink lips. She's like a life-size Barbie, all bright pink and bubbly. "Hmm, probably not. Brooks is pretty quiet, but Sara is a blabbermouth. You'll love her. Just you wait and see." She clutches my arm, and her eyes go wide. "But don't tell her I'm living in her apartment."

I snort as the elevator door slides open and she pushes me inside. "How does she not know?"

"She gave me a key to use one night when I was visiting, and I sorta just stayed."

Situating the stroller to one side of the small space, I side-eye her. "When was that?"

She bites her lip. "A month ago."

Head tipped back, I laugh. I haven't laughed this much in months. "But why?"

When the door opens on the ground floor, she peeks her head out and scans the lobby. "All clear."

"Who are you hiding from?"

"Sara!" she hisses, exasperated.

I scoff, even as I'm smiling. "I thought she was your best friend."

"She is, but she'll be all *Lennox, you need to grow up. Get a real job and stand up to your family.*"

"Oh, I get that. My friends are judgmental too." Just the thought of Chrishell and Taylor sends a bitter chill rolling through me that has me tugging my jacket tighter. I haven't thought of them since I got on the plane on New Year's and blocked their numbers. And good fucking riddance.

Lennox turns around and gives me a far too knowing frown. "That came out wrong. Sara really is the best. She'd be right to yell at me. I do need to grow up and stand up to my family. Just need a few more days—or weeks—to lick my wounds." She stares at me for another beat, then she spins and heads to the door.

Outside, I adjust Vivi's hat, pull her blanket up to her chin, and adjust the canopy of her seat to block the cool wind. April in Boston is still chilly, but the sun is out, and the breeze is mild. "Where to?"

She shrugs. "I've barely left the apartment—too afraid to be caught. You know where to get good coffee around here?"

I pull out my phone. "I just moved here, so Google it is."

We find a spot and head down the street, following the map on my phone.

"So Hockey Daddy?" she teases.

"Wow." I grip the stroller and shake my head. "You're like a dog with a bone."

"I could take my guesses, but if I do, you might blush." One eyebrow lifted, she smirks.

"No, please, have at it."

She rubs her hands together in glee. "Fine. If I had to guess, you've done just about everything with him, and it's not new."

I blow out a breath to combat the tightness in my chest. "It's definitely not new. In fact, it's so old it's over."

"No it's not." Her smile is kind. "It may feel that way, but I've known Gavin most of my life." She pulls the coffeeshop door open and holds it for me. "He's wildly protective of his brothers, so I can only imagine he'd be far more so with his daughter. So if he's allowing you to take care of her, to move in and be alone with her, then I promise, it's not over."

I ignore the way that lights a fire in my belly and how my heart races at just the thought of him allowing me to truly be part of their lives.

"How do you know him so well?" I ask as I push the stroller inside.

She points to the corner where there's a table lined with cozy benches. The sun filters in, softly highlighting the quaint space in a heavenly glow. "Go sit with Vivi. I'll grab food and drinks. What do you want?"

Once she's got my order and has popped into line, I park the stroller beside the table. As expected, Vivi fell asleep in her seat. It takes everything in me not to pull her out and hold her against my chest. Never wake a sleeping baby, they say, but *they*, whoever they are, have never spent time with this beautiful girl.

Snuggling with her was irresistible before. Now that I know that her mother just left her outside Gavin's door? Yeah, I get why Gavin doesn't put her down.

Last night, while I couldn't sleep, I finally googled his name. The images that populated included dozens of him skating around at practice and before games with her in a sling on his chest.

If I ever see that in person, my ovaries might just jump out of my body and latch themselves on to him, begging him to impregnate me.

It's wild. Only a few months ago, the idea freaked me out. But now...God, Gavin as a father? It's otherworldly and so damn hot.

Lennox plops onto the bench across from me. "I used to date his brother."

I tear my attention away from Vivi. "Huh?"

"You asked how I knew Gavin so well. His brother was my high school sweetheart."

Jeez, this girl's ability to pop from one topic to another makes it hard to keep up.

"Brooks?"

She laughs. "That'd be awkward, right?" Her lashes dip down. "No. Aiden." If I'm not mistaken, his name comes out softer.

"Ah, the funny one. I can see that."

She smiles.

"Is he still dating that vapid woman all the guys hate?"

Lennox lifts her shoulder in a shrug. "No idea. I don't really ask about him, and we don't talk."

Oh, hmm. Lennox doesn't seem like the type to leave a relationship on bad terms. She just seems...I don't know, direct, maybe?

"Was he a jerk in high school?"

Her blue eyes widen, and she laughs. "God no. I don't think that boy has a mean bone in his body."

"So what's the story, then?"

She pulls her shoulders back and smirks. "It's ancient history, that's what it is. Yours, on the other hand"—she looks pointedly at Vivi, then me—"is very much in play. So tell me, how do we fix things with Hockey Daddy and get you the happy you so obviously want?"

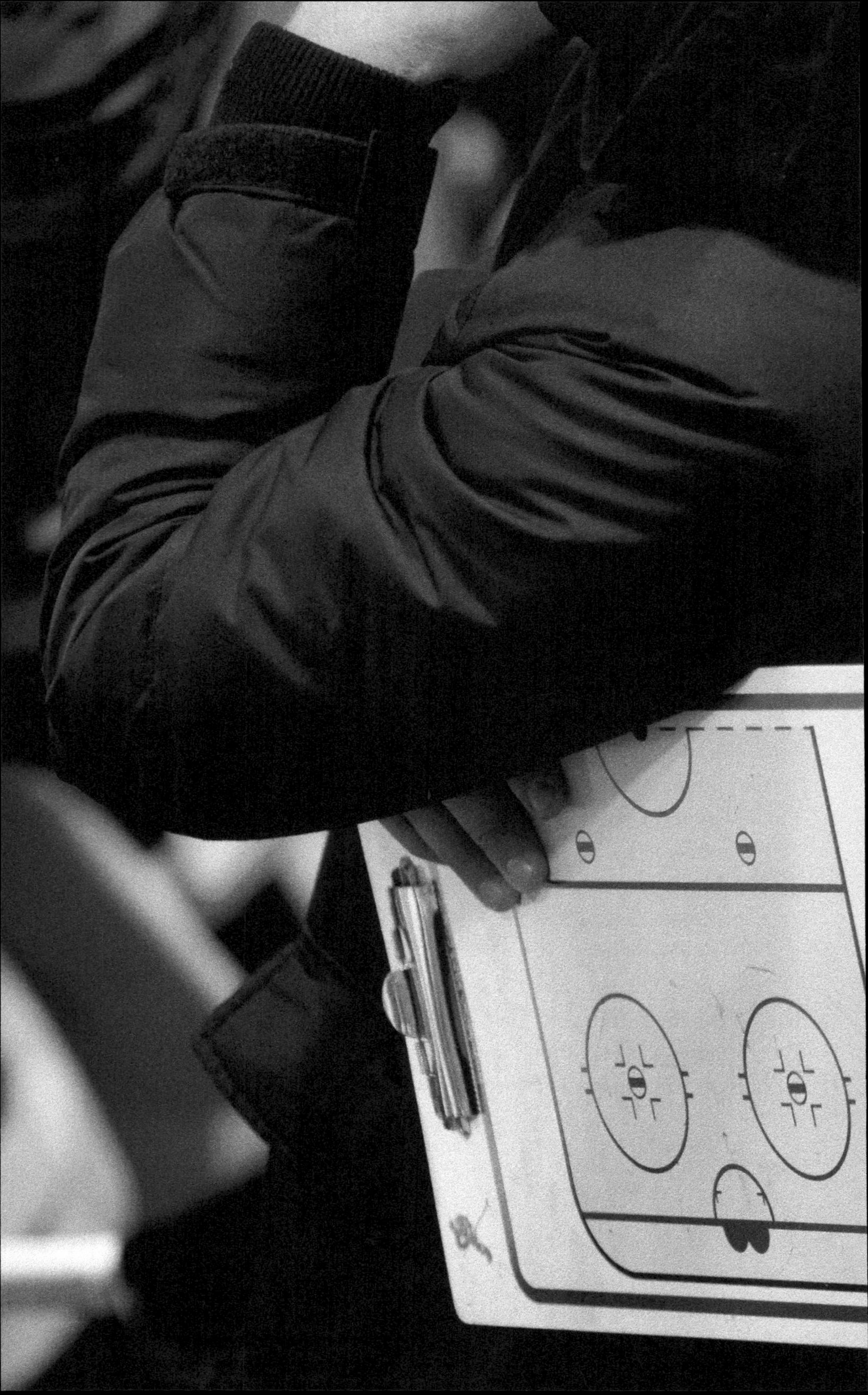

CHAPTER 34
Gavin

"WAR, you're favoring your left side again. New York knows it. Aiden, stop with the fancy shit. Hall, what the fuck?" My blood is pumping, and the cool air burns my lungs. This is exactly what I needed after this weekend.

"They're looking good." Beckett skates toward me with the twins strapped to his body.

"Are you nuts?" I growl, grasping his shoulder and pulling him toward the bench so that my nieces are out of the way of the guys who are in the middle of a fucking practice match.

He breaks out into a practiced smile and waves at someone behind me.

I follow his gaze to the edge of the rink and find Sara pointing a camera in our direction. "What are you doing?"

"You think you're the only Langfield who can wear your kid? The news is going nuts over how cute you are. Try wearing *two kids*."

"You realize you're insane, right? I brought my kid because I had no one else to watch her. Where's Livy?"

"She's at the office going over the travel schedule with Hannah. She stopped by with the babies, and I said I'd take them for a walk so she could relax. Let her feel like a human again instead of just a mom."

He stands tall and proud, chest puffed out as he adjusts the twins and then smiles again. But I know his games. The man never smiles like that. This is all for the fucking cameras.

"Does she know you brought them to my hockey practice hoping the media would plaster photos of her daughters all over the internet?" I tip my head toward Sara. "Or on the Bolts' Instagram account?"

"I didn't—"

I cut him off with a scoff. He *did*.

"Fine. Whatever. I'm leaving." He turns in a smooth circle and heads toward the gate.

"Wait." I skate that way too, catching up. "Don't leave. I—" I grit my teeth and swallow my pride. "I need your help."

Beckett's eyes shine. The last thing I want to do is stroke his ego, but he's got his shit together better than the rest of us, and that makes him my best resource. Even if he is mildly neurotic.

"Give me the twins and take off your skates, and then we can chat in my office."

Once we're off the ice, Beckett removes one twin from her carrier and hands her to me, then the other. It's wild how much more comfortable I am with them now that I have Vivi. Though she's about the size of the two of them put together. I holler to Fitz to take over and tell the guys I'll see them when they're done on the ice. We still have film to watch and plays to discuss for our game against New York this week.

In my office, cups of coffee in hand and a twin on each of our laps, I tell him everything.

"So she's going to live with you for the foreseeable future?" Beckett watches me with an all-knowing look that makes me squirm. "And travel with you?"

"Yeah."

"And Ford has no idea about you two?"

I bow my head. "You think I'd still have this perfect face if he did?"

Beckett chuckles and rubs a hand over Maggie's head. "True." With a huff, he shifts in his seat, repositioning her. "This is a ducking problem if I ever heard one."

"Tell me about it."

"You can't duck her."

I roll my eyes. "Obviously."

"Don't *obviously* me. It should have been obvious a year ago when you started a damn relationship with the girl—"

"I fell in—" I stop myself. I can't go back to that time. "I won't."

"She hurt you and told you she wasn't ready for this." He nods at June, who's drifting off in my free arm. "And can you blame her? Remember us at twenty-four?"

My laugh is short and sarcastic. "No. I honestly don't. Those years are a bit of a blur for me."

"Exactly. Not being ready doesn't make her a bad person. She's too young."

My heart revolts at that idea. She's not too anything when it comes to me. She's perfect. Which is why I can barely look at her. It's why I can barely stand watching her with Vivi. The life I wanted, the life I would have given up everything for, is a live dream playing out in front of me. A taunt. A tease.

I can touch it, and I can *feel* it, but in the end, it won't last. There's a time limit. An expiration date. She won't be ours forever, so I can't let her be ours for even a minute.

"Vivi comes first," my brother says, voicing my exact thoughts.

I keep my focus on the lid of my coffee cup and dip my chin. "I know."

He taps his foot against mine. "You can do this."

With a deep breath in, I look up. "I don't really have any other choice, huh?"

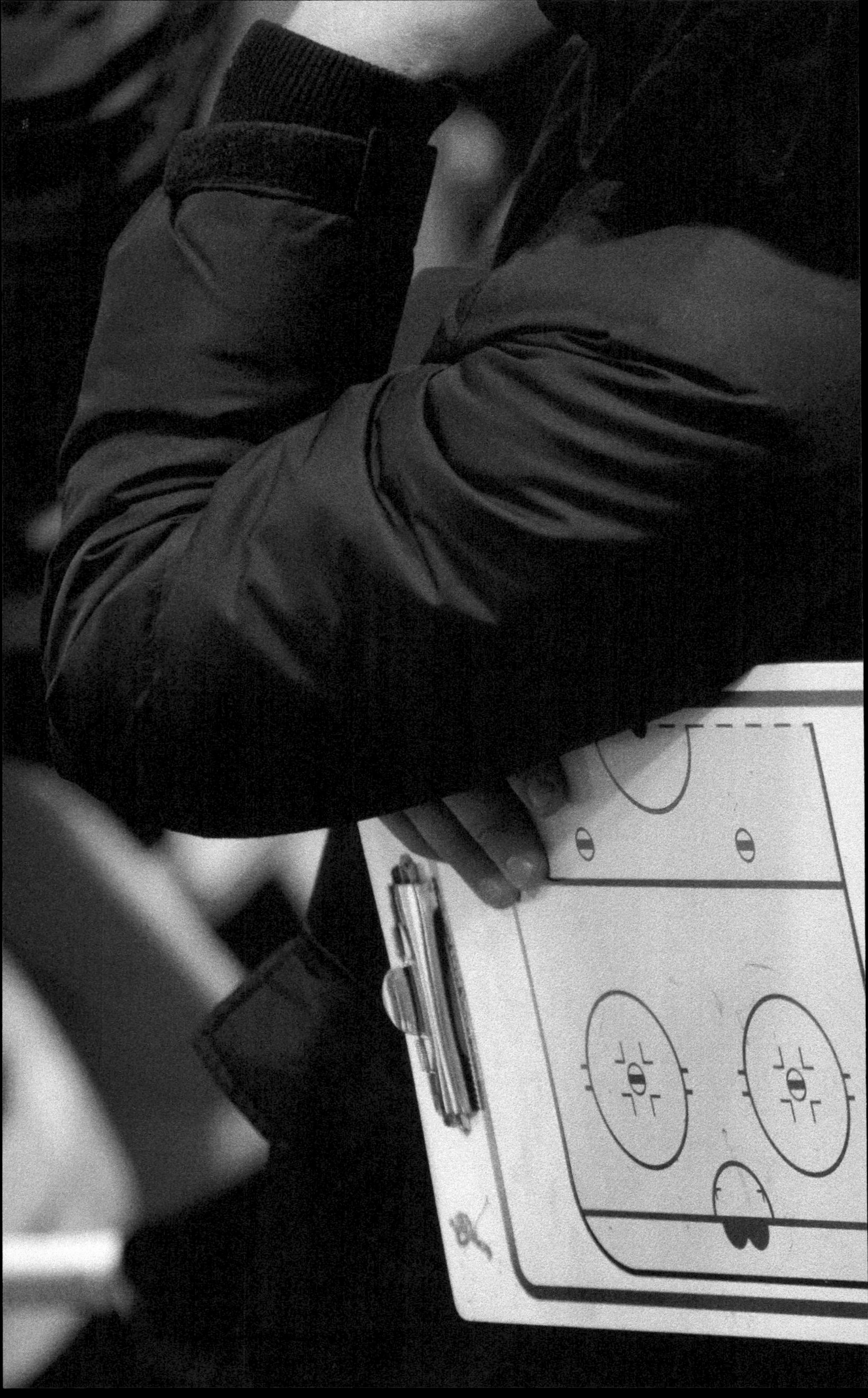

CHAPTER 35
Gavin

MY BROTHER CAME up with a fantastic plan to keep me from obsessing over Millie.

"Uncle Gav, are you as excited about this sleepover as I am? I brought my *Spiderman* sleeping bag, my toothbrush, seven bags of popcorn for movie night, orange soda, Hector, my blue shirt, and my John Cena shorts so we can wrestle later."

Uneasy, I stick the key in the lock and turn back to the little guy. "Who's Hector?"

Please tell me my brother didn't let this kid get another pet.

He's constantly collecting animals that are not actually pets: raccoons. Snakes. One time he even came home with a lizard. He brought it on the plane and everything after Beckett took all of Liv's best friends and their husbands to Florida for an early Christmas present.

"He's my robot."

Ah. A robot I can handle. With a relieved sigh, I open the door and usher Finn and his duffel full of prized possessions inside. I breathe easier when I don't immediately find Millie sitting on the couch, her hair up in a ponytail, teasing me.

God, even when she has her glasses on and she's dressed in sweats, I'm fucking obsessed. Especially when, in the middle of writing a piece, she pushes those glasses into her curly mess of hair and bites her lip, deep in thought. She'll be so focused I can do nothing but watch in awe of the melody she creates.

"Uncle Gav," Finn hollers from the guest bedroom. "Someone's been sleeping in my bed. Do you have a robot friend too?"

I laugh at the four-foot ball of energy. He's bouncing on his toes outside what used to be his room, sleeping bag in one hand, blue and orange robot in the other. A few years ago, my brother had to shave his head after an unfortunate incident with a pair of scissors, and for a while, he sported what we all referred to as *the Army Finn* look, but when Cortney Miller moved into the brownstone, the little guy was obsessed with his man bun. Throw Brooks into the mix, and there was no changing his mind, so he grew his hair out like two of his favorite guys. But Finn's isn't straight and smooth like Cortney "Man Bun" Miller's hair, and it isn't wavy like Uncle Brooks's. No, it's grown into a full-on bush on his head, and right now, as he bounces, it barely moves, making me laugh even harder.

"Remember how I told you Vivi has a new babysitter?"

He nods, head tipped back. "Yup."

"She sleeps here so she can take care of Vivi all the time, so she's been using your bed."

Finn's face lights up. "So I get to sleep on the top bunk?"

Uh, that'd be a no. The kid never stops moving while he's awake, and I don't have a clue what he does while he sleeps. The last thing I want to do is leave him unattended when he's suspended five feet off the ground.

Chuckling, I take his sleeping bag from him and head to my bedroom. "Nah, tonight we're having a bros' sleepover in my room."

Finn's responding *cool* is said in an awe-filled whisper.

Just as I'm shaking his sleeping bag out, the apartment door opens and closes.

"Honey, we're home," Millie sings in a teasing tone that has my back going ramrod straight.

Finn bounces and lets out a little gasp of excitement. "Is that the nanny and Vivi?"

I ignore the pinch in my chest that spreads at just the thought of Millie and my daughter together. Game face on, head held high, I walk toward the door. "Yes, Finn. That'd be them."

The apartment is shockingly silent after what can only be described as a very loud night. After kissing Vivi good night, I brought Finn into bed, and we watched a movie until he fell asleep. Now I've been sitting in my room staring at my phone, wondering if the coast is clear for me to go hang out on the couch for a bit. I've been reading a few parenting books, and I normally use this time of night when it's quiet to truly focus. Even if I only get a chapter done, it's better than nothing.

I slide out of bed and quietly tiptoe through the room, sighing when Finn doesn't stir. Any modicum of relief is quickly snuffed out when I spot Millie standing in the moonlit living room beside the grand piano.

For a moment, I hold my breath, afraid to make even the smallest sound when all I want to do is watch her unapologetically. The creamy expanse of her shoulder teases me as she presses closer to the piano, her fingers ghosting over the ivories.

"You should use it." The worlds tumble out of my mouth.

Millie startles and hits the keys, the sound jarringly loud. "Sorry."

I swallow and then double down. I'm a fucking masochist. "Not tonight, obviously, but feel free to use it."

She turns back to the keys, her fingers gliding softly against them, not pressing to make a sound, just maybe acclimating herself to them.

"It's so beautiful," she whispers, her voice filled with awe and longing.

It's how I feel every moment that I stand here staring at the woman I want more than my next breath, even as I'm perfectly aware that I can't have her. "Use it, Millie. I bought it for—" I clear my throat, looking away. *Fuck.* I'm sure my ears are tinged red as my entire body heats.

Millie's already walking toward me. "What?"

My fight-or-flight instinct kicks in. Allowing her close to me right now would be a disaster. I'm weak. Tired. Desperate.

I brush past her as I spot the book I came out to read on the table. "Nothing. Forget it. Use it or don't. I don't care either way." Then I grab the parenting book and head for the front door, hoping none of the guys are out here hanging in the common area.

I almost smile when I realize which parenting book I grabbed. *The Single Dad's Survival Guide.*

I'm already taking out my pen, knowing the note I'll be jotting in the margin and underlining three times: <u>Don't Fuck The Nanny.</u>

"Stop moving," I growl, eyes squeezed shut.

The kid kicked out of his sleeping bag minutes after I climbed into bed. I swear he's a trapeze artist in his sleep. My kidneys will never be the same after a night like last night.

"Uncle Gav, Uncle Gav."

At the urgency in his voice, I force my eyes open and focus on him in the dim early-morning light. He's sitting up beside me, holding a pillow over his head, worry lining his face.

I jackknife up, ready to face whatever has him upset. Once again,

I can't help but suspect that he brought one of his pets over and it's now loose in my bed. "What's wrong, buddy?"

He points at the mattress beneath him with a huff.

Holding my breath, I scan for a bug or another critter, but it looks like it's just the two of us.

"My tooth!" he shrieks.

I'm still half-asleep, so I'm a little slow, yeah, but I'm struggling to follow the conversation. "Your tooth?"

Finn opens his mouth wide and points to a hole along his bottom teeth.

Motherducker, how'd I miss that?

"It came out while I was brushing my teeth last night. I put it under my pillow just like I'm sposed to. Then I touched the red light on your clock and made my wish, but it didn't come true."

Pinching the bridge of my nose, I sit up against the headboard. "Touched the red light?"

"Yeah. Phoebe and Collette said you gotta touch the red light at 11:11 and make a wish."

"That's a different thing."

"My tooth is still here," Finn whimpers, his volume getting louder.

"Shh." I grasp his hand and check the clock.

Six a.m. I didn't hear Vivi get up in the middle of the night, and though I'd love to believe she slept through the night, I have no doubt Millie was up with her, even though I told her I'd prefer taking the night shift. Traveling with a tired nanny this week seems less than ideal.

"Bossman said this wouldn't happen again." Finn crosses his arms, a big pout on his face. He's wearing his John Cena pajamas, and as he promised, we wrestled as soon as he put them on last night.

Despite the panic rolling through me because I don't have a clue how to fix this situation, I can't help but smile at the kid. He's awfully fucking cute, even when he's upset.

"Finn, bud, I'm sure there's a reason the tooth fairy didn't come. Maybe she only comes to your house."

Finn's eyes widen. "The tooth fairy isn't a *girl!*"

Oh. Oh shit. I really am not winning here.

Instead of cringing, I play it cool and shrug. "Right. Of course. Your tooth fairy would definitely be a dude."

Finn growls, sounding so much like Beckett it's hard to believe he's not his biological child. "Sensei is not a dude."

"Finn—"

He holds out his palm. *See? All Beckett.* "Sensei is a fairy. Fairies are neither male nor female."

I nod and bite the inside of my cheek to keep from laughing. "Got it. So this Sensei character..."

Finn nods as if that's the correct terminology.

"Maybe Sensei didn't know that you were here."

"Sensei senses everything," Finn grits out.

I drop my head between my shoulders and squeeze my eyes shut. I am so in over my fucking head. "I'm gonna need coffee to continue this conversation."

"But what about my money?" Finn holds out his palm.

Ah. It's about the tooth fairy money. I can fix this.

I throw my legs over the side of the bed and shuffle to the dresser. "How much does Sensei normally leave you?" I ask as I open my wallet.

"Thousand," Finn says matter-of-factly.

I spin, frowning, and nearly trip over him. The ninja kid somehow made his way over from the bed without a sound.

"A thousand what? Pennies?"

Finn scoffs. "Dollars, Uncle Gav. What, do you think we're poor?"

"Bossman and I are going to have a chat. Does this money go to the swear jar account?" I stride back to the nightstand and pick up my phone. I've added plenty to the swear jar, so I'm sure I can find the info in my list of transactions.

Finn presses his lips together and looks at me like I'm an idiot, arms folded across his chest again. "Do you think I would let the Shining Twins have access to my tooth money?"

At a loss, I hold up my hands in defeat. "No idea, Finn. But I take it the answer is no. So where exactly do you want me to Venmo your money?"

Finn leans closer. "It's gotta be cash," he whispers.

"What?"

"Mommy won't let me have my own Venmo account."

I chuckle. Liv would die if she knew Finn was scamming me out of a thousand dollars cash, but I don't really have a choice, do I? I can't crush the kid's spirit. "Okay, Finn. We'll get cash on our way home." And then my brother will be reimbursing me. A thousand dollars for a tooth. Guy is nuts.

An hour later, Finn and I are scarfing down pancakes when Millie appears with a smiling Vivi in her arms. My little girl is dressed only in a diaper and kicking her bare legs happily.

"No clothes?" I say, zeroing in on my child, wishing I could block her nanny out completely.

Millie waltzed in here wearing a pair of shorts barely long enough to be appropriate in the presence of children. What's worse than the shorts and the creamy expanse of her thighs, though, is the oversized Bolts T-shirt she's wearing. Because the damn thing is mine. I know it's mine because I gave it to her when we were still together. It's one of the old-school ones in the original Bolts' royal blue. We've since shifted to a more muted hue. Even worse is the fact that she's clearly not wearing a bra—when does she ever?—and her nipples poke against the fabric.

When she turns, I swear the shape of her nipple has changed.

Like maybe there's something clamped onto it. But when I squint to get a better look, she turns again, and when I look up, she's smirking at me.

I avert my gaze and stuff a giant chunk of pancake into my mouth. Fuck, she's going to be the death of me.

Unfazed, Millie plops down in the seat beside me. "Figured our girl will just make a mess, so I'll give her a bath and get her dressed after breakfast. Right, Viv?"

Our girl.

Those two words are even more dangerous than the way the woman beside me is dressed. They have the power to send me tumbling into a fantasy I won't let myself imagine. It will never happen, so it's safer to avoid even considering it.

I'll just ignore it. Ignore her.

If Millie's bothered by my lack of response, she doesn't show it. Instead, she turns her attention on the toothless kid across from her. "How'd you sleep?"

Finn shoots me a look. "Well, this one snores," he points his thumb at me, "and I think he scared the tooth fairy away."

She giggles. "Oh, look at that. You did lose a tooth."

Finn nods, his head bobbing in an exaggerated way. "But the tooth fairy didn't leave me any moneys."

Millie sticks her lip out in a pout. "Don't you worry. Next time you stay over, you can have your bed back, and I'll have a sleepover with Uncle Gav instead." She winks in my direction.

Jaw clenched, I scowl at her.

"You don't mind his snores?"

Millie's smile is so wicked I almost laugh. "I sleep like the dead. It's all good."

"Cool," Finn says, his lips turned down in an impressed expression.

"No," I grit out.

"Why not?" Finn asks. "Millie is pretty. And I don't think she smells." He leans across the table and sniffs. "Oh, you smell good. Like pancakes."

"That's the food on the table," I bark, dropping my fork to my plate with a clatter.

Millie bites back a smile, but her eyes dance. "I don't know, Uncle Gav. Want to test it out for yourself?" She pulls her messy curls back, exposing the spot on her neck she knows I love.

"Witchy woman," I growl, only to instantly regret it.

Her brown eyes go wide, and her breath catches. Fuck. There's no way she isn't thinking about the night we met and everything that happened after she sang that song. I know I certainly am.

So much for forgetting. *Fuck.*

Hours later, after having a nice long chat with my brother about his kid's expensive tooth and a cold, cold shower, my mood has improved. We'll be on the road for the next week, which means I'll be surrounded by the guys almost constantly. Surely that'll keep me distracted from the nanny who never seems to leave my brain.

The coaches and our assistants typically sit near the front of the plane, and the players sit near the back. It's better this way. Gives us some distance from the ruckus. The guys tend to get a little rowdy in anticipation of a series. They're excited. I get it.

Since Ava isn't traveling with us, I made sure she's set up to order breakfast for the pediatric unit at the hospital this weekend. I owe her big time, and this is just a start. She's close to a girl battling cancer, Josie, and she and Sara visit with her as often as possible. When I told her I'd hired a nanny and that she wouldn't have to spend the next ten days on the road with us, she all but melted to the floor in relief.

War is sitting in my seat when I step onto the plane. "Vivi girl!" He holds out his arms.

She squeals and arches her back in excitement. She's quite possibly the happiest baby that's ever lived.

"You're in my seat."

"Come on, Coach. Figured you could use a break. Go hang with the team, and I'll keep an eye on our girl here." He points to Vivi, but I have the sneaking suspicion he's talking about the nanny who's walking up behind me.

"Nice try." I nod toward the back. "Beat it."

War pushes up to a stand, big smirk on his face, and leans in to kiss Vivi's cheek. "Your papa used to be much more chill, Vivi girl. We gotta work on him."

My daughter grabs hold of War's thumb and yanks, bringing it to her mouth. Before she can make contact, I gently pry her fingers off. "Get away from my daughter."

With a rumbling laugh, he saunters down the aisle. On one side of the aisle is a set of oversized leather seats with tables between them. The seats on the other side have no table.

Before Vivi, I would sit at a table. Always.

I'd have my coffee, talk to the coach—at the time my scumbag uncle—laughing or smiling the whole way.

But I'm not that man anymore. It's not lost on me that I don't smile as much. I'm trying. But it's hard to keep up the façade when I'm focused on keeping my head above water.

Millie waits for me to sit, still holding the diaper bag and her carry-on. What I want to do—what would put an instant smile on my face—is take Vivi and Millie to the corner in the front of the plane where it's just us. I want to hold Millie's hand during takeoff while she cradles my daughter. I want to smile at her while Vivi dozes in her arms, and I want to whisper secrets, tuning out the rest of the world.

What I'm going to do, though, is very different. "I've got it from here."

Millie's lips turn down and her brows pull together. "Huh?"

"Set the diaper bag on that seat right there." I wave a dismissive hand. "Then go sit in the back with your brother."

"Don't you need me to help?" Even as she asks it, she sounds resigned to my answer.

Yes is what makes sense. It's why I hired her. It's why she's on this plane and in my life. But I can't be that close to her. Not in such an enclosed space.

"No. You'll be with her all week. This is the perfect chance for you to have a break and for me to spend time alone with her before I have to deal with practice and games and the media circus." Without waiting for Millie to reply, I settle in the seat by the window and fix my attention on the tarmac. Even as I avoid her gaze, it's impossible not to feel the shock radiating off her.

It eats at me, this uncontrollable feeling, making me hate myself with every second that I don't return her gaze.

"Baby Hall, you're traveling with us!" At the sound of Camden Snow's voice, I can't help but turn. Camden—"Ice" to his teammates and fans—puts a hand on Millie's waist and steps up close.

Mine, I want to growl. *Hands off.*

Instead, I bite down and keep my mouth shut.

Millie's frown morphs into a smile. "Sure am. Can I sit with you? Apparently, I'm not needed up here." Her tone is sticky sweet and fake as can be.

We're both playing roles that we don't want to perform, but it's better this way.

Or at least that's what I'll keep telling myself.

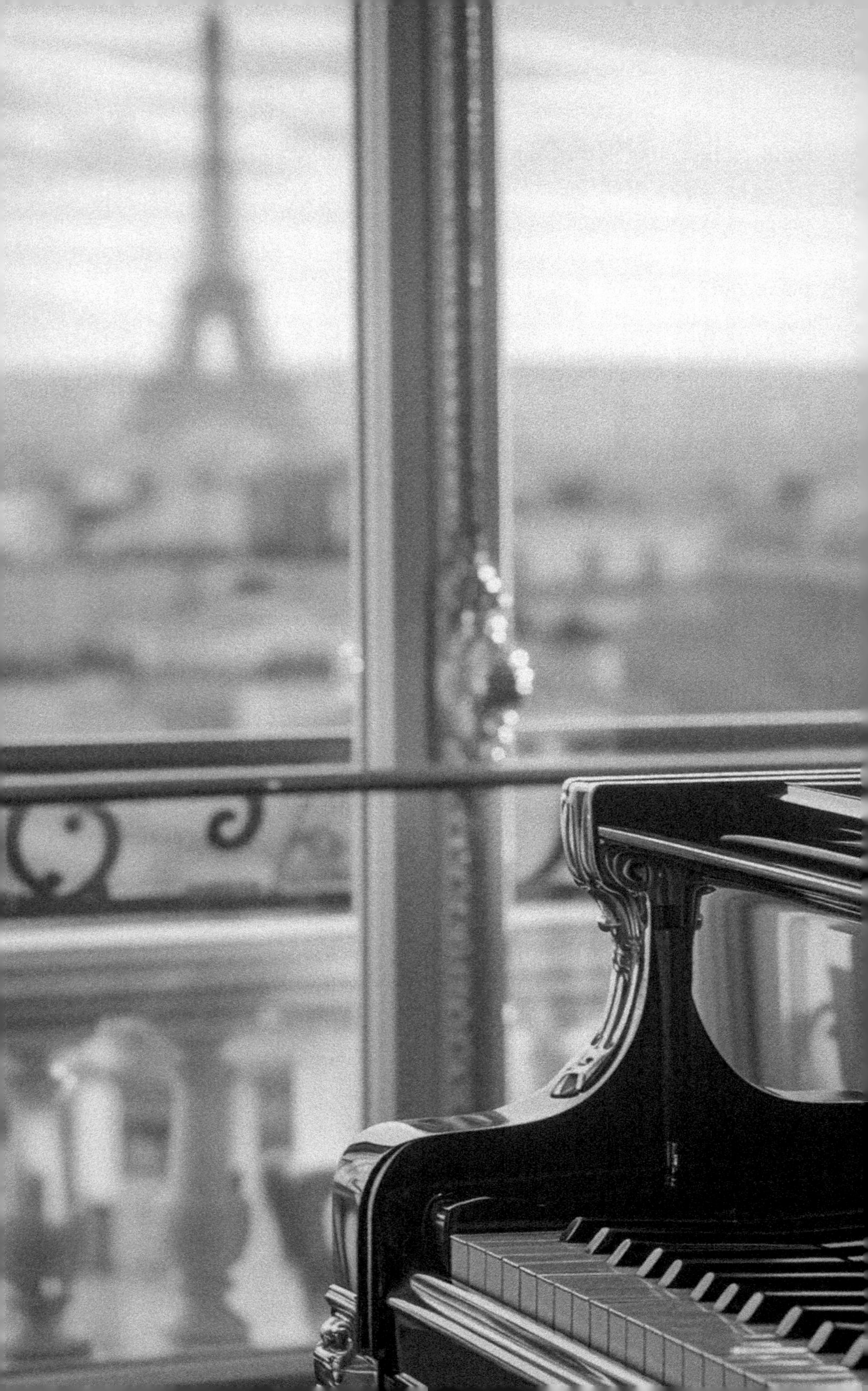

CHAPTER 36
Millie

CAMDEN DROPS into a seat and pats the empty one beside him, signaling for me to take it, his smile nothing but genuine.

"She's sitting with me," Daniel says, motioning to the empty spot beside him and zeroing in on me. "I want answers, and you've been avoiding me."

Stomach in knots, I settle in beside Camden. I've had just about enough with the attitudes of the men in my life today. I'm not answering my brother's inquisition any more than I'm dealing with the asshole up front.

We had a moment last night with the piano. I know we did. I don't even know what to make of his admission that he bought it for me. When? Why? His vulnerable admission was a slip of the tongue, obviously, but it was something. Which just means that now he's putting even more distance between us. One step forward, seven hundred back.

"Oh, looks like you're hanging with me, Playboy." Aiden plops down next to my brother.

My brother shoots daggers at me, then turns to Camden and holds two fingers out, motioning from his eyes to his buddy and back in the universal sign for *I'm watching you.*

The guy beside me laughs. "We haven't officially met. I'm Camden." He holds out his hand, and when I slide my palm against his, he squeezes it gently.

A gentleman. How nice.

"Millie, or as everyone here likes to call me, Baby Hall."

He grins, and his dimple pops. His nose is crooked—probably from being broken a time or two—but he's pretty all the same. "How's working with Coach?"

My smile is a bit more forced this time. *Terrible. Awful.* Yet I wouldn't want to be anywhere else.

If the term *glutton for punishment* had a face, it'd look like mine.

"It's fine. Vivi's a peach, so it makes my job easy." The minute the words are out of my mouth, I regret them. How is it that one man could single-handedly destroy a saying—hell, the name of an innocent piece of fruit—like that?

I'm going to need a new drink of choice if our relationship doesn't turn a corner soon.

"She's a cute kid. Still can't believe someone could just dump her like that."

Aiden scowls at Camden in a way that looks so foreign on his typically cheerful face.

Oblivious, Camden keeps talking. "I was there, ya know? It was crazy."

Nibbling on my lip, I consider whether to ask when this was. If anyone knows who the mother is. Whether Gavin has spoken to her. But that would be inappropriate. It's none of my business. And also, Aiden might bite our heads off if we keep this conversation going.

"Hey," I say to Aiden, another thought popping into my head. "I met someone who knows you."

Aiden's smile is back in place, his warm brown eyes relaxed. He's got the same chiseled jaw as Gavin does, along with the rest of the Langfield men, but his golden-brown curls give him a boyish charm that softens the severity of the feature. "Oh yeah? Who?"

"Lennox Kennedy."

His eyes flash bright, and he opens his mouth, but no words come out.

"When did you see Lennox?"

The feminine voice startles me, and I spin in my seat.

The woman in the seat behind me is dressed in black slacks and a blue sweater and has blond hair pulled into a ponytail and vibrant blue eyes.

Beside her, Brooks Langfield nods to me. The man is a beast. Thick wavy brown hair just a smidgen longer than Aiden's and wise green eyes. If it was possible to make a copy of Aiden and enlarge it by about 20 percent, it would look just like Brooks. He's built like a giant—perfect for his position as goalie—but he's got the gentlest personality of all the Langfields.

"This is Sara, my girlfriend. She heads PR for the team."

Sara...Sara...why does that sound familiar?

Oh shit, Sara is Lennox's best friend. The one whose apartment she's squatting in. "Oh, I met her in a coffee shop," I fib.

Sara looks at Brooks and frowns. "When did she get back into town?"

Aiden clears his throat. "She mentioned me?"

Brooks barks out a laugh behind me. "Could you be more obvious?"

I shimmy my shoulders, still turned halfway around. "Obvious about what? What's the tea?"

Sara sits back in her chair, her shoulders lowering, and eyes Aiden, then me. "Just that Aiden has a little crush he doesn't want to talk about."

"Do not." Aiden's tone is comical, like a five-year-old saying he doesn't have cooties.

I arch my brow. "That's too bad, because she certainly seemed—" I tap my finger on my lips, searching for the right word—"wistful."

"Yes. You thought so too?" Sara scoots forward and leans around my seat. "Because she acts so strange every time I bring him up."

"Yeah, I could see that. Like maybe she has a lot more to say but is afraid to talk about it?"

Sara slaps her hand on my armrest. "Exactly."

"Hello! I'm right here." Aiden waves, making us all laugh.

"Dude, dump Jill," Brooks says.

Those three words are like a bucket of cold water. Aiden clams up, and the rest of us shift in our seats a little awkwardly.

"Switch seats with me," Daniel says to Camden.

"Oh my god, are you serious right now?" I glare at my brother. "There's nothing to tell. No need to grill me. I'm nannying, and now I get to travel with you to your games. Don't drive me nuts, or I'll hang with Camden tonight instead of you."

My brother glowers at the man beside me. "Wipe that damn smile off your face. You aren't spending any time with my sister alone."

I laugh as I lean back in my seat and pull out my phone to put it on airplane mode. "I'm done with you." I slip an earbud into the ear closest to Daniel and turn to Camden. "So, tell me about yourself."

Camden stretches out beside me, his arm bumping mine on the armrest, and tells me all about his life as a professional hockey player. It takes real talent to keep from full-on beaming at the daggers my brother is launching at us the entire time. We're about forty minutes into the hour-long flight to New York, and I'm laughing hard at yet another of Camden's stories, when Vivi lets out a wail. An instant later, a red-faced Gavin appears next to my seat, bouncing an equally red-faced Vivi in his arms.

"Is she o—"

"Could you come help me, please?" Gavin growls, his eyes dark. "And you—" He glowers at Camden, and when he notices how close our arms are positioned on the armrest, his expression goes murderous. "I told you to stay away from my nanny."

"Hey," I hiss, quickly unbuckling and reaching for a now screaming Vivi. I rub circles on her back and storm to the front of the plane.

It seems we've taken another seven thousand steps back.

The hall is silent as Gavin waves the key card in front of the sensor. After a solid hour, Vivi finally settled down and fell asleep. When we checked in, Gavin told the front desk to move us to a room where we wouldn't disturb his players or other guests in case the crying started up again, so we're at the end of what looks like a deserted floor. I'm just thinking it's a pretty great setup when we step inside and realize this is a one-bedroom suite with a single king-size bed.

"I'll go lay her down," I offer, glancing at the couch and hoping like hell it pulls out.

Gavin's jaw ticks as he eyes it too.

The blinds in the bedroom are already closed, and the light at the door casts enough of a glow to allow me to see what I'm doing as I settle Vivi on the bed and stack pillows around her to keep her there for a moment while I set up the playpen. Poor thing wore herself out with all the crying.

Out in the main room, I find Gavin pulling out the couch. "Here, let me help." I tiptoe to the closet to find the bedding, and when I return, the bed is out and the cushions are thrown beside it haphazardly.

"I've got it." He reaches for the bundle of bedding in my arms.

I pull them to my chest and turn away. "I'll do it. It's my bed."

"You're not sleeping on the pull-out."

I grip the bedding tighter and take a step back. "Well, you certainly aren't."

Eyes downcast, he heaves out a breath, his chest rising and falling. "We're *not* sharing a bed."

I can't hold back the aggravated sound that works its way from my throat. "Oh my god, Gavin. I'm not trying to share a fucking bed. It's my job to watch Vivi. You need sleep so you're ready for the game. I'll set up the playpen by the couch and sleep out here with her. Shut the door and put on headphones or something."

"No."

"Do you realize how unreasonable you're being? You've made it abundantly clear that I'm the help. So it makes sense that I belong on the couch."

Gavin works his jaw, and then he deflates. "You're not—"

My phone rings, and he snaps his mouth shut.

Dammit. I silently groan, frustrated that, for the first time, he seemed like he might say something worth hearing, but my damn phone had to interrupt the moment. I quickly pull it out of my pocket and silence it.

When I do, Gavin is already across the room, standing in front of the bedroom door.

"Take it outside," he murmurs. "I don't want to wake the baby." With that, he steps into the room and shuts the door behind him.

I squeeze the sheets in my fists and hold in another silent scream. This man and his mood swings are going to be the fucking death of me.

THE HOCKEY REPORT

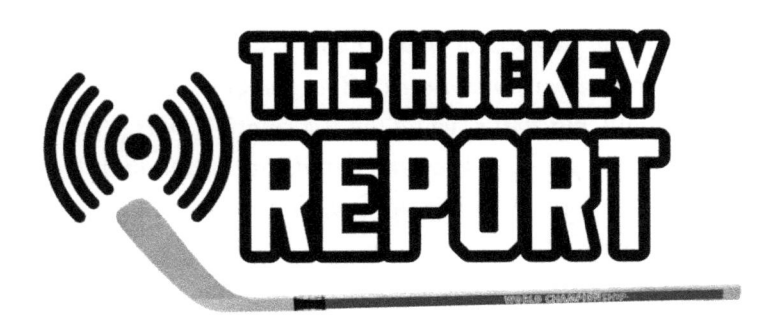

"Good Morning, Boston. Colton and Eliza here, and we've got the Hockey Report."

"This is a nerve-racking weekend in Boston, for sure. Tomorrow, the Bolts face New York for the first time since either team's change in leadership."

"And they're playing on New York's ice," Colton adds.

"The last time they faced off, Sebastian Lukov was still the coach of the Bolts. Now he's taken over as head coach in New York."

"For those of you who don't remember, the last time these teams faced off, Vincent Lukov instigated an altercation which had Bolts goalie Brooks Langfield leaving the net and charging to the boards, where he then took swing after swing at Sebastian Lukov," Colton says. "Lukov was let go as Bolts coach that weekend and then, as we all know, Gavin Langfield appointed himself as coach."

"Rumor is that if the Bolts make it to the playoffs, Lukov is entitled to a rather large bonus. Clauses like this are typical. It discourages teams from firing coaches near the end of the season to avoid paying bonuses when they make it so far. Of course, that's not what happened here."

"No, Eliza. There's been a lot of speculation surrounding Sebastian's termination. We know that Lukov, who was married, had an affair with Sara Case, who works in PR for the Bolts and is now dating Brooks Langfield, but that's where the information ends. Bolts ownership has said they prefer to keep the details out of the public eye, but that if Sebastian chooses to stir the pot, they're more than willing to provide all the facts."

"Sounds like it will be a tense game on and off the ice. Let's hope our goalie stays where he's meant to this time around and the fighting is limited to possession of the puck. We'll be back with a more in-depth look at the lineup for tomorrow's game after a word from our sponsors."

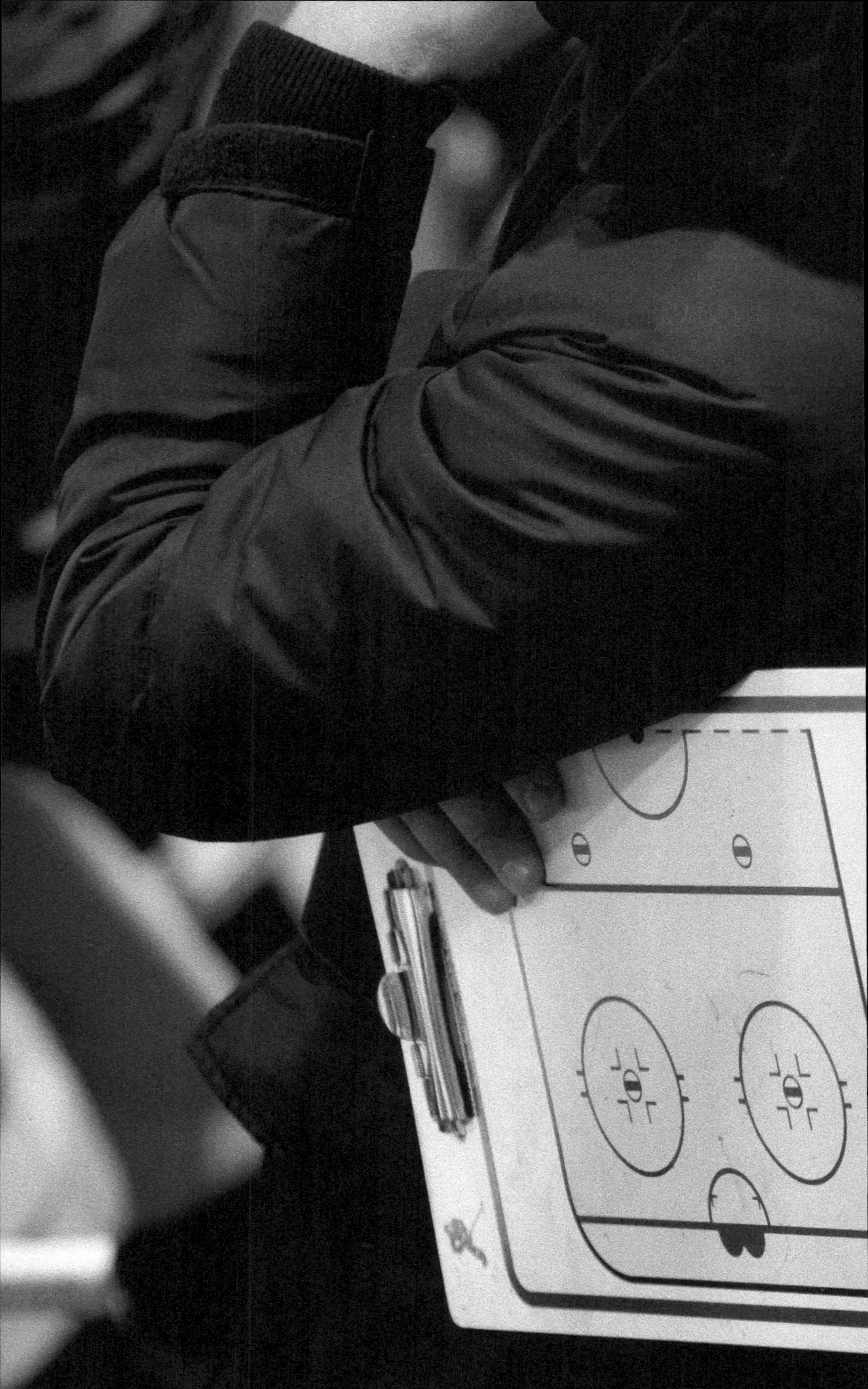

CHAPTER 37
Gavin

Me: Anyone want to grab dinner?

Aiden: Is Millie coming? I have more questions about Lennox.

Brooks: Dude. This is getting concerning.

Beckett: I'm with Brooks, and I'm not even there.

Me: Dinner?

Aiden: Baby Hall?

Me: Don't fucking call her that.

Brooks: He didn't even use ducking. You're screwed.

Aiden: Peaches?

I GRIT my teeth and squeeze my phone, resisting the urge to throw it across the room. Motherfucker.

> Brooks: What are you smoking?
>
> Beckett: Aiden, tread really fucking carefully right now.
>
> Me: Do you all fucking know?
>
> Brooks: Know what?
>
> Aiden: <side-eye emoji>
>
> Brooks: Wait, you told Aiden and Beckett a secret and not me?
>
> Beckett: You don't want to know this secret.
>
> Me: Fuck it. I could use the advice.
>
> Beckett: No you couldn't, because nothing is going to happen.
>
> Brooks: Sara says I'm an idiot.
>
> Brooks: Does she know the secret too?
>
> Brooks: Holy shit! Millie IS Peaches! Princess Peaches?
>
> Me: She's not Princess Peaches. That's just what Finn calls her.
>
> Beckett: Don't blame this insanity on my son.
>
> Me: Okay, Papa Bear, calm down. You know what I mean.
>
> Beckett: The only papa bear you should be worried about is Ford. Keep Gavin away from Millie, boys. That's your only job this week.

> Aiden: Jeez, I thought I was here to score goals.

> Me: Your job is also to score goals.

> Brooks: Also?

> Me: Dammit. No one needs to babysit me. SHE'S the babysitter. Is anyone going to join me for fucking dinner?

> Brooks: This is Sara. Secret's safe with us. We'll meet you downstairs at Cru. Is Millie coming?

> Me: No. She went out to dinner with Daniel.

> Aiden: See ya in ten.

> Beckett: I'm serious, Gavin. Do not ducking touch Princess Peaches.

Somehow, even when I'm ready to crack a tooth over my aggravation with these idiots, they make me laugh. I heave out an unsteady breath and watch Vivi, who's lying on the bed with her legs scrunched up, pulling at her toes, lost in her own little world.

Twenty minutes ago, Millie texted to say she was going to grab dinner and could be back in an hour if I needed her. She didn't even knock on the bedroom door to tell me. When I responded, I told her to take the whole night.

Needless to say, I'm an asshole. I don't have a choice, because when I'm kind, she gets comfortable and acts like the Millie I used to know, and I can't resist her.

I can't see her smile. Can't hear her laugh.

I almost told her she could never be just the help. That if I had my way, she'd be my everything. Thank fuck the phone rang before I could lay my heart on the line and beg her to love me. Beg her to forgive me for being such a goddamn dick to her all the time.

She made it clear months ago that's not what she wants. She

never loved me that way—*if she loved me at all*—and I need to keep reminding myself of that.

At least when she's pissed at me, she stays away. It's better like this. It *has* to be this way. Even if I hate every fucking second of it.

Vivi squeals, and I turn to her and smile. "Hey, Vivi girl. You want to go have dinner with the fam?"

Another squeal.

Scooping her into my arm, I press a kiss to her cheek. "Daddy loves that sound."

She does it again, as if she knows how happy it makes me. Fuck, she really is the perfect kid.

Vivi's rocking a blue sweater dress tonight, along with a ridiculous pair of fur-lined boots. This outfit is one of many Sara and Lennox picked out for her. I threw on a navy sweater and a pair of dark jeans, and for the first time in a while, I'm feeling like I've got this.

We're going to be okay.

I can't help but grin the whole way through the lobby. Every person we pass smiles and waves at Vivi or stops to tell me what an adorable little girl I have.

As I step past the hostess stand, my stomach sinks and the smile falls from my face.

"Just the person I wanted to see," Sebastian Lukov says as he saunters up to me.

For most of my life, I looked up to the man. I was a teenager when he married my aunt. Back then, he played for the Bolts, and I practically worshipped him. Then I considered him a friend. For ten years, we worked together to create and foster a program that allowed us to win the cup. Not once did I ever imagine he could be such a liar and a cheat.

Swallowing past the lump in my throat, I hold Vivi tighter. "Hate to disappoint you, but the feeling isn't mutual. So if you don't mind—"

I step to the side to pass him, but as I do, he grabs hold of Vivi's hand.

Instantly, ice runs through my veins and my entire body goes rigid.

"And who is this?" he asks, focus fixed on her.

"Don't touch her," I grit out.

Even Vivi senses the inherent evil inside this man. My always happy, friendly girl curls her body into my chest and rubs her face against my sweater, as if she doesn't want to look at him.

"Where's the girl's mother?" He tilts to one side, as if he's waiting for someone to miraculously appear behind me.

"Not in the picture."

"Heard she was left outside my old apartment door," he muses, one brow lifted.

With a hand on Vivi's back, I rub comforting circles. The move is just as much for me as it is for her.

"Better you than me." His steely blue eyes meet mine. "Though you seem to have everything now. My old job, a mysterious child who just so happened to be delivered to you at my old door." He pauses as he lets that sink in. "Sign the papers, Gavin. All I'm asking is for my fair share. No need for things to turn nasty."

"They turned nasty when you cheated on my aunt, you piece of shit," I hiss, my anger getting the best of me.

Sebastian's lips tip in an amused grin, his gaze going to Vivi again. "We both know there is way more at stake. I'm sure you'd hate for that little girl to be the one who suffers."

I nearly swallow my tongue. "What the hell are you insinuating?"

"Sign the amended contract. I get my bonus. I get what I'm owed. You shouldn't keep things that don't belong to you." He zeroes in on Vivi again.

I suck in a harsh breath, frozen to the spot, unable to speak. Not that I'd have the first clue about what to say.

He doesn't wait for a response, though. With one more sneering smile, he stalks off.

What the actual fuck was that?

Rattled and also fucking pissed off that Sebastian had the audacity to touch Vivi, I slog my way into the restaurant and to the table where my brothers and Sara who are all laughing and chatting.

Sara stands and smiles as we approach. "Hey, Vivi girl. Come to Auntie Sar. Daddy looks like he needs a drink."

I cough out an annoyed laugh as she takes Vivi. "That obvious?"

"What happened?" Brooks asks, pushing a glass of whiskey toward me. "I ordered it for you. I'm drinking water."

I drop into the empty seat and take a big gulp of the alcohol. "I saw Seb."

Brooks's jaw goes rigid, and he lifts up, scanning the restaurant.

"He's gone."

Aiden hisses and rubs at his eyes. "Tomorrow is going to suck. I can't believe they hired the slimeball."

Brooks leans back in his chair and crosses his arms. "He'll fit right in with all those jerks."

Sara keeps an arm wrapped around Vivi's midsection and rests her free hand on his arm. "This has got to be hard on all of you."

Can't be easy for her either. The last time we played New York, Brooks found out that Seb had been running his mouth about his affair with Sara to his nephew. Vincent Lukov plays defense for New York, and he's always stirring shit up on the ice. When he asked if he could have a shot with Sara since she'd already been passed around the family, Brooks left the ice in the middle of the game and beat the shit out of Seb in front of the whole arena. It was a shit show and a night we all wish we could forget.

"Feeling good. I've got my head on straight. I won't let Lukov get to me." Brooks squeezes Sara's hand. "You still okay?"

Sara gives him a soft smile and snuggles Vivi closer.

"Duckhole," Aiden grumbles.

Vivi breaks into a smile at the sound of his voice, causing us all to laugh.

"I gotta be honest. Using duck really doesn't hit the same."

I chuckle and take another sip of whiskey. Then I roll my shoulders back. Seb is a duckhole. He doesn't know anything. He's making threats because he wants his money. I blow out a breath and will my nerves to settle. I'm glad I asked my brothers and Sara to join me for dinner. I need time with my favorite people to help me feel a little like the old Gavin. Gavin 2.0 kinda sucks. I need to be a better version of myself for Vivi, not worse.

Once we've ordered and the server walks away, Aiden arches a brow. "We gonna talk about the elephant in the room?"

"You want to talk about Lennox again?" I tease.

"Hey!" Sara cries, feigning annoyance.

I hold up my hands. "He's the one who won't shut up about her."

Unfortunately, my youngest brother won't be distracted. He sits forward and rests his forearms on the table. "No. The *peach* elephant."

My stomach sinks, but I keep my expression bland. "Nothing to talk about."

"Sure about that?" he counters, a little too confident.

"Easy." Brooks lays a hand on the table. "Why don't we talk about tomorrow's game?"

"Because I think if Gavin talks about this, he'll feel better," Aiden counters.

I grunt. "People in glass houses shouldn't throw hockey pucks."

Sara's laugh is light and her smile is wide. "This family. I swear you can make anything about hockey."

Vivi sticks her bottom lip out and fusses. Before I can grab her diaper bag and search for her binky, it turns into a full-on cry.

As much as I hate when she does, I can't be mad about the excuse to avoid the conversation. "Looks like I'm on daddy duty, Aiden. No time to chat." I stand and snatch her out of Sara's arms. I've just pulled her to my chest when she makes a gurgling noise. "Hey, Vivi girl," I coo. "Say bye-b—"

My words are cut off when I'm splattered by baby goo.

"Oh shit." I grasp her a little tighter, fighting my instinct to recoil, and wipe my face on my shoulder to get the vomit away from my mouth. As I turn back to her, there's another gurgle, and this time, the explosion hits my hand. The hand holding Vivi under her bum. The liquid that coats my skin is warm and foul, and suddenly, everyone at the table is groaning and backing away.

Sara claps a hand to her mouth. "Holy shit. Is that—"

"Oh my god," Aiden shouts. "Gav, you really are on daddy duty. Only it's doody covering the daddy!"

I scan the restaurant, taking in the horrified faces watching us and then look back at Sara. "I'm gonna go." I back away, ignoring the mess left behind, trying like hell to hold my breath and not puke.

Sara follows me back to the room, the two of us gagging all the way, and helps me give Vivi a quick wipe-down. Once we've used half a pack of baby wipes on the poor kid, I wave Sara off, then take the screaming baby straight to the shower.

"This is so not how I saw my life going," I tell my poor girl. A single dad spending my night in a hotel shower with my baby girl covered in shit. Doesn't get more glamorous than this. I've just gotten Vivi in a fresh diaper when my phone rings on the bathroom counter.

I scoop her up, wrap the towel around her to keep her warm, and rush to pick it up. "Can't they just leave me the duck alone?"

When Ford's name flashes on the screen, I hit accept and put it on speaker. "In the middle of something. Can I call you back?"

"What is Millie doing out with your hockey players?"

Guess that's a no.

"What are you talking about?"

"Lake said she saw a picture online of Millie sitting on Camden Snow's lap."

The fuck? Could this night get any worse?

I keep my tone calm, even as my anger spikes. "Why are you calling me?"

"Because you're supposed to be watching over her."

"No, Ford. She's supposed to be watching my child." I peer down at my baby girl who's gumming her towel, happy again. "The child I'm currently bathing because she just shit all over me and probably the table at the restaurant we just left."

"Oh shit." Ford coughs out a laugh.

"Literally. So how about I worry about my baby, and you can figure out yours?"

"Yeah. Um, sorry. That guy—"

"Hit on Lake. I know. You got jealous. I remember the night very well. It feels fucked-up that he's now hanging out with your daughter, but I seriously can't wrap my head around this shit right now because, once again, I was covered in literal shit ten minutes ago, and I'm still trying to come to terms with it."

"I'm sorry, Gav. I'll let you go."

I sigh. I don't mean to take my frustrations out on him. "It's fine. She said she was going out with Daniel, so for what it's worth, I'm sure he's watching out for her. And I've told the guys she's off-limits."

"You're the best."

Gritting my teeth, I squeeze my eyes shut. He wouldn't think that if he knew that the reason she's off-limits to them is because she belongs to me. Even if I can't have her.

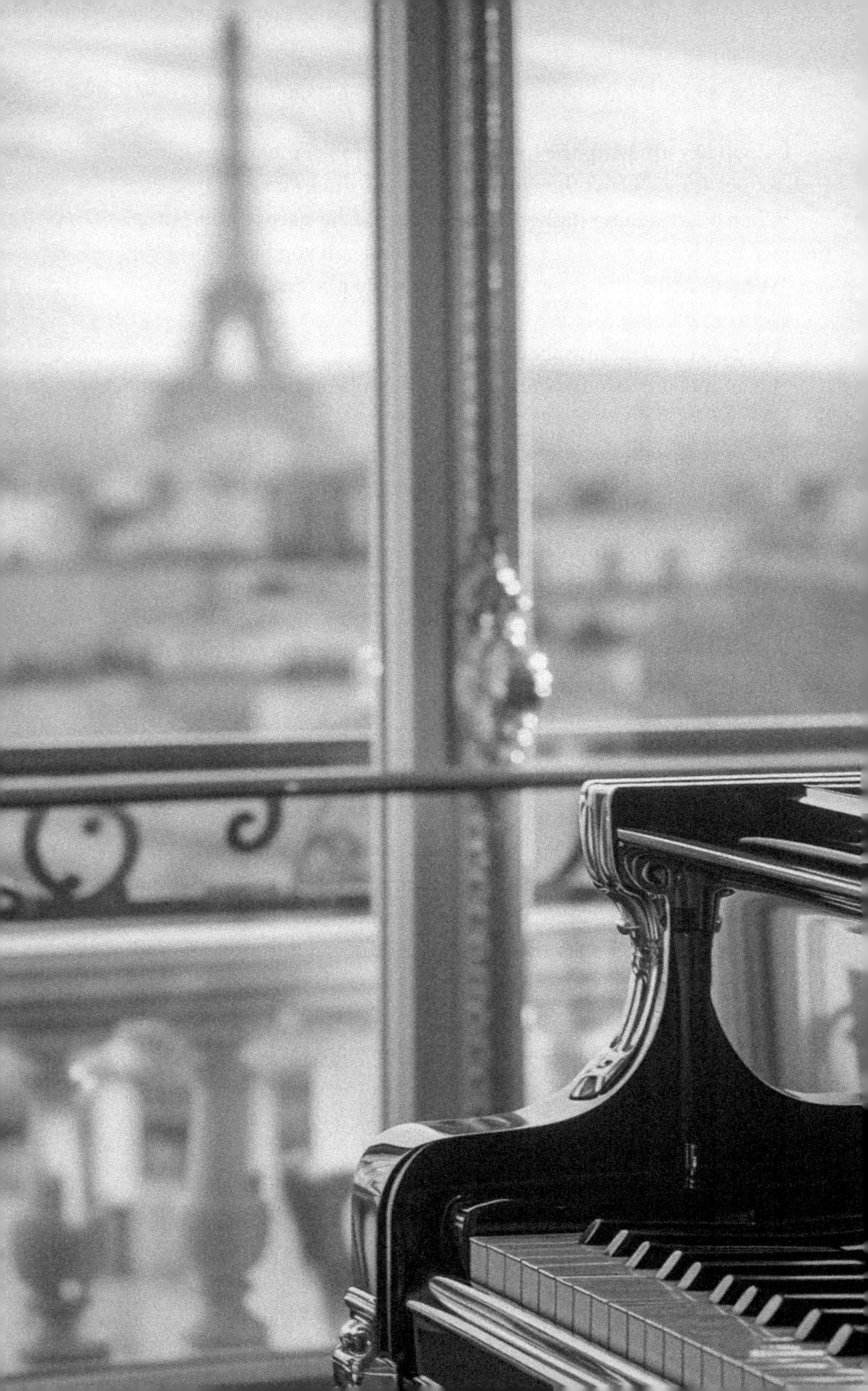

CHAPTER 38
Millie

I CHECK the time on my phone for the fifth time in the last two minutes. Have I waited long enough? I don't want to chance another run-in with miserable Gavin, but I want to be there in case Vivi wakes up. I missed her tonight.

Since dinner ended two hours ago, I've been sitting in the corner of the lobby, typing out fragments of lyrics into my phone. My brother and Camden tried to convince me to come out for a drink with them—risky, since they have a game tomorrow and they have an early curfew—but I wasn't interested.

And since I also had no interest in being glared at, I avoided our hotel room in hopes that Gavin would be asleep when I returned.

It's after eleven now. With the early morning he has, I'm sure Gavin is hiding in the bedroom, and I'll be able to quickly change and settle on the couch until Vivi decides she wants her middle-of-the-night bottle.

The sound of the lock clicking is loud in the dim, silent hall. I push the door open and blink at the light from the lamp in the corner. Gavin is perched there, with his attention fixed on his phone. Vivi is fast asleep in her Pack 'n' Play beside him.

Confused, I skirt the pull-out couch and peek in on her. Chubby fingers grip her binky loosely, and her face is relaxed as her chest rises and falls steadily.

I peer over at Gavin. "What are you doing?" I whisper.

He still doesn't look up from his phone. "Enjoy dinner with your brother?"

"Yeah, it was fine."

"Was it just the two of you?" He finally lifts his chin and locks those dark eyes on me.

For a moment, I forget how to breathe, and I drop a knee to the edge of the bed to keep from wobbling. Gavin's eyes don't warm as they meet mine, but I can't stop my perusal of him. He's in a Bolts T-shirt, and his brown hair is mussed. His eyes widen as if he's waiting for me to answer him, but I've forgotten his question.

"Um, what?"

As I move to sit on the bed, he holds up his hand. "I'm staying out here with Vivi. Take the bed."

This again? I sigh as I push to a stand. "It's my job to wake up with her. You have to be up early with the team. Go sleep in the bed. I got this."

"No." His voice is clipped, his face a hard mask that doesn't even resemble the man I once knew.

"Are you upset with me?"

His glare hardens further, if that's possible. "I'm *nothing* with you. I thought I was clear about that. You work for me."

The words are sharpened, thrown with the intent to maim. To draw blood. To hurt.

And they land perfectly, flaying me open, making it difficult to breathe. When his expression remains angry, the pain intensifies, like he's pushing the knife in deeper. Unable to take his wrath for even a second longer, I spin on my heel and head for the bedroom door, slamming it shut and pressing my back to it. A breath later, Vivi is crying and Gavin is muttering a not so quiet *fuck*.

Fuck is right.

Now not only do I not feel like I'm enough, but I feel worthless too.

This is so not working.

My plan for the next ten days is to avoid Gavin as best as I can. Fortunately, when we arrive at the next hotel, there are two bedrooms in the suite. Despite my protests, he brings Vivi's playpen into his room, making it clear that he's going to fight me on her sleeping near him every night.

The next morning, hoping to gauge how our day will go, I ask how she slept. He merely glares at me. Without knowing, though, it's hard to be tuned into when she needs a nap or to determine whether she's eating enough to satisfy her.

So I resort to a little stalking. I noticed at home that he had a few parenting books on the counter that were suspiciously gone when we were leaving the apartment to head to the team plane. I wait until Gavin leaves for the arena and then tiptoe into his room, my eyes darting in every direction like I'm in a James Bond film.

Though my body aches to lie on his pillow and soak in the scent of him, my mind is wise enough to know I have little time and that would only derail any progress I've made on the *be strong* front.

For Vivi and for Gavin, I need to not be a lovesick twenty-four-year-old girl. I need to be a woman on a mission. And I am. Gavin didn't make it hard either. The books are stacked on the nightstand, a pen pushing the top of one up, letting me know precisely what he was reading last night. When I open the book and see blue underlines throughout the page and his messy writing in the margins, my heart breaks.

The section relates to an infant's memory and how using bright objects could help stimulate their brain.

At four months, infants can remember an image of an object for a week. They can remember photographs of faces for two weeks. Your baby will be able to remember objects or faces for longer periods of time as they grow older.

His notes: *Ask doc how much a baby will remember at six months. Does she remember her mother? Will she know she was abandoned? What signs should I watch out for? How can I make sure she knows she's loved?*

Tears stream down my face. While I've been focused on how Gavin treats me, he's focused on this. As he should be.

I go through each one of the notes in the margins of his books, promising myself that I'll spend the day researching the answers. Then I do a crazy thing, and I leave a response to a few of the less heart-wrenching questions.

Is she getting enough tummy time? He wrote on the next page.

In blue writing, I reply. *She doesn't love it, but if I lay flat on my belly and sing to her, we can normally get fifteen minutes done.*

I hold my breath practically all night, worrying that I overstepped and he'll walk into my room and fire me on the spot. But the next morning, he watches me for a long moment as he's saying goodbye to Vivi, and then, if I'm not mistaken, he almost smiles.

I practically run into his room as soon as he leaves and search for the page in question.

There is no response to my note, but on the next page it says: *Vivi slept through the night for the first time.*

The grin that takes over my face is completely irrational. Like the man wrote me a love letter in those nine words.

It can barely be considered progress, but over the next few days, we exchange notes back and forth in the margins of his books. It gives me the tiniest bit of hope that he doesn't hate having me as Vivi's nanny anymore.

During our last stop—in LA—it's hard not to soak in the perfect weather, even if I am ready to head back to Boston and get back into a routine. Vivi and I are sitting outside. She's in her stroller, gnawing on a teething toy while I once again play on my phone, working on my latest song.

"Oh, Vivi girl, what rhymes with pick?"

"Dick!" Sara sings as she saunters up, wearing a big smile. When she spots Vivi, though, her face goes red. "Oh shit. Don't tell Gavin I said that." She cups her mouth and winces. "Shit, not shit. I meant duck."

I giggle. "Don't tell duck you said that?"

"No. Duck instead of shit. And maybe instead of dick? I don't know. The Langfields confuse me sometimes."

I laugh. "Tell me about it."

Sara crouches beside the stroller. "Hey, little Viv. How's it going?"

The cutie's eyes widen, and she latches on to Sara's hand and pulls it toward her mouth.

"She's teething pretty bad," I explain as Sara gently extricates herself. I dig through my bag and pull out the Ziploc containing a cold, damp towel I brought for her to gnaw on.

Sara points to the seat beside me. "Mind if I join you?"

I shake my head and shift to give her more space.

"God," she says, lifting her face to the sun and closing her eyes. "It's a gorgeous day, isn't it?"

"It is." It's sunny and seventy. So very different from the weather at home.

"You must be ready to get back, though. Hotel life with a baby can't be easy." Sara turns to me, her blue eyes warm and her expression soft.

With a slow breath out, I let myself relax. I haven't spent much time with her, but she seems down-to-earth, and if she's as cool as Lennox says, I think we'll be good."

"She's not the problem. If not for the teething, I'm pretty sure this girl would be fine anywhere."

"So who is the problem?" Sara asks, giving me a knowing look.

"Oh, no one." I plaster a big, phony smile to my face.

"Hmm, I know a certain someone who also likes wearing a fake smile. Name rhymes with pick too."

I giggle. "Gavin's not a dick. He's just—" I breathe out a resigned sigh. "He's got a lot on his plate."

"And the woman he's obsessed with is now his nanny, and he can't touch her."

My jaw drops open, and all the air leaves my lungs. "How...?"

She grins. "I've been where you are, babe. Slightly delusional and unaware that a Langfield is obsessed. Want some advice?"

My chin tips up and down, like it's got a mind of its own, because my brain certainly isn't on board with discussing this so openly.

"You're his Peaches."

I cough out an uncomfortable laugh as my heart trips over itself. "What?"

A wistful smile crosses her face, and she pats my hand, rubbing her thumb over my wrist.

For a second, I'm distracted by the move, but I forget about the odd interaction when she continues. "Even when you were apart, he kept you close."

"How so?" As far as I know, we hid our relationship from everyone.

Sara shakes her head, her blond ponytail swaying. "Just..." She presses her lips together. "Just pay attention to the little things. He still keeps a piece of you close to him. He's not over you. And if you're here to prove to him that you're all-in, then you're doing exactly what you should be doing."

My heart thunders against my ribcage as I consider her words. "And what is that?"

Sara nods toward Vivi. "Putting her first. But," she says, bumping my shoulder, "can I give you a little hint as to how to maybe move this along a little quicker?"

Once again, I cough out a shocked laugh at her persistence. "Sure?"

She leans in close. "Do you know about the jersey thing?"

I frown. "The what?"

"Oh goodie. You don't." She claps, making Vivi grin and wave her hands, trying to mimic her. "I didn't know about it either until a few months ago, but let me tell you, it works." Teeth pressed into her bottom lip, she fights a grin. "Although you should encourage Gavin to sanitize his desk at the arena when we get back. It's *seen* things." The face she makes is half cringe, half starry-eyed smile, if that's possible.

"You've lost me."

"The first time Brooks saw me in his jersey, he fucking lost it. You should have heard the feral tone he used on me. I wish I had a recording of it. That sucker would come in useful on the nights when —" She shakes her head. "Actually, there's never really a night when he doesn't give me the D, so I guess I don't truly need a recording."

A surprised "oh" slips out of my mouth, and my cheeks heat.

"Am I making you uncomfortable?" She grimaces. "I'm totally making you uncomfortable. Sorry. Sometimes I go off on tangents and forget that not everyone is as insane and open as I am."

"I'm beginning to see that." I smile. "But it's good. Now tell me about this jersey thing."

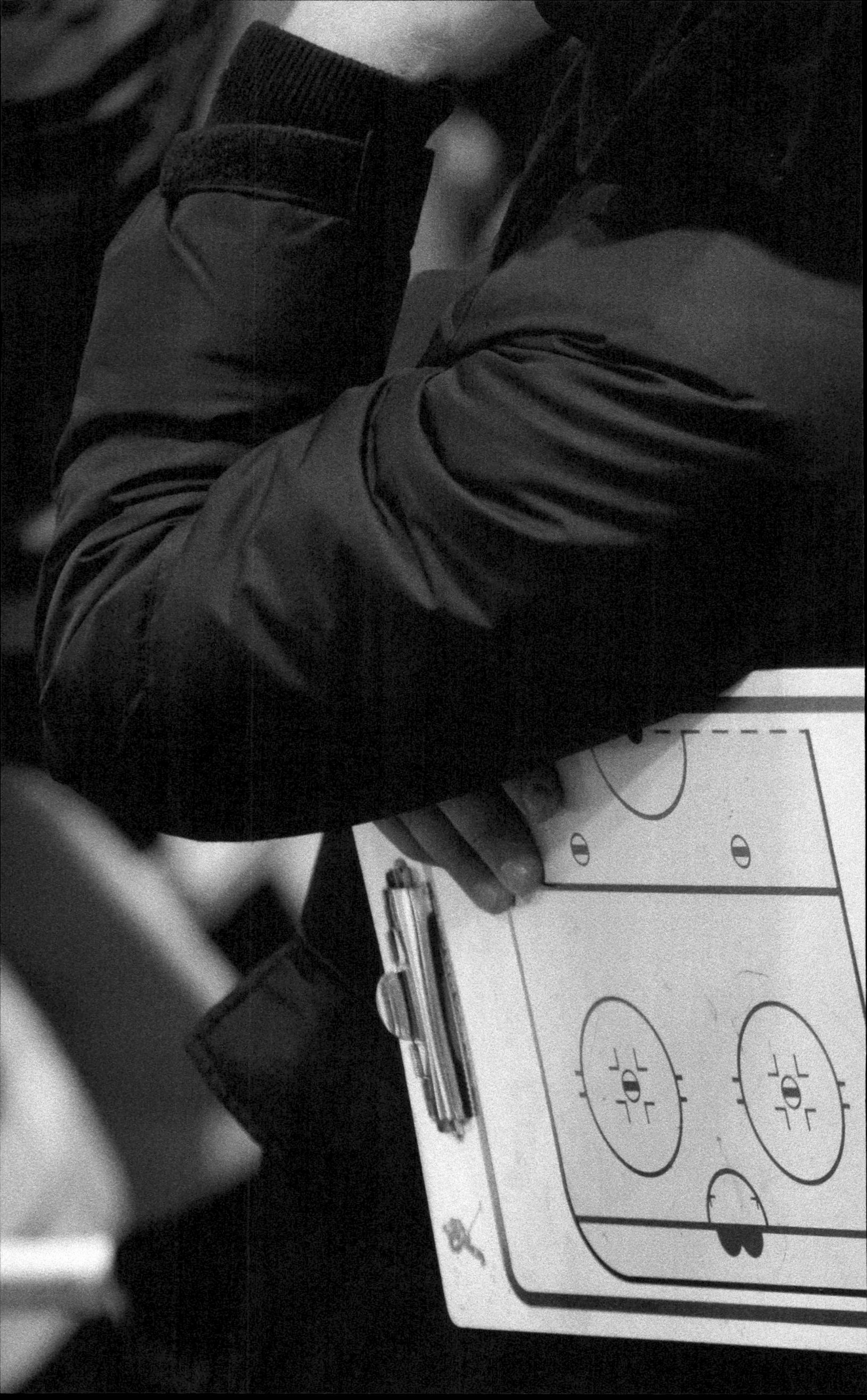

CHAPTER 39
Gavin

Beckett: War isn't playing tonight?

Me: He's got the flu.

Brooks: Everyone has the fucking flu.

Aiden: Not me. My immune system is steel. It's the vitamins. And the orange soda.

Brooks: You should donate your body to science when you die.

Beckett: I've never seen anyone eat more candy, and I once lived in a house with seven children.

Aiden: Thank you.

Beckett: that wasn't a compliment.

Aiden: And yet I have eight-pack abs and get to enjoy candy.

> Brooks: Like I said, medical miracle.
>
> Beckett: Anyone else not playing?
>
> Me: Better not be.

I POCKET my phone and turn my focus back to Fitz and Turner. They're going over the lineup now that our biggest instigator is out for the night.

"Bring Camden up?" Fitz suggests.

I want to say no. I'm still pissed at him for the incident with Millie. But that's unreasonable. "Yes. But have Pastanowitz ready to jump in if necessary."

Turner nods. "I'll let the guys know." He heads in the direction of the locker room.

I rub a hand over my head, too tired for a game day.

Fitz studies me. "You feeling okay?"

No. I feel like complete crap. My stomach is a mess because I've barely slept, and Vivi's teething is only partially to blame. Sebastian followed our little run-in up with an email that night. It's what I was reading when Millie walked in and I snapped at her. Again.

His veiled threats made it clear he has suspicions surrounding Vivi, and I'll die before I let him take her, regardless of DNA.

Fuck, I'm in so far over my goddamn head I can't see straight.

And the guilt over my words to Millie is consuming me. I've yet to apologize for how I treated her. I don't even know what to say.

Everything in my life is spiraling, and I'm scared to death I'm going to lose Vivi, and I was jealous that you had dinner with one of my players.

Absurd.

Her brother was with her too. It wasn't a date. Even if it was, I have no right to be mad at her. I sure as shit have no right to yell at her.

To make matters worse, she's so fucking good with my daughter. And she's good to me. The fact that she's taking the time to read through the parenting books, to reply to my concerns...it's just...fuck, I'm already dreading the day she says she's done.

The acid in my gut rises again, but I swallow it down, along with the rest of my worries. "I'll be fine. Just need to get through tonight. Then we've got the next four days off."

Fitz nods. "Damn, do we need it."

The season has been an incredible one, and we're still in line for the playoffs. But it'd only take a few bad games to change that. I nod toward the arena. "I'm going to head out there."

With a dip of his chin, Fitz wanders off in the opposite direction.

In need of a pick-me-up, I search out coffee first. Maybe it'll lighten this heavy feeling in my chest and the overall tiredness that won't let go of me. If I can make it through the game, we can all rest. I'll give Millie a few days off, get some space from these insane feelings, and just—

My thoughts leave my brain the moment I step into the arena and spot Millie standing with Vivi in her arms, swaying from side to side. She's just past the team bench, and each time she sways one way, the number 18 plastered on her back comes into view. *Hall* is emblazoned above it, but it's my fucking team's logo above her ass and my daughter in her arms.

The two of them like that—together—are quite possibly the most beautiful thing I've ever seen.

Vivi is also wearing a Bolts jersey. Millie layered it over a thick sweater. This one, I know, says *Langfield* above a single zero. There's no way I'd choose one brother's number over the other, so Vivi's got her own now.

Sara is standing beside them, talking a mile a minute. Millie's smile is genuine as she bobs her head in response. For too many seconds, I stand in place and stare. I imagine again the dream where this is my real life. Where Millie's jersey matches Vivi's, the name Langfield plastered on both their backs, and that the little girl in her arms is ours.

Millie laughs at Sara, who grins proudly, and my heart clenches tightly. That sound is so much better than the silence I've been receiving from her since I told her we're nothing. It ranks near the top of my favorite things in the world. Paired with the way my daughter is clinging to her, comfortable and at ease. It's utter perfection.

Sara catches me gawking and gives a knowing smirk.

Caught, I huff out a breath and stride their way. "Hey, Vivi girl. What are you two doing here?" I try to keep my tone even, my gaze on my daughter.

Millie's radiant smile won't have any of it. She catches my eye, and her cheeks go rosy. "She wanted to see her daddy before bed, right, Viv?"

Viviane smiles wide and reaches for me, her chubby hands opening and closing in excitement. Heart lifting at the pure joy radiating from her, I hold out my arms and step up close. Millie leans in, guiding her into my hold. It's only a moment, and the contact could barely be categorized as a touch. But when my hands scrape against her, I feel it so deep in my bones that a chill runs through my body. Her curly auburn hair swishes, and I'm hit with that fruity scent that is so her it makes my mouth water. The way I crave her is unreal. Unnatural. Unavoidable.

Just like the little girl in my arms, Millie Hall owns me.

"You feel all right?" Millie asks, pressing the back of her hand to my forehead. "You're really hot, Gavin."

I blink a few times, having trouble formulating words. The old Gavin would respond with "of course I am" or something equally cocky, but I'm struck stupid by her touch. By her proximity. We haven't been this close in I don't know how long. Since that day she appeared in Ford's kitchen, I've kept her at arm's length. It's the only way I've been able to resist stumbling over myself and begging her to try again.

"Gavin." She presses closer.

Now my gaze is focused on her lips. Those damn peach lips.

"Baby Hall! I woulda given you a signed number 22 to wear if you'd told me you were coming to the game tonight."

Instantly pulled out of my stupor and on edge, I focus on Camden, who is striding toward us in full gear.

Daniel, who's right beside him, hits him in the stomach, saving me from having to do it. "Eyes off my sister."

"Gavin," Millie says, drawing my attention again. She's still wholly focused on me, her brows pulled low in concern.

"I'm fine," I say, thankful the spell has been broken. I zero in on Vivi to keep from getting caught up in her again. "Make sure she gets to bed by eight, please."

When she doesn't immediately respond, I can't help it. I have to look. Her golden irises, so vibrant only seconds ago, have gone dull. She lets out a heavy sigh, her shoulders sinking. "Right. Just wanted to show our support. I'll let you get back to your job."

My heart pounds, at war with my brain, wanting to pull her against me, tell her I'm glad she brought my daughter here, that I'm glad she's here too. In my team's jersey.

I want to tell her that I want my name on her back, but more than that, I want my name attached to hers.

I want her to be mine.

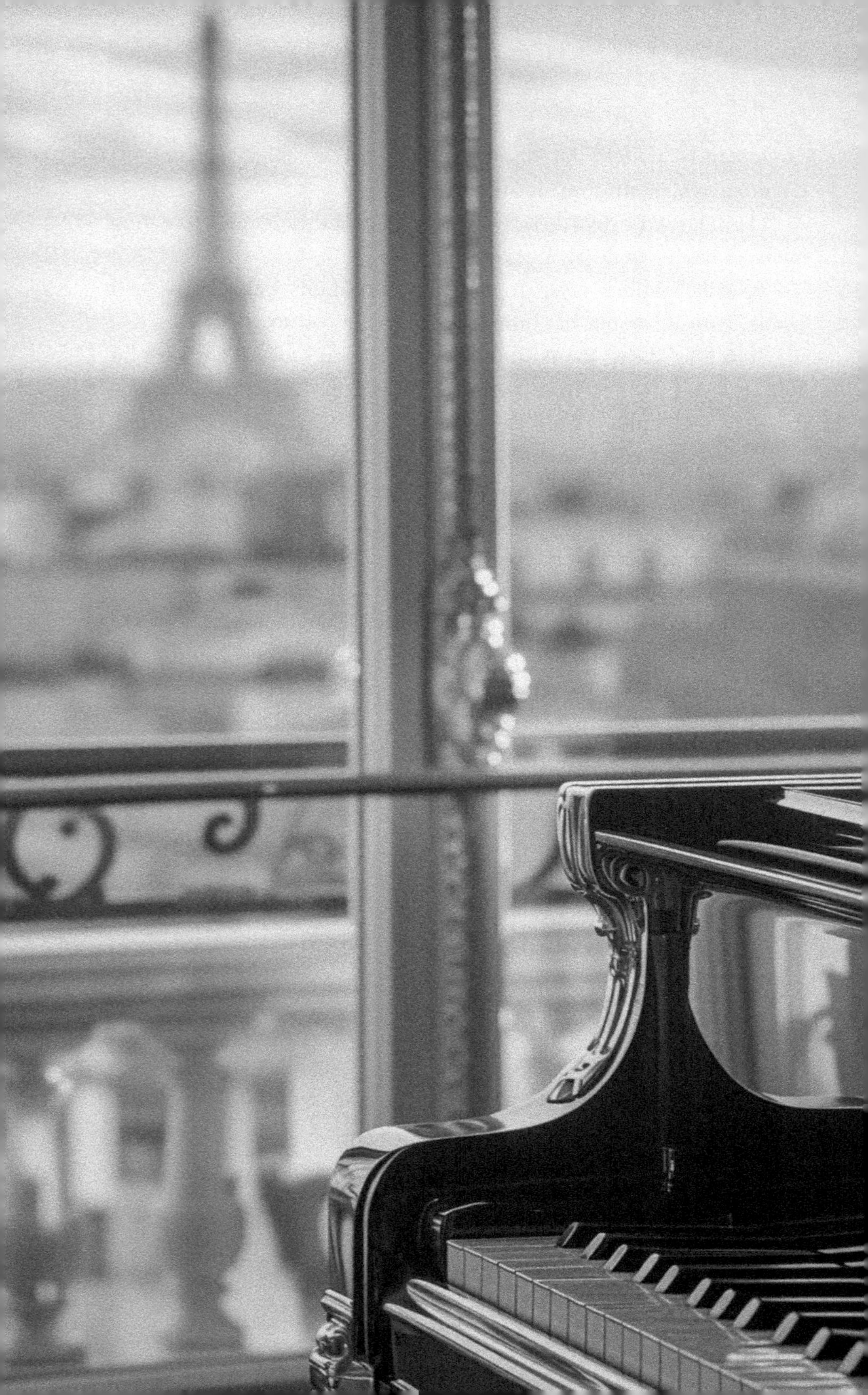

CHAPTER 40
Millie

"YOU KNOW your brother is over there."

Sara, Vivi, and I are set up in the Bolts suite, watching the game. Once the buzzer sounds, signaling the end of the first period, though, I'm heading out so I can get back to the hotel before the little lady's bedtime.

"Ha ha. You're hilarious," I deadpan, tearing my gaze from Gavin.

She flips her blond hair over her shoulder. "Just sayin'. The coach doesn't actually play in the game."

"Shouldn't you be more focused on Brooks? I've heard he's even got a pierced peen. I'm sure that keeps you occupied."

Her mouth falls open and her eyes go wide. "I'll kill Lennox."

"Please don't." I grasp her wrist, laughing. "I barely have any friends as it is."

"Now you have two." Sara bumps her shoulder against mine.

"But seriously, did you see the way Gavin reacted to the jersey? Was I right?"

I can't help but focus on the sidelines again, where Gavin is currently screaming his head off at his guys on the ice. "I was too focused on how pale he was." Frowning, I turn back to Sara. "You saw that, right? He was burning up."

She shrugs. "They're dropping like flies. Wouldn't be surprised if he has the flu."

"Shit." The second the word is out, I cringe and glance at Vivi, who's happily bobbing to the music on my lap. "I mean duck. Did I do that right?"

"You'll fit right in," Sara says, giving me a warm smile. "And since we're besties, I gotta tell you, the sparkly peen really is a bedazzling wonder."

A laugh bubbles out of me. "Bedazzling wonder?"

"The entire team has them." She wiggles in her seat, scanning the ice. "Can you imagine them all in the shower showing off their glittery penises? It's like Lisa Frank porn."

I choke at the visual. Ew. "Sara! *Please*. The last thing I want to do is picture my *brother's* penis."

Eyes wide, she slaps a hand to her mouth and turns in slow motion back to me. "Whoops. Forgot about that." The shock fades and is replaced with a look of contemplation. "Although I'm not sure if he has one. The guys got them before Daniel signed with the team."

"This was a *team activity*?"

She smiles. "Something like that. Gavin have one?"

"No." I giggle. "At least not the last time I saw it. Which was a while ago."

"I could have Brooks talk him into getting one while you aren't currently banging. It takes a while to heal, but when you finally stop all this 'we aren't together' nonsense, you, too, can ride the bling train."

"Oh my god." I flop back against my seat, being sure to keep a good hold on Vivi. "Has anyone ever told you that you're ridiculous?"

"Only every day," she practically sings, her face split in a grin.

Vivi went down easily, but I held her for a half hour or so after she fell asleep, relishing the baby snuggles. It wasn't until my brother scored a goal and I squealed in excitement and nearly woke her up that I finally put her in her playpen.

The Bolts won 2-1. Without War, it was a nail-biter, but Camden did well filling in for him. I shot him a text to congratulate him and sent another to my brother.

Then I stared at my contact list, at *Coach* specifically, just below Camden's name, wishing we were in a place where I could send him the same kind of text. More than that, I wanted to check on him. He looked like a ghost on the after-game show.

His responses to the media were clipped, his jaw rigid. When they asked if he planned to replace War with Camden for the rest of the season, I could practically see the fire in his eyes.

Stupid fucking reporters.

That's what he wanted to say.

After that, I spent a dumb amount of time scrolling the internet, looking for posts about him, only to discover that there is an entire fandom dedicated to finding a wife for Gavin Langfield and a mother for Vivi.

The number of women shamelessly using hashtags like #mommylangfield and #marrymegavin is sickening.

And yet I can't help but wonder if he would entertain any of them. He certainly used to. The thought of him with anyone else makes my stomach lurch violently.

I'm hiding in my room, already in bed for the night, when the door to the suite opens. I drop my phone face down, hit with a ridiculous fear that he'll catch me searching his name. Even though I'm behind a closed door and the man hasn't come close to me willingly since we broke up. That's not changing tonight, I'm sure.

A loud thud makes the wall shake, and when it's followed by a groan, I jump out of bed and rush out my door. In the living room, Gavin is hunched against the wall, his head hanging and his shoulders rolled in.

"Are you okay?" With my heart in my throat, I shuffle toward him, and as I get closer, the sheen of sweat coating his face makes my pulse take off. "Shit. Gavin, you look awful."

He merely groans without raising his head.

I flatten my palm to his forehead, and as the heat registers, I suck in a breath. Shit, shit, shit. "Let's get you changed, and I'll call down for some medicine."

"I—" He looks up at me, his eyes hazy. "I can. You go—don't want you sick," he stammers, his voice barely a whisper.

He's so weak he doesn't fight me when I lift his arm and slip under it, then guide him toward his room. When we've shuffled over to his bed, I turn him around so he's sitting on the edge of the mattress. He sways, so for several seconds, I hold him by the upper arms. Once the movement stops and I'm sure he won't fall over, I call the front desk and ask for a fever reducer. Then I run a lukewarm bath. It's what my dad always did when we were sick. Whether it really helps, I don't know, but he's covered in sweat, and I can't have him sleeping like that.

When I come back into the room, Gavin is lying on his side, still in his suit, eyes shut and knees pulled up.

"You have to stay awake for me," I plead, settling next to him but being sure not to touch him. He's told me to keep my distance, but if I don't get him up, he can't take the medicine, and I can't get him into the tub. "Gav," I say softly, giving in and pressing my hand to his forehead again.

He groans in response to my touch, but he doesn't recoil. I swipe softly at the perspiration coating his skin and rake my fingers through his damp hair to get it off his face.

He lets out a whimper. "Don't stop," he rasps.

God, the way those words steal my breath. I do it again, digging into his scalp, spreading my fingers wide and then closing them again.

This time he moans in response.

I lean down so my mouth is next to his ear. "Gav, let's get you in the bath, okay?"

He moans again and opens his eyes, and now we're just staring at one another. His eyes are bloodshot and smudged with dark circles. Even so, he's still the most breathtaking person I've ever seen.

"Can you get up for me? I really think a bath will help."

He swallows and gives me the smallest of nods, but his eyes don't leave mine, and he doesn't get up, like he's been entranced.

"You can go. I'll be fine." His voice is like sandpaper, scratchy and rough.

I ignore the shiver it sends down my spine. It's not the time to be turned on. "No. I don't trust you in the bath by yourself."

"You can't—"

"Gavin," I huff, "I've seen every inch of you. I swear I'm not going to try anything."

He grunts and closes his eyes. "Fine."

My heart screams as I push away from him. Already, I miss his proximity, but I have to get up so I can help him. For a few short seconds, it was like we were lying in bed together. Just like we used to. Heads on the same pillow, talking late into the night about everything and nothing at all.

Gavin splays one hand on the mattress and pushes, but his arm shakes as he tries to rise, leaving me vindicated in my push to help him.

"Come on, big guy," I say, going with a flirty tone to mask my concern.

With a heavy breath, he tries again, and this time he manages to sit up and brace himself with a hand on the bed on either side of him. I grasp one hand and tug on the cuff of his jacket's sleeve, then do the same to the other side. As I angle in and work the buttons of his shirt loose, he studies me, his attention fixed on my face.

"Hi," I say rather awkwardly. I work as quickly as I can. We're too close, and I can only handle so much.

As his bare chest comes into view, I have to bite back a groan. With both hands, I push his shirt over his shoulders, and then I undo the buttons at his wrist. That's when the bracelets he always wears come into view. Friendship bracelets he made with Finn and Winnie. They were obsessed with them last year, and his eyes had lit up when he recounted how thrilled Winnie was when her uncles proudly wore her creations. All four Langfield brothers wear them.

The ache in my chest grows stronger at the memories and loss—of the intimacy we used to share; I used to know everything about him—as I adjust them and read each one.

Best Uncle.

Boston Bolts.

Vivi Girl.

Peaches.

I hold my breath as I read and reread the word and examine the orange and white beads. My mind trips over the letters, as if certain I'm not reading them right. As if those seven letters put together in that order could spell anything else.

"Pay attention to the little things. He still keeps a piece of you close to him. He's not over you." Sara's words echo in my brain as I thumb the beads, rolling them. What he cares about most is represented here. His team, his status as an uncle, *his daughter*...and me.

Trembling at the thought, I look up, unsure of whether he'll be wearing an angry expression or something wholly different, but his eyes are closed and his brows are pinched in physical pain. He's oblivious to what I've found.

My pulse thrums at this new information. It's hard to tamp down on the elation that rushes through me. Because, though I'm still worried about him, I'm no longer worried about us.

He's not over us. He hasn't given up on us.

And there's no way in hell I'll give up on him.

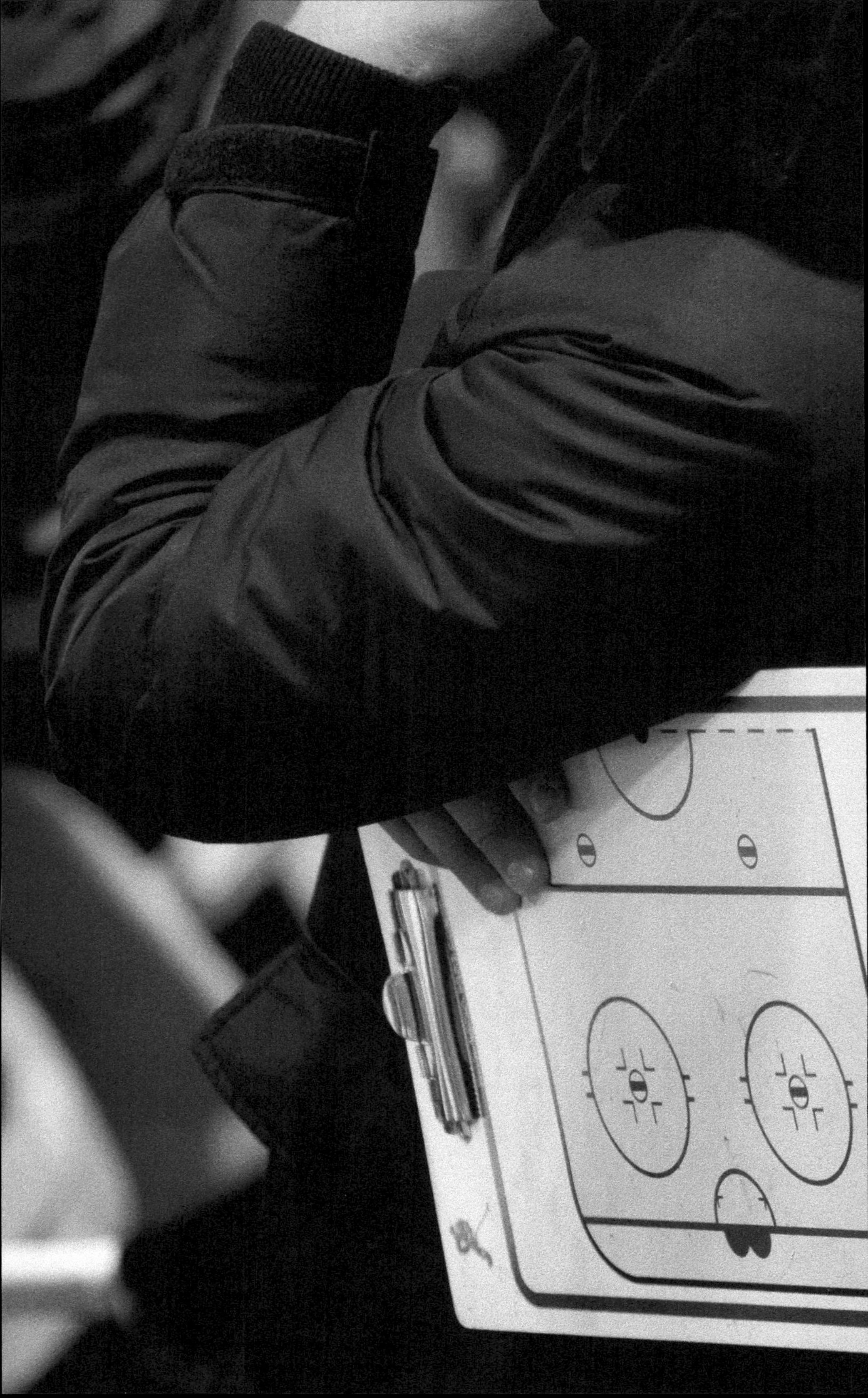

CHAPTER 41
Gavin

MY HEAD POUNDS and feels like it's underwater. I deserve to be tortured this way after what I put Millie through.

She steps out of the bathroom, cast in light from the doorway, wearing a ribbed pink cropped tank that exposes the curves of her stomach and a matching pair of light pink pajama pants that sway as she moves. The sight of her sucks all the air from my lungs, making the sensations plaguing me that much stronger.

"Come on, Coach. Bath is ready." The worry in her tone as she approaches me makes me want to tell her to leave. I've been so horrible to her, yet she's here, taking care of me. I'm such an asshole.

Her wild, curly hair is pulled back in a messy bun, with loose strands framing her face, and like an idiot, I reach for one and tug on it gently like I used to. When we were in bed. Or when she was playing the piano, focused and writing a song. Her eyes would glint like she knew I was a schoolboy just after some attention. I'd pull her hair, and then she'd press her lips to mine or tear off her top and grace me with the sight of her gorgeous tits. Inevitably, she'd end up riding my cock, teasing me while I made her come at least three times.

Despite how close to death I feel, my cock goes rock hard at just the memory.

Millie holds out her hand, but with a grunt, I ignore it and push off the bed and onto my feet. It takes far too much effort, but I keep myself from swaying, even though I immediately feel dizzy.

The soft, defeated sigh Millie releases sends a similar feeling through me. I wish I knew how to act around her. I wish I knew how to stop hurting her.

This is a losing situation.

She doesn't want this. She doesn't want a family with me. To be tied down. Why won't she just give up on us already?

If she keeps pushing herself toward me, I'm liable to grab hold of her, and the moment that happens, I won't let go.

I can't do that again. I can't get lost in the devastation. Vivi needs me.

The bathroom is all white and blinding, making my head throb with more force.

Clad in only my black slacks, I lean against the wall with a grunt, staring at the bubbling bath through slitted eyes. Damn, it looks enticing. With a grunt, I work my belt buckle, pushing away my concerns about Millie seeing me naked. She's right. We're both adults, and she's seen everything.

The bright light above goes out, leaving us shrouded in the dim glow of the single light over the shower. The change eases the pain in my head almost immediately.

"Thanks," I grind out, sliding my pants off and leaving them in a heap on the floor.

Millie faces the other direction, as if she's trying to give me privacy, but the mirror covering the wall reflects the image of my naked body, so it's a useless gesture.

Every step I take toward the bath is excruciating, so I get little enjoyment out of seeing the flush creep up her neck. As I steady myself with a hand on each side of the tub and sink into the water, every cell in my body screams in relief.

"Fuck," I murmur when I'm fully submerged.

Millie is still facing the mirror, frozen to the spot, her shoulders rising and falling as if her breaths are labored.

I rest my head against the tub and turn it so I'm facing the wall, intent on not staring. "You can go. I can call for you if I need help." My eyelids flutter shut, the ability to hold them open a losing battle.

"Not safe," Millie murmurs, closer than she was a moment ago. Her fruity scent mingles with the lavender fragrance of the bath water.

I blink my eyes open and turn, finding her seated on the side of the tub, worry etching her face.

"You gotta stay awake until we get you back in bed."

Eyes heavy, I let them close again, and my head lolls against the cool porcelain beside her thigh.

"Gavin," she says, her tone a bit more urgent now.

I try to open my lids, to obey, but the task is an impossible one.

Fingers scratch at the top of my head, and I whimper in appreciation. "So good," I mutter.

She does it again, and I moan.

"Feel good?" she teases.

I force my eyes open, fighting against the heavy weights keeping the lids lowered, and find her watching me with a smug smile. But it's the way she studies me that stops me from telling her to leave again. The caution that's missing from those golden hues.

That's Millie, though. She loves big and gives herself to the people she cares about, even when they don't deserve it. It's what drew me to her years ago. The way she gave her attention, her heart, to people who were too busy to notice made me want to give her everything.

"You know it does," I rasp.

Her chest swells with a surprised breath, the movement drawing my attention to her tits again. There's no denying it now. She's done something. "What's on your nipples, Mills?"

Her smile widens. "Wouldn't you like to know."

"Fuck." The curse is sharp under my breath.

She shakes her head and laughs silently as she turns away. Then she leans over the tub, cups her hands, and pours water over my head. It feels so fucking good I forget everything else.

Like how I'm supposed to be staying away from her. Like how I can't love her again. Like how naïve that idea is, because I never stopped.

She pours another scoop of water, this time onto my chest, and rubs slow circles over my pecs. I silently watch her, giving up the battle. Her touch feels like heaven. With every swipe of her fingers, my cock hardens and my resolve weakens.

Openly ogling her now, I clear my throat. "Why'd you come back?"

An almost aggravated huff of breath slips through her lips. "I thought that was obvious."

"Brat," I mutter.

She smiles, and then I do too. Immediately, I regret it. The slight movement makes my head throb. With a breath in, I school my expression and wait for the pain to ease again.

"Tell me," I beg.

Her golden eyes shimmer. "It was time." She slides her hand lower, continuing her soothing ministrations.

When she dips beneath the water. I hiss. She sucks in a breath and slides her hand up again, but I grasp her wrist to stop her, holding her fingers right on my abdomen.

"*Gav*," she pleads.

I hold her gaze and squeeze. "Time for what?"

A knock at the door cuts through the silence, startling her so badly she pitches forward into the bath. Before she can hit the water, I catch her. We stay like that for a moment, heads close and our breaths mingling.

"Shit." She blinks and pulls back. "That's probably room service with your medicine."

She gently disentangles herself from my hold and points toward the door, the wall coming down between us again. "I'll go handle that. Don't get out until I'm back."

I nod, though I have no intention of staying in this bath now. Not after our close call a moment ago.

When she returns, a bottle of water and pills in her hand, I'm seated on my bed, toweled off and in a pair of shorts.

"You're a terrible listener," she murmurs, handing me the water and medication.

I point at her with the neck of the bottle, my lips tipping up. "Pot, meet kettle."

With a snort, she looks away and points to the door. "I'll be in the other room if you need me."

"Could you—" I clamp my mouth shut before any other words slip out.

Millie turns back, her golden eyes open and shining, her heart laid out for me, allowing me to take from her again. "Anything, Gavin. I will do anything you ask."

Pain lances my chest at her words. I close my eyes and breathe through it. I'm really starting to believe her. Truly starting to believe that not only would she do what I asked, but she'd do it happily, and not just because it would make me happy. That maybe it would make her happy too. That *I* could make her happy too.

So I say what I should have said months ago. The single word that's been burning a hole through my body, trying to escape. "Stay."

Without hesitation, she rounds the bed and sits on the other side of the mattress, her head tilting my way. "Of course."

What she doesn't know is I wasn't talking about for the night. What I need more than anything is for her to stay with me *forever*.

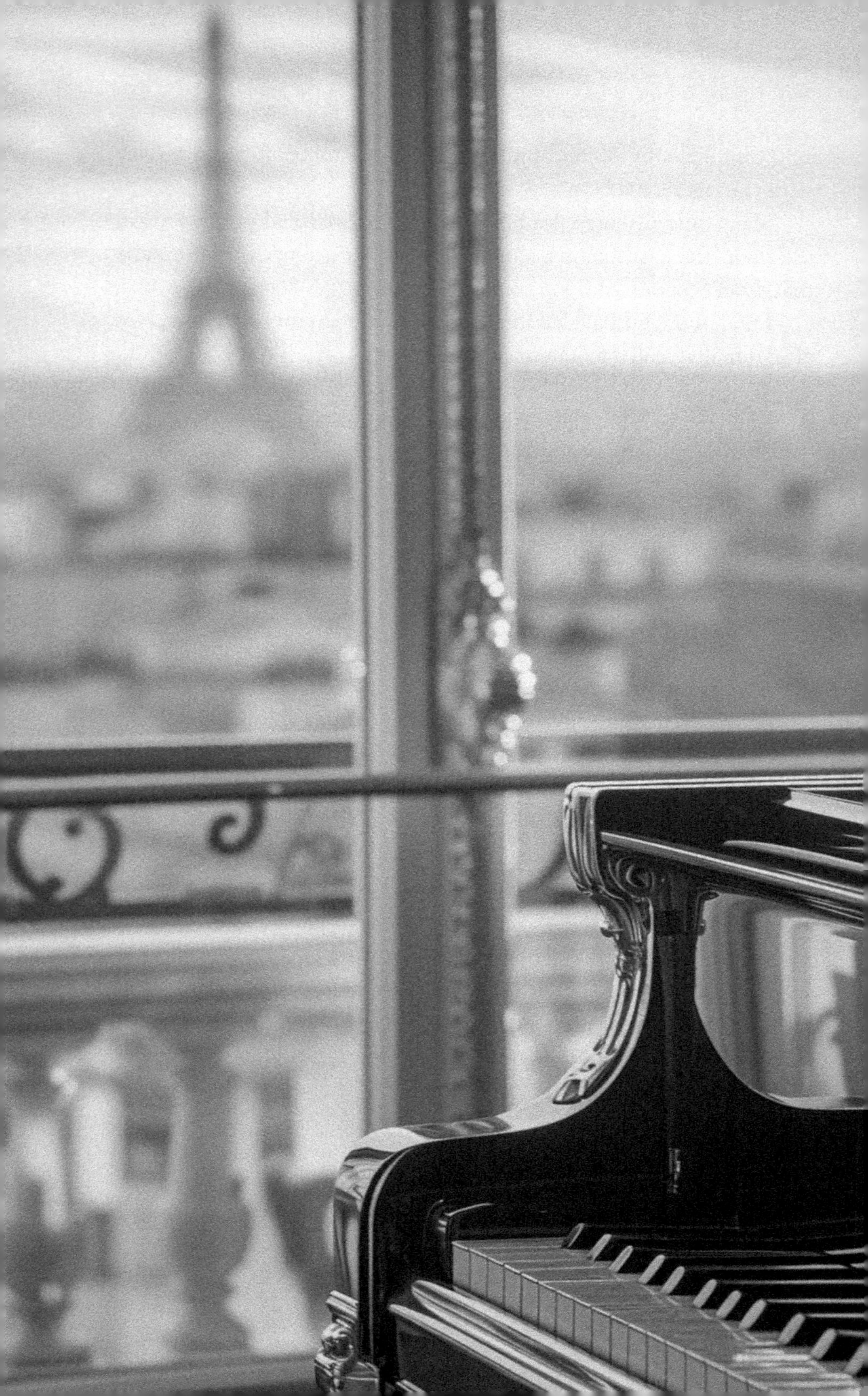

CHAPTER 42
Millie

GAVIN'S FEVER broke around three, and once we were all up and Vivi was fed, we boarded his private plane to head back to Boston. The rest of the team returned after the game. Even before Gavin got sick, we'd planned to return separately so Vivi wasn't up all night traveling.

By the time we walk into his apartment, I'm dead on my feet. Between checking on Gavin all night and dealing with a teething Vivi, I don't think I got more than an hour of sleep.

Gavin is still sick, and someone needs to watch the baby, so sleep is the last thing I'll be getting right now.

"Go lay in bed. I'll place an order for soup and more meds."

He slumps, his head hanging. "You've got to be exhausted. Let me check with my brothers and Ava. Maybe one of them is available to watch her."

I press a kiss to Vivi's soft head, irrationally annoyed that he sees me as nothing but her sitter. Easily replaced by anyone he knows.

"It's fine," I say, keeping my tone even. "No sense in potentially exposing anyone else to the flu."

"You think—" His brows pinch. "You think she'll get sick?"

My heart softens. He is such a good dad. "If she does, we got this." I give him a small smile. "I want to take care of her. I wouldn't be able to sleep if someone other than you or me is with her."

Gavin nods and thumbs over his shoulder. "Okay, I'm just going to—" With that, he disappears down the hall.

"Okay, Vivi girl. How about we order some groceries? Then maybe you'll want to take a nap."

Vivi had zero interest in napping, so once the grocery order is placed, we head out for a walk. As I enter the hallway, a flash of pink appears next door.

"*Psst*, c'mere!" Lennox is peeking out into the hall, her eyes darting left and right comically.

I can't help but laugh at her theatrics. "It's just us."

"Come in!" She steps back, leaving the door open, clearly assuming I'll obey. And because I've got no real plan and a heck of a lot on my mind, I do.

In hot-pink spandex, Lennox crouches in front of the stroller and smiles at Vivi. "How are things with Hockey Daddy?" she asks, pulling herself up again.

I roll my eyes even as my heart sinks. "The same."

She eyes me, and my cheeks burn under her perusal. "Nope. Something happened."

I snort. "Nothing happened. Promise."

My pink-haired friend shakes her head. "Nope. You saw him naked." She taps her finger to her cheek. "Water was involved."

My mouth falls open. "How do you do that?"

With a squeal of laughter, she claps. "It's my superpower." She snags an oversized water bottle off the counter and starts toward the door. "Come on. We're going to the gym, and you're going to tell me why, even after seeing Hockey Daddy's cock again, you're all frowny faced."

"I'm frowny faced because I haven't slept in like forty-eight hours."

"A workout will do you good, then," she says without even the slightest bit of remorse.

I follow her because I'm too tired to argue.

As we approach the gym, she steps to the side and juts her chin at the door. "You go in first and make sure the coast is clear."

I laugh. "Sara really is awesome. I don't think you have to continue hiding from her."

She purses her lips and hits me with a glare. "Go."

Smirking, I slip into the empty gym. "All clear," I sing, not at all surprised that the facility is empty. It's the guys' first day home in ten days. They're probably taking it easy.

She stalks in, eyes narrowed and peering over her shoulder. While she sets her water down and tightens her ponytail, I lay a blanket out on a mat, lift Vivi out of her stroller, and settle the both of us on the floor. Immediately, Vivi reaches for her toes and pulls them to her mouth. I grasp her hands and gently pry them off, then hand her a teething toy. "Don't eat your toes, bestie. I got you."

"You're so good with her," Lennox says, clipping her shoes into the stationary bike.

I shrug and look down at Vivi, who's gurgling and cooing at her toy now. "She makes it easy."

Lennox shakes her head. "No, babe. She's a baby. Even if she's the cutest one I've ever seen, I'd be losing my mind. You haven't slept in two days, and her father has been an ass to you, yet you're so chill and serene when you're with her. You're everything she needs."

My throat closes up, and I have to blink to stave off tears threatening to spill over.

Everything she needs. *Just me.*

The idea—that I could ever be enough for someone—slices through me.

The door to the gym swings open, startling me. I wipe at my face, even though I haven't shed a tear, and turn at the sound.

"Hey, Baby Hall," War hollers, stepping into the room. His eyes are bright and his smile is wide. Apparently, he's over the flu. Hopefully that means Gavin will be feeling better soon too. "Yo, Sar," he calls over his shoulder. "Your new bestie is here!"

Lennox squeaks and wiggles one foot, then the other, trying to dislodge herself from the bike. Frantic, she gets one free, then practically falls off the bike in one very un-fluid motion. "Shit, shit, shit," she mutters as she rushes past me and darts into the storage closet.

Sara appears then, scanning the space. "I swear I saw someone wearing bright pink on a bike when we passed the window a second ago." She shakes her head. "Am I losing it?"

Shrugging, I scoop Vivi off the floor. I'm a terrible liar, so looking away as I do is my best bet. "Just Vivi and me here right now." Not exactly a lie.

Brooks follows behind her, his size immediately making the room feel smaller. He kneels beside me and offers a fist to Vivi, even though she doesn't have the coordination for fist bumps just yet. "Hey, Vivi girl. How's it going?"

I sigh but smile at the baby. "She's teething, and her daddy is still sick."

"Oh, that's fun," Sara mutters.

Brooks smiles. He's always smiling. "Hiding from him?"

I snort. "What gave that away?"

He squeezes my wrist, then runs a finger along Vivi's cheek. "He's trying," he says as my eyes catch on the friendship bracelets circling his wrist. *Best Uncle, Saint,* and *Crazy Girl.*

I take a steadying breath when a flash of Gavin's bracelets hits me, specifically the one with my nickname on it. But before I get too lost in the memory, I remember that Lennox is still hiding in the closet. "Hey, any chance you guys can help me really quick?"

They all eagerly agree as I rack my brain for an excuse to get them out of here. I blink at Brooks, then Sara, then War, searching for inspiration, but my mind is blank.

"You need something?" Brooks says slowly, brow furrowed.

"What the girl needs is sleep," War says. "Come on, Baby Hall." He looms over me and holds out his hand. "Let's go up to my place. We can watch Vivi while you take a little nap."

I put my hand in his and hold tight to Vivi, letting him help me up. Now that sounds like a plan.

After spending the afternoon at War's, I return to the apartment, feeling marginally better. According to her text, Lennox made it back to Sara's apartment without being spotted. I promised to catch up with her later, then pocketed my phone to ensure Sara didn't see the messages. When she discovered I'd never seen *Dawson's Creek*, she just about lost it and forced me to sit through the first four episodes.

I get Vivi set up in her baby swing, and while she's cooing and smiling at the spinning butterflies above her, I heat up a bowl of soup, then take it and another dose of meds with me down the hall. "Gavin." I knock on his door. He doesn't answer, but I figure he's sleeping, so I press inside. "Hey, Gavin—"

The words die on my lips as I come face to face with a soaking wet Gavin who is stepping out of the bathroom in nothing but a towel. His head shoots up, and his brown eyes settle on me.

Rivulets of water travel down his shoulders and between his pecs, then disappear where the towel clings to his waist. I can't look away from the V that leads to the most perfect cock. One that is very clearly growing hard the longer I stand here ogling him.

"Fuck," Gavin mutters.

Caught in the act, I tear my eyes away and instead zero in on his face, which is etched in severe lines.

Lip caught between my teeth, I wince. "Sorry—I, uh—" I point to the door. "I'll just leave the soup here and get out of your way."

"Millie, wait." Gavin takes a single step closer, his expression easing. His damp hair is a mess, but his skin looks less pale. "Let me get dressed, and I'll take over with the baby."

"You're sick."

"I'm feeling a lot better. Sleeping the day away will do that."

I smile. "I'm glad you're feeling better, but seriously, rest. You can take over tomorrow."

He sighs. "You sure?"

"Yes. Vivi and I are going to eat. Then I'll give her a bath before we both crash for the night."

He nods and swallows audibly. "I really appreciate it. I'll be out in a bit to say good night to her, at least."

"Okay." We watch one another again. There's so much to say, but neither of us dares to interrupt this ceasefire we seemed to have entered. I catch a glimpse of the bracelets on his wrist again and feel another swell of certainty that we're going to be all right.

Then I book it out the door before I launch myself into his arms.

"Please, Vivi." We're both crying now. She's been up every hour since midnight, drooling and gnawing on her hand. This damn tooth is so close to breaking through. Every time she falls asleep, I collapse into bed and set the monitor beside my head on the pillow. I'm so delirious from lack of sleep, I worry I won't wake up the next time she cries.

But I do. And every freaking time, I fling myself up too quickly and bang my head on the top bunk.

I pace back and forth in her room in the moonlight. "We both need sleep, baby girl. Please."

Viviane's whole body shudders with each sob, pitiful and heartbreaking. I continue rubbing soft circles on her back and murmuring soothing words. When her cries grow louder, I try singing. At this point, I have to do something to keep myself awake. The exhaustion is so bone deep I'm not even sure what time it is or how many times I've been woken up.

After several minutes, her cries quiet, and she drifts off. "Oh, thank god," I murmur into the top of her head, holding her close.

After setting her back in her crib and begging her silently not to wake up again, I hurry back to my room, praying for sleep. My head throbs from exhaustion, and continuously banging it on the top bunk has only exacerbated it. So I grab a pillow and blankets, then trudge back to Viviane's room and curl up on the floor, determined to get some rest.

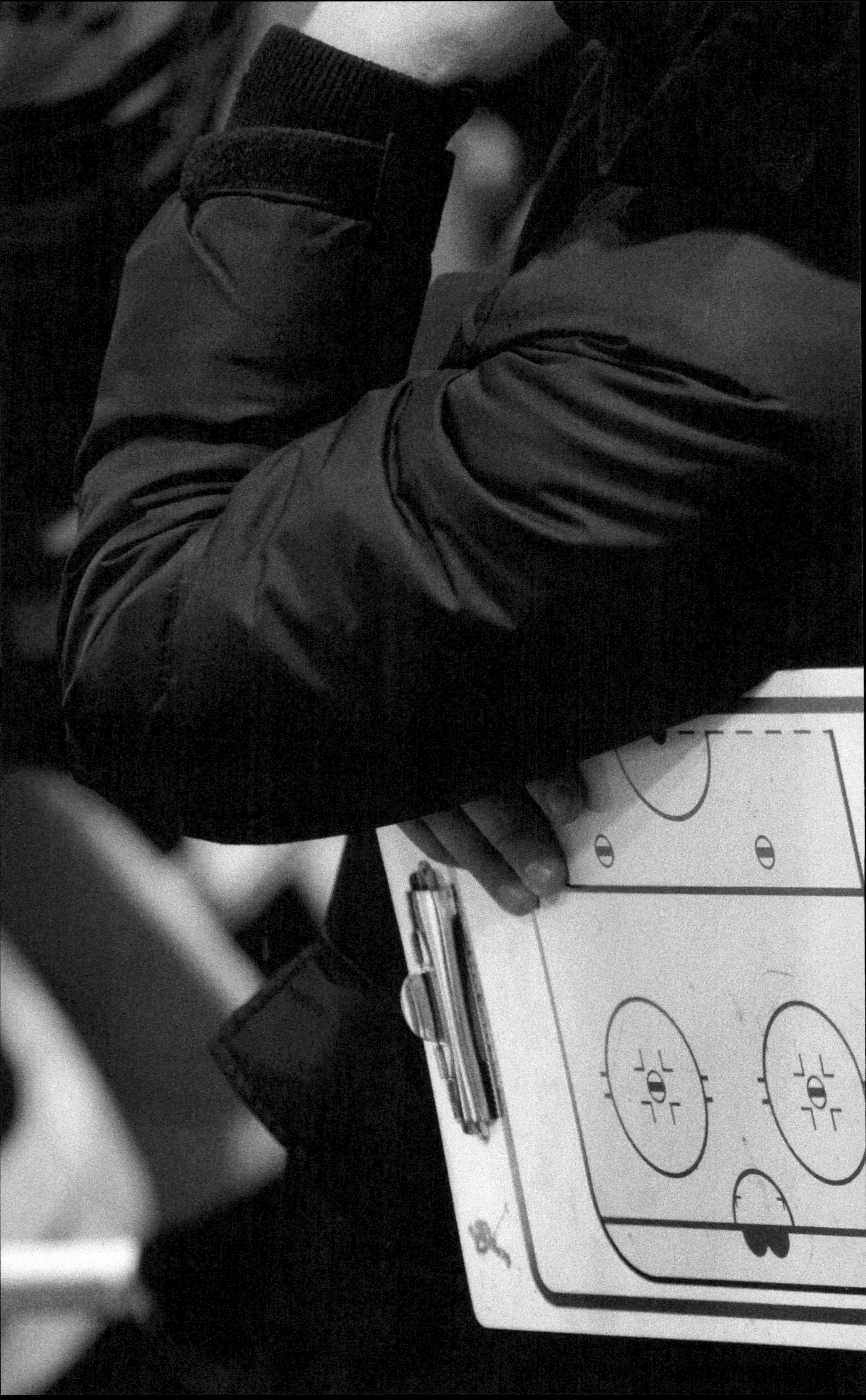

CHAPTER 43
Gavin

THE APARTMENT IS SILENT, my cock is hard, and the memory of Millie's touch the other night is playing on repeat in my head. The way she rubbed her hands across my chest, down my arms, through my hair, and lower—until we were interrupted.

Fuck, even delirious from a fever, I was hard as she touched me.

I slip a hand under the sheet and grip my cock. With a firm tug, I bring to mind the way it felt when she was wrapped around me. Hot. Squeezing me. Fucking me.

Fuck, it's been too long.

Too long since I tasted her. Touched her. Kissed her.

With a groan, I pump harder, imagining her lips wrapping around my head, how she'd twirl her tongue and then smile when I'd curse. I squeeze my eyes shut and conjure the way it felt when I'd fist her hair, and in response, she'd suck me harder. The light tugging turned her on so much that she'd grind against my leg, looking for relief. I'd flip her around then and eat her out until she came all over my face.

I need her so badly. My spine tingles and white lights burst behind my eyelids as I hurtle closer to my release. But the sensations are interrupted by a cry.

"Fuck." Just one more minute and I'll be—

Vivi cries again, this time louder and more pained. The desire drains from me quickly. With a grunt, I release my cock and swing my legs over the side of the bed. I adjust myself and rush into the bathroom to wash my hands. Then I march down to her room, determined to get to her before Millie wakes up.

I didn't hear Vivi at all last night, which means either she magically slept through the night or I was still so out of it that I didn't hear her, so Millie got up with her. I'd bet on the latter.

My suspicion is confirmed when I open the door to my daughter's room and find a sleeping Millie curled up on Vivi's rainbow rug, the blue comforter from Finn's bed wrapped around her.

Shame and anger flood my veins. I'm a fucking asshole.

Chest heaving with frustrated breaths, I silently move to the crib. I force my body to relax, though, before I pick up my baby girl. Once she's in my arms, I soothe her. "Hey, Vivi girl. Let's get you a bottle."

On the couch, I change her, and once she's finished her bottle, I settle her in the swing, then return to her room, determined to start fresh with the angel on her floor.

She deserves so much more than I've given over the last few weeks. Hell, the last few months. I walked out when she was struggling. I turned my back on her because she wasn't ready for all of this. And the moment she finds out what I'm going through, she doesn't hesitate to drop everything to help me.

To help my daughter.

To love us both, even when it's the last thing I deserve. Even when I've made it nearly impossible for her.

I bend down and pull Millie into my arms. She opens her eyes, blinking in confusion, and her first words crack my thawing heart. "Vivi—is she okay?"

"Yes, Peaches. She's okay. Come on." I press my lips to her forehead. "Go back to sleep."

She relaxes in my arms with a sigh and buries her head in my neck. "Just need a few minutes," she murmurs, her breath hot on my skin, sending tingles down my spine.

I shuffle into my room and lay her on my side of the bed. This is exactly where I want her. On my pillow. In my bed. Under my sheets. Smelling like me.

Forever.

Her lashes flutter for a moment before she finally forces her eyes open. "Wait. I can go to my room. I'm sorry I—"

"Sleep, baby." I press my lips to her forehead. From now on, she won't be sleeping anywhere but here.

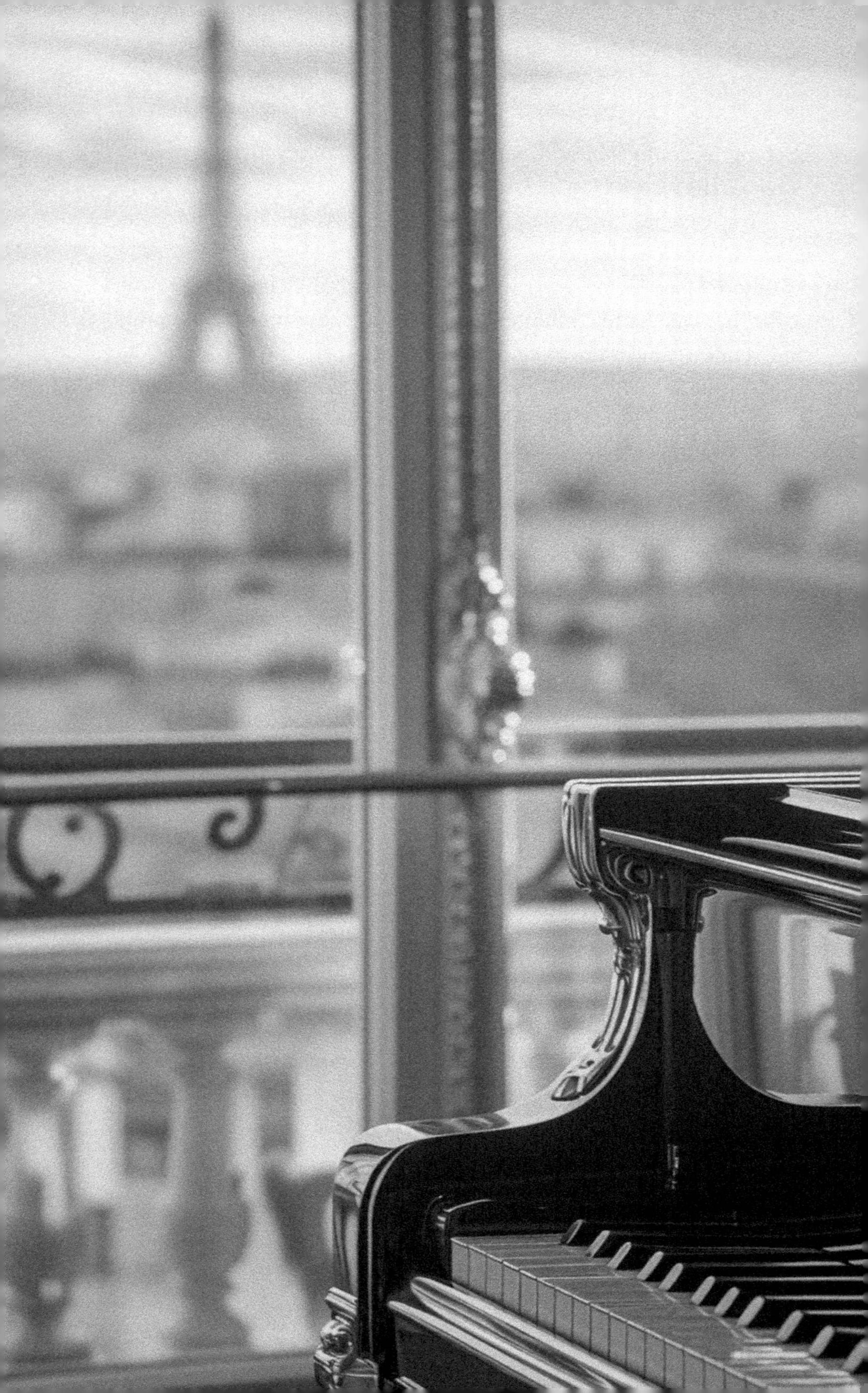

CHAPTER 44
Millie

HOVERING ABOVE ME, his lips only an inch from mine, Gavin smirks. "This what you been waiting for, Peaches? My lips? My tongue? My cock?"

I buck my hips, desperate for him, but he keeps himself just out of reach. "Please, Gavin."

"And what will I get if I let you rub that sweet pussy against me?"

Desire floods me at the tease, at his tone. "Whatever you want. I'll give you whatever you want."

"What if all I want is you?" His eyes glow with sincerity, making the ache in my heart almost as fierce as the one between my legs.

I need him, and the idea that I could truly be enough for him, that we could finally be us again, has my heart racing.

"I'm yours. Now please, just kiss me."

With a hum, he dips close again, his lips millimeters from mine. Finally, I get to feel them again—

A baby cries, and then Gavin is gone. Disappearing into thin air.

"Coming," I say, willing my limbs to work. My body is sluggish, though it feels like I got some sleep during this stretch. I wonder what time it is. I throw the blanket off and stretch out my shoulders, knowing I'll pay for having slept on the floor. When I finally open my eyes, I jackknife up and curse. Dammit. Why am I in Gavin's room? Fuck. Did I sleepwalk?

Oh my god, Gavin's going to think I was trying to seduce him. What the hell, Millie?

A quick glance at my surroundings tells me I'm alone, so I jump out of bed and rush out of his bedroom. Maybe he won't—

"Sleep okay, Peaches?"

I jump at the sound of Gavin's voice. "Shit." I slap a hand to my chest and glare at him where he's reclined on the couch. "You scared the shit out of me."

He laughs, and it's such a familiar and beautiful sound that my heart skips like it's a record caught on the best line. I could listen to that sound all day. And I could stare at that smile for the rest of my life.

He's wearing navy gym shorts, his legs spread wide. His hair is mussed, his brown eyes glinting mischievously. A five o'clock shadow coats his chiseled jaw, and his chest is fucking bare, with my favorite little girl lying on it.

My swallow is heavy. "You—you're—" I point at him. "No shirt."

His smile grows wider. Cockier. *Gavinier.* Is that a thing? Can someone be an even more potent version of themselves? I think so. In this moment, when he's looking at me like this, he's more himself than he's been in months.

Or maybe I'm delusional from lack of sleep.

"I read that it's good for bonding."

"With me?"

He chuckles, his eyes crinkling and his chest rumbling. "With Vivi. Although I'm sure you'd appreciate snuggling up against my bare chest too. You always did."

His words are *strange.*

Right? He's different. Flirty.

Am I still dreaming?

"I'm so confused."

With a nod, he gestures to the cushion next to him. "Come sit. You're probably still tired."

Ignoring his confusing offer, I stumble into the kitchen. I need coffee. Or water. Or—I blink at the clock above the microwave. "What time is it?"

It's six. Six a.m. or six p.m.? I haven't quite figured it out when a knock sounds on the door.

"I'll get it," I say, already heading back in that direction. "You guys are really adorable all snuggled up on the couch. I'm kind of jealous."

Gavin bites his lip, and I swear to god I'm going to melt into a puddle. "No need to be jealous, Peaches. There's room for you here too."

My stomach flips, and my smile is so fucking big as I grasp the doorknob and pull. The smile slips, though, when Camden comes into view.

"Hey, Baby Hall." His focus dips, reminding me that I'm still in my pajamas.

"Camden." I cross my arms over my chest to cover myself. "What's up?"

The back of my neck prickles, then Gavin is clearing his throat.

"Everything all right?" he booms, suddenly appearing behind me, still holding Vivi, who's wide-eyed and drooly, wearing nothing but a diaper and a smile.

Out of habit, I swipe at the moisture below her mouth, and she latches on to my hand, holding me close.

"Hey, Viv. You're looking much happier than you were last night."

Camden clears his throat, and I turn back his way.

"Sorry. It's been a long few days." I let out a light, uncomfortable laugh. "I'll get out of the way so you guys can chat hockey or whatever." Turning, I hold my arms out, reaching for my little bestie. "Want me to take her?"

"Actually, I came to see you," Camden confesses.

Frowning, I turn back around. He's dressed in a button-down shirt, and he's gripping his coat in one hand, his fists almost white.

Is he nervous?

He wets his lips, and my stupid eyes follow the movement. I definitely need more sleep.

"Me?"

His mouth quirks up in a lopsided, boyish smile. "Yeah, thought maybe we could go grab dinner and a movie."

Oh shit.

Chest suddenly tight, I glance back at Gavin.

His jaw is taut, and the easy demeanor and smile from moments ago have vanished.

"I have to work," I stammer, wishing I'd never answered the door. Wishing Gavin was still smiling and teasing.

"Can she have the night off, Coach? She's been going nonstop."

At Camden's plea, Gavin fixes his brown eyes on me. He studies me, appraising, and, I hope, finally seeing who I've become.

For a moment, I think he's going to tell Camden to fuck off. That he and Vivi need me. Or maybe even that he *wants* me to stay. I press my lips together and silently will him to do just that. I beg him without words to understand what's written in my heart. But when he lets out a soft sigh and a resigned smile forms on his lips, I know I'm going to hate whatever he says next.

"He's right, Millie. You deserve a night off."

"I just woke up," I almost whisper, my voice caught in my throat, looking from him to Camden with a frown.

"That's okay. I can hang with Coach while you get ready. That work?"

Gavin nods and motions for Camden to follow him inside. As the men settle on the couch, I force my feet to move and make my way down the hall, ready to scream about how time never seems to be on our side.

It isn't until hours later, when I'm sitting in the movie theater, hands clasped tightly in my lap, that I remember Gavin's first words to me today.

That I recall his demeanor when I woke up.

Those few moments when he was cocky and smiling and *flirting* with me.

And he called me Peaches.

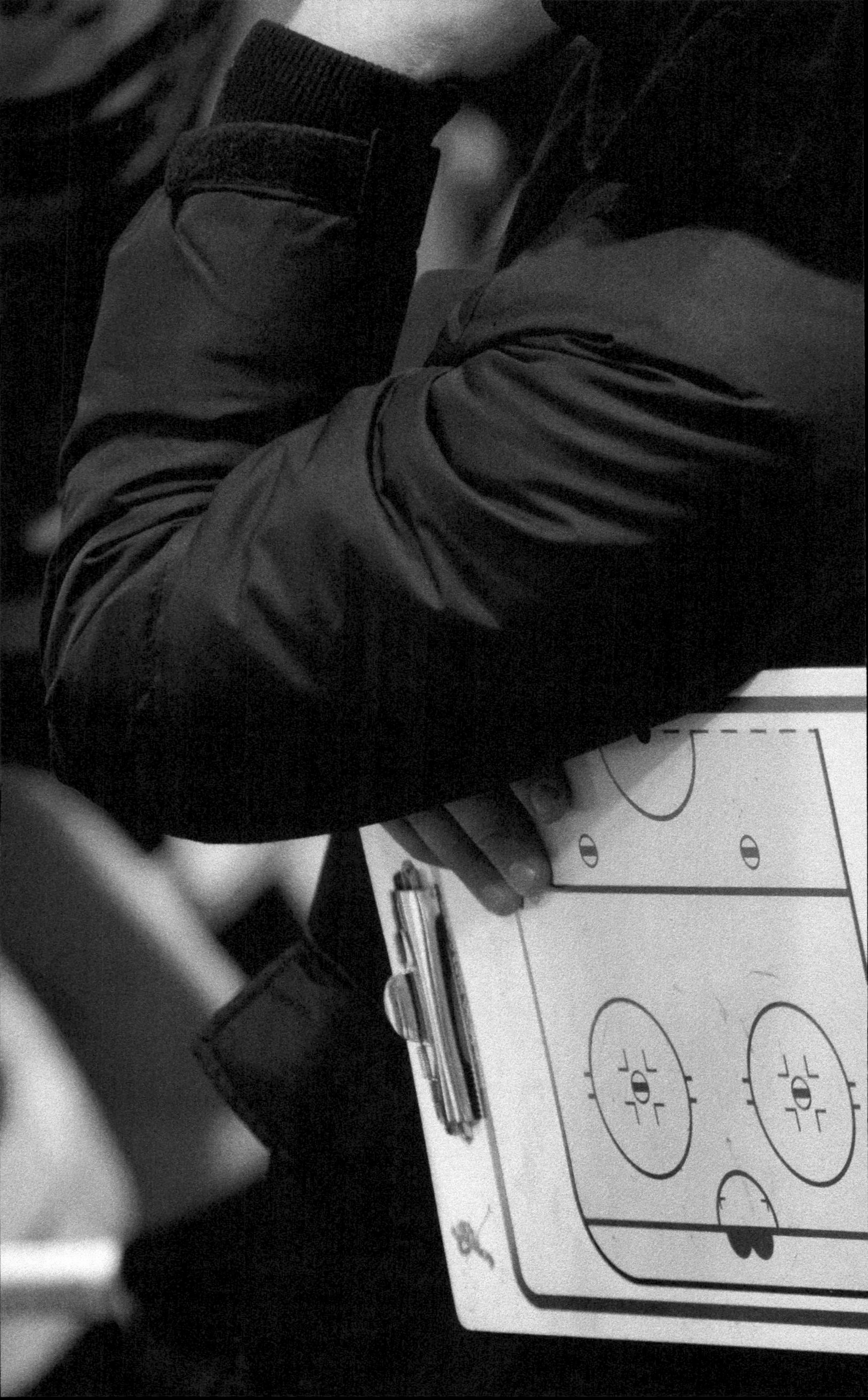

CHAPTER 45
Gavin

> Me: What do you know about Camden Snow?

> Brooks: He's a right winger with a wicked good slap shot?

> Beckett: We pay him too much to have him on second string…

> Aiden: He's currently on a date with Millie.

FUCK. I grip the bottle of whiskey I just swore to myself I wouldn't drink and pour two fingers into the tumbler. After a heavy sip, I lean against my kitchen counter and brace for everyone's commentary.

> Beckett: Duck. Really?

> Brooks: This kind of situation warrants more than just a duck.

> Beckett: I know. My ducking phone auto corrected.
>
> Beckett: Duck.
>
> Beckett: DUCK
>
> Aiden: You make this too easy.
>
> Aiden: Goose.
>
> Me: Are you done yet?
>
> Aiden: He's a good guy. He'll be good to her.
>
> Me: The fuck he will.
>
> Beckett: So I take it we aren't staying away from Millie?
>
> Me: No. I'm done with that idea.
>
> Beckett: Do you like your face?
>
> Me: Ford will come around.
>
> Brooks: LOL
>
> Brooks: Sara says that was mean. Sorry.
>
> Aiden: I mean, you weren't wrong the first time.
>
> Brooks: This is Sara. All I want to say is FINALLY!

I chuckle into my whiskey glass. Exactly. That's the energy I'm looking for. But as I stare at the clock, watching the time slowly drag on, I worry that I might have real competition now. Camden is a catch. Obviously. He plays for the NHL. Though I *could* change that. I grunt as I force that idea from my head.

So yes, he plays for the NHL, he's closer to her age, he doesn't have a kid, and he isn't best friends with her dad.

Fuck. This situation really is shit.

And he also hasn't treated her like absolute garbage for the past few weeks like I have.

I glance at my phone again, wishing Millie would text me and tell me she's having a terrible time. Or that she regrets going out. Fuck, even if she texted to ask about Vivi right now, I'd be happy. At least then I'd know she's thinking about us. That we matter.

This is ridiculous. Why am I just staring at the clock? Dropping the phone onto the kitchen counter, I grab my whiskey and head into the living room. Bypassing the couch, I go straight toward the grand piano I bought for the only woman I've ever loved. Then I settle on the bench in front of the instrument that has never been played, and in my dark apartment, I run my fingers across the ivory keys.

The sound that comes from the instrument is jarring, making me pull back with a sharp breath in. I glare at the damn thing, then curse under my breath. I'm a fucking idiot. The last thing I want is to wake Vivi. It's after eleven p.m. With my luck, she'll be up in another hour or so anyway. I should be reading up on how best to handle teething. Maybe searching the margins for Millie's replies. There has got to be something out there that will take Vivi's pain away.

Mentally, I add it to the list of the thousand things I want to do tomorrow. I hang my head and let out a resigned sigh. Every inch of my body is buzzing with adrenaline. I'm desperate to tell Millie how I feel, to tell her father that I'm in love with his daughter, and her brother that he's just going to have to deal with it. *I'm ready to tell the world that she's mine*, and she's out on a fucking date with someone else.

Keys jangle in the hall, and then the knob is turning and the door is opening, and there she is, her auburn hair wild. The relief that hits me is so bone deep I rub my legs to soothe the ache. In doing so, I hit the keys on the piano, startling us both.

"Shit." Millie jumps and spins, her eyes wide. Then, wearing a confused frown, she steps forward. "What are you doing?"

"Did he kiss you?"

"What?"

"Did. He. Kiss. You?" I grind out.

She tilts her head, her shoulders lowering. "Gavin," she says, her voice soft, placating.

My blood is pumping as I wait for her response. "It's an easy answer, Millie."

"No." She clasps her hands in front of her. "We grabbed dinner and watched a movie."

I spin on the bench so I'm facing her. Like this, with me seated and her standing, she's barely taller than me. My mouth waters as I get a hit of her fruity scent, as I get lost in the way she licks her full lips. The moonlight filtering in makes her golden eyes glow and brings out the freckles dotting her skin like constellations. She's effervescent, her dark curls so perfect I have to clutch my thighs to keep from pulling on one.

"Did you want him to kiss you?"

Millie juts her chin out defiantly. "What do you want me to tell you?"

"The truth. Do you think about kissing him? Does the idea of your lips touching his make you ache? It makes me ache, Millie. Makes me sick to my stomach. Makes me want to trade the kid, but only after I beat the shit out of him. But I can't really do that just because he's looking at my nanny."

She presses closer to me, her knee bumping mine. "Your nanny? That's all I am to you?"

Tipping my head back, I grasp her by the backs of her thighs and hold her in place. "You know you're more than that."

"You called me Peaches," she taunts, one brow arched. "Earlier, when I walked out of your bedroom, you said, 'Sleep okay, Peaches?'"

I suck in a breath at the sharp pain that lances my chest. I did.

Gently, she strokes my cheek, her expression softening. "And you wear a bracelet that says Peaches on your wrist. How long, Gavin? How long have you been wearing that?"

I close my eyes, relishing the feel of her hands on me again, soaking in her heat and inhaling her scent. I want to commit every detail of this moment to memory. Millie drapes one leg over my thigh, then the other. I grip her waist so she doesn't fall as she settles on my lap, straddling me. The heat between her legs has me stirring to life and squeezing her tighter, holding her to me, trying to wrap my brain around what's happening right now.

She clutches at my shoulders. "How long are you going to pretend we're nothing when we both know that, you and me, we're explosive together?"

"Exactly," I say, my throat thick. "Explosive. We'll blow up our lives. We'll blow up the lives of everyone we know. I was willing to do that, Millie. I was willing to destroy my relationship with everyone I knew so I could have you. But then you destroyed me."

Eyes glistening, she presses her palms to my cheeks. "I destroyed me too. But I wasn't ready."

My gut twists, and so does my expression. "And I'm supposed to believe you suddenly are?"

"No," she whispers, ducking and giving me the most earnest look. "You're supposed to *see* that I am. For weeks I've been here every step of the way. Not because I'm your nanny, but because I'm your person. I'm your person, and you're mine. Please stop punishing me and touch me. *Kiss me.* Because the only person I ache for is you."

Her golden eyes are imploring, begging me to believe her. In those eyes, I see my future. I saw my future in them a year ago too, when I showed up at her apartment in Paris. I think I saw it the day on the plane when I found out who she was.

If I hadn't, I wouldn't have risked blowing up my friendship with her father. I wouldn't have risked my reputation. She was worth it all. And though she broke my heart when she told me she wasn't ready, I'm not even upset that things turned out this way.

Because when Vivi showed up at my door, had Millie been here, had we not gone through these tests and trials, I would have wondered if she felt obligated to stay. I'd have worried that she was settling and that she'd one day regret being forced to mother a child who wasn't hers.

But now? Now I know she loves my daughter. She chose my daughter even when I didn't choose *her*.

We'll be stronger because of our time under tension. I'm confident in us, in our future. And I'm not worried, because even in the face of my hostility, Millie loved me and fought hard to get us here.

I press a thumb against her bottom lip, and she moans in response, her hot breath washing over me.

"Please, Gavin."

"Please what?"

"Soothe the ache. Make me feel better. Make *us* feel better." She sucks my thumb into her mouth.

Heat washes over me, and my need for her threatens to take over all logic. "You drive me fucking crazy, Peaches."

She bites down on my thumb and swirls her tongue again, making my cock throb.

"So punish me," she taunts. "Spank me, bite me, fucking devour me. But don't shut me out." She rolls her hips. "Don't deny me. I can't—"

The pressure against my hard length makes my control snap. I spin her and lift her onto the piano keys, the sound jolting and yet so perfect for the uncontrollable sensations taking over. With my hands on her thighs, I hold her in place.

"You can't? What about me? What about what I need? You want me to punish you, but I want to worship you. I need to apologize for how I've treated you. I failed you. Failed us. I should never have walked out that door. And I never should have let you end us because you were scared. So baby, please say I can have you. Promise me you're mine. Put me out of my misery and tell me you'll never let me walk away again."

The air between us grows so thick I may suffocate as I wait for her to promise me forever. Whether she understands the implications or not, that's what I'm taking. Her forever.

"I've only ever been yours," she whispers, slipping a hand down her chest. "My body." With a pinch to her nipple, she gasps. "My heart." She uses her free hand to tip my chin up. "Me." Her lips ghost against mine. "You have owned all of me since the day you took my virginity."

"And I always will," I promise her.

I don't take that responsibility lightly. I may not be the man her father would have chosen for her, but I'll protect her. I'll care for her. And I'll love her every day for the rest of my life.

Finally, I wrap my hands around her waist and pull her closer, barely registering the dissonant sound of the piano keys as she brushes against them, because the moment her lips are on mine, she's all I feel, all I see, all I hear. Our tongues tangle together, and our moans mix, creating the most beautiful tune.

From this moment forward, it's the two of us and Vivi. No one else matters.

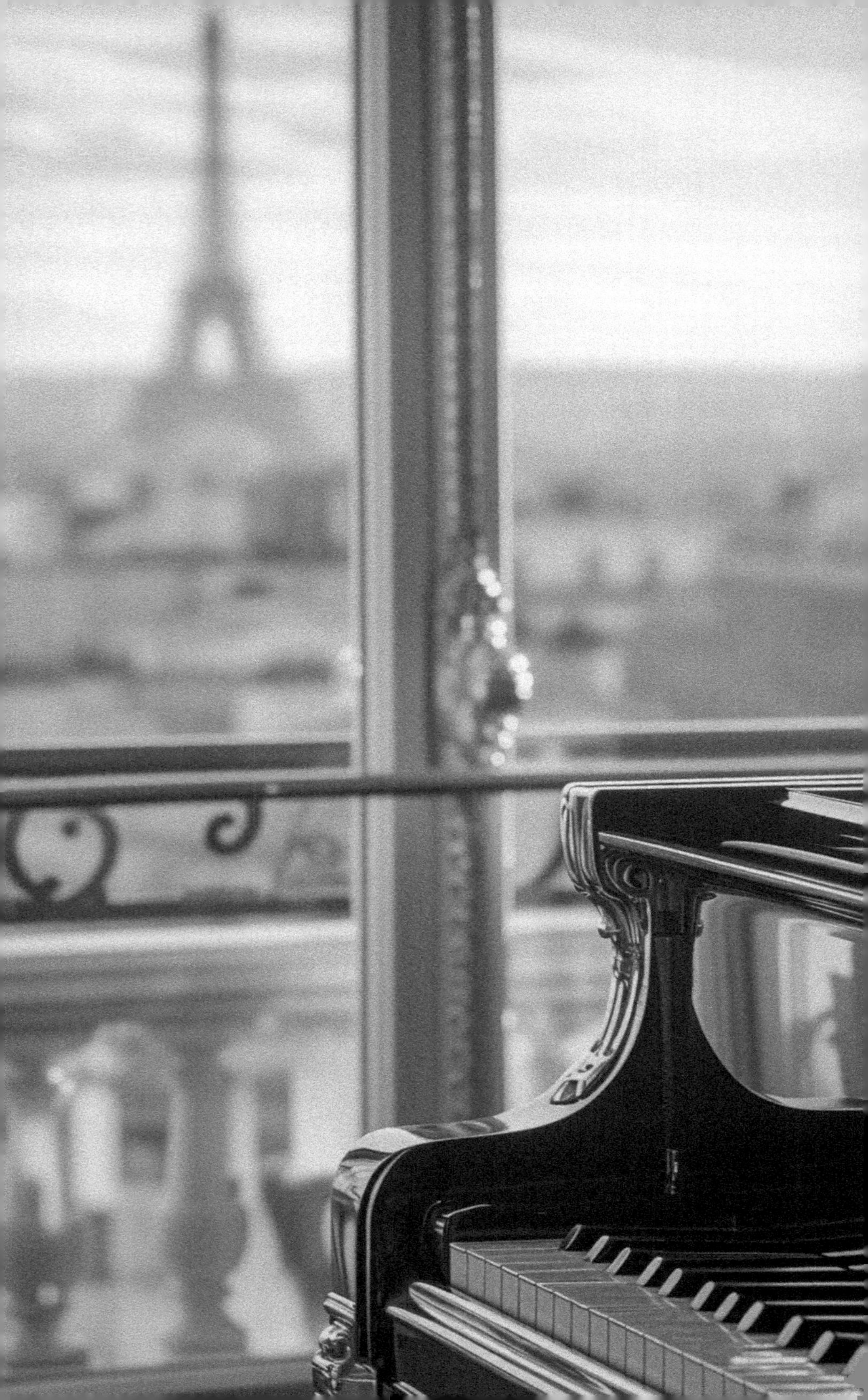

CHAPTER 46
Millie

THE TASTE of whiskey and remorse mixes with hope as Gavin kisses me. His apology is unnecessary. We've both been in the wrong, and yet neither of us would be here, doing this, if not for the mistakes we made.

And that's all I care about. Finally, we're on the same page. Finally, our lips are locked together, our moans all there is left to say.

My hands dig into the fabric of his shirt, and I cling to him. I can't get close enough. I want him to sink inside me and hold me all night. To fuck me slowly and never stop, even if there's no way either of us will last. We've barely touched, barely had a taste, and I am already on the precipice of an orgasm.

Gavin shifts, and suddenly, I'm on my back on top of the smooth lacquered surface of the piano.

"Need these off." He grits out the words as he tugs on my leggings.

With my hands planted on the cool surface of the piano beneath me, I lift up so he can yank my shoes off and then shimmy my pants down. Ignoring my panties, he goes for the hem of my sweater. I heave myself up so he can tear it over my head.

"Holy shit, Peaches," he says when I'm topless. "What did you do?" His eyes go wide as he takes in my piercings. Then he smiles, and his full black lashes flutter when he brings his attention back to my face. "Can I touch them?"

I nod. "Please."

His touch is gentle at first, tentative, his thumb grazing over one slowly. That brush sends a bolt of lightning to my core. Spasming, I cry out in ecstasy.

"Oh fuck," he murmurs. "And I thought I loved your tits before." When he touches them again, he's far less gentle. He squeezes one breast roughly and tongues the other with a moan. A wave of lust crests when he clamps his teeth down on my nipple ring and tugs.

In an unsteady breath, I hiss. "Yes. Fuck, that feels good."

"You feel good." Gavin looks up at me, his eyes pools of inky-black desire. "I want to fuck you so bad, but I also want to tease the orgasms out of you."

Panting, I tug on his shirt again. "Yes. Please, Gav."

His smile is devious, corrupt, as he half turns and reaches for his whiskey glass. All that's left is a few pieces of ice and half a finger of liquid. "Open, but don't swallow," he instructs, holding up the glass.

Breaths coming fast, I open my mouth, allowing him to press the glass against my lips and tip it back. As the zesty vanilla flavor dances on my tongue, his teeth replace the glass, and he bites down on my lip, forcing my mouth open. With a groan, he brings his lips to mine and drinks the whiskey straight from my mouth, his tongue teasing me endlessly.

He pulls back and hits me with a look so wicked a shudder racks me.

"That was just a little test. Let's try again." Without waiting for me to reply, he presses his thumb down on my bottom lip. This time he pushes an ice cube into my mouth. "Hold it with your teeth," he instructs, his tone dark.

Holy fuck. Bossy Gavin is hot.

I obey, shivering at the sensation, and he steps back and slides his shirt off, exposing the muscles that were teasing me only hours ago. Then he slowly slides his shorts over his hips, revealing his hard cock. Once he's kicked his shorts to the side, he stands straight again and gives himself a firm tug. "Look at you, Peaches. Spread out on my piano, your legs spread wide and begging for *my* cock, your nipples so hard they could cut glass."

The moan that rips from deep inside me is so violent I almost swallow the ice.

"Careful," he warns, his tone sinful as he grips my panties. In one quick motion, he slips them down my legs. Then he bunches the fabric and presses it to his face, inhaling.

I squirm at the sight and bite down harder on the ice.

"You're so fucking turned on, aren't you? This better all be for me."

I nod, sending a rivulet of cold water dripping down my chin. When it hits my chest, I suck in an unsteady breath.

Gavin leans in close and puts a hand behind my neck, angling so that he can take the cube from my teeth with his own mouth. He runs a line down my neck with the ice, over my already sensitive nipple, then down farther.

"Oh fuck. I don't think—"

With a hand on my waist, he pushes me back and silently shakes his head, telling me not to think.

Just feel, his expression says.

Letting my eyes fall shut, I wait, focusing on my breathing, knowing what's coming next. When he glides the ice over my swollen clit, I hiss. "Shit." I may have known what he was going to do, but I couldn't prepare for the forceful sting shooting between my legs. When he slides the ice cube inside me, I moan and shake, desperate and needy. He pushes it in farther, and just as the coldness becomes too much and I'm about to beg for him to remove it, he suctions his hot mouth to my clit, and I almost explode on the spot.

When he takes the warmth away, I throw my arms out, grasping, but my fingers slide as I push myself up. "What the—"

"You need more?" He arches a brow in challenge.

"You know I do."

He forces one finger inside me, his eyes still ensnaring mine, and I suck in a breath.

I fall back, head thrashing. "Ah."

"That's my perfect girl. My Peaches. Soak my hand, baby."

He spears me with another finger. The zap of electricity that shoots through me causes my back to arch, and I slide against the piano's surface.

"I'll never be able to look in this corner without picturing you naked and begging for me. Your tits are magnificent." He leans down and pulls one into his mouth, his tongue rolling over the piercing and pulling until I cry out.

"Shh, Millie. Don't wake the baby." His tone is pure tease. He knows it's almost impossible for me to be quiet when he has me this worked up.

He doesn't relent, winding me up and pushing me to the edge, then pulling back. I want to grab his head, hold him in place, and fuck his face, but the surface beneath me is slippery from not only the ice but also my desire, so I can't anchor myself enough to take control.

"Please, Gavin," I beg as my legs tremble beneath his hands.

Power rips through his eyes. "Please what?"

"Make me come. Please fuck me. Anything, please."

"Tell me you're mine. Tell me this is it. It's you and me forever."

Delirious with lust but anchored by love, I give him the truth. "Forever, Gavin. Tell me you're mine forever, because I am yours."

"Mine," he growls against me. Then his tongue is on my clit, swirling and massaging. My climax grows closer, and when he adds a third finger and sucks me into his mouth, I explode, tremors racking my body as the orgasm rolls through me.

Even as he removes his fingers, he continues to rub soft circles against my clit, prolonging my orgasm as he lines himself up. And then, in one swift move, he presses inside me, spearing me to this moment.

"Fucking finally," he groans as I contract around him. It's nearly impossible to breathe. He's stolen all the air from the room.

Angling over me, he holds us both in place for a moment. "You are the perfect woman. This is the perfect pussy. If you ever keep it from me again, I will die."

I smile at his dramatics, even as a wave of desire washes over me, and push his hair out of his face. "Deal. Now fuck me properly, Coach."

The grin he gives me is the easy one he used to wear all the time. Like the man has finally come back into himself.

I can't help but feel a swell of pride at the knowledge that I helped him get here. I helped bring him back.

He presses his lips to mine, and for a moment, we kiss, breathing in the same air, sharing the same space. It doesn't take long before I'm rubbing against him, needing the friction. Needing more.

Gavin bites my bottom lip and chuckles. "My girl need it rough?"

I nod and tug at his hair. "Yes, please."

He grabs me by the hips, pulls me to the edge of the piano, and positions one of my ankles over his shoulder. Holding me by one ankle and one hip, he slides out and then slams back into me.

Sparks of pleasure collide, pulling a moan from me. He does it again, then again. Soon, his pace is relentless as he fucks me hard, thrusting in and out in powerful strokes meant to bring me right to the edge again.

"You feel so fucking good, Peaches. Squeeze me, baby. Soak my cock and show me you're all mine."

Those words fling me over the cliff. I cry out and spasm around him, pulling a guttural groan from deep in his chest. I milk him until he comes, filling me and proving, once again, that I'm all his. And I always will be.

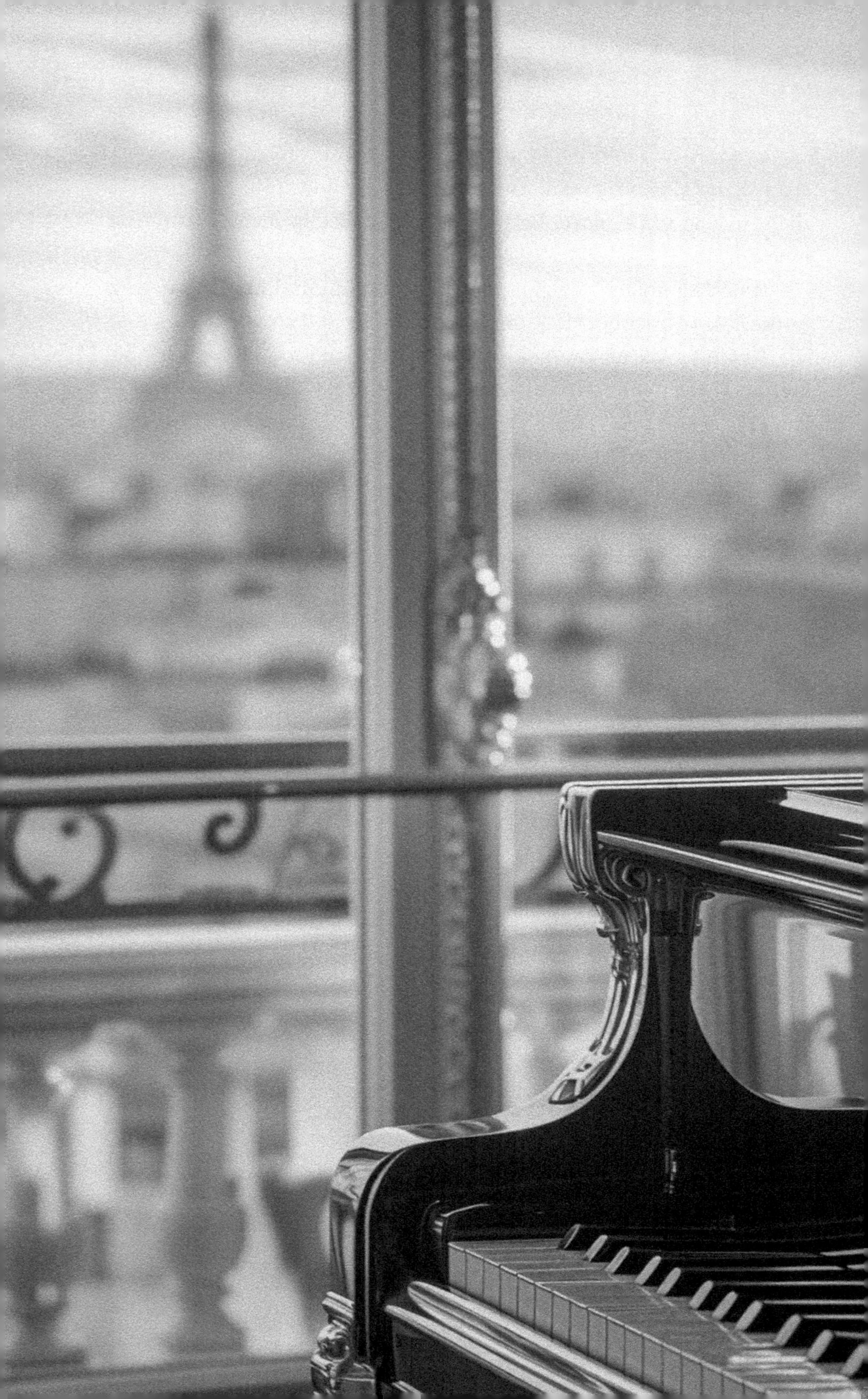

CHAPTER 47
Millie

GAVIN LIFTS me up and carries me to his bedroom. Rather than dropping me on the bed, he heads straight to the shower.

Still clinging to me, he angles to one side to turn the water on, struggling a bit to reach the knob with me still in his arms.

I rake a hand through his hair. "You can put me down, you know," I tease.

He presses a kiss to my forehead and continues his task. Once the water is running, he looks at me, his eyes hungry still. "Didn't want you to think I was done with you like you did the first time we had sex."

God, that night—when I sat in his bedroom at the penthouse, listening to the water run, believing he was done with me—was a lifetime ago.

"I'll never be done with you," he murmurs, as if reading my thoughts.

Warmth spreads through me. "I know."

Gavin holds me tighter with one arm and tests the water, then steps inside the oversized stall. Only then does he set me on my feet. Almost immediately, I feel the evidence of us between my legs and go to wipe it away.

With a hiss, he grabs my wrist. "Let me."

He snakes a hand between my thighs and lowers his hooded eyes. "My cum stays in you," he says as he pushes two fingers inside me.

"Oh," I moan, my legs going weak.

Gavin grips my thigh with his other hand and holds me in place. "One day, when you're ready," he murmurs, head still bowed, focus still on what he's doing to me, "maybe you'll let me do this again."

"One day," I whisper back.

His gaze shoots to mine, and his lashes flutter three times. "Yeah?"

I smile. "Yes, Gavin."

"Fuck." His body visibly shudders. "I just had you, and already, I'm starving for you again." He slides his fingers in and out of me, working me up again. Then he drops to his knees at my feet.

"What are you doing?" I ask, palming his cheek.

He looks up at me, dark eyes so full of desire and earnestness. "Apologizing."

"Gavin." His name comes out on a laugh. "I already accepted your—"

He sucks on my clit, stealing my words and pulling a moan from me.

His breath is hot against my sex. "You were saying?"

"Okay, yeah. You can apologize," I pant, grasping his hair.

His resounding chuckle sends shivers up my spine. He dives back in, feasting and apologizing, until I've come two more times.

By the time we're slipping into bed, me in one of his T-shirts because we couldn't separate even for a moment so I could run to my room for pajamas, it's after midnight.

"Who's her mother?" I whisper once we're beneath the covers, my head on his chest. I've been scared to ask, mostly because, before tonight, he would have bitten my head off. But now I need to know.

Gavin rubs soft circles on my back. "I don't know."

My heart pinches. I wish that Vivi was mine. Either way, I'm glad I'm here now. I'm so incredibly thankful for the time I get with her. "You're a wonderful father."

His arms tighten around me. "Thank you for saying that. Most days, I know I'm failing her, but having you here—it makes it almost bearable. Like maybe she'll be all right because we've got you."

"Gavin," I say softly, my heart squeezing tight. "She really left her at your door?"

He nods, his expression grave. "One minute, we were having dinner with the team, and the next, we were reading a note from Vivi's birth mother, and I was a dad."

"Holy shit."

He hums, his cheek pressed to the top of my head. "The moment I laid eyes on her, it was like I just knew; I'd been put on this earth to be her father."

Tears well behind my lids. "She's pretty special."

Fingers dancing lightly on my back, he brings his hand up to my neck, then buries it in my hair and maneuvers me so I'm looking at him. Expression intense in a way I've rarely seen, he studies my face. "The same thing happened when I met you. Can't explain it, but I was drawn to you. I knew you were special. Knew you were mine."

I blink back the emotion. "What do we do now? My dad—"

"I'll talk to him."

I sigh as nerves skitter through me. It won't be easy. "And Vivi?"

Brows pinched, he frowns. "What about her?"

With a hand pressed to his chest, I swallow and ask, even as I worry I'll upset him. "Are you worried her mother will ever come back?"

Scoffing, he gently guides my head to his chest again. "Not if she knows what's good for her."

I sigh and close my eyes. So many things remain uncertain. So many obstacles still stand in the way. But Gavin is right. One thing remains true: I am his, and as long as he'll have me, I'm not going anywhere.

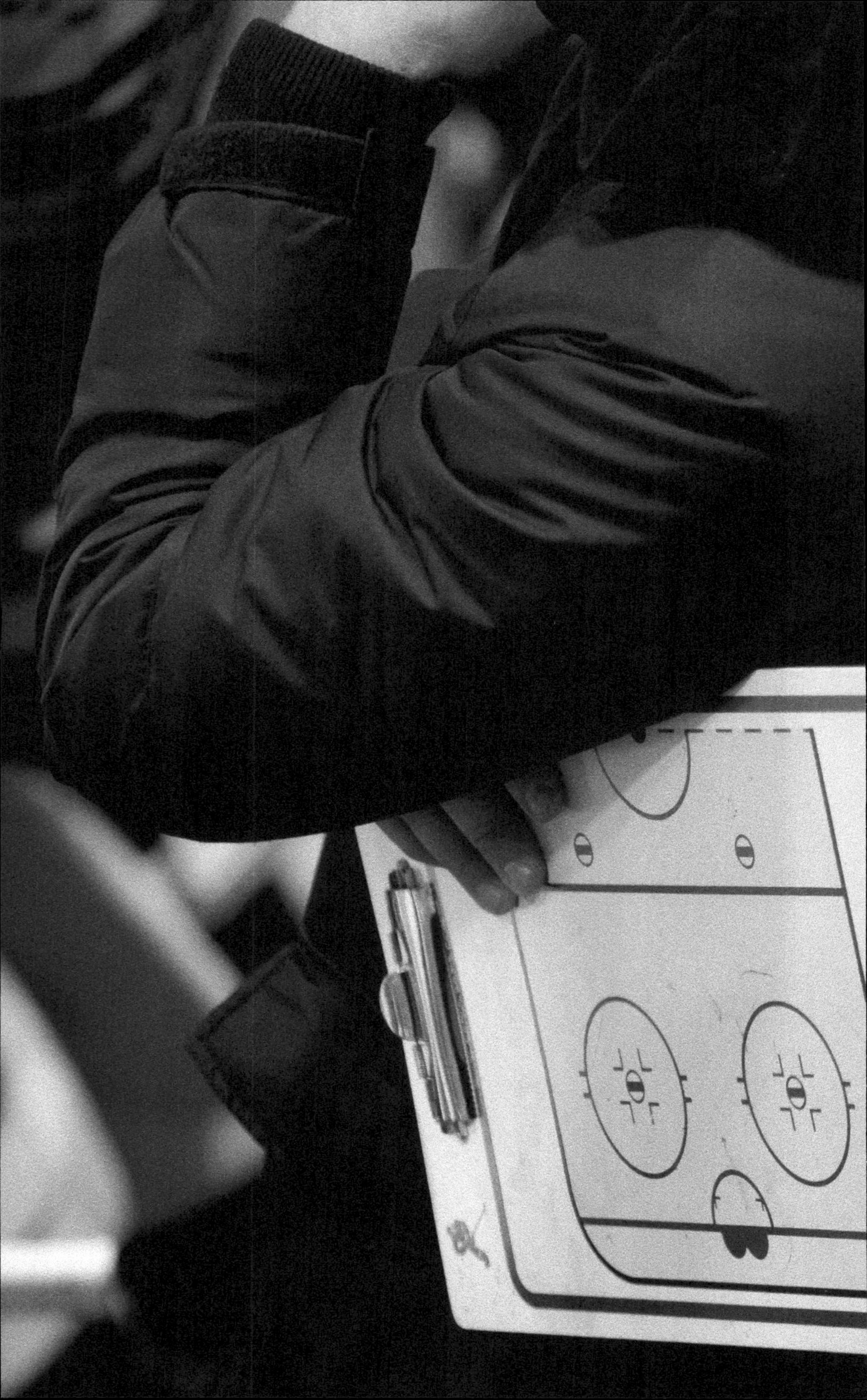

CHAPTER 48
Gavin

LIFE DIDN'T MIRACULOUSLY CHANGE the moment we came together and decided this was it for us. In fact, less than two hours after we finally drifted off, reality hit in the form of a baby's cry. Only tonight, that meant that while Millie went to comfort Vivi, I made the bottle, and then we sat on the couch together, my arm wrapped around Millie while she fed our girl.

Once she was down again, we went back to our shared bed, snuggled, and slept until my alarm went off.

"You sure you don't want to meet me for lunch?"

Millie smiles at me over a cup of coffee. She's still got my Bolts Stanley Cup shirt on, but her bare legs have me wanting to drop to my knees in front of her in the kitchen and eat her for breakfast.

She smiles up at me, coffee mug in hand. "I have plans."

I press a kiss to the side of her neck. "What kind of plans?" I ask, rubbing my nose along the sensitive skin below her ear. Then, because I'm a jealous prick, I add, "Better not be with Camden."

Goose bumps erupt down her arms, and her laugh is breathy. "He'll be at practice with you, dummy."

I glower, which makes her laugh harder. Behind me, Vivi gurgles in response, laughing right along with her from her highchair.

"And I wouldn't be with him anyway. I told you, we were just friends. Besides, I'm a taken woman."

"Damn right you are. And tell me this, who are you taken with?" I brush my nose against her neck again, getting lost beneath her curls.

"This really hot dad. We call him Hockey Daddy."

With a grunt, I nip at her neck. "No one is calling me Hockey Daddy."

She shakes with quiet laughter. "Lennox does."

"Lennox is a troublemaker."

"That's so accurate."

"Enough distracting me," I say, pulling back and smoothing a hand along Vivi's head. "What are you doing today?"

Catching her lip between her teeth, she sobers and settles her coffee cup on the counter. "Lake is coming over to hear some of my songs."

"Really?" I step closer and grasp her arms.

Pensive, she worries that lip and dips her chin, avoiding my gaze. "Is that all right? I probably should have asked whether if it's okay to use your piano."

I tilt her chin up so she's forced to look at me when I speak these next words. "Your piano."

Her face is lined with confusion as she searches my eyes.

"I bought it for you."

"For me?" she asks, splaying a hand over her heart. "But we weren't together. In fact, I'm pretty sure you hated me when you moved into this apartment." She looks around as if the room will agree with her, like the walls will tell her I was toasting her absence on move-in day.

"I hated that I couldn't have you. Hated that you were hurting so much and I couldn't fix it. Hated that I walked away from you when I maybe should have just held on tighter. But hated you?" I shake my head. "Never."

Her golden eyes well with tears as her throat works, like she's trying to swallow back the emotion.

I kiss her forehead. Fuck, I hate when she's sad. "And when the interior decorator asked for the must-haves in the apartment, the first thing on the list was the piano. A grand piano, to be exact."

"Why?" she whispers.

My focus settles on her face again. On the beautiful, trusting eyes that watch me, that have let me in, despite how undeserving I am. "I want to listen to you play music every day, Peaches. And whether you want to play for just us, maybe teach our girl to play when she's old enough, or if you want to write music or sell out stadiums, I'll be here beside you, in awe." I cup her cheek, brushing my thumb across her smooth, freckled skin. "Your dreams are my dreams. All I've ever wanted is for you to discover what those dreams are. I guess I just thought if the piano was here—I don't know—maybe you'd come back to me one day."

"Gavin."

"It was a mistake walking away. Letting you believe that you alone aren't enough. Because you are everything, Millie."

A tear slips down her cheek. "I still don't know exactly what I want. Outside of you and Vivi, my life feels so up in the air. Is it weird that I'm nervous?"

I brush the tear away, then pull her close. "Not at all." I lean my head on top of hers. "You are going to do great. And like you told your father, if Lake's not interested, there are thousands of other musicians out there. Someone will be. This isn't a one-shot deal."

Millie tilts her head up and presses a kiss to my lips. "Thank you."

"For what?"

"For being here. For believing in me when I didn't." Her freckles get lost among a pretty pink blush. "For caring."

Care doesn't begin to scratch the surface of what I feel for her, but now isn't the time to say it. I have a hockey practice to get to, and when I finally tell her exactly how I feel, it won't be as I'm running out the door.

I kiss her softly and remind her that I'll always be here. Then I drop a kiss on Vivi's head as I pass her highchair and head out the door.

"Aw, no Vivi today?" Aiden whines as he skates up to the bench, lip pushed out in a pout.

I laugh. "No. She's with Millie."

Camden and Daniel are just past him, stretching on the ice. War and Brooks are close by too, locked in a friendly competition to see who can do more push-ups. My idiot brother has continued his "tradition" of doing push-ups before home games with Sara on his back. If the guy can do that in his full game day goalie gear, I don't know why the Canadian bothers trying to keep up.

"Did someone say Baby Hall?" War is off the ice and on his skates in one fluid motion.

I fold my arms across my chest and affect my coach voice, ensuring all the guys are paying attention. "This is the last time I'm going to say this. Her name is Millie. Next person to call her Baby Hall," I say with an irritated growl, "will be doing suicides for a week."

Daniel claps. "Yes, Coach. Thank you."

I hold back my wince. The guy wouldn't be thanking me if he knew what I did to his sister last night on my piano.

"And if any one of you goes near her..." he adds, holding out a gloved hand and moving it slowly, from one guy to another.

Camden nudges him in the arm. "Except for me, since you gave me the okay to ask her out."

That sends my blood pressure skyrocketing. I grind my teeth to keep myself from doing anything rash, like knocking the kid out.

"As friends," Daniel adds. "I told you it was okay to go to the movie as friends so she had someone to spend time with other than me."

"We gonna actually practice hockey, or is this an episode of *Sex and the City*?" Brooks chimes in.

Aiden spins around. "Is that what you're watching with Sara this week?" He skates up to Brooks. "I wanna watch. Can I come over?"

"No," Brooks says quickly.

I chuckle despite the annoyance that has a stranglehold on me. "If you guys are done talking women and television, maybe we can play some hockey?"

"Right." Aiden nods, affecting an expression that on anyone else would be jovial but is about as serious as he gets. "No one mention Peaches, and no *Sex and the City* marathon with Sara. Got it." With that, he takes off for center ice.

My stomach bottoms out, and Brooks's eyes are wide as he looks from our little brother to me.

"Who's Peaches?" Daniel asks, frowning.

Fuck.

Aiden whips around, mouth dropped open and eyes filled with shock.

"Peaches and Cream," Brooks sings.

I swear I've never wanted to kiss one of my brothers, but right now, Brooks is my favorite of them all.

Daniel shakes his head and barks out a laugh. "Ah, shit. That's a good one. Leprechaun," he says, skating off toward Aiden. "Can't wait to hear what lyrics you put to that one."

I blow out a breath as I watch him go. Dammit. That was a close one.

"Huck, don't run too far ahead," my brother yells.

Finn hollers something unintelligible over his shoulder as he and Deogi dart off toward the empty baseball field in the middle of the park. Winnie is walking in front of us, holding Addie's hand, and the twins are content to watch the world around us from the stroller my brother is pushing.

"I'm so ducking happy it's almost summer."

Beckett smiles over at me. "Tell me about it. Having five kids inside all winter has been hell."

Winnie turns around with a smirk on her face.

Beckett sighs and digs his phone out of his pocket. "Duck. I'll Venmo the jar."

"Is this still the one the twins set up, or did you start a new one once you all moved out?"

Beckett side eyes me. "You think the Shining Twins would allow me to do that? No. They control the investments. I'm pretty sure all the brownstone kids will be set for life by the time the girls turn twelve."

I laugh. My brother's nicknames for the kids who lived with his family in the brownstone from hell—his words, not mine—always make me smile. "You need to give Vivi a nickname."

Beckett slips his phone back into his pocket, expression as stoic as always. "You mean Rosie? I picked the moniker the day she showed up on your doorstep."

I study my brother as we continue following the big kids. "Rosie?"

"Yeah, the Riveter. You know, 'We Can Do It.'"

I scratch my head. "I don't get it."

"Girl's got tenacity. She settled you down with one look and made you smile again. Despite the shitty cards life has dealt her, she's always smiling. Kid is a fighter."

Shit. Tears burn behind my eyes. I don't know the last time I cried, but suddenly, I worry I might break down right here in the middle of the park. My brother's right. No matter how much I hate that she has to be, Vivi is a fighter. I'd fight all her battles for her if I could. I want to make her life a beautiful one. Want to give her both a mother and a father. It's what she deserves—*everything.*

I swallow and look away. Last thing I need is my brother ribbing me for crying.

"I know," he says, keeping his focus on the path ahead of us and his kids. "I'm very wise, and you're lucky to have me as a brother, and Rosie will do just fine because she has you as a father."

Ah, fuck. That's it. I press my lips together to hold in a sob, but there's no stopping the tears that crest over and run down my face. I grab my brother's shoulder, pulling him from the stroller, and wrap him in a hug.

"You're an asshole, you know that?" I ask through an emotional laugh.

Beckett squeezes me back. "So I've been told a time or two."

I clap him on the back, straighten, and suck in a deep breath, pulling myself together.

"Hate to interrupt the moment, Uncle Gav, but you can Venmo the jar when you get home," Winnie says over her shoulder.

Beckett and I both laugh as I swipe at my eyes. "You got it, Win."

"So how are things with Millie?"

I smile. "Amazing."

My brother stumbles but rights himself quickly, eyes wide. "Weren't you freaking out last night about some date she was on?"

"Yeah." I rub a hand down my face. "I think it was what we needed to both realize we were getting in our own way. We're gonna give this a shot."

"Wow." He nods slowly and works his jaw like he's mulling something over. "I'm happy for you. Seriously. It's good to see you smile and all that, but what about the elephant in the room?"

Slipping my hands into my pockets, I watch Finn run the bases with Deogi at his heels. "Gonna tell him next week."

"Shit—" Beckett hisses the word under his breath, but he cuts himself off quickly and darts a glance at Winnie. Fortunately, Adeline has taken off toward her brother, and Winnie is chasing her. "Why next week?"

"Millie is meeting with Lake today. I want her to focus on that, and I want to give her a little time to think about what she wants to do with her music before we disrupt all of that."

I honestly have no idea how Ford will react, but I want to give Millie time. Just not too much time. I'm tired of living in the shadows, and I'm tired of other men thinking Millie is up for grabs. She's mine, and I'm hers. But most importantly, we're Vivi's family. Vivi deserves all our attention, which we can't give when we're constantly trying to hide.

Beckett nods. "And then what's the plan?"

"Then we live happily ever after like you and Liv and the kids."

Beckett eyes me with one brow raised. "So that's it? You're together? What about Vivi?"

My jaw ticks. "What about her?"

"A few months ago, she didn't want to have kids with you. Now she's okay raising another woman's child?" He stops in the middle of the path and locks me in his full CEO stare. "A woman who, by the way, you still haven't even looked for?"

Despite my best efforts, anger begins to bubble up, and my anxiety spikes. I don't want to think about either of Vivi's birth parents. If no one knows she isn't mine, then I can keep her. Fuck, I don't know that I can even tell Millie. What if she freaks out? What if...what if someone takes her from me?

I squeeze my fists, willing that idea to disappear. "Drop it, okay?"

"Gavin," he urges. "You need to get that resolved. I get that your girlfriend is young, but you need to stop acting like you are too."

"Duck you," I say, teeth grinding.

"Duck you too. I'm bringing this up because I *ducking* care. About you. About my niece. And about Millie."

My anger flares hot. He does, and his concerns are coming from a good place, but this conversation has me wanting to turn and run the other way. "How many times do I have to tell you that it doesn't matter? The woman—whoever she is—was dead to me the moment she left my daughter alone at my door. I don't care who she is. She didn't want Vivi, and we don't want her."

Beckett dips his chin, his mouth turned down in a frown, his voice dark. "It's not that simple, and you know it."

"Drop it. This isn't one of your matchmaking schemes. I'm not a project for you to pour all your time and energy into. I don't need to be fixed."

My brother's been known to meddle in not only our lives but the lives of his wife's friends. Sure, it worked for them, but this situation is wholly different. And I've got this handled. As in, we're *not* handling it. The woman doesn't exist as far as I'm concerned. And I don't intend on digging up that grave.

Finn sprints toward us and comes to a stop at my feet. He plants his hands on his knees and pitches forward, breathing heavily. "Uncle Gav, can I sleep over tonight?"

Before I can tell him no—because I have plans to do very depraved things to my new girlfriend; not that he needs to know that—my brother says, "Sure can, kiddo. Win, want to sleep at Uncle Gav's tonight?"

Winnie is headed our way, carrying a squirmy Adeline.

"I want to sleep at Uncle Gav's," Addie says.

I sigh and look at my brother, hoping he'll help me out of this.

He shrugs, but he's wearing a shit-eating grin. "You said you didn't want my help. Have fun tonight, Uncle Gav."

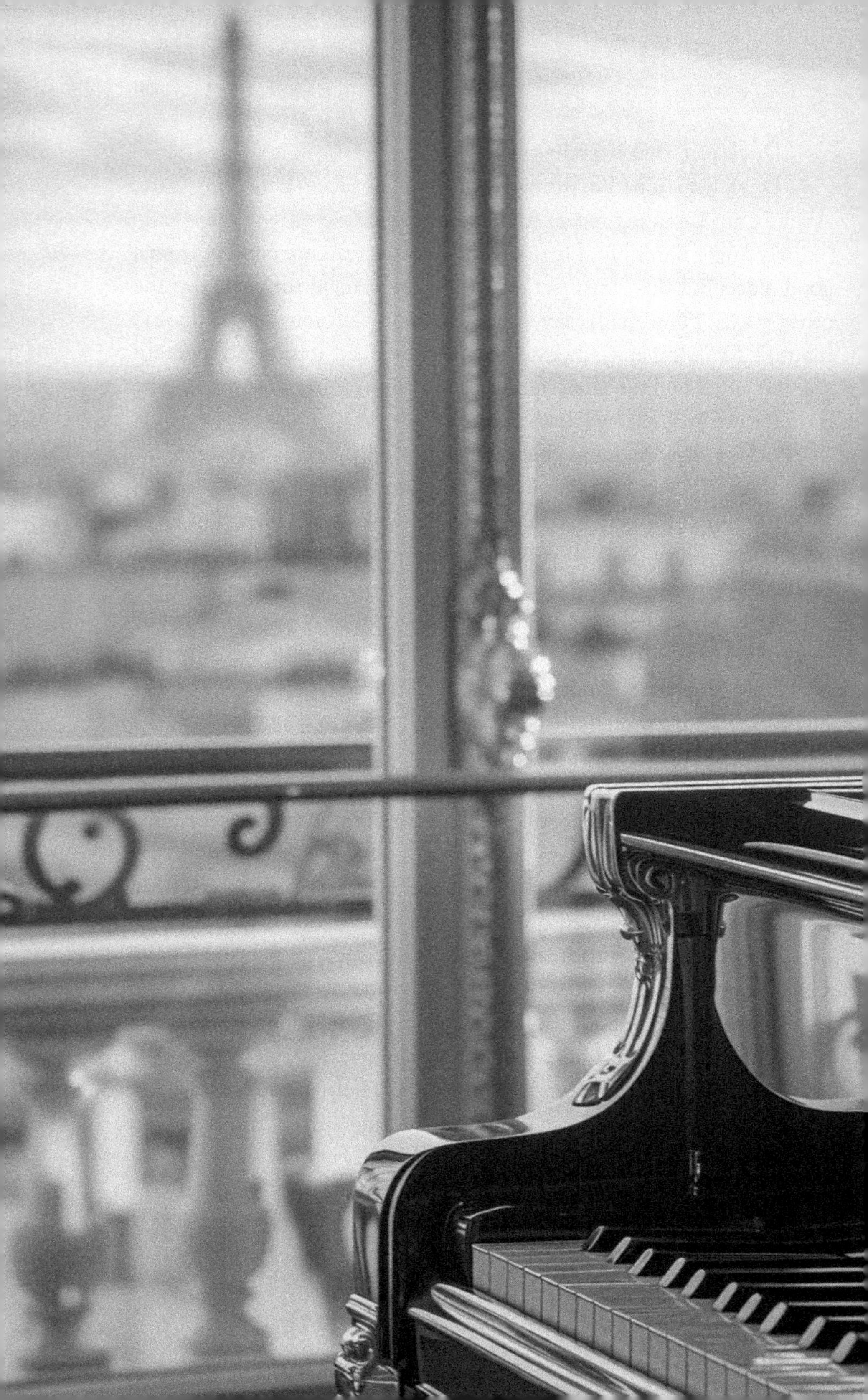

CHAPTER 49
Millie

> Mom: Did you hear what your father has planned for Lake's baby shower? Why is she even having one? It's tacky, if you ask me. They don't need the gifts. This is just another opportunity for him to remind everyone that he's young and hip. It's gross.

STOMACH SINKING, I turn over my phone. Dammit, I hope Lake didn't see the message.

We're sitting side by side at the piano, and she's helping me work through a bridge. I thought it was perfect when I finished it, and maybe the old me would have been upset that she's tweaking it, but as she plays the updated version, my heart beats wildly in my chest.

"You don't have to use that, but what do you think?" She turns to me, wearing a nervous expression.

"Lake, that was—" I stumble at a loss for words.

"Seriously," she says, ducking her head, "I shouldn't have stepped on your toes. Your way was great."

I put a gentle hand on her arm. I can see it now, how she's worked to gain my approval for the last two years. How she's put up with her husband's bratty daughter and his awful ex-wife, always keeping a smile on her face, because she truly loves my dad.

"It's perfect. The second you added that melody, the song transformed."

Her cheeks flush. "You did the hard work. I know how difficult it is to get it this far. I can't tell you how many times I've been ready to record, and one of the producers shifts my hands on the keys, and that little switch turns the song into a hit."

"I'm sure they're incredible without the input."

Lake's brown ponytail swings as she shakes her head. "Sometimes it takes another ear to recognize what we can't. But this is your song, and it's a beautiful one. I'd buy it in a second—"

My heart jumps, and I smile wide—

"But..."

That one word sends my stomach plummeting.

"I think *you* should record it."

Chest suddenly tight, I force a laugh. "What?"

Lake stands and leans against the piano, looking down at me. "You have the talent, Millie. I get why you've shied away from performing. You've seen the limelight, and you don't seem like someone who wants to live in it."

I shake my head. I definitely don't.

"But you have the talent. You could just record. You don't have to go on tour. You don't have to do"—she waves a hand up and down her body—"all this."

I laugh. "I don't think anyone can do that. You're one in a million."

Vivi screeches, drawing our attention to where she's swinging back and forth, reaching for her butterflies again. For a long moment, it's quiet. The two of us watch her, matching smiles on our faces.

When I turn back to face Lake, she's resting a hand on her small bump. "I think my days of doing that are pretty much done."

"Really?"

Eyes going glassy, she nods.

"Wow," I whisper. "You're really willing to give it all up?"

She shrugs, and when she responds, her voice is barely a whisper. "Doesn't feel like I'm giving up anything. I'm getting every dream I've ever had."

"Thank you for coming over." I take a deep breath. "And I'm sorry if I made these last couple of years harder on you than they should have been."

Lake shakes her head. "I get that me marrying your father—and now having a kid with him—is a lot for you."

"But you make him happy," I remind her. Then I smile big as I think of just how happy he'll be when this baby is born. "And he's the best dad in the world, so my little brother or sister will be extra lucky." Tears fill my eyes as I realize just how much I truly miss my dad. And how nervous I am that he'll be the one disappointed in me now.

Lake's eyes well with tears again, but the smile that spreads across her face is blinding. "Brother."

My heart stutters, and I shoot to my feet. "It's a boy?"

She nods, then her eyes go wide and she covers her mouth. "Oh my god, you have to act surprised on Sunday when he tells you."

I laugh. "Promise."

The door swings open, and Gavin appears, attention focused straight ahead. "Peaches, I'm home! We have an hour before Beck drops the kids off, so you better strip and—" He turns in our direction, and his jaw drops open.

"I'm going to pretend I didn't hear that." Lake laughs and covers her eyes. "Millie, seriously, I think you should record the song. But if you decide to sell, I want it." She lifts her palm from her face and turns to Gavin. "My lips are sealed, but get in front of this."

I grasp her wrist, heart pounding and knees suddenly shaking. "Is he ever going to forgive us?"

The smile Lake gives me is kind and understanding. "If anyone understands that you can't help who you fall in love with, it's Ford. But knowing you kept this from him is what will really hurt. Just be honest with him. He'll come around."

I throw my arms around her. "Thank you," I whisper.

For being so understanding. For being kind when I wasn't. But most of all, for loving my dad. Because she's right. If there's anyone who gets it, it's them. I just hope my dad remembers what it was like to be judged by the people around him and that he's a hell of a lot more understanding than I was.

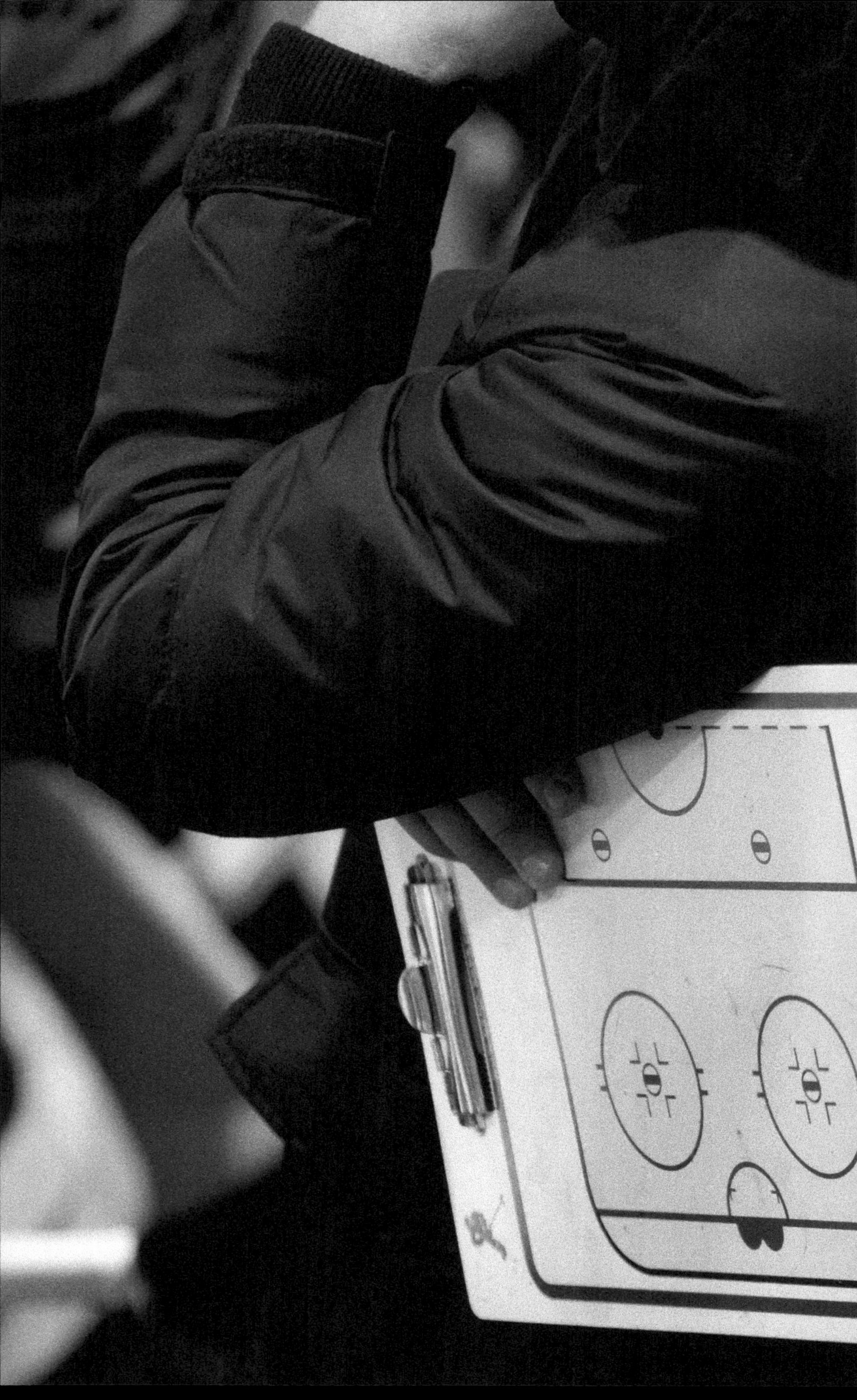

CHAPTER 50
Gavin

"WHY IS THERE a robot in the refrigerator?" With the door still open, I spin and take in all the children in the room. Vivi is in her highchair, and Winnie is helping Millie feed her a little container full of disgusting pureed food that I stupidly tried just like the damn formula.

Babies must not have taste buds, because Vivi is smiling and gobbling it up every time Winnie flies the airplane straight at her mouth.

"Don't touch Hector!" Finn jumps up and runs toward me, ready to defend his toy.

I narrow my eyes at him. "Robots don't belong in fridges."

Finn grins. "That's where you're wrong. Auntie Dylan told me the universe didn't want me to have orange soda every night after dinner, and Bossman told me it's going to rot my teeth. So Mommy said I can only have one orange soda a month, but she won't pay for it."

Lips pressed together, I tilt my head, waiting for the story to make sense.

He lets out a loud sigh. "So I saved all my allowance, and then Man Bun brought me to the store and gots me the soda with his money."

I chuckle. "Good moves, little man, but what does that have to do with the robot?"

Finn whips around and throws his arm out, pointing at Winnie. "Because she didn't get the memo that it's *my* soda, and she drank one. The robot is protecting this one."

Winnie heaves out a weary sigh. "I'm not going to touch your ducking soda."

Finn sucks in a shocked breath, his eyes going wide. "I'm telling Bossman on you!"

"I said duck!" she screams.

Vivi lets out a little screech of excitement, and then she opens her mouth, and out pops the most adorable sound. "Duck! Duck! Duck!"

Millie straightens and locks eyes with me from across the room, and for a moment, we're both silent.

Did my daughter really just say her first word?

And was it really a watered-down version of fuck?

With the back of her hand pressed to her mouth, Millie tries to hold it in, but the cutest snort slips out, and then I can't help but laugh.

"Uncle Gav." Finn pulls on my shirt to get my attention.

Bowing my head, I ruffle his hair and give him the *hold on a minute* finger, my feet already leading me to my little girl.

Vivi smiles at me as I approach, orange goo dripping from her lips. I scoop her up out of her chair and laugh. "Did you just say your first word, Vivi girl?"

She smiles. "Duck. Duck. Duck." She enunciates the *ck* over and over, so damn proud of herself.

My damn heart practically floats right out of my chest. She really is fucking tenacious. My little girl.

At the table, Millie is watching us with a big smile on her face. The warmth in my chest spreads. "Isn't she the ducking best?"

Millie stands and wipes Vivi's face. "Yup."

I breathe in her fruity scent, feeling the happiest I have in a long, long time. "We're doing okay, huh?"

She presses a quick kiss to our girl's cheek. "We're doing better than okay, Gav. We're doing ducking fantastic, right, Vivi girl?"

Vivi tangles her chubby fingers in Millie's curls, pulls her close, and presses her open mouth to Millie's face like a big, sloppy kiss.

"Love you, bestie."

My heart nearly stops in response to Millie's words. Something shifts into place in this instant, and suddenly, I'm hit with a feeling of peace I've never known.

Vivi arches back and says "duck" again and again, encouraged by the giggling fit it sends her cousins into.

Through dinner, I can't stop smiling, even as my cheeks ache. My girl loves my daughter. And I'm in love with my girl.

Beckett may have thought I needed to be punished for being a dick today, but it turns out having the kids over has made this the best night I've had in a long time. Maybe ever.

Everything is going to be fine.

"Want to join us at the pediatrician tomorrow? We could go from there to family day at the arena."

Millie's snuggled up next to me, exhausted after reading all three stories Winnie insisted on. When she came out of their room, Vivi was still wide awake on my lap, saying her favorite word.

I sat with her for far too long, enamored by our conversation, even if it was one-sided and consisted of only one word, before finally putting Vivi down for the night.

In bed beside me now, Millie tilts her head and studies me. "You want me to come to family day?"

"I assumed you'd be there with Daniel anyway."

She bites her lip. "I was—but..." She sighs.

I stroke her cheek. "What, Peaches?"

She gives me a soft smile. "Nothing. It sounds nice. Thanks for asking me to come."

"Of course. I want you everywhere I am."

A huff of a laugh escapes her. "That's because I'm super nanny."

I squeeze her side, making her squirm. "That you are. Tonight was fun with the kids, yeah?"

"They're hysterical."

"They're ducking awesome."

Millie's eyes dance as she ghosts her fingers over my bare torso. "I still can't believe her first word was duck."

"Me neither. We'll do better with the next kid."

Millie sucks in a soft gasp, the sound making my stomach sink.

"Sorry. I know we said maybe one day," I backpedal.

With a kiss to my shoulder, she eases my worries. "Don't take it back now, Coach. Be confident in your request."

"Fine." I loop my free arm around her. "I know tonight was crazy, but it was perfect. I loved seeing Vivi with her cousins. Loved seeing you with them. But I know it's a lot, and I don't want to pressure you about having kids of your own."

Millie tips her head back and locks those warm golden eyes on me. "I like to think of Vivi as my own." Her lashes flutter shut, and a blush creeps up her cheeks. "I know that's probably wrong."

When I don't respond—because I'm too lost to my own thoughts about how Vivi isn't really either of ours but we both want her, yet I may be setting us up for disaster—Millie continues, "She likely won't remember being left. I know you were worried about that."

I shift to look at her, loving that she somehow always knows just what to say to calm me. "The doctor says the same thing." I run my fingers through her curls, settling myself. "I'll just have to love her enough that she never feels that loss."

"You won't be alone in that." She lifts her head and presses a kiss to my jaw. "We'll both love her so much she'll never know anything but happiness."

My heart skips again. As often as this has happened today, I worry I should see a cardiologist. With a grunt, I pull her on top of me. I don't have the words to express how I feel about this woman. There's nothing that I've ever heard or read that could encapsulate the joy I feel with her by my side.

Love might be the closest I'll ever come to describing it, but even that doesn't touch this feeling. It's so trivial and overused.

I ache for her, and knowing she's mine leaves me with a sense of peace that I never believed was attainable. Being hers *is* my purpose.

Since I can't describe it, I show her instead. I kiss her, pouring every emotion I have into my actions, hoping she sees that she's not just my love and she's not just my family. She's my everything.

THE HOCKEY REPORT

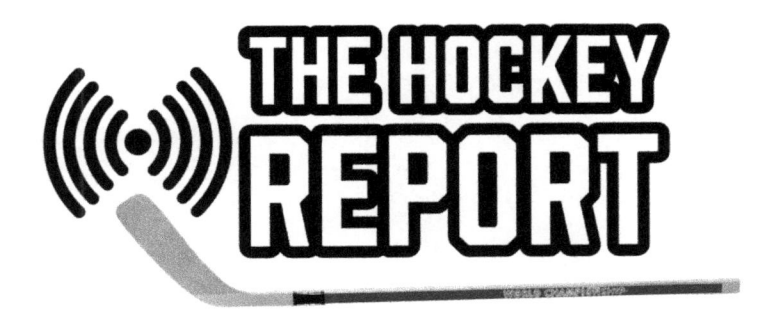

"Good morning, Boston. Eliza here, with my cohost Colton. Today we've got a special edition of the Hockey Report."

Colton chuckles. "You sound excited, Liza. And you took my line."

"I am excited. The Bolts are on fire. Even without Tyler Warren, the Bolts pulled off a win last week, and they're officially in the playoffs."

"Yes, the game against New York began the stretch of wins. It seems the team and its new leadership have found their groove, and it's back to hockey."

"It's not *all* about hockey, Colton. Tomorrow the team heads to the arena for family day, and fans are anxious to see pictures of Brooks Langfield with his girlfriend, the head of PR, Sara Case. If we're really lucky, maybe we'll get a shot of little Viviane Langfield with her daddy. And, since it's family day, the masses are wondering whether Gavin will finally introduce Boston to her mother."

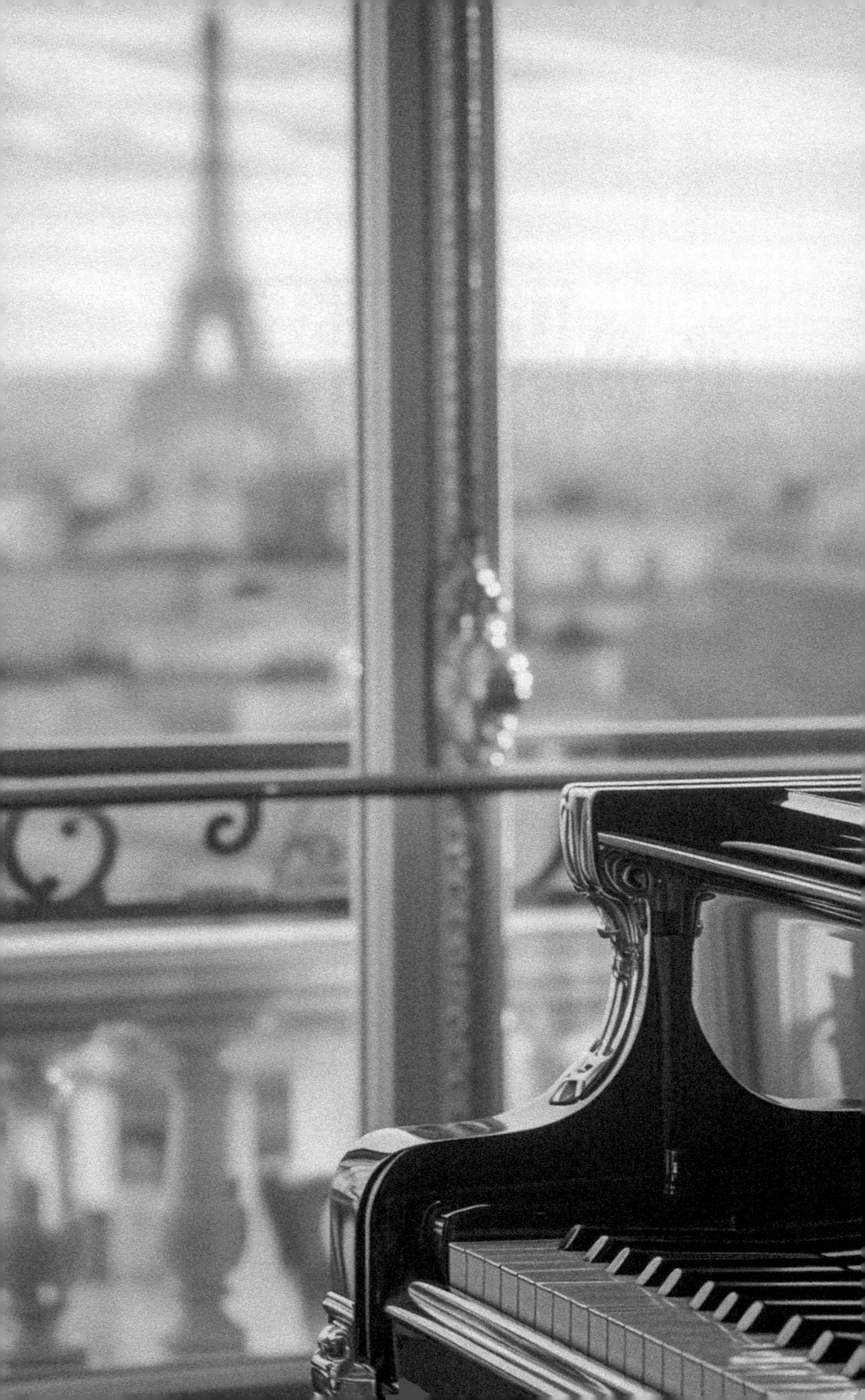

CHAPTER 51
Millie

"SHE'S ALREADY SAID her first word, and she's in the ninetieth percentile for weight and height. All in all, I'd say Viviane is doing great."

Gavin and I beam at one another as the pediatrician continues her assessment. Vivi said duck just as he stepped into the exam room, and at first, the doctor thought she'd said *doc*. I almost wanted to let him believe she was a little baby genius. I certainly think our Viv is the smartest baby around.

"How's she sleeping?"

"She's up about once a night now for a bottle. Last week was rough because of teething, but now that the tooth has broken through, she's sleeping well again. Any suggestions for how to handle the rest of them?" I smooth my hand over Vivi's, and she smiles at me, her lips shiny with drool.

Rather than respond, the doctor blinks at me in surprise.

Oh. Oops. That's right. I'm just the nanny. Gavin should be the one speaking.

"Sorry," I say with a wince at Gavin. "I'll let you handle the questions."

He drapes an arm around my shoulder. "We'd appreciate any suggestions, Doc. Like my girl said, Vivi is up about once a night."

I duck my head to hide my heated cheeks. The man seriously just claimed me in front of the doctor. We've hidden our relationship from everyone we know, so this is new, though I don't hate it.

I lean into his arm, and Vivi squeezes my hand.

"Duck."

We all laugh.

"Unfortunately, there's no magic solution to the teething. There are numbing gels that can help and cold toys during the day for her to gnaw on. Use a little trial and error and find what works best. As for the bottle at night, she's old enough to go longer stretches without eating. If she wakes up before about five a.m., try getting her back to sleep without one."

Gavin looks at me, wearing a small frown. He's probably thinking the same thing I am. As much as I'd love the extra sleep, I'll miss those late-night cuddles with Vivi.

"Sure, Doc," he says, clearing his throat. "We'll see what we can do."

After the doctor has finished his exam and leaves, I press a kiss to Gavin's cheek.

"What was that for?" he asks, adjusting Vivi so he can slide an arm around my waist.

I run a hand down her back. "It was just nice how you included me in that. Thank you."

Gavin makes an approving sound in his throat. "You're included. You're the one doing most of the work."

I smile down at our girl. It's how I've started thinking of her. "I love it."

When Vivi says duck again, we both laugh, and Gavin points to the door. "All right, let's get out of here so we can skate."

Vivi spit up all over herself halfway to the arena, so once we're parked, I hop into the back seat to change her into another adorable Bolts jersey and twist the teeniest bit of curls into a little ponytail on the top of her head. "There ya go, bestie. You're looking good."

Once I've climbed out and have her settled on my hip, Gavin steps in close. "Soon I'll have two curly-haired girls." He tugs on one of my curls and then leans in, lifts Vivi's jersey, and gives her a raspberry on her belly. Her laughter echoes through the team parking garage, filling me with so much joy I might burst.

Gavin, eyes bright with happiness, gazes at me for a long moment. The genuine adoration in his expression steals the breath from my lungs and sends my heart into a gallop. I'm so head-over-heels in love with this man.

I angle in, forgetting where we are, and press a soft kiss against his lips. Needing him. Wanting to tell him right now exactly how I feel. When he cups my jaw, deepening the kiss, I vow to do just that.

"*What the fuck?*"

I startle back at the booming voice and spin, coming face to face with my twin. His jaw is clenched tight and his eyes are shooting daggers at us.

"What the hell, Millie?" he says, his tone dripping with disgust. "Did you just kiss my coach?"

"Watch your tone," Gavin hisses, stepping in front of me protectively.

"Watch my tone?" Daniel scoffs. "Watch where you put your fucking hands."

"Daniel." My mind is going a million miles per minute trying to figure out how to spin this.

"Don't *Daniel* me. How long has this been going on? How long have you been hiding my sister like she's a dirty fucking secret?"

Gavin takes a deep breath and turns. "Can you take Vivi inside? I'll talk to your brother."

"You should take her," I suggest. "I'll handle my brother."

"Neither of you is going anywhere until you tell me what the fuck is going on." Daniel's scowl cuts deep lines into his brow.

Vivi grabs my shirt and kicks her little legs. "Duck."

I suck in a breath. Shit. This is getting worse by the second. "We have a baby here. Watch the language."

"How long?" he grits out, ignoring my request.

Exasperated, I huff and hold Vivi closer. "Like two years," I grit out. "Get over it. We're fine. I'm fine. Mind your business."

By the horror that crosses Daniel's face and the way he staggers back, that was not the right answer. "Did you cheat on my sister and knock some other girl up?" he shouts, taking a step closer to Gavin. "And now you're making her watch the baby?"

"Oh my god," I mutter. "That's not what I meant. Gavin, I'm sorry. I—"

He wraps an arm around me and pulls me in, keeping his head high and his focus locked on Daniel. "We weren't together the whole time. But we are together now. We didn't mean to hide it from—"

"Millie," my brother barks. "You're too good for this. You aren't some dirty mistress. What the hell are you thinking?"

"Enough." Gavin's tone is lethal. "She's not my dirty anything." He turns to me now, standing between my brother and me, attention fixed intently on my face. "I planned to bring this up tonight, but I guess now is as good of a time as any. I plan to talk to your dad tomorrow. I already invited him over." He swallows audibly and smooths a hand down my upper arm. "But if you're ready, I'd really like to go inside the arena and skate with my family."

Heart lodged in my throat, I scan his face. The brown eyes that have felt like home since I first lost myself in them. The affectionate smile. The lines that have formed beside his eyes from smiling and laughing as we talked late into the night.

"Your family?" I can't hide the hopefulness in my tone.

"Yes. You and Vivi. *My family.* What do you say, Peaches? Let's go inside the arena as a couple. I'm done hiding."

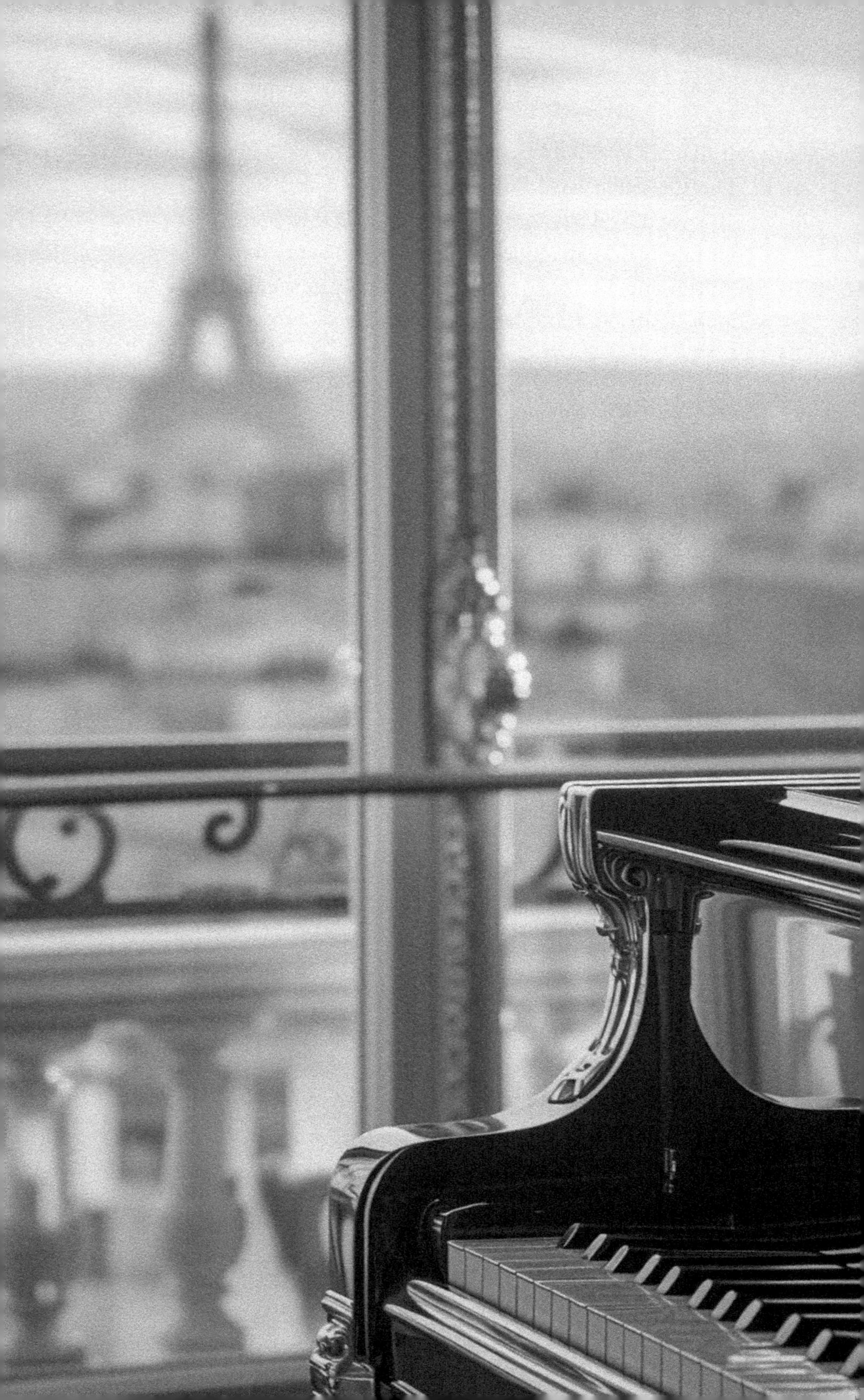

CHAPTER 52
Millie

"THIS IS A BAD IDEA," Daniel grumbles behind me as we step inside. "Can you at least not, like, hold hands?" he whines. "What if the press sees?"

Gavin, who's now holding Vivi, turns around and holds his hand out to me, palm up. "We're a very touchy family," he teases.

I place my hand in his and link our fingers. "Could you at least try to be happy for me?" I ask Daniel.

"And there's no press," Gavin assures us. "I'm crazy *about her*, not plain crazy. I have no intention of letting this get out to the public before I talk to your dad tomorrow."

"He's like Dad's age," Daniel whisper-yells, still trailing us. He's watching us with his lip curled on one side, like he smells something bad.

I ignore it. I get the reaction. The look he's giving us is probably identical to the one I wore for the better part of two years around Lake and my father.

Out of nowhere, Daniel cracks up, causing us both to frown at him over our shoulders.

"What now?" I ask, pulling up short in the hallway.

"Can you imagine Paul's reaction?" He slaps a hand over his mouth to muffle his loud laughter. "First, Dad steals his girlfriend, and now Dad's best friend is sleeping with his sister."

Gavin grins. "I'm sleeping with your sister too."

Daniel drops his hand, and his grin morphs into a scowl. "Not cool, man. Not cool. If this is gonna be a thing—"

Chuckling, Gavin pulls me in close and presses a kiss to my cheek. "How about you worry about hockey, and I'll worry about keeping my girl happy?"

With a sigh, Daniel straightens and holds a hand out to Gavin. "You better be good to her. No more hiding her like she doesn't deserve to be paraded around."

Gavin releases me and shakes Daniel's hand. "From here on out, everyone will know the two most important people in my life are right here." He bounces Vivi in his left arm and juts his chin toward me.

Butterflies take flight, leaving me feeling light and slightly drunk. Is this what love feels like? I thought I knew before, but there's something about living love out loud that makes the colors seem brighter. Makes my heart take flight. People say someone can steal your breath, but in this moment it feels like I've sucked in too much oxygen. I'm quite possibly delirious with how happy I am.

"Then we're good." Daniel nods once, and then he saunters into the arena, falling into his typical loud, boisterous persona as he high-fives everyone he sees.

Gavin turns his full attention to me. "That went okay."

Rolling my eyes, I try to hold back a laugh. "He was the easy one. The Energizer Bunny in him wouldn't let him stand still long enough to dig too deep into the details. His brain has already moved on to whomever he's going to drive nuts next."

Gavin's loud laugh hits me right in the solar plexus.

"Ducking yes. Gavin is back!" Aiden pumps his fist as he wanders our way with a grinning Brooks and Sara beside him.

"If it isn't the other Energizer Bunny," Gavin says. His tone is dry, but his smile is fixed firmly in place.

"Hey, Vivi girl," Sara coos to our sweet girl.

Like the little attention hog she is, Vivi makes grabby hands at Sara until Gavin hands her over.

When Brooks leans down and nuzzles noses with her, I swear I'm melting into a puddle of mush. What is with these Langfield men today?

"Is it finally out in the open? Can we tell everyone Princess Peaches is Millie and Millie is Princess Peaches?" Aiden asks, bouncing on his toes. "There's a song by Jack Black I've been practicing while I've been *waiting*, anticipating, this moment right here."

"Aiden," Sara says, giving him a pitying frown. "He's singing to Princess Peach, not Princess Peaches."

Aiden shrinks before my eyes, hurt flashing across his face, but Brooks saves the day. "Come on, crazy girl, we all know Aiden changes the lyrics. Let him have his moment."

Aiden brightens again. "So, can I? Is it? Are we?"

Beside me, Gavin frowns. "What the hell are you talking about?"

"Does everyone finally know that you're together?" He steps closer and lowers his voice. "Keeping this secret since I saw you on the beach in Aruba has been killing me."

"Since Aruba?" Brooks's shocked laugh echoes through the empty space.

"Vivi and I are going to take a walk. She doesn't need to know about what her daddy was doing in Aruba." Sara winks at me and disappears.

"Tell me he doesn't mean the time we were in Aruba for Lake and Ford's wedding." Brooks's expression is even, but he's a big guy—bigger than his brothers—so even though he's a complete softie, he looks slightly menacing at all times.

Gavin pulls me in close and presses a kiss to my neck.

"What are you doing?" I hiss.

Gavin clings to me. "Yes. Aruba. I'm talking to Ford tomorrow. I'd like to enjoy what might be my last day on earth with my girl and my daughter. Get all your questions out of the way now so Millie and I can skate."

Aiden's grin is so bright it hurts to look at, his eyes bouncing between Gavin and me. "I really love this for you. Ford will be fine. You got this, big bro."

I smile, even if I don't quite believe the sentiment. It's nice to know at least one person is for us, and it's nice to be out in the open with the man I've fallen for. Aiden isn't gaping at us like we're a circus show, and he isn't questioning why his brother would want to be with me. Not thinking that I must have seduced him.

I kind of did—but I know his feelings are real too. He wouldn't risk his reputation and his friendship with my dad if they weren't. This is more than lust and more than a mid-life crisis. I'm enough. Just me.

That's what I hold on to as we go in search of Vivi. As we step onto the ice and everyone stares, I take a deep breath and remind myself that their opinions don't matter. This man has fallen for me. We're happy.

Vivi is strapped into the carrier on his chest, facing out so she can enjoy the view. Gavin has our fingers twined as he guides us around the ice, a big smile on his face.

Aiden and War skate backward in front of us. War makes silly faces and gently taps Vivi's nose and feet while Aiden sings his newest tune about Princess Peaches and her no-longer-growly king.

Daniel eventually joins in. Like I said, the kid can't keep from jumping into the fray. His smiles are genuine as he teases Vivi and the guys. He's the best brother, and as long as I'm happy, he is too. That's how it's always been.

"You doing okay?" Gavin asks as we take another trip around the rink.

"Yeah," I sigh, giving him a warm smile. "I just wish I could skate backward so I could watch Vivi's reaction to this."

Gavin lifts my hand to his lips and presses a soft kiss to my knuckles. Then he lets go and spins so he's skating backward.

Vivi breaks into a gummy smile, her rosy cheeks lifting, when she sees me.

"Show off," I tease. "Hey, bestie. You having a good time?"

She squeals and kicks her feet. "Duck!"

A laugh bubbles out of me. It's so violent I stumble. For a second, I'm sure I'm going down, but then a warm hand grasps my elbow, keeping me steady. I turn to say thank you and am met by the steely blues of Camden Snow.

"You okay?"

"Yeah, thanks," I say, bringing a hand to my racing heart. I quickly peer at Gavin to gauge his reaction.

The smile Gavin has worn all day has been replaced by a scowl. I give him a small nod, silently signaling that I'm fine and he has nothing to be upset about.

"So you and Coach?" Camden asks slowly, his hand still on my arm.

I grab hold of the ledge, coming to a stop. Gavin continues and does some fancy footwork, which results in ice flying up toward Aiden.

"Someone call a penalty," Aiden shouts. "He just iced me!"

Camden laughs and shakes his head as he stops beside me, waiting for me to reply.

"Um, yeah," I say, lowering my head. "I'm sorry if you thought—"

He shakes his head. "Hoped. You didn't give me any reason to think there could be more. It's okay." He smiles, his dimple popping. "He's a lucky guy."

"Thank you." I grasp his arm and press a kiss to his cheek. "You're a good guy, Camden."

At the sound of a throat clearing, I pull back and smile at my very jealous and possessive boyfriend. I'm not even going to lie and say I don't like it. In fact, I love that he can be openly jealous and possessive now.

With a hand on my hip, he glares at his player. "Say goodbye, Camden."

In the true good-guy fashion, Camden smiles, looks his coach dead in the eye, and says, "Be good to her."

Gavin seems to respect the response and nods.

Once Camden skates off, I turn my attention back to my two favorite people. "Your daddy is ridiculous," I tell Vivi, rubbing my hands against her cold cheeks. "Think it's time to get this little lady home and warmed up."

Angling closer, Gavin presses a kiss to my lips. "I can think of a few ways I would like to warm up Vivi's nanny."

I pinch his side. "Stop calling me that or that's all I'll be, *Mr. Langfield*."

Gavin gives me his cheekiest smile. "But your brother told me there's a whole thing about single dads and nannies."

Eyes narrowed, I cross my arms over my chest. "You wanna be a single dad?"

With a chuckle, he kisses me again. "Not a chance," he says against my lips. "Completely taken with one woman and one woman only."

I smile against his lips and hum contentedly, closing my eyes. "Better be. Come on, Hockey Daddy. Take me home."

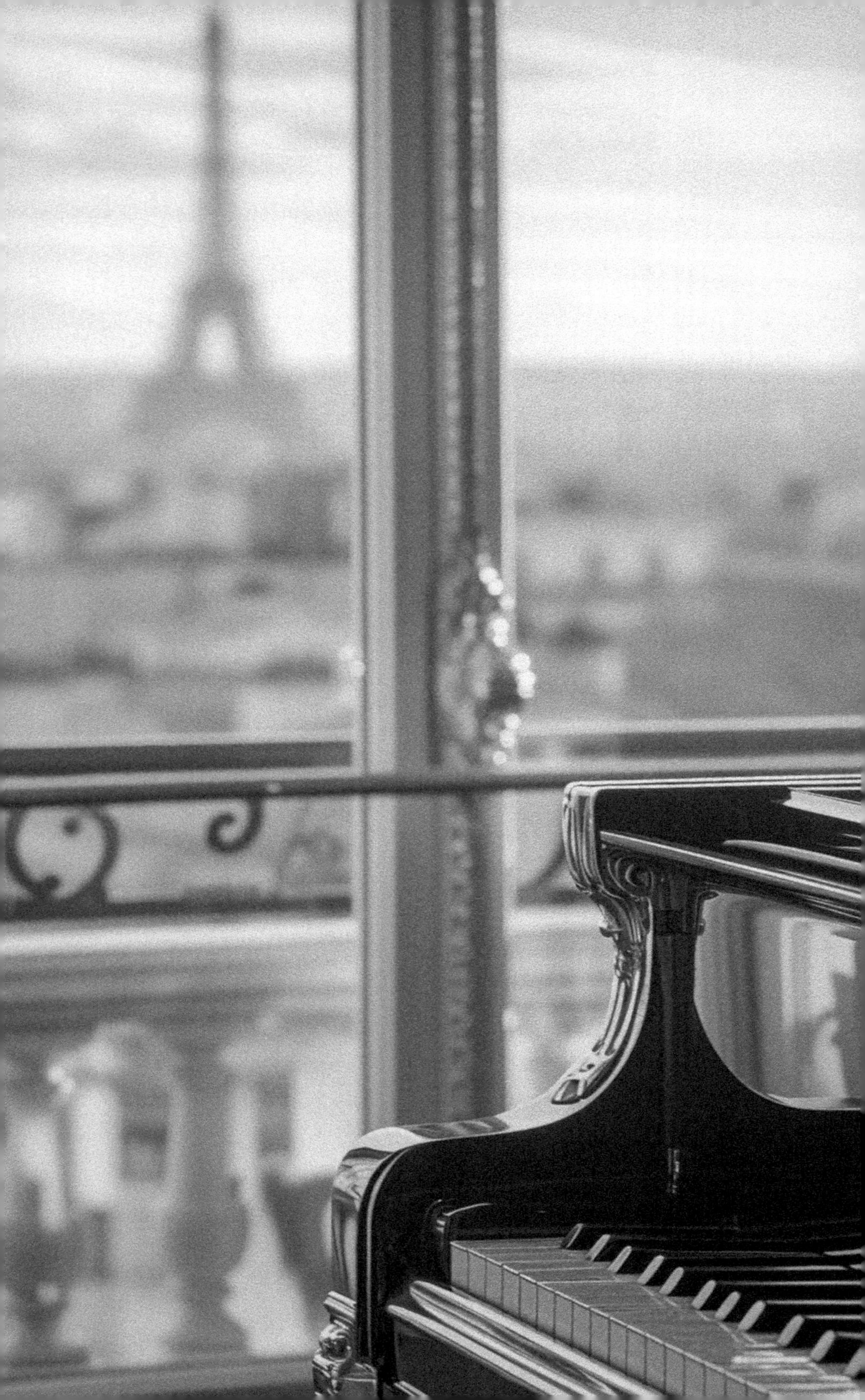

CHAPTER 53
Millie

IT'S late by the time we get home, and Vivi goes down easily. Then, for the first time since we decided we were going to do this, Gavin and I are completely alone.

"I don't know about you, but I'm fucking exhausted," he says as I step out of the bathroom after brushing my teeth.

I lick my lips, not even trying to fight the wicked smile that takes over. "Too tired for me, old man?"

Growling, he pulls me onto his lap on his side of the bed. "Never."

Straddling him, I work to undo his belt buckle and zipper. My mouth waters at the thought of touching him, and when I reach inside his boxers and roll my finger over the head of his hard cock, heat pools low in my belly. "I heard a rumor that the other Langfield men have piercings."

Gavin cocks a brow. "Yeah, and?"

I roll my thumb over his crown again. "Just got me thinking..."

"Thinking I need metal or toys to get you off?" His eyes go dark and devilish. Sinful. "Peaches, I ate you out on a bar top in Boston so thoroughly you kicked me in the stomach and knocked me on my ass."

"Yeah, I guess." I shrug. "But that was before. Back when you were more daring. Now you're a dad. Sensible, tired. Missionary sex is probably all I have to look forward to."

His laugh is sharp and dangerous. "You think I can't be wild? You think that because I'm dedicated to one woman and one woman alone, I'm boring?"

I lower my head demurely and look up at him through my lashes, egging him on.

"I'll show you how boring I am." With his right hand, he tears the black leather belt from his belt loops. Once it's free, he folds it, making a loud snapping sound as he pulls it taut.

"Are you going to spank me, Coach?" A zap of electricity shoots through me at just the thought of it.

He chuckles, the sound deep and raspy. "I should. You're being such a brat. I should smack the sass right out of you. But no, I have other plans for this belt."

He flips me onto my back and looms over me, crushing me with his weight. Before I have a chance to react, he grabs my wrists and pulls them above my head. With his eyes locked on mine, he binds my wrists together tightly.

"Holy shit," I mutter.

Gavin smirks as he slides down my body. "Still too boring for you?"

My breath comes out in gasps, my voice weak. "Yeah, I mean, I'm still clothed."

"Oh, I don't need you naked to get you off, Peaches. That's what you don't seem to understand. I don't even have to touch this pussy to make you cry out my name while you come."

He ghosts his lips across my pelvis, then he slips his thumbs beneath the hem of my shirt and pushes it up, exposing my breasts.

"Fuck," he says, working his way up. "I hate that you don't wear a bra when we're in public, but right now..." He flicks my piercing with his tongue, sending a bolt of need through me. "Right now I'm so fucking glad there's nothing covering these perfect tits."

When he gently sinks his teeth into my flesh, holding my nipple in place while he continues to flick the ring, I hiss.

"Shit." My breaths come out quicker. "Holy fuck."

His body is warm against mine, holding me in place, even as I writhe and buck. "You like this? Like how I'm using my tongue?"

"That's not where I want your tongue," I pant, tugging at my wrist restraints, desperately wanting to pull his hair and guide him to where I need him.

He chuckles. "Oh, it's cute that you think you're in charge."

"You're the one on your knees right now, Hockey Daddy. I'm the one who gets to watch you pleasure me."

He smiles devilishly, his brown eyes dancing as he stares up at me with my nipple between his teeth. With a final flick, he releases, and the kiss of relief shockingly burns. "Who said you get to watch?" Brow cocked, he hauls himself up.

Cool air rushes in, punctuating the loss of his warmth. "Where are you going?"

Gavin doesn't answer as he strides to his closet. With a flick of the light, he disappears inside. When he comes back out, he's dangling a blue tie from two fingers. "You were saying something about watching..."

As he stalks toward me, I let out a surprised laugh. "Wait. You're really going to—"

He presses his mouth to mine, cutting me off, kissing me long and hard. When he pulls back, he gives me only one more second of sight before he drops the silky fabric against my eyes and then lifts my head to tie it.

"That too tight?" he asks softly, his words tickling my ear.

"No. It's fine."

It's more than fine. The loss of my sight heightens my other senses. Not being able to anticipate his next move has me arching for him, aching for the moment his lips touch me.

He trails his fingers down my bare stomach, and then he's tugging my pants down.

"Thought you were going to make me come without touching me down there."

Gavin settles his weight above me again, his heat returning, his thighs straddling my hips. "Oh, I am. But I want to see how wet this beautiful pussy gets. I want to watch your clit pulse as I suck on your tits. And I can't do that when you're wearing pants."

Holy shit. My hips buck of their own accord. Even my brain is panting out my thoughts. I'm a fucking puddle.

The first swipe of his tongue against my nipple has me clenching my fists, squeezing the excess leather from the belt.

"That's it, Peaches. Grind that greedy pussy against me. Maybe if you rub hard enough, you'll get what you need."

"Gavin, please," I beg.

He ghosts his lips over mine. "You wanted this, so now you'll take it." He pulls on a nipple ring, and I cry out. The cry becomes a moan when he sucks it into his mouth, his warm tongue easing the pain he just inflicted.

He continues the pattern, teasing, then licking, torturing me, bringing me to the brink of orgasm until I explode and stars float before my eyes.

"Gavin," I cry. "I'm—"

His hot tongue suctions my clit, and I go over the edge, coming long and hard. There's no end to the pleasure. As I crest the wave, he thrusts his thick cock inside me. The fullness mixed with the tension of the restraints on my wrists sends me tumbling. I'm lost in euphoria, unable to brace myself as he doles out one brutal thrust after another. Being unable to see what he's doing makes it hard to breathe. Gasping for air, I hurtle right into a second orgasm, coming until I'm practically boneless.

Without warning, he pulls out and flips me over, his hand landing on my ass with a loud smack. "Still boring?" he teases.

"Fuck no. You win." I push my ass back, wanting more.

He doesn't disappoint. He smacks me hard again, this time on the other cheek. I pulse as the ache inside me grows, desperate to be filled.

"You done being a brat?" he growls, draping himself over my body and releasing the leather from my wrists.

I flex my hands but don't dare remove the silk tie that's still in place over my eyes. "For now."

Gavin's hot mouth presses to the flesh of my ass, making me go rigid while I wait to see what he'll do. He nips at it and growls. "Say you'll be good, Peaches."

I wiggle my ass against his face. "No."

He bites harder, making me yelp. "Say it." Before I can sass him, he runs his tongue between my cheeks.

Holy shit, that's dirty.

"No," I pant again.

"Do I have to fuck this peach of an ass, Millie? Will that get you to admit that I'm enough for you? That I can keep you satisfied forever?"

"Yes," I breathe out, shocking myself with the response.

Gavin's guttural groan has me pressing my ass toward him again. I'll do anything with him.

"Fuck, Mills. I didn't—" He slides a thumb between my cheeks.

I tense at the sensation, my breaths sawing in and out of my lungs. His warm body comes down on my back, and then his lips are beside my ear again. "Do you want me to tease this asshole until it's ready for my cock? I'll lick it and lube it up and make it feel so good for you."

"Holy shit," I mutter.

"Tell me, baby. Tell me what you want. Want me to fuck you all night? I'll fuck your every hole. Keep you satisfied. Keep us both young."

I turn my head and lift myself up the best I can so that I can kiss his lips, our tongues working in tandem. "You are enough, Gavin Langfield. No other man would ever be able to keep me satisfied. But yeah, I'd like all of those things." I can feel his smile against my lips, and then he's pushing me down, ready for the challenge.

Fortunately for me, I'm the lucky girl who gets to keep him on his toes for the rest of his life.

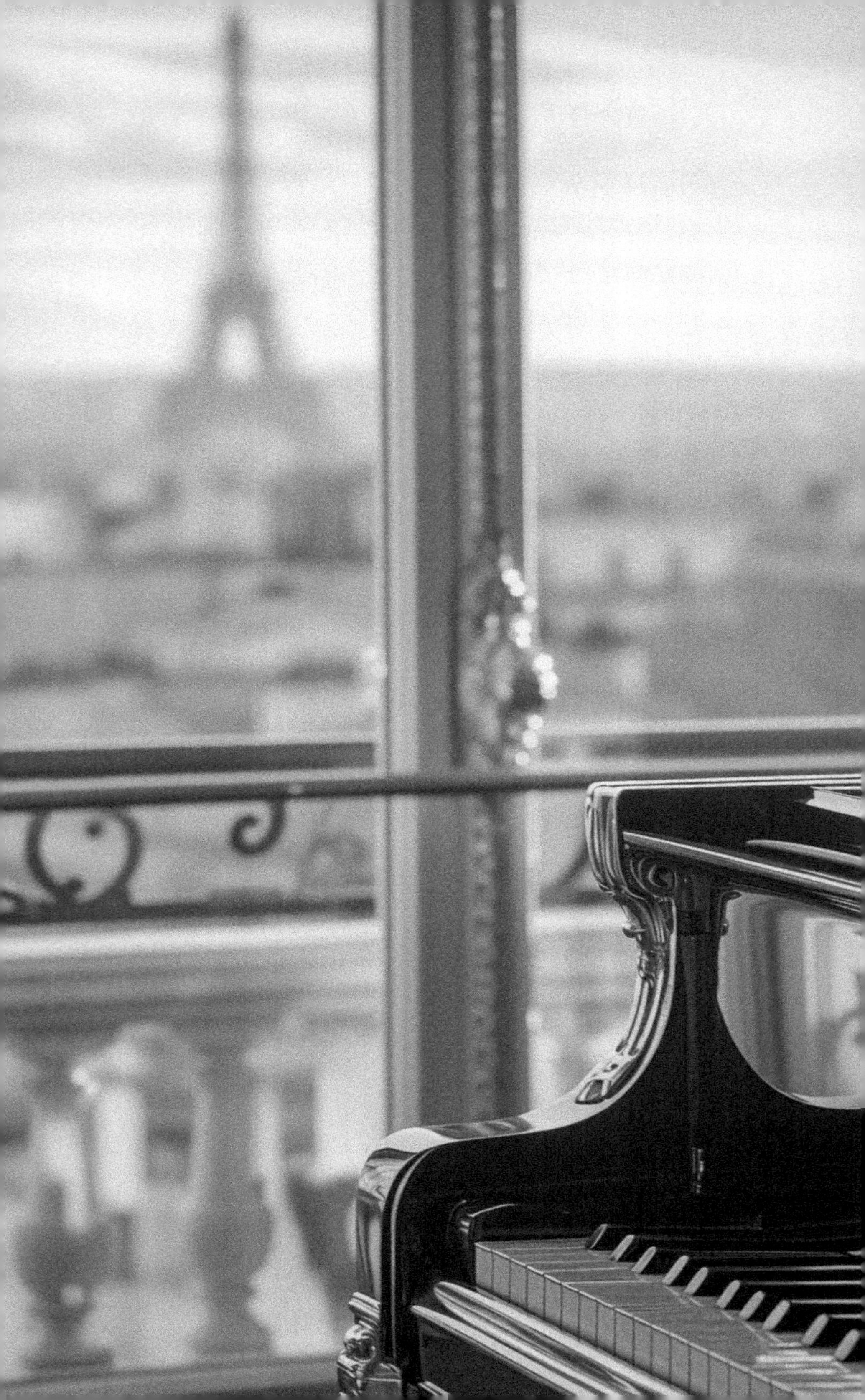

CHAPTER 54
Millie

"YOU SURE YOU don't want me to take Vivi?"

The Bolts don't have a game tonight, and after practice this morning, Gavin came home, declaring he'd taken the rest of the day off.

If I hadn't already made plans, I'd be up for snuggling with my two favorite people all day and soaking in the quiet time.

Gavin sets Vivi on a blanket on the floor with her toys and steps up close, placing his hands on my waist. "Nah, I like having her here."

I frown, and my shoulders sag. "I wish I could hang with you guys, but I promised I'd meet Sara." I pull my phone from my pocket and unlock the screen. "Better order the Uber now."

"Take the Bugatti."

A little shot of glee courses through me. "Your fancy Batman car?"

He laughs. "I haven't driven it since Vivi. I should really sell her. Poor thing needs to be driven."

I swat at his arm. "Aw, your poor baby girl isn't getting our attention."

Gavin rolls his eyes like the car is nothing but an afterthought. In reality, before Vivi came along, it was his obsession. I was almost jealous.

"Seriously, take it. I'm not going anywhere today. Your father will be here at three. Do you want to be here for that *or...*?"

My stomach knots as the words hang heavy in the air between us. "Should I?"

Gavin blows out a breath. "Honestly, I think it would help if I talked to him alone first."

"I'm nervous he's going to hurt you."

Gavin's response is a scoff and an arched brow.

"He's very strong, you know," I tease. "But really," I say, sobering, "I don't want this to ruin your relationship."

"I don't either," he says, brushing a hand down my arm and circling my wrist. "But in the end, the relationship I'm most concerned about—after ours, of course—is the one you have with your dad. You and Vivi are my priority. Everyone else comes after you two."

My heart aches at the sincerity in his voice. Eyes watering, I cling to him. "Gav."

Cupping my cheeks, he kisses me softly. When he pulls back, he stares at me quietly, his eyes saying so much. About how deep his feelings for me run. About what he wants for us in the future. My heart beats a tattoo against my breastbone in anticipation of the words I think are on the tip of his tongue. But when he shakes his head, I release the breath I'm holding, only slightly disappointed. It's not time yet.

But then he mutters, "Fuck it," and a smile ghosts his lips. "Every time I've felt like I'm toeing the line with you—worried that I'm pushing too far but do it anyway—it's turned out right. Those things that my mind questions but my heart wants?" He rakes a hand through his hair. "The moment I realized you were a virgin, right before I decided to take you anyway, promising myself I'd make it good, that no one else would care the way I did, no one else would deserve you. When you cried on the beach and begged for someone to see you, in my head, I questioned whether kissing you was wrong. My heart, though? It was positive that anything that ended with my lips on yours was right."

He grasped both of my hands and squeezed, his expression so full of warmth.

"When you told me you couldn't stop thinking about me and my mind screamed that Paris was the worst idea because I could never really have you, but my heart couldn't imagine spending another night not beating beside you..."

Tears crest my lashes and cascade down my face unchecked.

He shakes his head and swipes at them with his thumbs. "Every moment that mattered in my life may have seemed wrong at first, but my heart knew. And right now, my heart is telling me to do this before you walk out the door. It may be anticlimactic, and it isn't anywhere close to what I planned, but I couldn't have planned you if I was the greatest architect in the world. You are a glorious surprise. The eighth wonder of the world. *My* Roman empire. The love of my life."

He presses another kiss to my lips, chest heaving and hands trembling.

"I love you, Millie Hall. You are the greatest fuck-it moment come to life."

I sob out a laugh. "Gavin, I—"

He presses his mouth to mine. "After," he rasps.

I pull back, frowning, but he clasps my hands and holds them tight.

"Tell me after I've gotten your father's blessing. After I've shown you how much I love you. After I've earned your forgiveness by being honest with your father."

Warmth wraps around my heart, holding it in a precious embrace. "You already have my forgiveness."

A loud breath escapes him. "It feels so good to hear that. But I don't have my own. I need to make this right. With everyone. Then I want to hear you say it. I'll need to hear it. But just—after. When I deserve it."

This man. How can he not believe that he deserves it? He still doesn't think he's earned my love after the way he treated me when I came home from Paris. But love doesn't work that way. At least mine doesn't. It's freely given, and it's not based on preconditions or standards.

People make mistakes. They fail. Stumbling along the way is part of the journey. It's okay to love them when they're at their worst so long as I love myself enough to walk away if that love becomes toxic.

This love isn't toxic, though. Gavin is my champion. My partner. It just took us a little time to get here.

I kiss him one more time and leave it at that. He needs to do this his way. But with my lips, through my kiss, I tell him exactly how I feel. I love him unconditionally. And I always will.

I wander the halls of Langfield Corp, in awe, as Gavin's former secretary, Stacey, leads me to Sara's office.

She pauses in front of a door and knocks. "I'll leave you here, but if you need anything, stop by my office on the way out."

"Thanks," I reply as she strides away.

I'm still turned, surveying the hall, when the door swings open and I'm dragged into the office by a pink flash.

"What the hell?" I say as I steady myself.

"I said the same thing when this loud, bossy woman showed up here and told me she was joining us for lunch," Sara says, pointing toward said loud, bossy woman, also known as Lennox Kennedy, who is beaming like a lunatic.

Behind her is a woman I haven't met. She has vibrant red hair and she's dressed in all cream. Her lips are pinched, as if she can't quite find her bearings. She's lovely, with keen green eyes. She's clearly scrutinizing me silently, trying to read me without saying hello.

"Don't lie and say you aren't excited to see me," Lennox teases as she pulls me in for a hug.

"Am I supposed to lie and pretend I didn't see you yesterday?" I say, not nearly quiet enough to ensure the other women don't here.

She scoffs as she releases me. "No, I told Sara the truth."

I wave at the quiet woman behind her, and she says a muted hello.

"You didn't tell the truth," Sara quips, but her lips are tipped up in a smile. Her blue eyes are bright when she turns to me. "Caught her walking out of my bedroom naked as the day she was born when I stopped in to pick up a couple of things."

"Yeah, a couple of your 'toys.'" Lennox holds up a hand, pantomiming a rather large phallic-shaped item. "Don't let that innocent blonde persona fool ya, Millie. The girl's a freak in the bedroom."

Sara licks her lips and shrugs.

"Why were you naked?" the girl sitting in the corner asks in the most beautiful lilt. She's got a raspy voice that sounds a bit like an angel.

Lennox props herself up against Sara's desk with a *humph*. "I don't like wearing clothes when I'm at home." She runs her hands down her body, as if she's on display. "This all takes a lot of work."

I cough out a laugh. This girl is the opposite of modest. Lennox is bold in her personality and her wardrobe. Right now she's dressed in a hot-pink wrap top that accentuates her breasts and shows off a strip of her stomach. She's paired it with white-washed jeans that have more holes in them than fabric. Combine that with her hot-pink hair and glossy lipstick, and she's one hell of a sight. The woman demands attention, and I'm happy to give it to her.

Sara snorts. "Key words being *at home*. That isn't your home, it's mine."

"Please, you'll be married and popping out little hockey player babies any day now. You don't need an apartment on the singles floor."

Sara turns a shade of rosy pink. "Don't give Brooks any ideas."

Lennox lifts her chin and assesses her. "Like anyone needs to put that idea into his head. He's got googly eyes and dreams galore when it comes to you."

A brunette in sky high heels, a black pencil skirt, and a green tapered shirt appears in the doorway, causing us all to turn.

"It has been a *day*. Beckett is on the warpath because Cortney put a bucket of blue glitter above his door, and when he walked in, *poof*"—she holds her hands up and flashes her fingers like a fireworks display—"the man is a walking, talking Lisa Frank art project. I need lunch, and by lunch, I mean alcohol—oh my god," the woman says, her cheeks flaming. "There are a lot of people in here."

Sara stands and plucks her purse off her desk. "Hannah, this is Millie, Gavin Langfield's girlfriend and *Daniel Hall's* sister—"

The way she arches her brows and emphasizes my brother's name piques my curiosity. Lips pressed together, I study Hannah. *What's the deal there?* But then the other part of that sentence registers, and I choke on air.

"G-girlfriend?" I gape.

It's true, yeah, but we've yet to use that label. Plus, I had no intention of going public with our relationship until Gavin talked to my father.

Sara shoos me out the door. "Please, everyone saw you two holding hands at the family skate yesterday. Cat's out of the bag, Mills."

"And you know what they say about pussy," Lennox adds.

The redhead's eyes bulge, and Sara hisses.

"We don't say pussy in the office," Sara says. Then, in a louder voice, she adds, "But yes, once you've let that bitch out into the wild—"

Hannah slaps a hand over her mouth. "Can't say bitch either."

"Duck is an excellent replacement," a bedazzled Beckett Langfield says as he strolls by, hands in his pockets, full of swagger, as if he isn't reflecting the hallway lights like a blue disco ball. "Now if you'll excuse me, ladies, I have a bun to duck with."

"This must be a fun place to work," Lennox sings as she loops her arm through mine.

Behind us, Sara laughs, the sound echoing down the hall. "You are *not* working here. Don't get any crazy ideas."

Lennox leans in close. "But those are my favorite kind."

Lunch turns into an afternoon cocktail party, though I stick to club soda since I drove Gavin's beloved car. Even without the alcohol, I laugh entirely too much as the girls tell story after story about working for Beckett and Gavin. Surprisingly, Lennox tells us a little about her history with Aiden, which even Sara seems surprised about.

The redhead, Ava Erickson, is the head of charity relations for the company. She and I chat quite a bit, since before I came into the picture, she helped Gavin with Vivi. We make plans for her to come over later in the week so she can visit with my girl.

On our way back to the office, I'm feeling lighter than I have in months. Spending my days with Vivi has been far more rewarding than I could have imagined. My relationship will be out in the open in a matter of hours. And now I've met a group of wonderful women who I could see becoming my true friends. Women who are kind and caring and uplifting. No more Taylors or Chrishells for me, please.

They all insist we pop into Sara's office before parting ways, and once we've said goodbye, I stride down the hall toward the parking garage, anxious to get home to my family.

Halfway down the hall, I hear Beckett Langfield's loud voice and decide to stop in to say hello. Not only is he Gavin's brother, he's his best friend, as well as one of my father's, so it's important to me that we get to know each other and get along.

"And you're sure this is her?" he says.

Realizing he's on the phone, I hang back in the hallway, waiting for him to finish.

"Thank you so much. My brother wanted to put his head down and ignore it all, but it's important that we find Viviane's mother. I appreciate your help in the matter."

My heart lodges itself in my throat. Holy shit. He found Vivi's mom?

"She'll be there tomorrow?" He pauses for several seconds. "Amazing. I'll make sure he brings her too."

He'll make sure Gavin brings who with him? Viviane?

"No, this is the right thing to do. Gavin wants her to be a mother to Viviane. And Viviane deserves her, not some flake who will disappear the next time things get hard."

Beckett's words hit like a slap, and I stagger back, tears filling my eyes.

Gavin has been so concerned that I haven't forgiven him that neither of us considered that his family may not forgive me.

God, is that what they really think of me? I stumble down the hallway, swiping at tears as I go. I need to get out of here.

So much for being happy.

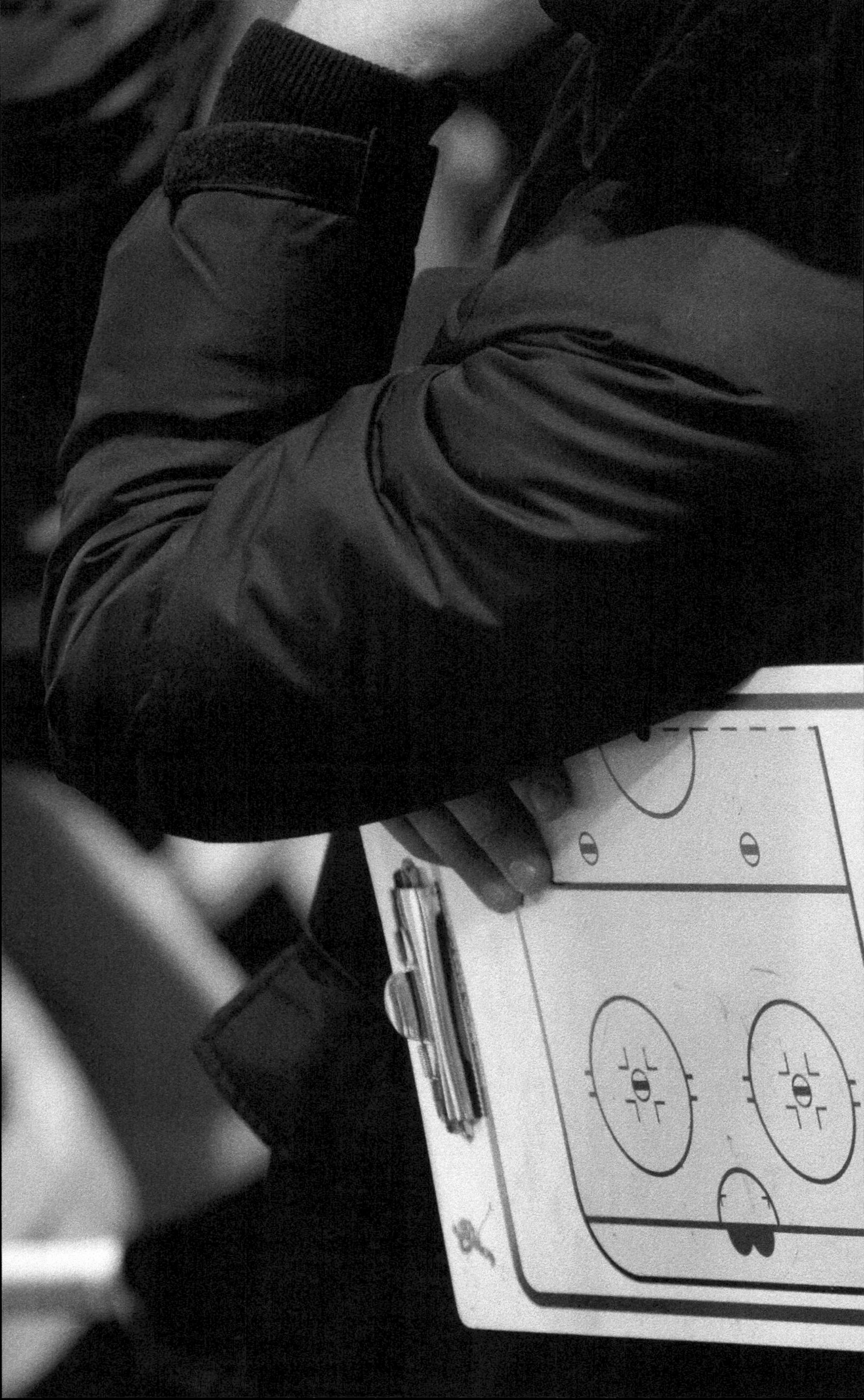

CHAPTER 55
Gavin

PACING the expanse of my living room, I will my nerves to settle as I wait for Ford to arrive. My time is up. This moment has been inevitable for two years. I wish I had known early on how impossible it would be to walk away from Millie Hall. If I had, I would have come clean immediately.

Now the lie has gone on for so long, I'm not sure Ford will ever forgive me.

Once the doorman calls up to let me know Ford is here, I rush to the bathroom and splash water on my face. Then I straighten my shirt and give my reflection a little pep talk.

I've never actually met the parents of a woman I'm dating. I've never cared for another woman enough to make it to this step. It's not lost on me that, of course, I already know Ford. We've been friends for years. We've shared whiskeys over late-night rounds of poker with my brothers and gone to bars and left with different women. Hell, he's been my wingman and I've been his. I was there the night he finally decided to go for it with Lake. I pushed him toward her, in fact.

And yet I feel completely unprepared for the meeting we're about to have.

Today I'm going to look into the eyes of the father of the woman I want to marry, and I'm going to hope like hell that he can leave our shared history where it belongs. That he can see how much I care for his daughter.

At the sound of the doorbell, I hustle to the foyer. Vivi is down for a nap, and with any luck, she won't wake up during this conversation. Though Ford would be less likely to hit me with my daughter present, I'd rather not use her like that.

When I open the door, Ford gives me a big smile and holds up a pink gift bag. "Lake sends gifts."

I take it, grateful to have something to do with my hands. "Thanks. Come in."

Awkwardly, I lead him into my living room, setting the bag down on the dining room table as we go. "Can I get you something to drink?"

Ford looks at his watch and shrugs. "Sure, but I'll stick to a beer. I'm hoping Millie will let me take her to dinner when she gets home. You up for joining us?"

I keep my focus fixed on my task as I stalk into the kitchen and pull two beers from the fridge. When I return, I hand him one, then take a long swig of mine. "Maybe. I'll see if Sara and Brooks can watch Vivi for a bit."

"Where is Vivi girl?" He scans the room, passing over the swing and the play mat and the baskets of toys. "Man." He huffs a laugh. "Never thought I'd see the day that your house would be filled with kids' toys rather than random women's panties."

The comment hits like a dagger to the heart. Wincing, I rub at my chest to ease the pain. "I'm not like that anymore."

He takes a sip of his beer and nods. "Obviously. Though I'm sure Millie wouldn't mind watching Vivi so you could take a real break.

Your life doesn't have to be all about diapers." He drops to the sofa and crosses an ankle over a knee. "You deserve to be happy. Now that you have a kid, have you considered maybe finding someone to settle down with?" He surveys the space again, his expression thoughtful, and takes a long pull of his beer. "Someone who could do all of this with you?"

The ball of lead in my gut that's weighed me down all day grows until it's so big I'm not sure I can speak around it. Fuck, this isn't easy.

"That's..." I clear my throat and suck in a deep breath. "That's actually why I asked you to come over."

Ford frowns, his brows pulled low. "You met someone?"

"Yes," I say, my voice breaking. "Millie." I sit up straighter and look him in the eye. "I'm with Millie."

Ford tilts his head, looking at me like I'm speaking another language. "With Millie how?"

I swallow past the boulder in my throat. "She's my girlfriend. We're together."

Ford grips his beer bottle so tight his knuckles are white and his hand trembles. "No."

"Yes. I didn't know who she was when we met, but I fell for her." I take a deep breath. "I'm in love with your daughter."

Ford scowls, and his face darkens. "You don't even know who the fuck the mother of your child is, and you've been sleeping with my kid?" His tone is gruff, his body vibrating with anger. He sets the beer down on the coffee table a little too hard and launches to his feet. For a long moment, he paces, ignoring me. Finally, he stops in front of me and fists his hands at his sides. "Is Viviane hers?"

"No." I shoot up off the couch. "You know your daughter. She would never hide something like that. She'd never abandon a child."

He scoffs and wipes at his mouth with his wrist. "Apparently I don't know my daughter as well as I thought. Never imagined she'd be stupid enough to sleep with a player like you."

I grip my own beer, willing myself to tamp down on my anger. "I'm not like that anymore. I haven't been for years."

"Viviane's existence is evidence to the contrary, Gavin."

"Don't mention my daughter's name if you're going to use it like that," I grind out.

"That's rich coming from the man who is fucking *my* daughter." The moment the words are out, he flinches. Even he knows he's crossed a line. He takes a steadying breath and schools his expression. "How long?"

"I met her two years ago. Before your wedding. I didn't know who she was."

His eyes cut to mine, and he stares down at me. "So you cheated on my daughter when you knocked up Vivi's mother."

I set my beer down and face him head-on. "No. I stayed away from her when I found out she was your daughter."

He huffs a sardonic laugh. "How big of you."

I grasp his shoulder, willing him to really listen. To see my sincerity. "If anyone understands what it's like to fall for the wrong person—"

He shrugs, dislodging my hand, and backs up. "Don't you dare compare what Lake and I have to *this*."

"Why?" Now it's my turn to scoff. "Because you were a saint when you slept with your son's girlfriend?"

Ford's eyes harden. "*Ex-girlfriend*. And it was different. He cheated on her."

"And you fell in love," I remind him.

Hands on his hips, he works his jaw, his nostrils flaring as he assesses me. "Are you telling me you're in love with my daughter?"

"Do you think I'd have you over and sit you down to tell you about our relationship if I wasn't? Come on, Ford, you know me better than that." I pull in a deep breath, then another, my heart practically beating out of my chest. "When was the last time you saw me with a random woman? When was the last time I talked about dating, period? I saw you and Lake together. Then my brother and Liv, and something just—" I run my hands through my hair. "It shifted. I got what you'd been saying all along." I let out a heavy sigh and meet his eyes, silently imploring him to consider that I could care about her. "And then I fell in love with your daughter."

His hands claw through his peppered hair. "You don't even know what love is." His words are harsh, but his tone has weakened.

Jaw clenched, I stare him down. I'll say it again. Over and over until he hears me. "I love her. I know it's hard to wrap your head around, and if it was just me I was worried about, I'd be okay without your approval. I wouldn't like it, but I'd accept your choice. But she needs your blessing. You don't have to think I'm good enough for your daughter—"

Blue eyes meet mine. "You're not."

I sigh, the adrenaline that's kept me pacing all day draining from my system. "I know. But I'm who she wants. And no one will ever love her the way I love her. She and Vivi are my entire world."

My phone chimes in my pocket then, startling me. I pull it out to silence it and catch sight of Daniel's name on the screen. My guys rarely call, and seeing as though I'm eyeball deep in drama involving his family, my gut instinct is to answer. "I have to take this. Give me one second."

Without a response, Ford walks to the window. Maybe the interruption is good. Maybe it'll give him time to really mull over our conversation. Hear my words. *Feel them.*

"Hey, Daniel. What's up?"

"Gav, you need to meet me at the hospital."

My heart plummets, then takes off at a sprint. "What? Why? Who's at the hospital?"

Ford spins around, the angry look on his face morphing to concern.

"It's Millie. She's been in an accident."

The room spins. Accident? I blink, and his voice fades in and out.

"Gavin," he says, pulling me back to the moment. "Get here fast." He pauses, and then as the room seems to get smaller, he adds, "It's bad, Gavin. It's really bad."

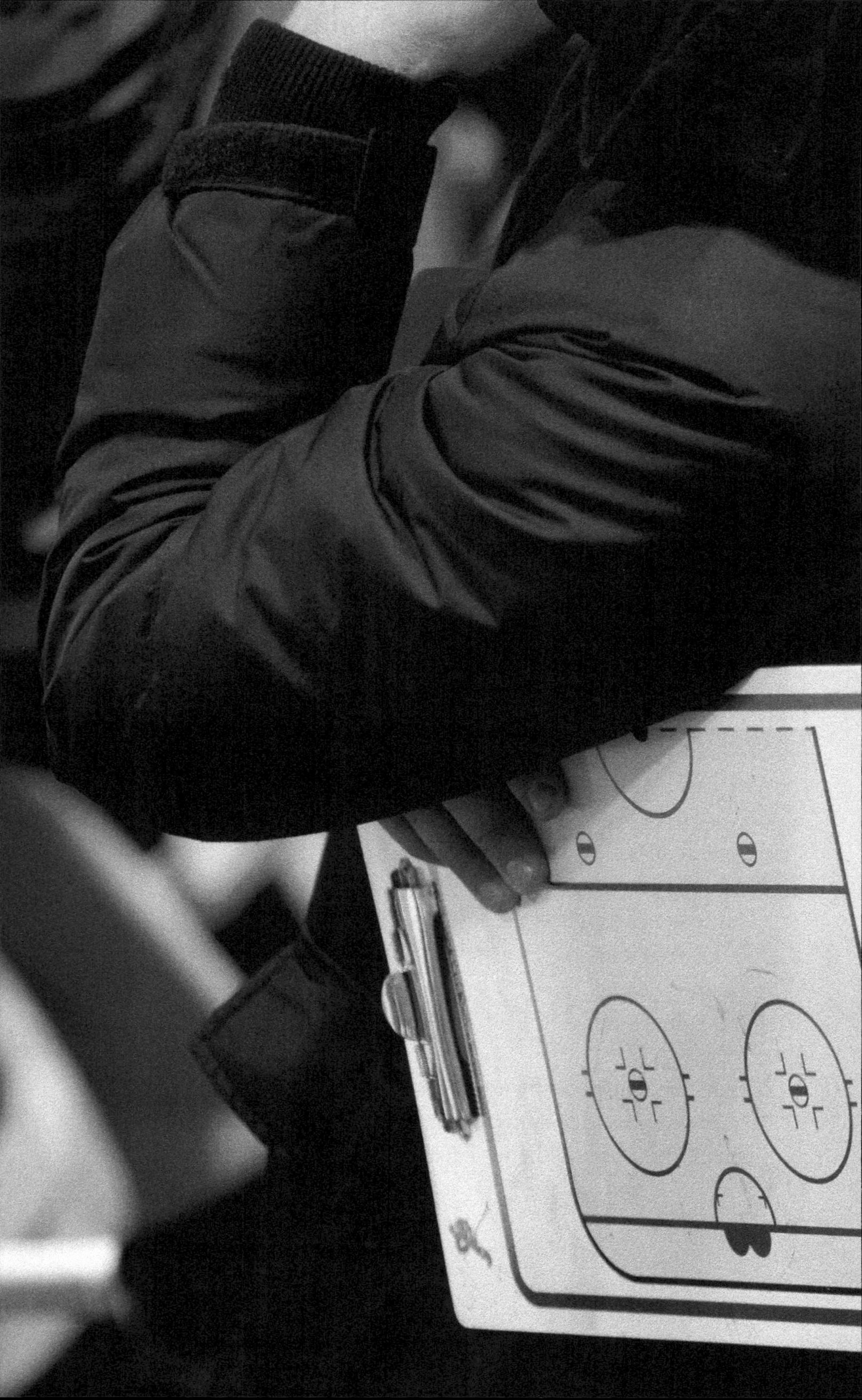

CHAPTER 56
Gavin

HEART GALLOPING at a million miles a minute, I race through the glass doors of the hospital with Ford on my heels. I spot Daniel first. He's huddled with Paul and their mother, Kyla.

"Where is she?" My desperation leaves no room for pleasantries.

When Kyla looks up, her face streaked with black tears, my stomach bottoms out.

Daniel points to the double doors behind him. "They took her through there. I got here right as the ambulance did."

"How?" I grit out, my mind still spinning out.

"I'm her emergency contact," he explains.

Chest tight, I force myself to breathe in deep. "Have they said anything? Who can we talk to?"

Kyla puts herself between Daniel and me and glares. "Why the *hell* are you so interested? Feeling a little guilty for letting her drive that fucking toy car of yours? The kid hasn't driven in years, and you send her on her way in a death trap?"

My heart cracks in two. Dammit. I should have hired a driver for her. Hell, I should have driven her myself.

"What did they say when you spoke to them?" Ford interjects, stepping closer, though he still keeps his distance from me.

I don't even care at this point. Nothing matters but her. I just need to know how she is. What we're dealing with here.

Paul is the one to speak up this time. "She was unconscious. They're running tests to see if there's brain damage."

A stab of pain sends me doubling over, making it impossible to breathe.

"Breathe." Suddenly, Lake is at my side, rubbing circles against my back as she talks me through the panic.

"Why is he freaking out?" Kyla asks, though her voice sounds distant.

I pull myself upright even as the world around me fades in and out.

"Now's not the time, Mom." I think it's Daniel who says that, though the voice is distorted, like it's being piped through a tube.

My vision blurs. I'm pretty sure I'm going to be sick.

A bottle of water appears in front of me, and Ford, I think, says, "Drink this."

My hands shake so badly I can't unscrew the cap. He yanks it back, opens it, and hands it to me again. As I take it, water sloshes over my hand and onto the floor.

Lake's hand settles over mine, and her blue eyes bore into me from under the ball cap she has pulled low. "She's going to be okay," she says, her tone soft, soothing. "You need to breathe and take a sip of water. She's going to need you when she wakes up. She's going to want you beside her, holding her hand. Okay?"

I suck in another unsteady breath and nod.

Ford hisses in a breath. "You knew?"

Lake gives her head a slight shake. "Not now."

Ford rests a hand on her shoulder and steps up beside her.

She turns, her mouth turned down and her eyes swimming with sadness. "She loves him. She *needs* him."

"Knew what?" Kyla hisses. She steps out of Daniel's embrace and pushes toward me. "What is she talking about?" She throws a thumb in Lake's direction, refusing to look at her.

"Now's not the time, Mom," Daniel says, grasping her arm gently.

Ford eyes him, his chest heaving. "You knew too?"

Red-faced, Kyla squeezes her fists at her sides and shouts, "Knew what?"

The group goes silent. Daniel and Lake blink at me. Ford is still glaring.

Eyes closed, I take in one breath, then another, and when I open them again, the world comes mostly into focus. "That I'm dating your daughter," I croak out. "She's my girlfriend."

"Like hell she is," Kyla screeches. "You're old enough to be her father."

I straighten and look at Millie's mother, then her father. "I *love* your daughter. She's the love of my life. So please, I can't do this right now. I need to know that she's okay. Then you can tell me what an awful choice I am for her. I'll never be good enough for her, but I love her anyway. And—" The words catch in my throat, and tears spring to my eyes. "And I can't lose her." When the weight of those words hit me, I double over again, hands on my knees, and give into the sobs that rack my body.

I can't fucking lose her. I just got her back.

"Of course," Ford mutters. "We'll talk about this later. We need to focus on Millie right now."

"Let me see if I can get an update," Lake offers. She squeezes my shoulder and heads for the front desk, tugging on her ball cap, probably hoping to stay incognito.

"I'm not surprised the two of you don't have a problem with this," Kyla scoffs.

"Enough, Mom," Paul grits out. His tone is serious enough to have me straightening again. "Enough. Millie is lying somewhere in this hospital, fucking broken, and according to Lake, she loves him. She'd want him here."

"Since when do we care what Lake says?" Kyla shrieks.

Paul groans and hangs his head. "Enough of that too."

Ford, Daniel, and I all stare at Paul in shock.

"Seriously. Lay off Lake. I was the asshole," he says, hitching a thumb at his chest. "Not her. She fell in love. I'm happy." He flings his hand toward his dad. "They're happy. The only unhappy one is you, and quite frankly, none of these relationships involve you."

"You're my son, and she's my daughter. Of course they involve me."

Daniel steps in front of his mother and faces her full-on. "Then be her mother and let the one person she'll want holding her hand into the room so when she wakes up, she's comforted."

I close my eyes and focus on my heartbeat. I'm so fucking scared, and I'm not above dropping to my knees and begging Kyla to let me in to see Millie. I need to know she's okay.

Please let her be okay.

"You should go home and shower. Don't you have a game to get to?" Ford's voice is scratchy, muffled too. Could be that I'm so delirious. Twenty-four hours ago, I got the call from Daniel, and Millie is still unconscious.

I scoot closer to the edge of my chair and silently will my girl to open her fucking eyes.

Beckett's in the corner, talking quietly to Lake. The coffees he brought are on the table next to Millie's bed, getting cold. I can't let go of her hand long enough to pick one up. I haven't left this seat since I was finally allowed in the room. The others have taken turns sitting where Ford is now. Daniel is currently pacing the hall while Kyla and Paul grab food from the café downstairs.

"I'm not going anywhere."

Ford clears his throat. "I can call you when she wakes—"

My spine snaps straight, and I shoot figurative daggers over the top of Millie's bed and straight at her father. "When she wakes up, I'll be sitting here, whether you fucking like it or not."

"I wasn't—" Ford hangs his head.

Standing, I sweep Millie's curls away from her face and press my lips to hers. "You're gonna wake up, right, Peaches? Vivi and I need you." My voice cracks, right along with my heart. It's already been pulverized. I didn't think it could break more, but every hour she doesn't wake up sends another fissure through it. "I need you, Millie. Please." I bury my face in the pillow beside her head and let another round of tears fall.

My world stops again when there's a brush against my cheek, and then a muffled voice more beautiful than anything I've ever heard says, "Vivi. Where's Vivi?"

"Doc!" Ford leaps to his feet. "We need a doctor!"

Lake hustles from the room, and Beckett puts his phone to his ear. I ignore it all, too lost in golden eyes zeroed in on me. The most beautiful eyes I've ever seen.

"Peaches," I whisper.

She licks her lips and winces, a flash of pain crossing her face. "Vivi," she croaks.

I press my finger to her lips. "Save your words, baby. Vivi is fine. She's at home with Brooks and Sara."

"I hear our patient is awake." The doctor strides into the room, pulling her stethoscope from around her neck. "Can I have a listen?"

A hand squeezes my shoulder. "You gotta let her go. Give the doctor some room," Beckett says.

I blink a few times, kiss Millie one more time, and then let go of her hand, allowing the doctor to check her. My hand tingles, and the cool air against my palm feels foreign as I flex it.

"You gave your family quite the scare. Fortunately, nothing is broken. You just hit your head on the window pretty hard. Can you tell me your name?"

Even with the blue-black bruise and the knot on her head, Millie, awake and somewhat alert, is the most beautiful sight. Her voice is husky and weak, but she has no trouble answering each question the doctor asks.

"Do you remember what happened?" Ford asks, settling back in his spot next to her.

Millie scans the room slowly before focusing on me again. "No. How's your car?"

"Who the fuck cares?" I grit out.

Millie clasps her hands over the blanket pulled up to her chest. "Did I total it? Oh shit. I'm sorry, Gav."

I push past the doctor and take her hand again. "I couldn't care less about the car. I just need you and Vivi."

Millie blinks, and her bottom lip quivers. "What about her mother?"

I can't help the scowl. "What about her?"

"Beckett said—"

My gaze swings to my brother. "Beckett said what?" My voice is deadly.

Millie squeezes my hand, drawing my attention back to her. "He said he found her mother."

My stomach lurches, and I claw at my chest, though it doesn't ease the piercing pain. I turn to Beckett, my gaze lethal. "You did what?"

My brother sighs, his shoulders sagging. "I didn't want to do this here. Maybe we should let the doctor finish her exam."

"I need to know," Millie rasps, her eyes welling as she sets them on Beckett. "I know I'm not who you would want in Vivi's life, but I love her. If her mother is going to have a relationship with her, then I need to know that she loves her too."

Jaw clenched so hard my teeth ache, I hover over Millie so I'm all she can see. "You are her mother. No one else." Angry, I straighten and turn, but I don't let her go. "Beckett, you had no fucking right."

"If you'd give me a second to explain—"

"I don't care what you have to say." Chest heaving, I fight the urge to stalk across the room and knock him the fuck out. "Get out. I'm done."

"She's not your daughter either." Beckett's words are a physical blow that almost takes me down.

"The fuck she's not."

My brother must have a death wish, because he steps closer, but he holds up his hands, placating. "She's Sebastian's. He's the coach the woman left the note for. She assumed he still lived there."

I shake my head as the room closes in on me. This can't be happening. Not like this. Not now. Vivi needs me. And I need her.

Fuck, I figured she was Seb's, but that scum doesn't deserve her. I can't lose her. She's *my* daughter. *My* baby. And I'm the only father she knows.

"You said it yourself," Beckett says, his voice eerily calm. "You had no memory of sleeping with anyone after meeting Millie. You've been infatuated with her since the first night. You gave up the drunken hookups. The playboy ways. It didn't make sense. We were together constantly that entire year after Ford's wedding."

Ford lets out a heavy sigh.

Beckett winces. "I'm sorry. But it's true. He was in love with Millie. From the beginning, this didn't feel right. So I did some digging."

"You had no right," I grit out, hands trembling and knees threatening to give out. "You think I didn't know we don't share DNA? You think I can't do simple math? Of course I fucking knew." I suck in one breath, then another. "But Vivi," I say, slamming my fist against my chest, "is mine." I pound on my chest again for emphasis. "*My daughter.*" Then I look toward the woman I love with all my heart, hoping like hell she'll forgive me for hiding this from her. "And Millie is going to be my wife."

Across from me, Ford's mouth pops open, but I ignore him. I cup Millie's tearstained cheeks. "I know this isn't ideal, and I know it's not what you signed up for, Peaches." With my thumbs, I wipe the tears as they fall down her face. "And, *fuck*, this is *not* how I planned to ask, but you and Vivi, you both stole my heart. I know it hurt to think I'd had a child with someone else. I'm sorry I let you believe that." I bring her hand to my lips and press a kiss to her knuckles. "I've known since day one that another man fathered her, but that's just science. What's real—what's true—is this. Us. You, me, and Vivi were always meant to be a family," I choke out. "Please be my wife and help me fight to keep our daughter."

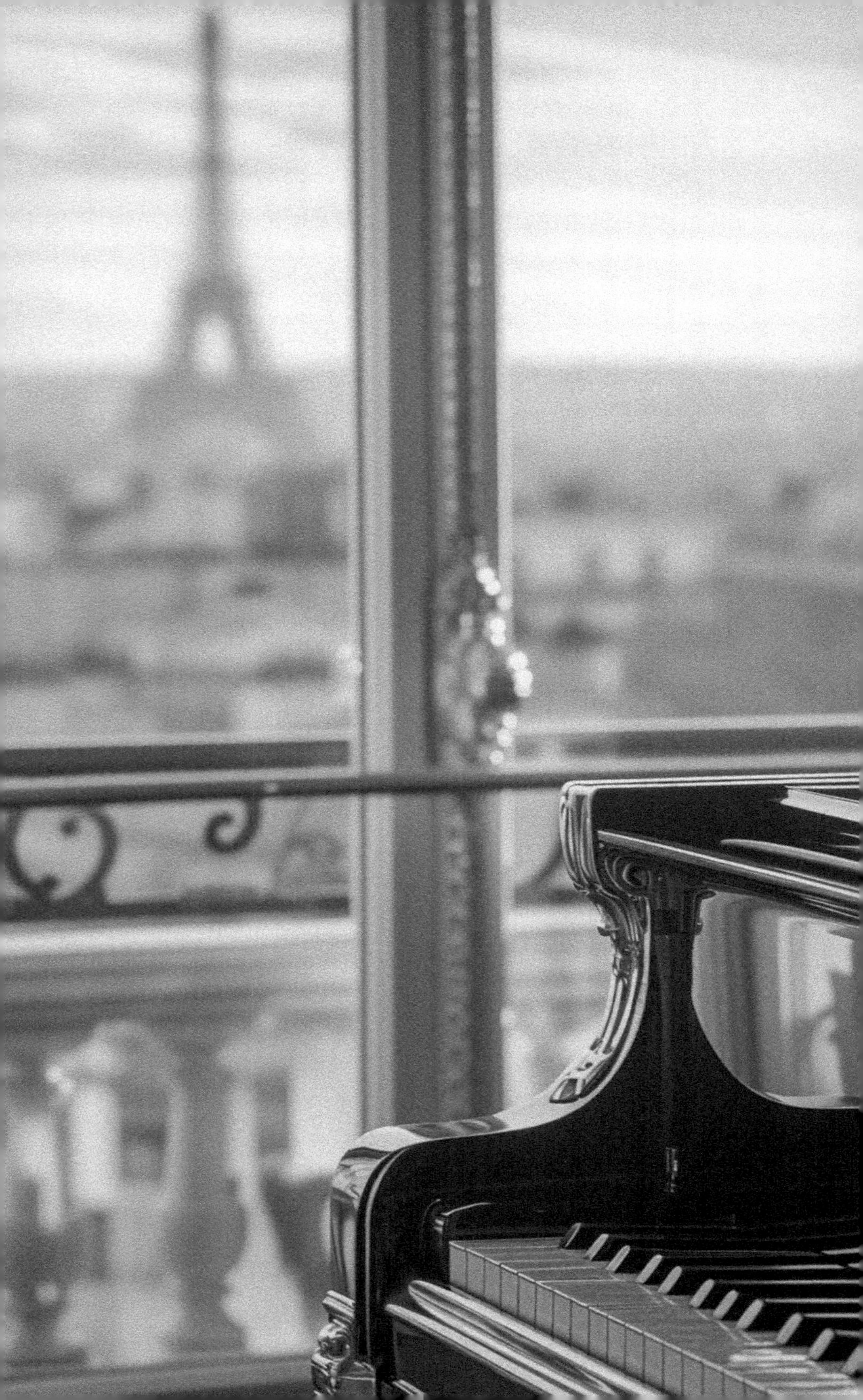

CHAPTER 57
Millie

MY HEAD THROBS as I process all the information being thrown at me.

Gavin isn't Vivi's father.

He never slept with anyone else.

His words jumble and blur together, mixing with my warring emotions and the tears welling in my eyes.

Gavin's frantic, his face etched in fear, his eyes swimming with pain and remorse, silently pleading for forgiveness. "Millie, please," he begs.

Tears continue to track down my face as I shake my head.

Panic flashes in his eyes, and he gasps like he can't catch his breath. He's clearly getting the wrong idea.

I press my hand to his cheek and channel calm, hoping he can feel it. "Can I speak now?"

He swallows and nods, his movements jerky.

With a hum, I brush my thumb along the length of his jawline.

"You didn't let me tell you the other day, but I need you to hear this." I clear my throat and pause to make sure he's truly listening rather than panicking. "I love you. I thought I loved you before, but now that I know what you did for Vivi, what you did for both of us? I love you even more fiercely. You deserve my love. You always have. We'll figure out a way to keep Vivi. She's ours. We'll fight for her together."

Gavin sucks in a shocked breath, then he stutters, his mouth working, but no words come out.

I smile up at him, hoping he can hear just how earnest I am about it all. We're doing this. "I love you," I rasp.

Angling over me, he presses a kiss to my lips. Then he pulls back, his expression filled with awe. "I love you too, Peaches. So much."

I grasp the front of his shirt to keep him close and press another kiss to his lips. Though I'm not ready to let him go, I press against his chest and shift my attention to my father.

"I know this isn't what you wanted, but please, Daddy, try to understand. Gavin and Vivi—they're what I need. Until I met Gavin, my life was filled with people who only kept me around because I was convenient or because I could give them access to the things they wanted. A way to get to you or Daniel, and later Lake. But Gavin—I was the most inconvenient person in the world for him to fall for, and he did anyway. Please be happy for us, Daddy. I love him, and I love Vivi. I'm happy."

My father's face crumples, and he takes a giant step closer. With his forehead pressed to mine, he wraps his arms around me. "Of course, Mills. I'm so glad you're okay. I love you."

"I love you too, Daddy. And I'm so sorry we lied to you. That we hid our relationship."

He takes a heavy breath, then presses a kiss to my head. "It's going to take some getting used to." He looks at Gavin, his brow furrowed. "But I've known Gavin for a long time, and I've never seen him the way he is with you."

Gavin deflates in relief and closes his eyes, and when he blinks them open, they're filled with tears. I squeeze his hand. God, I wish I could take the pain and uncertainty away from him.

"It's clear he loves you and, well, I guess that's the most a father could hope for. I'm just glad you're okay. Don't worry about me. I just want you to focus on getting healthy."

My heart beats wildly as the anxiety that's plagued me for months ebbs. All the secrets, all the hiding...it's over.

"Okay, now that we've resolved that," Beckett interjects, "can I tell you how I've already gotten Vivi's birth mother to agree to the adoption? I was supposed to have a meeting with Sebastian to finalize signing over his rights"—he snaps his wrist and tugs at his jacket sleeve, uncovering his watch—"five minutes ago. I told him we'd have to reschedule."

My heart stops, and I hold my breath.

Gavin grips my hand as he stares at his brother. "What?"

Chin tipped high, Beckett gives Gavin a smug smirk. "God, for someone who goes on and on about wishing people would talk, you do a terrible job of letting us do it."

"Beckett," Gavin grits out. "Speak clearly and slowly."

Beckett only smiles wider. "She's yours, Gav. If you want her, Vivi is all yours."

Swaying a little, Gavin bows his head and locks eyes with me. In this moment, our entire world shifts again.

"Ours," he says firmly, bringing my hand to his cheek and nuzzling against it. And then he utters the three most beautiful words. *"She's our daughter."*

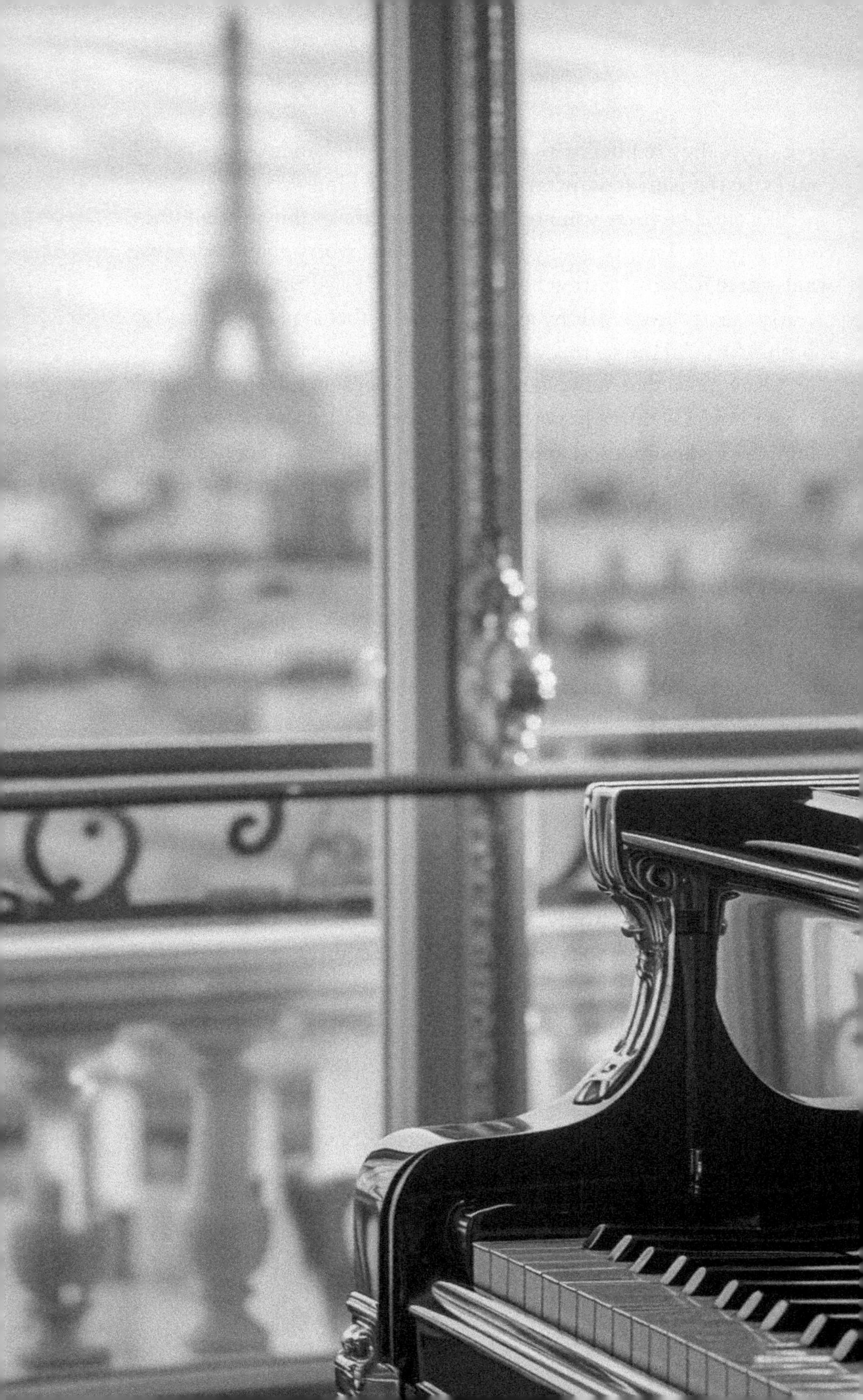

CHAPTER 58
Millie

"YOU DON'T HAVE to carry me. I *can* walk." Even as I say the words, I know the man won't put me down. He strides straight through the living room into his bedroom, pressing a kiss to my lips before depositing me on his bed.

"No moving until I'm back," he says with a stern glare. He knows me well. Vivi is in Sara and Brooks's apartment and I'm dying to see her. It's been three days since the accident. What if she's forgotten what I look like? What if she thinks I abandoned her?

Even as I scramble forward, I know it's a losing battle.

Gavin places a hand on my thigh. "Millie, I know you love to be a brat. It's our thing, and normally it works for me, but right now, I'm going to need you to fucking listen for once. I won't be able to breathe if something happens to you. Just stay." His words pierce me. The man is pure exhaustion right now. "*Please*," he adds when I have yet to reply.

I place my hand over his, trying to calm him. "I won't move. But when you get back, can you grab a pair of pajamas from my room? I want to shower the hospital off."

Gavin grunts. "Your room is here."

I let out a soft huff of a laugh. "Okay, big man, but my stuff is in the other room."

Gavin leans down close. "The closet is filled with your clothes. I hung them last night when they kicked me out of the hospital so you could rest. I also had Lennox pick up that shampoo and conditioner you like, and your toothbrush is in the bathroom. We'll buy anything else you need this week, but you aren't spending another minute in any bedroom that isn't mine."

"*Gavin.*" The words rush out like a prayer.

He splays his fingers over my cheek as he looks deep into my eyes. "I love you. Almost losing you nearly killed me. Please, baby, don't ever do that again. Promise me I die first. I can't live without you."

I don't argue with him, though I feel the same way. This man is my everything. Him, as well as his daughter.

Our daughter.

God, I miss her.

"I love you too. Go get our little girl."

Gavin presses one more kiss to my lips, then, with another squeeze of my thigh, he walks out of the room.

For ten minutes, I sit in complete silence, allowing thoughts of the last seventy-two hours to filter through my mind.

Vivi isn't his biological daughter. My father now knows about Gavin and me, and from what Daniel told me, Paul even stood up for me to my mom.

I shake my head. I truly hope she can find a way to be happy, but I'm done worrying about other people. Done trying to appease people who will never be content. I'm living my life for me.

The door to the apartment closes, and despite wanting to burst into the living room and run to my girl, I sit perfectly still like I promised Gavin I would.

Footsteps sound in the hall, and when they stop at the door,

Gavin lets out a heavy sigh. "Okay, Vivi girl. I'm going to need you to be extra good for Millie. She bumped her head and—" He huffs. "Why am I talking to you like you understand a word I'm saying?"

"Duck," she replies, and I imagine that she's squeezing his cheeks like she always does, hopefully making him smile.

"Duck is right," he says, sounding lighter.

God, I love them.

"I'm going to make everything better, though. You've got me, and you've got Millie. And that woman in there—" He cuts himself off.

I have to cover my mouth to keep my sob from escaping. I've never heard such concentrated emotion in his voice.

"She's the best mother around. You're so lucky to have her. And I'm so lucky to have both of you." He takes a deep breath. "Okay, we got this. No tears. Big smiles when we walk in, okay?"

When the door opens, I follow his instructions too. I paint a big smile on my face to hide my tears and pretend I didn't hear his sweet words to our daughter. Then I hold out my arms. "Hey, bestie! I missed you!"

"I can feel you watching me," I grumble from my pillow.

"So?"

At his cocky response, my eyes flutter open. I'm obsessed with cocky Gavin.

The man is sitting beside me with a bunch of beads on his lap.

"Why aren't you sleeping?"

"I was too worried about you to sleep. But look what I made." He holds up a little bracelet that says *Vivi Girl*.

"Aw, you made Vivi her own friendship bracelet." I pluck it from his fingers and spin the miniature beads, smiling at them. "We need one for her that says *bestie*, though."

"I made you one too," he adds, ignoring me.

I reach for it, noting the *M*. *M* for Millie makes sense. But I swear my heart stops when I see the letters that follow it.

"You can be her bestie too, but I think this title is more fitting." He slides the bracelet onto my wrist and turns it so the word, *Mommy*, printed on white beads, is on full display. The rest of the beads are peach, just like the ones on the *Peaches* bracelet he wears.

It's then that I catch sight of a new one on his wrist. One that says *Daddy*. That's when I lose it. "Gav."

He shrugs and gives me a boyish grin.

"You're going to need to put those beads away," I warn.

"Why?"

"Because in two seconds, I'm going to straddle you, and then they'll be everywhere. A clear choking hazard for our sweet Vivi girl."

With one big sweep of his arm, the beads clatter to the floor. "I'll get them with the vacuum," he says as he pulls me onto his lap.

"It's so sexy when you talk dad to me," I tease.

His chest rumbles with laughter, vibrating against me, and when he pushes my hair out of my face, his laughter transforms into a soft smile. "What do you want to do today?"

"Something with just you and Vivi. Can we get some fresh air?"

"How does the zoo sound?"

I can't help the smile that splits my face. "Really?"

"Yeah, the company just invested in a puffin exhibit at the zoo. Beckett showed me some pictures. They're actually pretty cute."

"Okay, seriously, stop. You just keep getting sexier."

I'm not even teasing him. Why is it that Gavin as a father talking about family time makes me instantly wet?

He scowls. "Puffins are sexy?"

I laugh. "No, Hockey Daddy is sexy."

He trails his fingers down my back and squeezes my ass. "The doctor said you need to take it easy."

I grind against him. "The doctor also said that I was cleared for sex."

"I can't believe you asked him that," he grumbles. "Your father was right outside the door waiting with balloons and flowers."

I smirk. "So you wouldn't like it if I did this?" I roll my hips again.

Gavin groans as I slide myself along his hard cock. "Millie," he warns.

"Please," I beg. I need him. Need to feel like me again. Need to feel like us.

He dips his fingers inside my panties and pulls them down.

I lift up and kick them off as he slides his boxers down.

"You know I can't say no to you," he mumbles as he grips my thighs and lets me control how quickly I take him.

Wanting to prolong the moment, I ease my way onto his cock, pressing a hand to his chest and holding his gaze as I slide down inch by fucking inch.

"Yes," I murmur when he's fully inside me. Filling me. Making me complete.

"Fuck yes," he mutters. "Fuck me, Peaches. Use me."

I shake my head. "No. I won't use you. But I will make love to you."

And that's what I do. We go slow. Making love. Making up for all of our lost time. Just as we're on the precipice, I tug his hands over his head and take in the matching bracelets that circle our wrists.

This is my forever. I have no doubt. Despite every obstacle we've had to overcome, we're exactly where we should be.

"Oh my gosh, bestie. Aren't they the cutest?" I screech as we watch the little birds that look like mini penguins with large orange beaks.

Vivi points her chubby finger at a bird waddling in our direction. "Duck! Duck! Duck!"

"She's do damn smart," Gavin mumbles.

"It's actually not a duck," Aiden says.

Brooks chuckles, and Sara hits Aiden in the chest.

"Vivi is the smartest," she says. "Don't even start."

Heart full, I lean back against Gavin. He presses his chin to my shoulder. "You feeling okay?"

The plan was to spend the day just the three of us, but when his brothers and Sara showed up with breakfast and flowers this morning, I invited them along to the zoo. I figured they'd say no, but Aiden practically squealed in excitement.

Then Beckett called and said he'd meet us here with his three oldest kids. When they arrived, though, Finn demanded they visit the snakes, so Beckett grumbled that he'd see us back at his house for pizza.

Despite the insanity of it all, I love every minute of my time with this family.

"I feel fine."

"Hi, guys," a pretty blonde says as she approaches. She's wearing a zoo shirt with a little puffin in the corner.

"Hey, Avery." Brooks dips low and presses a friendly kiss to her cheek. And soon, everyone in our group is doing the same.

"Avery is Coach Wilson's daughter," Gavin tells me.

"Coach Wilson?" I frown, trying to place him, but I don't remember a Coach Wilson on the Bolts' staff.

"He coaches the Boston Rev's," Avery explains.

"And Avery's dating the pitcher," Aiden says. "I *love* love," he adds with a dopey smile. "You think Beckett and Gavin were grumpy? You shoulda met Damiano before he finally won over Avery."

The blonde rolls her eyes good-naturedly. "He's a total softie. You guys want to meet *his* best friend?" She leans over the exhibit. "Hey, Puff, come say hi to some new friends." She twirls her finger, and the puffin in the back does a little flip.

"Oh my gosh, he does tricks, Viv!" I say as I bounce our girl.

"Oh no. Now my girls are going to want pets," Gavin grumbles, though his tone is light.

"His name is Puff?"

Avery giggles. "Chris—my boyfriend—calls him Puff Daddy, but I feel weird saying that."

I laugh. "Hear that, Hockey Daddy? I think we need a Puff Daddy too."

Gavin shakes his head. "All right, enough. Let's go look at the monkeys."

When the rest of the gang ditches us to get ice cream, Gavin and I take our time strolling through the zoo with Vivi. "Thank you for today," I tell him. "I really needed this."

"Not that I'm glad you were hurt, but the timing couldn't have been better. Having these few days off is perfect. With the playoffs..." He trails off, probably worrying about all the travel we'll be doing over the next two months. Playoffs are brutal, but this ain't my first rodeo. I know how the sport goes. I know he'll be busy.

"I've got Vivi. And we'll be there supporting you every day."

Gavin frowns. "You don't have to travel with us. I know it'd be better for her if we didn't drag her to a different city every night."

"We'll figure it out."

"What about your music?" he asks.

I shrug. "I'd like to get into a studio to record a few songs, I think."

Gavin's face lights up, and he stops in the middle of the walkway. "Really?"

"Yeah," I say, turning to face him. "I'm not sure what I'll do with it. Maybe nothing. But I'd love to have a chance to work with Lake before she has the baby. I'm not sure about anything, really. So long as I have you and Vivi..." I take in our sleeping girl. She's nestled against Gavin's chest with her head tucked beneath his chin.

We're both worried about the future. His games. My music. But most of all, we're worried that we won't get to keep this little girl.

"You'll always have us," Gavin says, somehow knowing I need the reassurance. He adjusts so he's holding Vivi with one arm, then grasps my hip and pulls me close with his free hand. There, in the middle of the zoo, we snuggle our little girl. Right now, in this moment, I have everything I'll ever need.

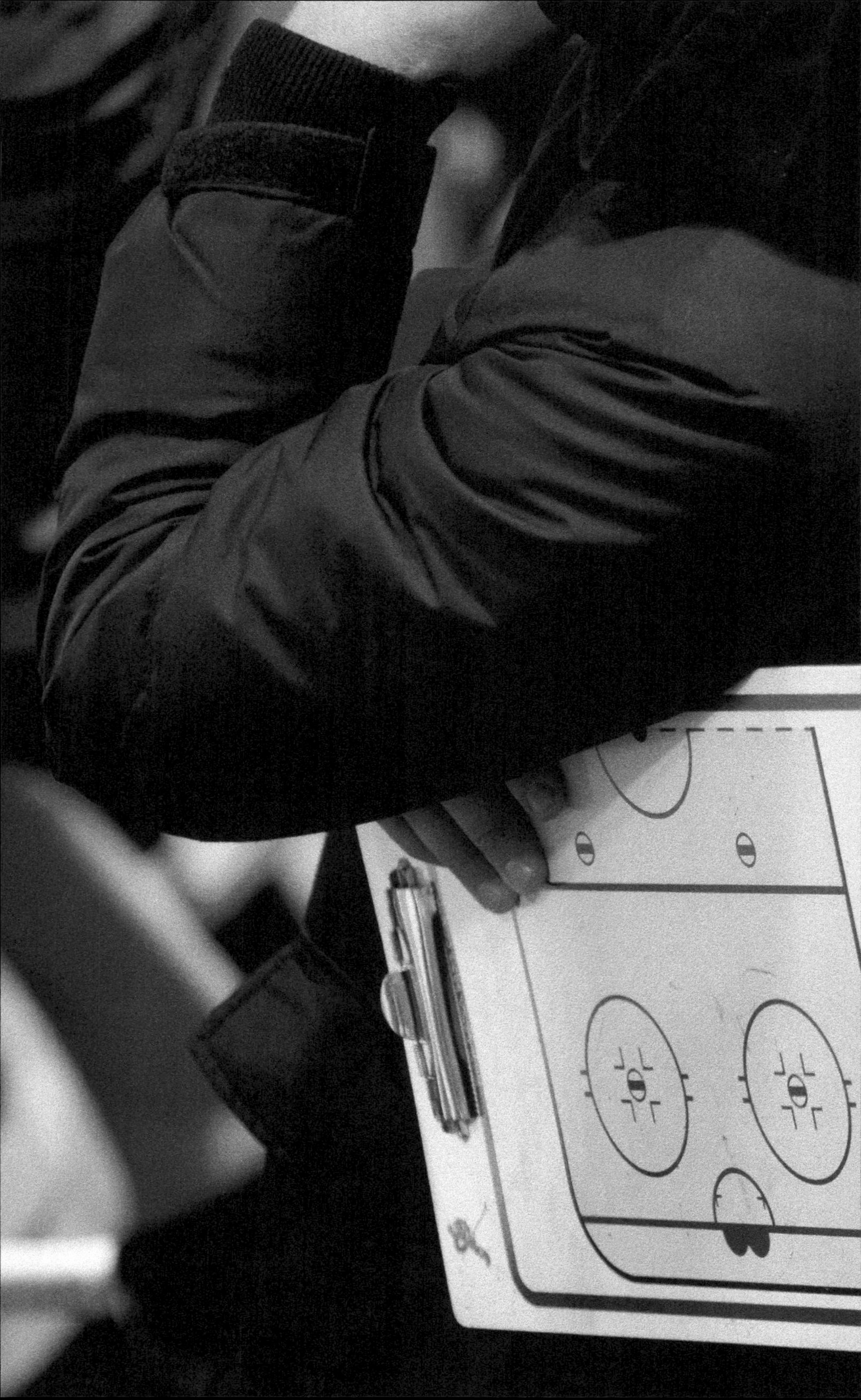

CHAPTER 59

Gavin

> Brooks: Good luck today
>
> Aiden: Proud of you, brother. Vivi is lucky to have you and Millie as her parents.

AFTER I TYPE out a quick thanks, I slide my phone into my pocket, then focus my attention on my older brother.

"You ready?" he asks.

I blow out a breath and assess the door. It's just a simple piece of solid wood. Nothing special. But the man on the other side holds my future in his hands. "What if he refuses to sign?"

Beckett frowns. "He doesn't want a kid, Gav. And you heard the lawyer. You've established an emotional connection with Vivi. If push comes to shove, we have legitimate arguments."

"But I stole a kid," I whisper.

Beckett chuckles in response to that confession. Fucking *chuckles*.

I practically swallow my tongue. Now is not the time to laugh.

"It really does seem like something I'd do, not you."

My lips tug up into a surprised smile. "True. Though there are fates worse than turning into my big brother."

Beckett adjusts his tie and blinks a few times. "Duck. Why'd you have to go and make this emotional?"

With a hand on his shoulder, I look him dead in the eye. "In case I haven't said it yet, thank you for helping me keep my daughter. For caring enough to do all this. We're all lucky to have you."

Beckett pulls me into his chest and hugs me tightly.

"Everything okay?"

We pull apart as Ford approaches. He's wearing a navy-blue suit, and he's got his hair slicked back like he's ready for negotiations.

I straighten, still a bit nervous in his presence now that he knows the truth. "Yeah, we're just heading in to meet with Sebastian. What are you doing here?"

Ford glances at Beckett and then zeroes in on me. He straightens and tugs at his jacket cuffs like he, too, is nervous. "I figure I'm going to be a grandfather. Have to make sure nothing goes sideways today."

Another wave of emotion washes over me, but I swallow it back. "That means a lot to me."

Fuck, it's hard to keep the tears at bay. It's one thing for Ford to accept my relationship with Millie, but it's something entirely different for him to claim my daughter as his grandchild. It means Vivi gets a real family. And between Millie and me, my siblings and parents, Millie's brothers, and all of our extended family, Vivi is going to have one big, beautiful, crazy family.

When Ford holds out his hand to me, I grasp it and pull him in for a hug.

He claps me on the back and says, "They're both lucky to have you."

The door to the conference room opens, and we all straighten. When Sebastian's smug face comes into view, the tension of this moment settles over me like a heavy weight again.

Before my brother walks in, I grab his arm. "We give him whatever he wants," I murmur. I'd trade every dollar in my bank account for my little girl.

Beckett hits me with a look that's pure ruthless CEO. "I've got this." He nods once, confirming that he understands there is no limit. Then he smiles deviously. "And if he becomes a problem, we can always call Jay."

I cup a hand over my mouth to stifle a laugh. Our best friend Jay Hanson went up against the mob and won. I suppose my brother does understand the lengths I'll go to for my little girl.

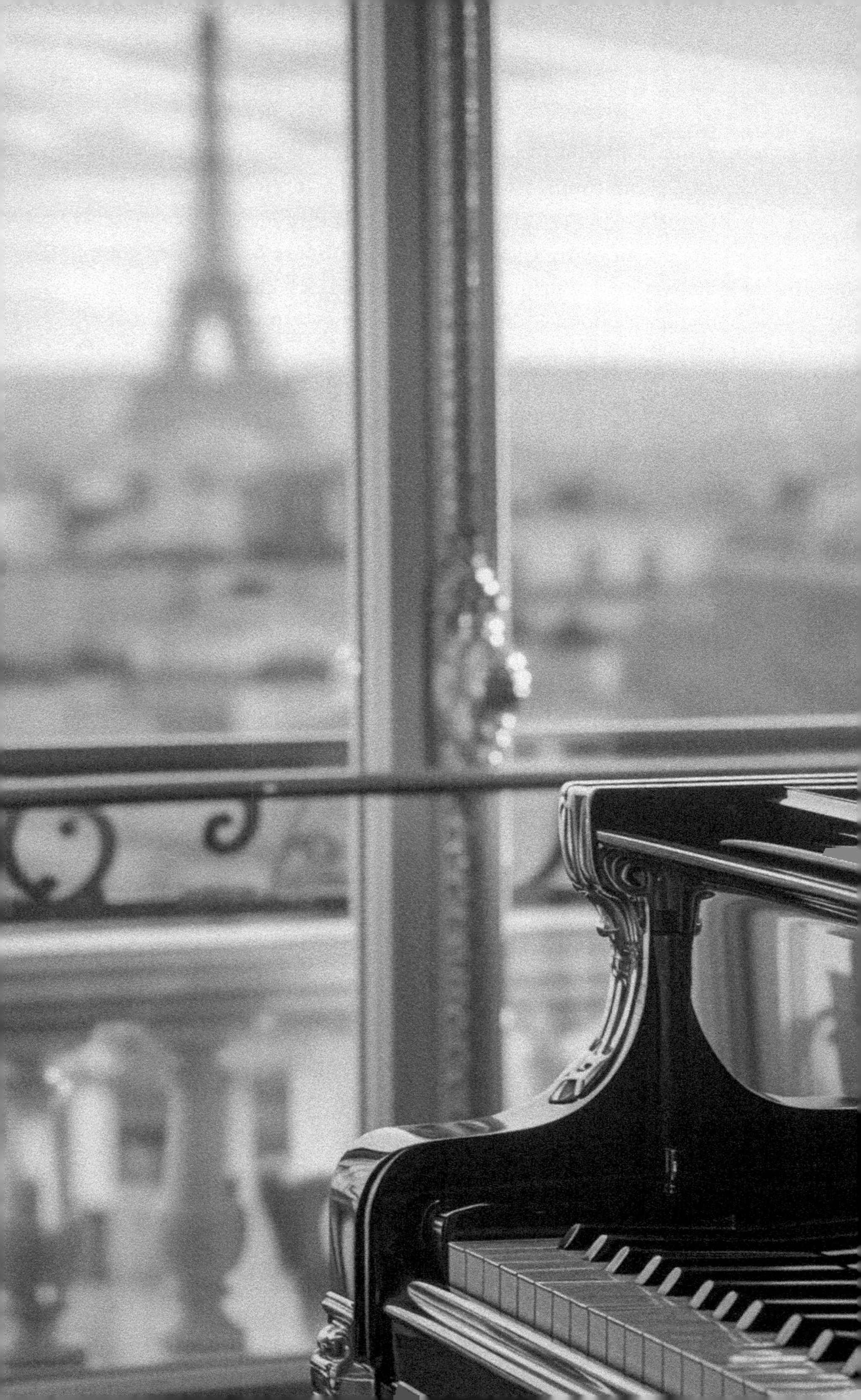

CHAPTER 60
Millie

"ALL RIGHT VIV. Apparently Daddy has plans tonight, so you're going to hang with Lennox and be a good girl, right?"

With a gummy smile, Vivi tugs on my sparkly earring.

"We're going to have a great time," Lennox says, holding out her arms. My traitor of a best friend sees the oversized pink Barbie and launches herself at her.

"Jeez, I'll miss you too," I grumble, fixing my earring.

Gavin chuckles from the door. "You're worse than the baby."

I turn around and stick out my tongue in rebuttal but almost stumble when I see how handsome he looks. He's in a black suit, his thick arms crossed over his chest as he leans against the open doorway. His brown eyes shine with pure love. His hair's a bit of a mess, though. I don't mind. It makes him look a bit more real, a bit more mine. I take a deep breath, reminding myself that he is mine. All mine. Then I step closer to him and press a kiss to his jaw. "Hockey Daddy, you clean up nice."

He rolls his eyes, and behind me, Lennox snickers.

"Told you the name would stick."

Gavin wags a finger at her. "You're a bad influence."

She holds Vivi up so their cheeks are pressed together and pouts. "And yet I'm watching your daughter so you can go get freaky—"

"Lennox!" I hiss.

She laughs as Gavin spins on his heel, ignoring her.

It's been a month since my trip to the hospital. A month since our world flipped on its head and we thought we were losing the little girl who makes our life complete. But instead, thanks to Beckett, she's ours for good.

Well, she will be once the paperwork is finalized. Then we'll officially be Vivi's mom and dad.

Only a few months ago, the idea of being a mom sent me running to the other side of the world. But now if anyone tried to tell me Vivi wasn't mine, I'd run through fire to prove them wrong.

I wouldn't change things, though. It was always meant to be this way. Vivi and I were meant for one another. My whole life, I never felt like I alone was enough. But then that little girl looked at me like I was her whole world. And I intend to spend the rest of my life making sure she knows she's enough. Making sure she knows she's loved.

And I know Gavin will too. I just hate leaving her tonight since I've been so busy the past two weeks in the recording studio with Lake. Still have no idea what I'll do with the recordings, but there was something incredibly special about sitting in a booth and recording while Gavin and my father smiled on the other side of the glass.

It's still not completely normal between them, but we're getting there.

Kind of like Lake and me. I suppose we're all a work in progress. But isn't that what life is? A work in progress?

"Peaches." Gavin says my nickname in a soft, flirty whisper, then presses a kiss to the spot below my ear he knows I love. He tugs on a curl when I don't immediately respond. "You're doing an awful lot of thinking in that pretty head of yours."

I smile up at him, looping my arms around his neck. "Just thinking about how happy I am. But I'm ready."

He presses his lips to mine, and for a moment, the world fades away.

Twenty minutes later, the car stops. Gavin has been awfully secretive about the plans he made for tonight, but when Jacob, his driver, opens the door and the entrance of the bar where we first met comes into view, I give my man a knowing look. "Bringing me back to your old playground?"

With a dark chuckle, Gavin holds out his hand and helps me out of the car. "Rented it out for the night again."

Jacob shuts the door and rounds the car, leaving us alone again. I stare up at the restaurant as memory after memory flits through my mind, then shake my head. "I can't believe you rented this place out again. What could you possibly have planned for tonight?"

His responding smirk is wicked. "Figured maybe I'd get down on my knees again for you."

I roll my eyes and huff a laugh, but when he tugs on my hand and drops down onto a knee on the sidewalk, I suck in a breath.

"What are you doing?" I whisper-hiss, looking one way, then the other in confusion.

Gavin simply smiles up at me, his eyes never leaving mine. "I was upset that when I told you I loved you for the first time, it was on a whim. But for so long, I couldn't put into words my feelings for you. These feelings were so much bigger than what any one person had ever spoken. Any word I'd ever read.

"Infatuation. Obsession. Love." He shakes his head in dismissal of each one. As if they're beneath him. Beneath us.

"*Infinitely and endlessly yours.* Love wanes. Obsession tires. Infatuation can be toxic." He bows his head for a moment, rubbing soothing circles over the back of my hand. "When I call you mine, that encompasses my feelings. We belong to one another. Your heart and mine. I am infinitely and endlessly yours, Millie. I know I asked at the hospital—on a whim, once again—but you deserve me on my knees, begging. Please be mine for eternity. Marry me. Be my wife."

I'm nodding before he even finishes. Then I tug him until he's on his feet and in my arms, crushing myself against his chest as I cry.

"Peaches, I need your words," he whispers into my hair. Hands cupping my cheeks, he gently forces me to look at him.

"Yes, I'll marry you," I sob out, my vision blurred and my breaths stuttering.

He presses a kiss to my lips, then sticks a hand in his pocket. When he pulls it out, he's holding a gold band adorned with a beautiful round diamond. "Give me that finger."

Watery laughter bubbles out of me as I hold out my shaky hand, and he slides the diamond ring on. The smile that overtakes him is so wide it makes my heart ache.

God, have I ever been this happy?

"I have something else for you," he adds with a squeeze, his own hand trembling along with mine.

I wipe under one eye, then the other. "Yeah?"

"The paperwork came through this afternoon. We're Vivi's parents. It's official. You're her mom."

Screw trying to collect myself. My whole body ignites in delight, and tears flow down my cheeks. "Really?"

Gavin nods. There was a moment when we thought it would be a real battle—when Sebastian Lukov intimated that he may actually want to be Vivi's father—but his true motive was money. When the Bolts agreed to pay him the full amount his contract had stipulated, even though he was fired mid-season, he signed the papers. Knowing he gladly traded his child for it makes me sick, but we'll spend our lives ensuring that Vivi is loved and cared for. She never has to know that part of her story.

The only thing that little girl will know is that Gavin and I loved her so much we had to have her, and whether she's my biological child or not, she'll always be my little girl.

"Ready to go inside, Future Mrs. Langfield?" Gavin swipes the tears from my face.

Pressing my cheek against his palm, I laugh. "Oh, a new nickname? I like it."

He kisses me again and then taps my ass, urging me toward the entrance. "So what are we actually doing—" As Gavin pulls the door open, my words are drowned out by a chorus of *surprises*.

Teetering on my heels, I latch on to Gavin for support.

He circles his arms around me, swaying as he leans down and whispers in my ear, "We're celebrating, Peaches. It's Mom and Dad's night out to celebrate."

My dad approaches and shakes Gavin's hand, then pulls me in for a hug, telling me how happy he is for me. Lake is next, with a hand on her belly, already listing wedding ideas.

My brothers appear after her, along with my mother, who seems to be on her best behavior. Paul brought his new boyfriend—*not* the manager Lake fired, but a new guy who seems to be a bit more down-to-earth and is even smiling and chatting with Lake.

The women at a table in the corner, Sara, Hannah, and Ava, have become close friends. The kind I always wished for. They're always up for mimosa Sunday brunches and helping with Vivi when I need them.

Lennox and Vivi make an appearance via FaceTime, and for a moment, when my girl gives me a smile that shows off a couple new teeth, I consider leaving the party so I can snuggle with her.

Gavin's brothers are congregated by the bar, all holding tumblers of whiskey. Beckett has one arm wrapped around his wife, who waves at me with a smile.

Gavin puts his hand on the small of my back, interrupting my perusal, and guides me toward the group. "I think my sister is here too." I search the space, and sure enough, I spot Sienna standing between Brooks and Aiden, laughing as Aiden gestures wildly.

There's a man I don't recognize standing among them, but as

soon as we approach, his eyes light up as he beams at Gavin. "This Princess Peaches?"

"Henry?" Gavin's voice sounds surprised.

"Wait, how do you know one another?" Beckett asks.

Gavin eyes the white-haired man in a navy suit. "Met him in the park with Finn a few months ago. We became friends."

The man laughs. "He thought I was homeless. Tried to slip me a couple hundreds so I'd have somewhere to sleep that night."

Beckett laughs so loud heads turn around us. "You thought Henry Rose—venture capitalist and the owner of the bank where we do all of our business—was homeless? Oh, that's too ducking good."

Gavin groans. "Shit, really? Wait, why are you here?"

Beckett wears a smug grin. "He's here as Aunt Zoe's date. I introduced them."

Liv nudges her husband and, under her breath, mutters, "Oh god, another matchmaking scheme."

Henry doesn't seem to hear, though, and with a big grin, he turns to Gavin. "Congratulations. I'm so happy for you."

Gavin shakes his hand and then formally introduces us. After catching up for a few moments, Gavin leans against the bar to order drinks for us. "Peach margarita for my fiancée," he says with a squeeze to my hip.

It's impossible not to giggle. He's going to be so obnoxious, and I love it.

"And I'll take a whiskey."

I poke him. "You don't want to test out new drinks? Figure out what you really like?"

Gavin looks down at me, a smile in his eyes. "What I like is you, witchy woman. Now go get up on stage and sing me a song."

I don't hesitate to give Gavin exactly what he wants. I never will. Last time I was in this room, I had no idea who I was or where life would take me. Tonight, as I settle my fingers on the piano keys, I know exactly who I am.

A musician. A mother. And the love of Gavin Langfield's life.

And there is no one I'd rather be.

EPILOGUE

"PLEASE TELL me you're not replacing my lamp with that." Sara points at the lamp Lennox has just turned on. It's white marble in the shape of a woman's body and covered with a hot-pink fringed lamp shade with pink crystals hanging from it.

Tilting my head one way, then the other, I survey it. "I actually kind of like it."

Lennox grins. "Thank you. Had to spice up the apartment a little now that it's mine." She shimmies her shoulders and turns in a circle. "You really don't mind me staying here?"

Sara snorts. "Like that would stop you."

Lennox adjusts a photo frame on the bureau. The picture is from last week—another boozy Sunday brunch with the girls. Ava, Hannah, Lennox, Sara, and I are all smiling big at the camera. The rest of the girls are holding champagne flutes in the air, but I'm holding Vivi. She was in another blue outfit, courtesy of Aiden.

It's been a few weeks since the adoption was official, and the boys are in the Stanley Cup Finals. We're going to game one tonight, and I couldn't be more excited.

Lennox started a new job, trying her hand at wedding planning, and has decided to stay in Boston for good.

My phone buzzes, and I roll my eyes when I see the text.

"Those girls really don't take a hint, huh?" Lennox says, eyeing me.

I shrug. Chrishell and Taylor have been blowing up my phone for the last few weeks. Apparently now that I'm engaged to Gavin, I'm worth their time again. Too bad they aren't worth mine. Today's text is about the game.

> Chrishell: Hey babe, Taylor and I got the three of us matching jerseys. Can you get us tickets to sit with you in the box? It will be like old times.

Sara grins devilishly. "Oh my god, you should totally tell them yes, and then when they get there, have security tell them their names aren't on the list. I'll have so much fun waiving at them from inside. Of course, my waving would be with my middle fingers."

I giggle. "No. Seriously. If I've learned anything, it's that the best revenge is being happy. And I am."

"Aw," Lennox croons. "Look at our Millie, all grown up."

"Please come tonight," Sara begs her for what has to be the fifth time since we arrived.

Lennox spins and lets out a loud sigh. "No, and you know why."

Sara glares at her. "One of these days, you and Aiden need to talk, but I'm not saying it has to happen tonight. Just come to the game. What's the worst that can happen?"

"Oh, I don't know," Lennox says, her tone dry. She taps a pink painted nail against her lips. "The boy could run into the glass, miss a winning shot, and end up with a concussion."

"Knock on wood! Where the hell is wood around here?" Sara whips her head from one side to the other, grimacing at every surface in the room.

Lennox replaced all of Sara's serene furniture with sleek white pieces with glossy surfaces that are decidedly not wood.

"Where's your shower dildo?" Lennox teases. "That counts as wood, right?" She scurries into the bathroom.

My mouth falls open. "She's joking, right?"

Sara scowls at me. "Obviously I didn't leave my shower dildo in *her* bathroom."

So she does have a shower dildo. Damn. Lucky Brooks.

In a louder voice, she calls for Lennox. "Babe, seriously. You can't avoid him forever. The kid is obsessed with you. One day he'll wise up and break up with that vapid woman Jill. Then you'll have your second chance at *love*." She draws out the last word, all girly like, and we both laugh.

Lennox appears in the bedroom doorway, giant pink dildo in hand. How in God's name does she fit it? "Do I literally knock on it or, like, rub my hand on it?" She glides her hand up and down the silicone toy like she's jacking it off, sending all of us into a fit of giggles.

"Stop. Seriously," I say through tears. "Do you really use that?" I whisper.

Sara rolls her eyes. "She wouldn't have to if she'd come to the goddamn hockey game and let Aiden see her for freaking once. What are you so afraid of, anyway?"

My phone buzzes in my pocket, and Sara's starts singing at the same time. Aiden stole her phone the last time we were out and programmed it so a recording of him singing his version of "Fergalicious"—Sara-licious, naturally—plays every time she gets a notification.

We let it play for a few seconds, because it's just as hilarious today as it was a week ago, before either of us looks at our phone.

> Aiden: Okay, fam jam, I've got news!
>
> Beckett: Did your adult teeth finally come in?
>
> Brooks: LOL

> Gavin: No news, Aiden. You're supposed to be heading to the arena right now. Unless that's your news, we've got issues.
>
> Brooks: True. Where are you?
>
> Beckett: Uh-oh. Did you get stuck in the bathroom?
>
> Brooks: Burn.
>
> Aiden: You all suck. Girls, are you here yet?

Sara smiles at me. After my engagement, Aiden added both Sara and me to the family chat. I'm sure they have a chat without us too, because I see Gavin rolling his eyes and laughing all the time while my screen is blank, but I appreciate the sentiment.

> Me: We're here. Be nice, boys.
>
> Beckett: Hi Millie, Hi Sara. We'll see you both tonight, right?
>
> Sara: Obviously. I'll be the one with the blue hair.
>
> Brooks: Crazy girl!

She grins at me. "We should totally do it!"

I giggle as I look back down at the phone.

> Aiden: Can I speak now?
>
> Gavin: Please. We're all waiting on pins and needles.

"What are you two smiling at over there?" Lennox asks, sidling up close to me.

I tilt my screen so she can catch up on the thread. As I do, another text pops up.

> Aiden: We're adding another girl to the family! Jill and I are engaged! She said yes!
> <picture of vapid Jill holding out an oversized diamond>

"Holy fucking shit." Sara mutters the words running through my head.

Lennox's mouth pulls into a tight smile, and her usually bright blue eyes go dull. "Well, I guess that's that. Now you can all stop playing matchmaker. Looks like that second chance with 'the love of my life' is over."

Want to find out what happens when Lennox is tasked with planning Aiden's wedding?
Preorder A Pucking Disaster NOW!

Want to see more Millie and Gavin and find out about his jersey?
Read the extended epilogue HERE!

ACKNOWLEDGMENTS

Beckett: Well, I think we can all agree, I did it again.

Gavin: Oh God, what are you going on about?

Brooks: This should be good.

Aiden: I think he means how he is to thank for first setting himself up with Liv, then you Brooks and now you Gavin.

Beckett: I couldn't have said it better myself. Thanks Aiden.

Aiden: I'm going to frame that. Pretty sure this is the first time you've thanked me.

Brooks: LOL

Brooks: Not sure how you are taking credit for my story with Sara.

Beckett: Clearly you need to revisit it then. Fake dating for revenge. Ha. It was all me. It was so much more than Pucking Revenge.

Gavin: I definitely think I should get credit for you and Liv. I forced you to admit to your feelings when dad told you that you needed a wife. If you need a refresher, I've jotted it all down here in Mother Faker.

Aiden: Well none of you can take credit for my love story with Jill.

Beckett: Thank duck. I'm not touching that with a ten foot pole.

Aiden: Duck you! My story is awesome. It definitely won't turn out to be A Pucking Disaster.

Beckett: Truth is, if we want to get technical, I can even take credit for our friend Jay Hanson's marriage.

Gavin: Oh this will be good.

Beckett: It's too long to text. Read about it here though in Dirty Truths.

Gavin: Well if you are taking credit for that, then I definitely get credit for Ford and Lake.

Brooks: Oh! He's trying to one up ya, Beck!

Gavin: Don't act like you don't know I'm right. The talk I gave him. Come on. Lake may have been in her Revenge Era when she went after her exes boyfriend but we all know it was always love for Ford.

Aiden: Your friends are all a bunch of simps. I'm here for it. But I know all these stories, got any other good ones for me?

Beckett: How about a story about a real matchmaker who falls for her client? Oh did I mention she's married...

Gavin: Sounds dramatic.

Brooks: Like you don't like dramatic.

Aiden: Give me the TITLE!

Beckett: Whiskey Lies.

Aiden: Downloading now. Thanks Bros. Let's do this again soon.

Another Langfield bites the dust. And can I just say, he was one of my absolute favorites. Although every time I write another Langfield brother they become my favorite. This series, these men, there obsession with their women and the texts chains, give me life. Thank you to every single one of you for loving them with me and allowing me to have so much fun bringing you these characters.

This book would not have been possible though if not for some really amazing people. Sara, my ride or die partner in crime who helps me plot, chats me down when I think of crazy ideas, talks me up when I think of crazy ideas, supports me, formats for me, manages my socials, commiserates over our 'love' for tiktok daily, and is basically just my human support person, I LOVE YOU. Jenni, basically everything above minus the doing my socials and formatting. The two of you are my people and I appreciate you immensely.

To my amazing beta readers who offered insight and helped make this book better, I can't say thank you enough. This story wasn't an easy one, it was angsty but I also wanted it to have joy, it was a long timeline which meant we needed to keep readers invested, and thanks to these lovely women I hope we met that mark. Becca, Glav, Anna and Andi, I can't thank you enough. And as always, your commentary on the spice had me kicking me feet in excitement.

To my lovely editor Beth who literally never says no when I ask if she can squeeze in another word, another paragraph or another project. You are an integral part of my success and I can't thank you enough for always making my books better. I will never stop singing your praises.

To my Book Babes and Swoon Squad, my street team, every release gets better because of you! I am always in awe of your friendship and support.

And to my amazing readers, thank you for all of your messages, your Tiktoks, your dms, your posts and your rants. There is nothing I love more than hearing from each of you how a character affected you, or a storyline made you laugh. I love your reviews, your anecdotes, and the notes you send to me.

I have so many more stories coming to you this year. If you want to follow along on my writing journey and have sneak peeks into all the characters in Bristol and Boston, follow me on Instagram, join my awesome Facebook group, sign-up for my newsletter and follow me on TikTok.

ALSO BY BRITTANÉE NICOLE

Bristol Bay Rom Coms

She Likes Piña Coladas

Kisses Sweet Like Wine

Over the Rainbow

Bristol Bay Romance

Love and Tequila Make Her Crazy

A Very Merry Margarita Mix-Up

Boston Billionaires

Whiskey Lies

Loving Whiskey

Wishing for Champagne Kisses

Dirty Truths

Extra Dirty

Mother Faker

(Mother Faker is Book 1 of the Mom Com Series, but is also a lead in to the Revenge Games alongside Revenge Era. This book can be read as a Standalone, or after Revenge Era and before Pucking Revenge)

Revenge Games

Revenge Era

Pucking Revenge

A Major Puck Up

Standalone Romantic Suspense

Deadly Gossip

Irish

Find Brittanée's Books Here